CASTLE CHARMING

TANSY RAYNER ROBERTS

For my Patreon subscribers
Who made all this possible

For my Sheep Might Fly listeners, who got attached

For my Kickstarter supporters
Who made it a book

But most especially for my favourites
Who were all three

CONTENTS

GLASS SLIPPER SCANDAL

DANCE, PRINCES, DANCE

CHARM OR DARE

LET SLEEPING PRINCES LIE

DEAD QUEEN WALKING

GLASS SLIPPER SCANDAL

AUTUMN

Autumn 1499
Price: 3 Copper Toads
Castle Charming #1
est. 1066
THE UNTOLD STORY!
GLASS SLIPPER SCANDAL!
Tansy Rayner Roberts

1

CASTLE CHARMING AFLUTTER FOR AUTUMNAL FLING! (WHO WILL MARRY OUR PRINCES GONE WILD?)

"The best thing about magical ink," said Amira, "is that it smells different to everyone. They say that if you ever find a person who smells the same thing that you do in the ink, that person is your soulmate."

Kai craned his neck around the Charming Herald printer room, taking in the swoops of paper overhead, the scratching of quills, the splashes of black ink in courier font, all crashing together in mid-air to make the news and gossip of the day into a tangible, readable object.

He had always had an affinity to ink, something deep and primal that bubbled under his skin, but he had never given any thought to what it smelled like. He inhaled, and caught a scent of wet feathers with a touch of vanilla, along with the raw weave of the paper itself. "That's not actually true, is it?" he asked.

Amira laughed at him. "Sure it's true. Also, if you sleep with a violet under your bed, you'll dream of your best love, and if you find a stray glass slipper on a staircase, you should either marry or murder its owner within 24 hours."

Kai blinked up at the grand floating wheels of paper, and

the day's headline — CASTLE CHARMING AFLUTTER FOR AUTUMNAL FLING! It made a change, at least, from the variations on PRINCES BEHAVING BADLY that had dominated the Herald's front page over the summer. "You don't actually believe all of that gossip bullshit the paper publishes about the royal family?"

"Hey," said Amira. "I write the horoscopes. You'd be amazed the level of bullshit I can stomach on a daily basis."

"So what does magical ink smell like to you?" he ventured. He had been here a few hours, and she was the only one who thought he was worth talking to. It was a good idea to get a measure of what kind of person she was.

Amira turned her pretty, round face up to his. Possibly she was flirting. It was hard to tell, with girls. "Vanilla and wet feathers," she breathed.

Kai hesitated, not sure whether to be horrified or suspicious. As ever, his default was awkward.

Amira fell apart in a heap of giggles. "Oh, Kai. The look on your face!"

"I can't help my face."

"You totally fell for it."

"I didn't fall for anything, you were super obvious." He couldn't help grinning, though. A prankster. He'd much rather work alongside a prankster than a flirt. "Everyone smells vanilla and wet feathers, then?"

"Everyone who hasn't been snorting pixie dust, yeah." She looked terribly pleased with herself.

"You almost had me," Kai said generously. It wasn't true but hey, he was on the verge of making a friend here, and it was his first day. You took what you could get.

"You're a good sport," Amira decided. "You can eat lunch with me, and I'll only prank you once or twice a week."

"Thank you?" he ventured.

She patted him on the shoulder. "Believe me, pet, you're

getting off lightly. Now, let's get you a desk before they send you out on the rookie run."

That sounded like something to be alarmed about. "What does a rookie run involve?"

"Throwing you into the lion's den, dressed as a lamb chop." Amira smiled at him from under her very dark eyelashes. "Oh, and I wouldn't talk too loudly about the bull-shit nature of gossip around here, if I were you. This is a kingdom built on a fairy tale. Stories are important to us, even the silly stories about who's snogging whom, and whether an engagement is forthcoming. Spoiler: an engagement is *always* forthcoming."

2

ENTER THE DOGHOUSE

"Welcome to the Doghouse," said Corporal Jack, leading the way. She was tall, a solidly built wall of muscle and judgment with amazing hair. It was a rare thing for Dennis to look at a woman not much older than him and think 'yep, she could totally crack my skull with her thighs.'

"I hope you don't mean that literally," Dennis joked as he followed her into the stone building — a former stable, by the look of it, still pungent with old straw.

Jack gave him a sideways look. "How else do you think I mean it?"

That was the other thing. Corporal Jack had no sense of humour. Dennis had been trying to get a laugh out of her for the last half hour, and nothing. Maybe she was made out of the same granite as the castle. It would explain a lot.

Sure, he wasn't here to joke around. He took himself and this job very seriously. Getting a promotion out of the general guards to the royal family's personal service was an amazing opportunity. But… was it too much to ask for a partner who didn't get a pained crease between her eyes when he said something funny?

"What's the boss like?" he asked, since they were there before everyone else. There was little contact between the castle guards and the Royal Hounds, so he had nothing but rumour to go on (and the rumours were… kind of terrifying).

"Sarge?" Jack shrugged. "He's a broken down hack with a drinking problem, but he knows his shit, and he's not an arsehole most of the time."

Wow. She didn't mess around. Dennis barely managed to close his mouth after this revelation of brutal honesty before a voice like a rusty nail broke into his silence.

"He's also standing right behind you, Corporal."

Corporal Jack didn't twitch, but Dennis was about ready to crawl under the floor from embarrassment. Seriously. Time to revisit the theory that Jack was entirely made out of granite.

"I knew you were there, Sarge," Jack said calmly.

The Sarge circled them both. He was about an inch shorter than Jack: sandy hair and wiry muscle, and while his uniform was crisp and pressed almost as sharply as theirs, he clearly hadn't shaved that morning. He was somewhere between 30 and 40 if Dennis had to guess, but his eyes were cynical enough for a man twice that.

"That," said the Sarge in a low growl. "That is why you're my favourite, kid."

Jack smiled — a businesslike, brief flash of a smile. "I know."

"You must be one of the new pups. I've seen you around the castle. You do good work." Dennis had been expecting military formality, but the Sarge shook his hand with a boyish enthusiasm. "Welcome to the Doghouse."

"I already said that," Jack added. "I did the slow walk and the dramatic flourish and everything."

Sarge pointed a finger at her. "You don't get to say that part. I get to say that part because I am the boss. You have at least another five years before you get to challenge me for the top spot, kid."

"Give me four," she replied, cool as you like.

Dennis was busy having a heart attack. Corporal Made-of-Stone did have a sense of humour after all. The issue was that he hadn't been plumbing a deep and dark enough well.

"Right," said Sarge, with a cheerful smack to Dennis' shoulder. "You're in good hands with our Jack. The newbies who make it through as her partner have a higher survival rate than the others. Come to me if she makes you cry. I've got a handkerchief somewhere."

More Hounds milled into the Doghouse now, and Dennis hoped that meant that they were done with this strange initiation rite.

Like him, the Hounds wore the formal dress tabard of Castle Charming — red hearts and black spades against blinding white cotton, with red linens underneath. Dennis spotted several other new recruits in the crowd, in tabards so new they squeaked.

It was a far cry from the plain grey uniform he had worn as a castle guard. He was a Royal Hound now.

"All right, sweethearts," barked Sarge, standing on an upturned apple crate. "Let's leave the gossip for the bastards in the press gallery. It's the start of the season and you know what that means — tonight's Autumnal Fling is the first in a parade of butt-scratching, dull as dog-shit fancy events bringing hundreds of well-dressed strangers into the castle and making trouble for us. Unlike the rest of the year, our Princes Gone Wild are expected to behave themselves in public, and we all know what that means."

There was some muttering in the crowd. Dennis could take a guess — he read the Herald as much as any other kid his age, and the outrageous antics of the royal twins were a matter of public record, not to mention castle gossip. The platinum-haired, silver-eyed Princes Chase and Cyrus Charming were in some kind of screwy contest over which of them could fuck themselves up worse before their twentieth birthday.

Everyone knew that the royal family was a goddamned tragedy — what with the king in a haze of endless melancholy, the queen still buried in an enchanted sleep, and the princess hidden from public view since childhood with a mystery illness. It was down to those two beautiful, broken princes to stand as the public face of Castle Charming.

Dennis knew when he signed up for this that keeping those reckless boys alive and in one piece was one hell of a job. It was only just starting to sink in that it was up to the Royal Hounds to keep the boys from drunkenness and debauchery as well as protecting them from gold-diggers and assassination attempts.

Huh. And here he had been thinking the worst shit he'd have to deal with was a crossbow bolt to the back.

Sarge was finishing up his speech. "As ever, we have some new muscle joining us for the season — six shiny recruits, hand-picked from the trough to join the family's personal service. There are only two permanent positions available in the Hounds once the season closes, but let's face it, most of these newbies will fall by the wayside when they realise how bloody thankless this job is."

Sarge's second-in-command, a senior Corporal called Marie, took his place on the crate and started yelling out duty rosters. It was gobbledegook to Dennis, but he took it from the groans and cheerful fist-pumps that corridor and roof duty were far more prized than positions inside the ballroom.

Their names weren't called, and Corporal Jack's impressive musculature began to slump. "I can't believe they're doing this to me again," she muttered.

Dennis nudged her with a question in his eye but she shrugged him off, not giving him a clue.

"And finally," said Marie with a vengeful tilt of her head. "Personal prince detail, eight till two. Fergus and Dante on Cyrus, Jack and Dennis on Chase."

"Sonofabitch," swore Corporal Fergus. His partner, another newbie, looked alarmed.

"Best of Charming luck to you all," said the Sarge cheerfully, blowing a kiss. "Two years since a ballroom fatality in this castle! Let's try to make it three."

SMASHING PRINCESSES PARADE IN PUMPKINS! THE INSIDE STORY.

"So they weren't kidding about the pumpkins," said Ziyi of Xix. She wasn't sure what smelled worse, the princesses or the carriage they rode in on.

At the kingdom border, each princess had alighted from her own intricate (and well-ventilated) carriage in the drizzling rain to be crammed four apiece into the official Charming Pumpkins.

Here they were, all damp antique lace and slow-drying wool capes, their hair brittle with unguents from four different kingdoms, their faces smeared with powder and polish that should have been washed off and reapplied three rest stops ago, trundling along inside a gilded, horse-drawn... well.

It was a bloody pumpkin, wasn't it?

Everyone knew that the kingdom of Charming was proud of its fairy-tale heritage — just like Ziyi's empire was unreasonably proud of the things its citizens could do with tea leaves — but this was ridiculous. Did the farmers grow the pumpkins this large deliberately? Was magic involved? Whose idea had it been to grow giant pumpkins for coaches, instead of sensibly building a simulacrum out of wood and steel?

Ziyi considered herself lucky that she had scored a place by the door, so she could inhale occasional mouthfuls of dusty air through the small latched gap instead of the heady cocktail of royal musk and dried squash.

The rain hadn't helped. Princesses always smelled terrible in packs. On their own, they would not be too rank, their scent belonging to the entire package of clothes and hair and manners so carefully designed to attract a mate, and/or impress his elderly relatives.

But *en masse,* and damp? Ugh. Every perfume of the known world, jumbled together in a single carriage, warring for attention. It was like sitting in a cosmetics factory that had been unexpectedly invaded by scented silk marigolds and pollen monsters.

Apart from herself, Ziyi's coach contained one veteran princess — Laurana of Thalm, a long-necked blonde hardened, like Ziyi herself, by multiple campaigns across multiple social seasons in multiple foreign kingdoms — and two newly 'out' young princesses whom Ziyi had mentally named Ninny 1 and Ninny 2.

Laurana and Ziyi had never met before, but they shared a curt nod of mutual understanding upon first introductions. Thalm was almost as far away as Xix. You didn't hunt for a marriage over such a distance if you were considered a good prospect in your own territory.

Finally, the coach rattled to a stop. Ziyi and Laurana immediately acquired a lapful of Ninny each, as the younger girls clambered forth to peer through the window.

"Are they reporters?" Ninny 1 squealed. "Will there be monochromes?"

Ninny 2, not quite as aptly named as her companion, realised the ramifications of this and hurled herself back on to her own half of the bench, rummaging for what cosmetics she had left in her vanity pouch. "This is awful. They can't monochrome us like this. I'm a wreck!"

"I wouldn't worry about it," Laurana said dryly. "They'll only use images from this scene if nothing of any import happens tonight at the ball… or if one of you manages to flash her knickerbockers while alighting from the pumpkin."

Ziyi ignored them all. This was it. Had to be. She wasn't going through it again. Charming would be her final kingdom, and her last season.

She had to catch a prince or die trying.

Even thinking that made a little piece of her soul die. Her life was so embarrassing.

REPORTING LIVE FROM CASTLE CHARMING

Kai felt like a seagull pecking at crumbs on the shore as he stood with the press gaggle on the steps of the Palace. "Will they even want to speak to us?" He couldn't imagine wanting to talk to strange reporters after travelling for several hours — in some cases, several days — to reach Castle Charming.

"It doesn't matter whether they do or not," said Amira, rising and falling on her feet beside him. She was shorter than Kai, despite her alarmingly high heeled boots, and he could see her calculating whether it was better to stand up on the steps from the carriageway — thus being higher and having a better view — or to be down and close as the pumpkins approached. "The important thing is that we are here, witnessing their arrival, reporting live from Castle Charming. We catch the quotes, describe the frocks and styles and excitement, and we move on to the big event tonight."

He nodded, quill pen hovering over his notebook. "Got it."

"Stick to positive flattery for the most part," she added. "Unless something hilarious happens, like a knickerbocker flash. Word is the princes aren't going to be allowed to escape this season without mating, which means that one of these girls will be our future queen. No reason to put the poor peahens offside from the start."

Kai considered that in light of what he had read in the Herald over the last few years, the endless trash-talking of the boys in the palace. "So, no one minds pissing off our future king?"

She glanced around to check no one was close enough to hear what she said. "You've obviously never tried to piss off one of those princes. It's like water off the back of a gold-plated duck in a raincoat. Besides, every reporter at the Herald has been holding back for years, just in case King Iolchas comes out of his fog and starts reading newspapers again."

Kai blinked. "The coverage over the last few years has been the Herald holding *back*?"

"Oh, honey. I don't think the magical ink could actually handle some of the scandals we've discreetly reworded for public consumption."

He wasn't sure whether to be shocked or impressed. "So we go easy on the princesses. For now."

"Exactly. Apart from the general ethics of not slamming them too early in the season — some of those wenches are crazycakes. They're ruthless, ambitious, and unlike our local Royals, perfectly capable of sneaking into the Herald offices in the dead of night and setting fire to your desk."

Kai stared at her in horror.

Amira shrugged. "It only happened one time, but if we don't learn from these experiences, we're no better than animals." She leaned into him, discreetly pointing at the cluster of their co-workers and competitors. "Keep an eye on Llew at the front there, the one in the green tunic. He has an eye on the Assistant Editor's job when Maggie retires, so he'll be going big or going home this season. Don't let him near your quills and parchment, he's been known to rewrite other people's copy to leave out the juicy deets, and save them for his own stories."

Kai took note of the heavy-set reporter in the front row. "Is everyone here from the Herald?" There were more than a dozen reporters, and at least eight monochromists setting up heavy equipment along the steps.

"And the Kingdom Weekly. They pretend they're too highbrow for gossip, but when the season hits they're not too proud to squash a few frocks on to their front cover. A few of the stragglers on the edge there are from the outer town gazettes, and there's one or two representatives from the newspapers of border kingdoms — Mountainside have two princesses joining us for the season this year, and the River-lands are so bored of reporting flood damage that they usually send a few quills across to collect gossip. Their royal family is too young to play for the season, so they live vicariously through our national sport."

"And the kids?" Okay, Kai was barely of age himself, but he was certain that the youngsters juggling some seriously vintage monochrome cameras down on the lowest step weren't even old enough to read the Herald, let alone work for the paper.

"Oh, they're from the Whistler," Amira shrugged. "Up at the Academy. Didn't you work for the school newspaper when you were there?"

"I didn't go to the Academy," Kai said, startled.

"Huh. You just have that look, you know."

"What look?"

"Like you went to a fancy private school. Something about the eyebrows. Also the accent. And the politeness. But mostly the accent."

"My mother was a governess," he growled, not liking her

assumptions at all. "We travelled all over – pretty much everywhere but this kingdom."

"There you go, then. Fancy."

A hubbub sprang up from the crowd as the first of the Charming pumpkins rattled precariously up the carriageway.

"Cheer up, Kai, you have the best job in the world," Amira said breathlessly. "Get in there, my son." She promptly elbowed him out of the way and darted at the coach. Llew in the green tunic gasped and swore as Amira's high heel drove into his foot.

The foreign princesses emerged from the lopsided root vegetable on wheels, smiling and glowing. If their gowns were somewhat wilted (and honestly who decided they should travel in floor length dresses, that seemed unnaturally cruel?) then they hadn't noticed — their chins stuck proudly upwards, with feathered headdresses swooping over their beautifully coiffed hair.

As if they were preparing for battle. Or some elaborate hazing ritual.

The air filled with the pop and crack of monochrome explosions, tearing up the space between the reporters and the princesses with flashes of ink and light, recording their calculated smiles on silver plates for printing.

Questions shot out from the cluster of reporters, even as more pumpkins rolled up and more noblewomen levered themselves out, blinking in the autumn sunshine. Only two of the pumpkins contained genuine princesses; the rest were a more general assortment of aristocratic debutantes. There were even a few young men here and there — it was the height of rudeness to send too many unmarried princes or lords to a season like this when it was known that the host wanted his sons married off, but no one wanted to be left without suitable dance partners in the meantime. Some wily kingdoms sent sons as chaperones to their sisters, well aware that the Charming princes could only take one wife apiece and there would be plenty of disappointed leftovers who might be bought for a bargain.

The male guests were ignored entirely by the assembly of reporters, who knew where the kingdom's real interest lay. Half of their questions were about what the ladies were wearing right now, and the rest were about what they would be wearing for the ball that evening.

Frocks, frocks, frocks.

Kai's eye was drawn to one of the princesses from the first coach. Her smile was every bit as practiced and pretty as the others, but there was a sharpness to her as she surveyed the crowd. He immediately dubbed her Princess Most Likely To Be Smuggling a Shiv. She became aware of his gaze and met it with a challenging stare.

As the noblewomen made their way up the steps, the reporters and monochromists fell back to make an avenue for their procession.

Kai finally got up the stones to holler a question of his own, and blurted the words "Are you going to meet the prince of your dreams tonight?" to the Princess Most Likely To Stab Me In My Sleep.

She gave him a searingly sarcastic expression, then batted her eyelashes at him. "It's what we were born for," she drawled.

Oh, he liked her.

"Are you going to meet the prince of
your dreams tonight?"

THE CARE AND MAINTENANCE OF PRINCESS HAIR

Ziyi was the only princess who had not brought a retinue of relatives, maids or ladies-in-waiting with her to the castle. Her reasoning was simple: everyone she brought from her own kingdom was likely to be a spy for her family, and might put a spoke in the wheel of her plans.

So, she was given the impoverished step-cousin of suites, in a crumbling corner of the castle. She was provided with the service of Abigale, who was called in to 'do' for visiting ladies at Castle Charming during the season, and spent the rest of the year as a shepherdess. Or possibly a milkmaid. Some sort of healthy outdoor job involving dairy product or lanolin, anyway. Her hands were terribly soft.

Abigale had two hairstyles she could master: three-strand braids and four-strand braids. She faltered at the array of pearl pins and jade clasps that Ziyi usually required for formal hair attire.

"I thought we could tie fresh jasmine into your hair," said the maid, biting her plump lower lip. "Tuck it into a braid, like."

"Goodness, why?" asked Ziyi in alarm. She hated the

cloying smell of jasmine. It reminded her of her mother's funeral.

"To let them know where you're from," said the maid. "You're of the Jasmine Empire, ain't you?"

Ziyi flinched. "Is that what you call us?" It could be worse. The first time she travelled abroad, she discovered that her home was often referred to as Gunpowder Isle by outsiders. Still, she would rather be the gunpowder princess than be named after a sickly sweet flower.

"Why?" said Abigale in surprise. "Ain't that what you call yourselves?"

"We call ourselves Xix," said Ziyi.

"That's not nearly as pretty as the Jasmine Empire," Abigale decided, brushing Ziyi's hair so hard that static electricity flew around them. "What's your name mean, then, in your tongue?"

"It means ziyi," said the princess, refusing to translate. "Put my hair in the jasmine," she decided. If Castle Charming expected an exotic cliche of a Xixese noblewoman, then she would meet their expectations. The best thing about a disguise was that, once you removed it, you could disappear entirely.

DRUNK PRINCE IN GAZEBO SHOCK!

"How could you lose him?" Corporal Jack demanded. She had two inches on Dennis in height and used both of them to great effect as she loomed over him. "Chase of Charming is a drunken sot of a prince wearing fuchsia satin. He's not exactly camouflaged!"

"I swear," said Dennis desperately. "He was right here!"

His first night as a Royal Hound was not going well.

Prince Chase had seemed amiable enough when he joined his entourage for the evening, making a point of remembering Dennis' name and sharing a joke or two with Jack before they joined 'the fray' which was the two-hour receiving line before the Autumnal Fling began.

Then there was the dancing. Jack and Dennis had stood by the sidelines and watched as Chase and his brother Cyrus — who was similar in aspect but wore less glitter powder in his hair and had restrained himself to a jacket of emerald satin instead of the fuchsia — paraded an endless swirl of marriageable damsels around the ballroom decorated with thousands of gilded autumn leaves.

An easy night in theory, if you didn't mind standing to

attention for hours on end, but now he had stuffed up good and proper. It had been Dennis' job to supervise Prince Chase while Corporal Jack made the eleven o'clock check-in with Sarge, and in that tiny window of time he had somehow been talked into a 'breath of fresh air' on the balcony that led them — well, here. Wandering around the well-lit castle gardens, searching for an errant fuchsia prince.

"Sarge is going to have our ears for this," groaned Jack.

"Excuse me," said a polite voice. "Are you — uh, looking for a fellow in satin?"

Dennis whirled around to see an awkward-looking boy with dark hair and very bright blue eyes. "Have you seen him?"

The stranger gestured with a thumb. "He's throwing up in the gazebo."

"Oh, brilliant," said Jack, and took off at a run.

Chase was in a sorry state when they found him on the floor of the ornamental gazebo. He had indeed been emptying his stomach into one of the large antique urns.

"I swear I found him like that," said Mr Helpful.

"No one thought otherwise," snapped Jack.

Dennis stared down at Chase's glazed eyes. It was impressive, how dedicated the prince was to getting off his face. "He was out of sight for fifteen minutes. How did he drink so much?"

"He was already far gone when the evening started," said Jack through gritted teeth.

Dennis had enjoyed his share of wild nights with friends, but he was starting to think he was a doe-eyed innocent compared to everyone else in this palace. "He looked fine," he ventured.

"He always does," said Jack with pained cynicism. "Here, you two, help me get him to the fountain for some clean up."

Dennis came forward to catch one of Prince Chase's

flailing arms, and their new friend helped to lever the nearly dead-weight of the prince upwards. As the three (four) of them manoeuvred themselves awkwardly out of the darkened gazebo and out into a pool of light from the paper lanterns along the avenue, Jack sucked in a breath.

"Oh hell," she growled. "I thought you were one of the foreign princes."

"No," said Mr Helpful. "I just sound like I went to one of those schools. I'm quite ordinary, really."

"You're a quill," said Jack, like it was a dirty word.

Quill meant reporter. That was bad, right? *We have to protect them from more than assassins.*

"Do people actually call us that?" asked the stranger. "It's my first day."

"It's my first day too," Dennis broke in. "But I can already tell when Jack is about to punch someone, so maybe it's time to make yourself scarce, mate?"

It was a shame, really. Their helpful stranger was about Dennis' age, and very nice to look at. (He had promised himself he wasn't looking, not this year. He had enough to manage without bringing down that kind of trouble on his head.)

"Sorry," said the quill, letting go of his half of the prince. "Look, I can push off if you like, but I promise I won't write about this."

"Is anyone interested that I'm about to throw up again?" demanded the prince, opening his eyes long enough to collapse into the nearest hydrangea bush.

"I didn't push him," said Jack calmly.

"No one thought otherwise," said the quill, and smiled a beautiful smile.

Trouble, Dennis told himself sternly. *Don't.*

"Jack," said his corporal gruffly, holding out a hand. "This is Dennis. Thanks for your help. And your silence."

"Kai," said the quill, gripping her hand with his own. "Don't mention it. Only an idiot would try to start out with a *Drunk Prince in Gazebo Shock* byline his first day."

"They generally prefer you to work up to those," Jack agreed.

"Besides," said Kai, growing bold. "We all know it wouldn't be a shock to anyone."

"Still lying in a bush!" announced the prince.

"Exactly what you deserve," said Jack, yanking Chase to his feet again, and draping him decoratively over one of Dennis' shoulders.

"I miss when you used to be fun, Jax," sighed the prince with a pout.

Huh. That was interesting. Exactly how well did they know each other? Dennis pretended not to notice the weird intimacy between Prince Chase and his Hound, and he spotted that Kai was pretending not to notice the same thing. Their eyes met for a moment, and they exchanged awkward smiles.

BREAKFAST OF QUILLS

"*...* And then we took turns scooping water over the prince's head until he sobered up, and the Hounds dragged him off to bed."

Kai finished describing his evening to Amira over breakfast rolls. She had dragged him out of his digs first thing to steer him into the Queen's Bishop, a small and only slightly seedy coffee house near the Herald offices. He was pretty sure this meant that they were not merely two people whose desks were parked next to each other, but officially friends.

"Aww, most of us have to be with the Herald at least a month before we get our very own drunken prince encounter," Amira said, refilling their tiny glasses from the communal coffee pot. "Let alone a tasty Hound to flirt with."

"There was no flirting!" Kai protested. He would, he suspected, always regret letting her know that he now had a thing for men in uniform.

"She was right, though," Amira went on. "You can't write it. *Prince Gets Trashed in Gazebo* is barely even Page 6 material — and besides, while you were hanging out with Hounds and Royals, you missed the biggest story of the week. Maybe the season. The story that's going to swallow us whole and spit us out after."

"What?" said Kai. "Did someone break a punchbowl in the ballroom?"

"Better than that," said Amira with glee. "We're talking a glass slipper situation. Accept no substitutions."

LIVING THE FAIRY TALE

Everyone knows the story of the Rags to Riches Queen… the glass slippers and the fairy godmother, the ball and the mice and the Happily Ever After.

No one ever talks about how long Happily Ever After lasted.

Magical happy endings come at a cost, and this was hers: cursed that if her heart ever broke, she would fall into a terrible sleep until it could be mended again.

It seemed no risk at all, at the time of their marriage. Their future was golden. As the new king and queen of Castle Charming, they had wealth and power, the boundless love of their people. They had silver-eyed twins, as happy and joyous as any children could be. Then the second pair of twins, the dark-haired babies that the kingdom took to its heart.

The king and queen thought themselves immune from heartbreak. But one of their babies was stolen, and nothing that they had — the magic, the wealth, the Hounds — nothing could help them find that child.

The queen's heart broke, and she was lost forever to the enchanted sleep.

Those left behind — her king, their sons and their daughter, remained awake and breathing, but equally broken.

They're still breaking. Every day. Before the eyes of the kingdom.

No one ever tells that part of the story. No one can bear to say the words aloud.

WHO IS THE MIDNIGHT PRINCESS? YOUR MOST POPULAR GUESSES, INSIDE

"A glass slipper situation," Kai repeated.

"Pure and beautiful," confirmed Amira. "The full bit. A mysterious, masked princess arrived in the ballroom shortly before midnight. She danced with Prince Cyrus three times, and then — this is where things get weird. She legged it out of the ballroom the second that the clock struck midnight."

"And she left a shoe behind."

"I see you're familiar with the trope."

Kai shook his head, breathing disbelief into his coffee glass. "But who would —"

"I know."

"Seriously, who —"

"I *know*."

"Who would have the balls to do the glass slipper thing in Castle Charming?"

"The Midnight Princess, that's who," said Amira. "The name was my idea," she added modestly. "Front page head-line, thank you very much."

"It's so tacky," Kai said, turning it over in his head.

"Get stuffed."

"No — not the Midnight Princess, that's a genius name, obviously."

"That's better," she said, blowing him a kiss. "Drink up, pet, we have to get into the office. Time to run through mugshots of the candidates."

"Do you think it's some kind of protest?" Kai asked, following her dutifully, though it pained him to leave the last few inches of coffee in his glass. He swallowed it down hard, scalding his throat. "Or satire?"

"Live action theatre, you mean? Graffiti of the ballroom variety. A one person flash mob."

"She can't be seriously intending to marry a prince with this technique. Not in this kingdom. What was the king's reaction?"

"He wasn't there. Retired early due to boredom, or ennui, or whatever it is that makes him ghost through the castle, ignoring his sons," said Amira. "Sorry, did I say that out loud? Sometimes I have to get these things out before I step into the office."

"I heard nothing," said Kai dutifully. "So. Midnight Princess?"

"If we can find her," said Amira. "Then we can ask all these questions and more. Story of the century. Want to team up?"

"Why would you pick me?" Kai asked, and then thought about it for two seconds. "Oh. I'm new and no real threat to you."

"Good boy. Also, your arms are longer than mine and believe me, we'll be logging more than a few hours hauling boxes in the archives. We need to know everything about all the girls of the season if we're going to blow this story wide open."

THE FIRST RULE OF GLASS SLIPPERS IS YOU DON'T TALK ABOUT GLASS SLIPPERS

Dennis worked at the castle for a year before he was tapped to join the Hounds, and in all that time he had never seen the king so angry.

To be honest, he had never seen the king express any feelings at all. The man had a fog about him — he was broken-hearted due to grief, so everyone said, but he functioned well enough when there were practical decisions to be made, or conversation to be had about the weather.

He showed up, but never seemed to care about anything.

Today, the king cared. He had been in the Doghouse with Sarge for more than twenty minutes, shouting and blustering, while the Hounds gathered outside, finding minor tasks to busy their hands with, so as to pretend they were not eavesdropping like champions.

Finally, the door opened and the king stormed out, his seneschals clinging to the hem of his fur-trimmed velvet coat. "You will find and arrest this disrespectful wench before the next ball, or I will send everyone of those grasping, diamond-studded hussies back to their kingdoms and cancel the season!"

"Your Majesty," said Sarge with a calculated, neutral sort of deference.

"Do your fucking job, or I'll find someone else to do it for you!"

"Glad you're not overreacting at all, Father," broke in a drawling voice. The Hounds parted to let through a blond, gorgeously jacketed prince — not Chase, Dennis realised. The other one. They were technically identical, but the elder prince, Cyrus, was a dedicated athlete as well as a party boy. Unlike his brother, he had some muscle about his shoulders and legs, which he showed off with sharply-cut clothing.

They looked nothing like their father — his hair was dark and neat, his eyes a sharp blaze of sapphire blue instead of their otherworldly silver matched with blond. They must take after their cursed mother, the one that no one ever talked about.

"Don't start on me, boy," growled the king. "This is all your fault, as usual."

"Don't let me interrupt your rant," said Cyrus, his eyes glittering. "It's so fascinating to see you up and about, expressing opinions to the staff. The same staff who will have to clean up the mess when your egocentric bullshit pushes us to the brink of war."

King Iolchas lurched angrily towards his son — they were the same height, and Dennis spotted the exact moment that this fact came as a surprise to His Majesty. "Don't lecture me on what you don't understand, you little degenerate."

"I know that arresting a princess for dancing without tact is not the best move for a kingdom as small as ours," said Cyrus, smiling with all his teeth.

"Don't think I haven't considered the possibility that this is one of your childish, attention-grabbing pranks," the king snarled, close enough now to embrace his son, though it was clear that wouldn't be happening.

"Ah," said Cyrus, mocking. "Because I live to hurt you, apparently. Funny. I thought it was the other way around."

The king stood frozen for a moment, hand raised at waist-height, as if to cuff a child. Without saying anything more, he thundered away.

Cyrus squared his shoulders, disregarding that the Hounds around him had witnessed such an intensely personal exchange between he and his father. He nodded to Sarge. "Permission to attend your briefing, Sergeant Clay? I feel that it's pertinent to my interests."

Sarge surveyed him critically. "Can you sit still in the corner and keep your yap shut?"

"Stranger things have happened," the prince declared.

"Go on, then. Let's give it a whirl."

The Hounds filed into the Doghouse, more subdued than usual. Dennis stood close to Corporal Jack, who was visibly seething. Did she resent the prince's presence so much?

"Right," said Sarge, stepping up on his crate. "I'll keep this brief. There will be no arrests. If any of you come across evidence of the identity of the — *person* that the Herald has dubbed the Midnight Princess, you will bring that evidence directly to me." He gave Prince Cyrus a hard look. "That includes you, Your Highness."

Cyrus reached into his jacket, and pulled out a glass slipper. An actual — it gleamed like a diamond. Dennis couldn't stop staring at it. "It stinks of magic," Prince Cyrus said, holding it by the heel. "Do you mean to say we won't be going door to door, trying it on the feet of ladies? I was so looking forward to that part."

"We'll hold off on that for now," said Sarge, holding out a small burlap evidence sack for the prince to drop the shoe inside. "No arrests. No confrontations. His Majesty might not be concerned with the diplomatic fallout from treating visiting princesses like criminals, but our primary job is security of the royal family, and that goes further than dragging them out of gazebos in the middle of the night." His eye fell briefly on Dennis, he smirked.

One of the new recruits — Dante — raised a hand. "Sarge, do you think the Midnight Princess poses a significant threat to the royal family?"

Sarge huffed at that. "Depends on what you mean by threat. She was close enough to assassinate Prince Cyrus last night, and she didn't try it."

"My heart is thoroughly protected, if that's what you mean, kid," put in Cyrus, who had to be only a year or two older than Dante himself. "I know better than to pledge marriage and eternal love to a girl because she's excellent at waltzing and has decided to enact the courtship of my parents."

"Whatever this girl's game is," Sarge went on. "I don't think she represents a physical threat."

"But how can you be sure?" Corporal Jack demanded.

Sarge gave her a weary look. "Because I'm an old, old man, and I've seen everything," he told her. "Glass slippers mean that the so-called Midnight Princess has got herself tangled up with fairies, and that means she's got bigger problems than you or I can handle with a crossbow and a short sword."

"What should I do?" spoke up Prince Cyrus. "If I should happen to see her again."

There was something haunted in Sarge's face. "Try not to kiss her," he said finally. "In fact, it would be wise not to kiss *anyone* for the next 48 hours. If you think you can manage that, Your Highness."

11

PROWLING WITH HOUNDS

"I t's my second night," Dennis said aloud because really, it had to be said. "My second night as a Hound, Jack. I haven't even drawn my first pay yet."

"Well aware," Corporal Jack said evenly.

"We're stalking our boss through the seediest bars of the city. On my second night."

"Shhh now."

They were not stalking so much as waiting. Both of them had signed off from their day's shift and were supposed to be resting up before the next Grand Event of the season, tomorrow night.

"You're going to get me fired," Dennis complained.

"Sarge respects initiative," said Jack.

"More than he respects his own privacy?"

Corporal Jack blew out a breath of annoyance. She terrified the rest of the Hounds into constant compliance, but Dennis was not yet trained into blindly following her orders, especially orders that were not entirely work-related.

Which begged the question: why had she chosen him for this particular expedition?

"I'm worried," Jack admitted.

"About Sarge?"

"It's fairies. He has a thing about fairies. Last time we had a case that maybe — only maybe — involved a fairy godmother, he went on a bender for two days. So yeah. I want to keep an eye on him." She gave Dennis a sly look over her shoulder. "Also I have a pathological need to know what the hell is going on at all times, especially when it relates to the smooth running of Castle Charming and its security. Are we on the same page?"

"Fine, yes. I'm curious too."

"Good lad."

They leaned against a wall outside a bar charmingly titled The Lunatic Arms until Sarge rolled out, several sheets to the wind. He did not see either of them, and headed off down the street at an unsteady angle.

"He never drinks on duty," Jack said in a low voice, and Dennis realised to his surprise that she was embarrassed on behalf of their boss.

"I'm not judging," he said softly.

She punched his arm, which might be a sign that he'd said the right thing.

They didn't talk as they trailed Sarge back to the castle. He didn't look terribly drunk, though he listed to one side and walked with a slower rolling of the hips than usual. He did not head for the Doghouse or the guard quarters, but made directly for the ornamental gardens.

"We can make fun of him if he ends up in the gazebo, right?" Dennis whispered.

Jack choked on something that might have been a laugh. "Only behind his back and forever."

Ahead of them, Sarge broke into a run. "I knew you were around here!" he hollered through a flowering archway. "I could smell your bluebell bullshit a mile off. Come out here and face me, you bastards!"

12

SPITTING WITH PRINCESSES

Ziyi was so angry she could spit — if a princess was allowed to spit — if there was anywhere in any royal castle that allowed for the possibility of discreet princess spittage.

Ziyi was so angry, she wanted to set the world on fire.

She sat through a day of gossip and finger sandwiches, and tamped down the fury inside her with many tiny cups of tea. She allowed Abigale to lever her into a fluffy nightgown that belonged in a dusty attic (or possibly a museum of antiquities) and stayed docile while her long black hair was twisted into hundreds of tiny 'pin curls' that she would regret by morning.

As soon as Abigale moved on to the next foreign princess on her schedule, Ziyi hauled the midnight gown out from under her bed and stuffed it — trailing lace fronds, sequinned buttons and all — into a large handkerchief bag.

Oh, and the glass slipper. Mustn't forget the damned glass slipper.

Ziyi slithered out of the window and down the ivy trellis

until her feet hit grass, and then she was off and running, past the fancy hedge maze and the brick wall of alcoves containing statues of every king and queen of Charming, rendered perfectly in white marble and smug.

Finally, she found a secluded grotto beyond a series of flowered archways, a cozy nook of a meditation pool decorated with crystal flowers, far from the lanterns and public paths. Here, she could light the blue candle without fearing that she might be seen from the many, many windows of Castle Charming. It smelled of bluebells and sugar and broken promises.

"Godmother, godmother, I have a bone to pick with you," she said aloud.

"And here I am, reporting for duty." The voice was warm and sensual and unquestionably male. It was not the voice of her fairy godmother.

Ziyi leaped back, staring at the shelf of stone that ran around the top of the grotto, and the man who was suddenly draped across the stone shelf like a cat. "Who are you? You're not Miss Clover."

"Why, thank you for noticing. My name is Master Foxglove." His eyes gleamed purple in the darkness. "She's otherwise engaged tonight. You don't think you're the only princess who has demands on her time?"

"I might have known," Ziyi retorted. "First I have to share a maid, and now a godmother. Welcome to the end of the century."

"Never mind, sweetling, I may not be your fairy godmother, but I am *a* fairy godmother, and I am well acquainted with Miss Clover's open cases." Master Foxglove leaped suddenly, landing on his feet with a terrifying grace. "You're the Midnight Princess, aren't you? Frock and glass slippers and magical perfect timing — I can't believe you have any grounds to complain."

"No grounds?" Ziyi was furious. If Miss Clover wouldn't show her face, then she would happily take it out on the nearest godmother available. "I went along with this appalling charade because I needed to secure a fast marriage. Miss Clover convinced me it would be *cute*, recreating the glass slipper story of Castle Charming."

Master Foxglove considered the matter. "Sounds freaking cute. Sweeping one of the princes off his heels with the same storyline that worked for his mum and dad? Epic."

"It wasn't cute," Ziyi hissed between her teeth. "His family didn't think it was adorable and romantic. Turns out the entire kingdom is highly *traumatised* by how that love story ended, and I'm the airhead who mocked their misery for all the world to see. The king has put out an arrest warrant, and is one throbbing forehead vein away from having the guest rooms searched. Will you stop laughing at me?"

Master Foxglove snickered wildly, hanging on to the wall of the grotto to support him. "You don't think it's hilarious?"

"Was this deliberate?" Ziyi snarled, close to belting him with her bag. "Is this one of those 'careful what you wish for' stings that the fairy tales warn against? Because *I thought* Miss Clover was sincere in wanting to help me, and instead I'm screwed six ways to Sunday."

The fairy godmother peered at her from between his fingers, like a child playing games. His voice was deadly serious. "How important is it that you marry this prince?"

"I don't care about the prince," Ziyi said impatiently. "I can't go home, and I thought marrying a prince was the best way to assure that."

"Interesting." He tilted his head, his purple eyes glowing even more intensely than before. "I suggest you take that incriminating bag of yours, and make a run for it."

"Why?"

"Because I'm about to get punched in the face by a man

with the power to arrest you." Master Foxglove looked pleased at the very idea, even as the shouting started, from some distance away.

"I could smell your bluebell bullshit a mile off. Come out here and face me, you bastards!"

13

HUNTING WITH QUILLS

K ai could not believe the luck of it. The story of the century had fallen into his lap, and this time he wasn't going to let it go.

He had tried pitching several original pieces to the editor, who turned all of them down flat. Amira shook her head at him afterwards. "If you're not writing about the Midnight Princess right now, pet, you're invisible."

"But *everyone's* writing about the Midnight Princess," Kai said in frustration.

"There's always a new angle."

A new angle on the story that had been done to death in less than 24 hours? Sure.

So Kai returned to the castle, walking the path that the fleeing princess must have taken after the ball, trying to get his head around a 'new angle'. He didn't question why he needed to be here, why the castle was tugging at him, until he noticed that his ink was itchy.

Kai had a magical tattoo on the small of his back: his mother had always told him that in the kingdom they came from, it was traditional to have a fortune tattoo bespelled to each child, marking out their destined path in life.

His had never made a lot of sense: it was a literal blot of ink most of the time, shimmering and occasionally splashing, as if a new drop had been added. Sometimes it resolved itself into words, though they were hard for him to read and he had rarely been in a position to ask others to translate for him.

On the few occasions he was drawn to the changing images by the itch of the ink, and held a mirror up in time to get a good look, he had caught what looked like newspaper headlines: Castle Charming Princes Go Wild and the like.

This had been enough to convince his reluctant mother that his path lay here after all, that being a quill was a profession he could excel at, though she would have preferred something more highbrow for him: a writer of ballads, perhaps, or a scholar of journals.

Kai had never in his life regretted following where the ink urged him. Tonight, it clearly wanted him here, in this garden behind the castle, for whatever reason.

It certainly wasn't for inspiration. He had been walking around in circles to no avail for hours.

Just as he was about to give up, he spied a girl in a nightgown climbing down the trellis and running off into the garden. He wasn't sure if it was her — the actual Midnight Princess herself — until he crept closer and heard something of her conversation with the sinister, beautiful fairy gentleman.

This was pure gold. Story of the century. But it was all too fanciful to write up for the Charming Herald without something solid to tether it.

An interview. He would have to interview the Midnight Princess.

"I could smell your bluebell bullshit a mile off. Come out here and face me, you bastards!"

The princess fled the scene as soon as she heard that yell in the distance. Kai went after her, scrambling around urns and hedges until he got in front of her. She was hurrying too fast to stop, smacked directly into him and fell into a silver pear tree.

"Oof!" The princess stared up at him in horror. "I know you — aren't you one of those quills who were sniffing around the staircase my first day?"

"Yes," Kai said breathlessly, to the Princess Most Likely To Poison his Coffee. "And I can find a hiding spot where the Hounds won't find you. Interested?"

Why had he said that? He barely knew this castle at all. And yet… and yet, the ink was tugging at him, and he always followed where the ink led. It brought him to this kingdom, this job, this castle.

The princess glared at him for a moment, then lifted one hand imperiously so he could help her out of the bushy tree. "What do you want in exchange?"

"Your story," Kai blurted. "I want to tell your story to the world."

Her eyes narrowed. "Can you make the king of Charming hate me less?"

"If I can't," he promised in a moment of valiant exaggeration. "No one can."

14

MIDNIGHT PRINCESS EXPOSED!

Z iyi must be crazy to trust this stranger — a reporter, no less — but she didn't fancy sticking around while the Hounds and her feckless substitute fairy godmother went at it tooth and claw in the gardens.

So, she followed the quill.

"Kai," he told her, as he led the way through a copse of trees to a tower she had never noticed before, well away from the castle. "My name is Kai. I'm new around here, like you."

"Not a lot like me," she observed.

He gave her a lopsided grin. "No, not a lot like you. Um. Your Highness."

"*Don't*," she winced. "If you can't be on first name terms with a scandalous young man who rescued you in a garden, then what's the point of being a princess?"

"If you say so." Kai seemed bemused to be labelled a scandalous young man.

"Ziyi," she told him. In for a pearl, in for a diamond. "I'm not much of a princess."

"That's all right," he told her. "I'm not much of a quill. I'm working on it, though."

As she watched, Kai found a key under a loose paving stone and opened up the tower.

"Have you been here before?" she asked.

There was a pause that went on a little too long before he said "No," in a confused voice.

"Then how did you know —"

"Look, a kitchen," he announced, pushing through the door to a small, shabby room with the basic requirements of a kitchen, including a wood stove that burned low, as if it had been abandoned for the night.

"If that's your way of offering me a cup of tea," said Ziyi. "You can have my firstborn child, if you like."

So the chipped sapphire of Xix sat at a clean but small kitchen table and rested her chin on her hands while the young reporter lit a cozy fire in the grate, and heated up a kettle of water. "How did you even know about this place?" she asked.

"I don't know, exactly," said Kai, sounding frustrated. He plucked aside a makeshift curtain and gaped for a moment into the next room. "Oh. Actually, that explains a lot."

Ziyi followed him, peering around his shoulder. She had expected this to be some kind of servant's quarters, or a space for the gardeners to take their tea during the day, not… well. An artist's retreat?

The studio was the canvas. Every inch of wall, ceiling and floor was covered with strange, arcane drawings in vivid black ink. Ziyi saw dragons and fairies, historical battles, flowers and knights. The ceiling blazed with what might have been a royal family portrait from the old days — when the princes were toddlers, and their siblings babes in arms — but a large smear of ink had ruined the image.

There was a chill to this room, despite the warmth from the stove in the kitchen behind them. They had both made footprints in the dust.

"Ink," Kai said, sounding subdued. "That's why I became a quill, you know. I've always had an affinity with ink. It speaks to me — like, literally, I could hear these walls halfway across the garden, pulling me in."

"A useful talent," Ziyi observed.

"You don't think it's strange?"

"I'm not sure if I can judge what's strange any more. Not since I put my life in the hands of a fairy godmother."

"I used to make art like this," Kai said dreamily, his eyes on the ink-daubed walls. "My mother disapproves of art almost as much as she does of magic — she thinks that sort of thing is all aristo indulgence. Not for ordinary folks like us."

"So," said Ziyi thoughtfully. "You came to write for a newspaper, where you would be surrounded by magic and ink all the time. To torture yourself, I presume?"

"Mother hates that I spend my days hunting royal gossip and scandal," Kai said. "She was furious I wanted to move here for this job. Once I turned eighteen she couldn't stop me."

"It's a shame that families can have such an effect on your future prospects," Ziyi mused, as they returned to the kitchen. "I don't know if princessing counts as a trade or a profession, but I'm not cut out for it. I sat through a thousand different Imperial Education classes and did everything I was told, but… somehow it didn't work. The only part I was ever good at was the war and weapons training, and now there's no war. I've had maids who were more convincing princesses than I am."

"The Midnight Princess scandal wasn't a great move, that's for sure," Kai said awkwardly, pulling his eyes away from the studio to return to his tea-making duties over the stove.

Ziyi sighed, leaning on the doorframe. "It's a disaster, that's what it is. Can I have tea yet?"

"Water's boiled, I'm just brewing," he said, adding tea to a pot and topping it with the hot water.

"Your newspaper thinks I'm a nutcase," Ziyi accused him. "Or a gold digger, I suppose?"

"Isn't that what you all are?" Kai asked absently, busy about his task.

She sucked in a breath.

"Oh, I didn't mean to insult you or anything. But you came here to marry a prince, didn't you? That's pretty much a definition of — well. Um."

She glared at him. "All this friendliness will be wasted if I have to slap you before I've had my tea. Tell me more about how the ink invited us in."

"The artwork in there," said Kai. "It's ink, the same kind of enchanted ink we use to make the newspapers. I felt it scratching away at me, like a cat wanting to be let in the door. When I stepped inside, I felt safe."

"Good to know someone does," said a third voice, filling the kitchen. "Hello, strangers. Is there tea? I'll forgive your trespassing if you've made tea."

Ziyi froze in the act of accepting a cup from Kai. He looked horrified.

"Oh," said Ziyi. "Have mine." She immediately regretted the sacrifice.

"No, I'll pour another," said Kai desperately, to cover his embarrassment. "My lady, I'm — I wouldn't have set foot in here if I thought it was someone's home. I'm so sorry. It looked abandoned."

"Indeed," said their unexpected hostess, stepping down from the shadowy stairwell in the corner, to join them. "That was deliberate, to keep people away."

She was a young lady of quality from the look of her, old enough to have been presented at court, though her dark hair spilled down her back like she had never been out in public.

She wore a bohemian smock and a beaded belt, but her accent was pure cut glass. The kind of voice that elocution instructors insisted upon, once the foreign languages had been mastered.

Ink patterns spiralled up and down the lady's arms, tattoos that danced and moved as if alive. She was quality, and she was magic. A rare combination.

Ziyi might be a failure of a princess, but she knew how to act royal in a jam. She sipped her tea as if nothing in the world could bother her. "Ziyi of Xix," she introduced herself. "One of the visiting princesses, here for the season."

"But of course you are," said their hostess, accepting a cup from Kai as her due, and taking a seat of her own at the kitchen table. "Camilla of Charming," she added. "I'm what they call the home team."

Kai dropped the teapot, which smashed in a small explosion of hot water and leaves all over the floor.

"Damn," said Camilla, the hidden princess, the younger sister of Chase and Cyrus, the one never seen in public. "I liked that teapot. Never mind, there's another above the cheese barrel, if we require more tea. We *will* require more tea," she added to Ziyi, with an air of exchanging confidences. "I never feel right until I have at least two cups. Didn't your people invent it? They must all be terribly clever."

15

FAIRY GODMOTHERS FIGHT DIRTY

"I could smell your bluebell bullshit a mile off. Come out here and face me, you bastards!"

There was a splash of water, and a thud, and a grunt.

Dennis and Jack ran after the Sarge, to find him in a grotto, rolling around in the contemplation pool with yet another beautiful boy — seriously, why were all the men in this castle so attractive, it was like the universe was trying to tell Dennis something.

They fought like equals, no holding back, all elbows and teeth and fury, though the fury was mostly on Sarge's side. His opponent with his wild dark hair and clothes made of — oh, flower petals — was enjoying himself far too much, with a bloodstained grin and fiercely bright eyes.

"Where — is — Illyria?" Sarge growled into his opponent's neck as he pinned him in the water, about to shove his face under.

"That's not her name any more," laughed the fairy. Of course it was a fairy. "You know how to find her, sweetling. Light a candle in her new name, and make a wish."

Sarge snarled at him. The fairy kissed him on the jaw,

laughed again, and vanished, leaving the angry human alone in the shallow pool of water.

Dennis and Jack exchanged silent looks, then came forward to help him out.

Sarge pushed them away once his feet were on dry land, then shook himself like a dog to get the water out of his sodden clothes and hair. "Not a word of this to anyone," he growled.

"If it helps," said Dennis. "I saw which way the Midnight Princess went."

Jack gave him a sharp look. "Oh really?"

He nodded, and managed not to confess that he had taken particular note of the direction when he saw her collide with that boy he liked, the quill from the night before.

There was something about Jack that made Dennis want to confess all his sins while crying on her shoulder, but not today.

"Right then," said Sarge. "Let's catch ourselves a princess."

16

A RIGHT ROYAL TEA PARTY

K ai tried not to panic. He was surrounded by ink — the paintings in the studio, the tattoos on the arms of this unexpected princess. The smell of vanilla and wet feathers was a comfort, and more than that.

The ink was inside his head in a way he hadn't allowed it to be for a very long time. And it was telling him that he belonged here.

Here, in a kitchen, taking tea with two princesses. This was not what he had expected when he decided *newspapers* as the compromise he and Mother would both have to live with.

"It's a stepmother thing," said Ziyi of Xix, the dishevelled foreign princess who had finally stopped looking like she was about to pull out a hidden weapon.

"Oh, stepmothers," sighed Camilla. "I was spared that at least."

"I have at least twelve," said Ziyi. "My father's latest wife has a son of her own, the kind of horrid creature who likes to pull wings off beetles for the fun of it, and I'm very much the third spare daughter unmarried in the palace. One more failed season is all it's going to take for my father to be convinced that marrying my stepbrother is a safe, sensible choice for me."

"Kings never listen," Camilla said in grim agreement. "Not to daughters. They have dozens voices commanding their attention, and ours are so far down the list of priorities that they don't feel the need to even tune in to the words. Never mind that royal women are trained from an early age to spot social dangers and subtle problems long before they become diplomatic disasters."

"That's my story," said Ziyi, spreading her fingers wide. "The one you can never write about," she added with a stern look at Kai.

This evening was so surreal already, it didn't hurt to give her that promise. "We can find a better story," Kai said. "If you really want to — if you need to find a better alternative. It's going to have to be romance, not practicality."

Camilla and Ziyi gave him equal expressions of disdain, as if it should have been obvious to him that romance and practicality went hand in hand, with princesses.

"I'll shut up now," he volunteered.

"I have an idea," said Camilla brightly. "I shall introduce you both to my mother."

17

LET SLEEPING QUEENS LIE

This was.

This was without a doubt.

This was without a doubt the most difficult social situation that Ziyi had ever navigated, in her entire world-weary history as a princess on the marriage market.

Queen Ella of Charming lay on a bed made of glass, in the room at the very top of the tower.

It was an exquisite piece of artwork, that glass bed. It had pillars and platforms and blown roses. But to Ziyi, who had seen her own mother buried before she was ten years old, it looked like a coffin.

In every way, except that the glass panel nearest the queen's pale lips occasionally clouded over from her sleeping breath.

"So," said Camilla, who sounded bright and cheerful and not at all as if she were about to cry. "This is the curse that broke our kingdom."

Kai stood by the doorway, not wanting to even step inside the room. Ziyi did not blame him. This was the woman she had wronged, without realising it — the woman whose epic love story she had copied for her own selfish needs.

If her mother was like this, trapped in an endless state between life and death, she would break. It was amazing that Camilla's eyes remained dry. Ziyi wanted to cry for her.

"I'm so sorry," she whispered, not exactly to Camilla.

"Never mind that now," said Camilla. "We need to resolve this Midnight Princess business. The question is, how are we going to do that without marrying you off to one of my silly brothers? Unless you really do want to marry one of them. I suppose someone has to."

"No," said Ziyi, mortified. "I mean — I couldn't *now*."

There was a thud at the door, and then again, a massive boom of a sound, and the breaking of wood.

"Oh, hell," said Camilla of Charming. "More visitors."

Kai moved closer to Ziyi. She would have him as her witness, at least, someone who could swear blind she hadn't tried to hurt the queen, or the princess.

"Royal Hounds!" shouted a voice from below.

"You'd better come up!" Camilla called into the stairwell. "Take your shoes off, this carpet can't hold up against mud."

They burst through the door a moment later, without their boots — the Sergeant with the bluebell fixation, his two junior Royal Hounds in casual clothes that didn't fool anyone, and a platinum sylph of a young man in an embroidered silk dressing gown and a knowing smile that wouldn't quit.

One of the princes, Ziyi realised with a flame of embarrassment. She couldn't even tell if it was the twin she had danced with.

If only she had developed the art of the fake swoon, instead of spending all her training hours on useless princess arts like duelling, and rope climbing. Now would be an excellent time to have some damsel skills to fall back on.

18

TOMORROW'S HEADLINES

This was the greatest story that Kai would never be able to write. First, the two princesses, sharing confidences over tea. Then, the glass coffin of the cursed queen. He could not imagine that many quills had been allowed into this private sanctum.

Now there was the sight of three tough-nut Royal Hounds in their socked feet, pretending they had the situation under control.

Kai didn't even have time to indulge in his awkward crush on Dennis, the wide-shouldered blond boy, not now, not with so much going on.

Not with a Prince Charming in the room, smirking like he planned to write the headlines himself.

FOREIGN PRINCESS CAUGHT IN CURSED QUEEN'S BEDCHAMBER came to mind, and Kai was instantly ashamed of himself.

"Cyrus," said Camilla, and kissed her brother's cheek. "I haven't seen you for an age. Why did they dig you out of bed?"

"Sergeant Clay didn't dare break into your private quarters without a royal permission slip," said Prince Cyrus. "We know how you value your privacy, darling."

The Sergeant, who was dripping wet for some reason, looked annoyed at this summation of events.

Kai fell into a new wave of panic, because he had strolled in here as if he owned the place, just because he smelled some interesting ink, and the princess surely had every right to…

He was so caught up in his thoughts that he missed the most obvious and newsworthy event of the evening, when Prince Cyrus was formally introduced to Princess Ziyi of Xix.

"Awk-ward," Dennis muttered in an undertone. Kai had been creeping close and closer to the Hounds, as they stood between him and the door.

"More tea!" announced Camilla, clapping her hands as her brother and the Midnight Princess stared at each other with a mixture of hesitation and suspicion. "So much tea. Kai, will you be godmother? Sorry, Sergeant," she added, patting him lightly on the shoulder. "Didn't mean to raise old ghosts. Let's trot down, shall we?"

Tea. Because of course that made sense.

19

WAR AVERTED: CRUMPETS IMPLICATED

This was how war ended and marriages were made, Dennis decided — over tea and crumpets and sardine sandwiches at midnight with the representatives of royal families and their advisors, chewing over a problem until it quietly went away.

Prince Chase turned up, grumbling, looking for his brother Cyrus, who welcomed him to the party. Chase was sober for once, and mocked the awkward situation between his brother and the Midnight Princess so expertly that there would be no puns left for the newspaper to use in its headlines for a week.

Princess Ziyi dropped her own embarrassment sometime around Prince Chase's third inappropriate joke, when she threw a sardine at him, and his brother and sister laughed so hard that they almost choked on their own cups of tea.

Royals, Dennis thought, had a different code of what was appropriate, and they bloody well made it up as they went along.

Sarge, despite his soaked clothes, was obviously a trusted ally to the Charming siblings. He won several brownie points with Princess Ziyi when he agreed without question that her family emergency was just as important as their homegrown King Iolchas Is About To Screw Up Years of Diplomacy With His Hissy Fit situation.

Corporal Jack stood near the fireplace, wearing her generic facial expression of 'I'm not even listening to any of you' which Dennis longed to master. He and Kai stood near each other, almost certainly because it put them in the best position for the plate of sandwiches, and not for any other reason.

"On a scale of one to ten, how much are you longing to take notes right now?" he whispered.

Kai gave him a sardonic look. "I'm waiting for them to remember what I do for a living and chuck me out," he replied, just as quietly. "I'm pretty sure they shoot quills for sport around here."

"Assuming the two of you don't actually want to get married," Camilla was saying thoughtfully.

"NO," said Ziyi and Cyrus in unison, and then looked apologetically at each other.

"No point to it," drawled Chase. "It would solve this young lady's problem, but not our own diplomatic crisis. What we need — what both parties need — is for the Midnight Princess to disappear without trace."

Sarge gave the prince a dirty look. "We don't do that in this kingdom, Your Highness."

"Certainly not!" snapped Camilla.

"Um," said Ziyi, looking alarmed.

"Oh, how adorable, you thought I meant to assassinate her," said Chase. "No, my sister doesn't have the skill-set to clean blood out of furnishings, and besides, too many witnesses." He gave Dennis an arch look over his shoulder.

"Good," growled Sarge. "I've hidden enough bodies for this family."

All of the Royals looked startled at that, and only Camilla laughed.

"He was joking," noted Corporal Jack, making Dennis jump. For a woman made out of stone, she was pretty sneaky.

"I got that," he replied.

"Making sure that your friend did," said Jack, giving Kai a dirty look.

"I'm surrounded by aristos and their guard dogs," Kai sighed. "I'm just going to assume that 90% of what everyone says tonight is sarcasm, metaphor, or a personal threat."

"Chase has a plan," announced Camilla. "I knew it was a good idea to bring him in on this. Cyrus, pass Chase a cake."

"*Whose* idea was it to bring him?" teased her brother. "Chase doesn't need more cake, he won't fit into his favourite waistcoat."

"The Midnight Princess needs to disappear," Chase said loudly. He gave Ziyi a very undiplomatic once-over. "How attached are you to the label of princess?"

"I'd have ripped it off at birth if I could," she said instantly.

"Have you any useful skills, as an ordinary citizen? We all know you can run fast."

She frowned. "The usual princess things. Porcelain painting. Religious dance. Poetry recital. Twelve different forms of martial art including special weapons and anti-kidnapping techniques. Tinkling conversation…"

"Oh," said Sarge softly, and shook his head. "Got it. You'll have to marry me," he added to Ziyi.

She took that in stride, smiling. "I think that will do nicely."

"What?" Jack demanded. "I mean, *what*?"

"Calm your knees, corporal, I'm not actually going to marry her."

"Good, because she's half your age, Sarge, I was either going to have to punch you or arrest you…"

"The good Sergeant is suggesting that I should write home and let them know I have eloped with someone most unsuitable to my station in life," said Ziyi softly. "He is offering his name, which means his protection, which is kind but unnecessary. It would be better, I think, if I was seen to leave the kingdom of Charming altogether before my unfortunate imaginary marriage."

"But where will you go?" Dennis blurted. He had sisters, and the thought of one of them disappearing into another kingdom with nothing but a letter full of falsehoods made him sick to his stomach.

"One of our newbies quit after the Autumnal Fling," said Sarge. "No stomach for it. There's always one. Slip this lass into a tabard and a helm, cut her hair, no one will spot her as a princess in hiding. Not if she can throw an opponent as well as the Xixese warriors I've met before."

"I believe I can be adequate to the task," said Ziyi. She glowed all over, as if the very thought of freedom had set her on fire.

Corporal Jack looked angrier at this idea than she was about the fake marriage, but she said nothing.

Dennis felt Kai shift beside him. "It's not enough," said the serious young quill, finally calling attention to his presence. "I'm sorry, but it's not. The Midnight Princess is the story of the season. The Herald is never going to stop hunting for her, and as long as their — *our* headlines are screaming that story, I don't imagine the king will calm down, either."

Chase and Cyrus turned their faces towards him, so similar that it made Dennis shiver.

"So, we need a better story," said one of the princes as if it was obvious.

"A bigger story," agreed his brother, "To swallow the

Midnight Princess whole, and push her back to page 6, then page 12, then page 24."

They stared expectantly at Kai.

Kai gulped.

"That's easy," said Camilla, and she might be darker than her brothers in hair and skin tone, but she looked like their reflection as she leaned in to share her idea. "I think it's time, don't you?"

Everyone in the room went very still. Chase and Cyrus both got an odd look on their identical faces, a softness despite their sharp features.

"Really, darling?" said Cyrus.

Camilla smiled brilliantly, and motioned Kai to come and sit beside her. "I've dumped this whole royal burden on the two of you for years. Time I shared the load. The hidden princess is coming out into the sunshine. How does that sound?"

"Story of the century," said Kai approvingly.

Dennis stood there with Jack, two watchful Hounds, as tomorrow's history was planned out with meticulous precision. Sarge drew Ziyi aside, almost looking cheerful as he dared her to show him a few of her defensive moves.

Kai sat with Princess Camilla and both of the Princes, talking animatedly — and finally allowed to take notes! The four of them plotted out what should be said, and written, practically finishing each other's sentences as they worked. Dennis could not take his eyes off Kai, how alive he seemed in this moment, crafting the story that would surely make his career.

For a moment, a brief moment, he allowed himself to *want*, fiercely.

Beside him, Jack drew in a breath. "Do you see that?" she whispered. "Am I imagining that?"

Dennis could not see anything but Kai in his element. "What do you mean?"

"Oh, I —" she shrugged, and rolled back against the wall, her defenses drawn up like a drawbridge. "Nothing. It doesn't matter."

DENNIS DIDN'T REALISE what Jack had noticed until later, much later.

Sarge dragged Ziyi off to reinvent her as a new recruit for the Royal Hounds. He insisted Jack join them 'to provide a girl's opinion,' a phrase for which Sarge would pay dearly, in the weeks to come.

Camilla and her brothers disappeared back up into the tower, planning her grand coming out at the next ball two days hence. She would wear the Midnight Princess gown and mask, dance with both of her brothers, and finally her father, if he hadn't called the Hounds to arrest her already.

She would allow herself to be revealed, the hidden princess coming home to her family and her kingdom and her castle.

Kai's story, Dennis imagined, would be written and filed ahead of time, guaranteeing he would be the first quill to capture the story of the century.

The Midnight Princess Exposed.

NOW IT WAS ONLY the two of them left, sitting on the steps outside the tower as dawn came, sending fingers of light across the beautiful gardens of Castle Charming.

"I just," said Kai, and laughed with a hint of hysteria in his voice. "I'm coming to terms with it, I suppose. These are the sorts of things that happen when you move to a fairy tale kingdom."

"You'll get used to it," said Dennis, leaning back on his elbows.

"Pumpkins and godmothers and princesses and — really? Those are things you get used to?"

Dennis had lived in this kingdom his whole life. "Talking cats, too," he remarked.

"I almost believe you."

The early morning sunlight hit the tower, and when Dennis next looked across at Kai, the other boy was lit up all over, haloed in sunlight. For one giddy moment, Dennis thought about breaking his promise to himself and kissing, touching, letting this unspoken thing between them unravel.

Except.

There, in a halo of sunlight, sprawled comfortably on the steps of a tower that contained a cursed queen, two fairy tale princes and their beautiful, strange, inked-up sister, Dennis realised how very familiar Kai looked.

Dennis swallowed. Jack must have realised this in the kitchen, the odd similarity. In the sunlight, his dark hair all glossy and reflective, Kai looked a great deal like the Princes Charming. He had the cheekbones, the nose — the colouring was wrong, but not after you had spent the evening around Princess Camilla, with her spill of black hair, her olive skin tone closer to that of their father than the pale complexion of the golden-haired cursed queen.

The age was right. Kai spent his childhood travelling, away from Charming… he couldn't have guessed who he was. If Dennis' horrible guess was correct.

Because yes. This was the kind of shit that happened to you when you lived in a fairy tale kingdom: the boy you wanted to kiss started to look a lot like a long-lost prince.

Dennis had no words for this. He didn't know what to say.

Perhaps, he thought desperately, he didn't have to say anything at all. It wasn't his place. Let someone else break the next story of the century, the one that left the Midnight Princess forgotten in the dust.

He wasn't a quill. *This wasn't his job.*

Kai winced into the brightness of the sun, and looked like himself again, beautiful and serious and ordinary. Not the least bit royal. "Hey," he said, letting his hand brush against Dennis' knee. "Do you want to grab breakfast?"

"Sure," said Dennis, when breathing became possible again. "I could eat."

He was a Royal Hound, charged with protecting and serving the royal family. Keeping them safe. And keeping his mouth shut.

For now.

MIDNIGHT PRINCESS REVEALS ALL

Camilla of Charming's Years of Silence, Her Family Tragedy, And The Glass Slipper That Ended Her Exile

EXCLUSIVE INTERVIEW
BYLINE: KAI FOSTER AND AMIRA CHAUDRY
ONLY IN THE CHARMING HERALD
6 COPPER TOADS SUPPLEMENT ON SATURDAYS
BRINGING THE NEWS TO EVERY DOORSTEP
IN THE KINGDOM OF CHARMING AND BEYOND

DANCE, PRINCES, DANCE

WINTER

Winter 1499
Price: 3 Copper Toads
Castle Charming #2
est. 1066
YOU WON'T BELIEVE YOUR EYES!!!
DANCE, PRINCES, DANCE!
Tansy Rayner Roberts

1

ARMOUR UP!

They called her Ziggy or Zig, close enough to her original name in their flat accents that it didn't feel like she had become a different person… though of course, she had. The sharp, sarcastic princess from the exotic island empire of Xix had disappeared, to be replaced by a quiet, diligent Royal Hound cadet.

She had aching muscles from the hard training that was expected of a royal bodyguard. She had friends. She had work she enjoyed. The martial arts disciplines she had inhaled as a child were finally useful. No one was ever going to insist that she married a prince. Life was good.

Only –

No one had warned her about *this*.

"I don't think there's enough armour," Ziyi gasped as Dennis and Corporal Jack tightened the thick leather straps around her, shoving a helm with a mesh face-guard over her head.

"You'll be fine, Zig," said Dennis, smacking her helpfully between the shoulder blades. That boy kept forgetting how strong he was. Normally she liked that he never treated her like some hothouse flower. "Get out there, try not to get hit, and make us proud."

"I'm not ready!" Ziyi insisted. "There must be someone else who can…"

"It's tradition," Jack and Dennis chorused, and what was with that? Dennis had been a Royal Hound for maybe a week before 'Cadet Ziggy' joined up. How was he suddenly an expert on what was and was not castle tradition?

"Does this helm have actual horns on it?" Ziyi demanded.

"You can do it, kid," Jack told her. She was also wearing the thick leather padding, the helm and the horns. "I'll be with you every step of the way. Head up, eyes bright, grip your stick… and don't drop the ball."

"Why would I be anywhere near the ball?" Ziyi yelped, but it was too late. Dennis had one of her arms, Jack had the other, and the ground whooshed past her feet until she landed on the grass, in the midst of the game.

Somewhere, a whistle blew. Ziyi failed to see how that was constructive.

ROOKERY WAS a sport invented by bored princes three generations ago, which should have been the first red flag. Castle Charming had a particular sympathy with bored princes, enabling their more destructive tendencies and protecting them from the worst consequences of their actions.

The relationship between castle and princes was less than healthy; this should surprise no one.

Prince Cyrus spent more time on recreational athletics than he had ever spent on his royal duties. Prince Chase preferred to get his athletic training via sneaking out to clubs in the city or in neighbouring kingdoms, dancing for hours, and hooking up with strangers.

One prince rose early to train before breakfast; the other slept until noon or, on many occasions, nightfall. They lived hard, played harder, and defied their father at every turn. At nineteen, barely a couple of months away from coming of age as heirs to the kingdom, they were both set in their ways.

But every year, as autumn gave way to the chill winds of winter at Castle Charming, the two princes came together with their friends to play a weekly rookery championship against a team of their own bodyguards: Royals vs. Hounds. It was the social and sporting event of the winter, for those who played and those who watched.

The winter half of the season was more relaxed than the frantic autumn whirl of dances and receptions and matchmaking. Many attractive young people had already found their future spouses and sat upon their smug laurels to plan a wedding. The rest mostly embraced the more intimate potential of house parties in the country until well after New Year — Castle Charming was chill in winter, and less than hospitable for guests. The only outsiders remaining were those hardy young women still set upon bagging a prince. They had managed to get their families to send them chests of furs and woollen layers so they could participate in the traditional winter sports of ice skating, flirting on frosted balconies, and cheering on their chosen rookery champions.

Kai Foster learned all of this from Amira, his mentor and closest friend at the *Charming Herald* since he signed on as a junior reporter or 'quill' a few months ago. She wasted a whole twenty minutes explaining the rules of rookery to him, of which he only absorbed 'five-player teams' and 'they wear a lot of leather' and 'chances are high you will see one of the princes thrown in a pit'.

"So, audiences aren't usually this big?" Kai asked Amira, as a mob of teenagers shoved past them to get to the few remaining seats.

"Nope," said Amira. "It's usually just us, a few diehard statistics nuts, and the last handful of marriage hopefuls." She indicated the row of beautiful debutantes shivering under thick blankets and furs on the front bench with homemade signs indicating their preference for Prince Cyrus or Prince Chase. "Everyone reads about the games and talks about the games but no one bothers to actually attend. Still, you know. Everything about this year is different."

This year, the Royals team wasn't only made up of Cyrus, Chase and their closest friends and cousins: this year, they had a princess on their side.

Seventeen-year-old Princess Camilla of Charming had recently returned to public life. Her dark hair was now styled into something trim and fashionable, but she still looked more bohemian artist than Royal, with her tattooed arms and her mocking, sarcastic ways. Kai glanced across to her now, just as Camilla shared a fist-bump with two of her teammates: Serena, Countess of Argyll, and Gawain of Gaheris. Both were distant Charming cousins, and favourites of the family.

Kai liked Princess Camilla a lot. Her life had become so busy and complicated recently when she embraced royal duty, but she still made time to teach him about the magical connection to ink that they both shared. He could not quite believe that she had let her brothers talk her into playing sport — but Camilla was laughing now as Cyrus shoved a spiky helmet over her fashionable hair.

"She's pretty," said Amira with an arch expression.

Kai rolled his eyes at her. "Please don't." Camilla of Charming was 100% not his type.

"Don't worry," smirked Amira. "No one will accuse you of treason or journalistic bias if you cheer for the Hounds instead."

Because yes, there was Kai's type, on the other side of the pitch. The blond, wide-shouldered Hound cadet Dennis. All wrapped in leather and about to take to the field in a crazy game of spikes and kicking. Kai let his gaze linger for a moment before he blushed and looked away. "That's not happening either."

He had thought it might, but they had settled comfortably into being friends, and that was fine. It was enough. He knew better than to expect more.

"Such a disappointment to me, Kai," Amira said gravely, shaking her head. "If I can't live vicariously through your romantic exploits, I'm going to have to get myself a date-friend, and who has time for that nonsense?"

The whistle blew, and the game began. Kai tried to follow it, but there were three spiked leather balls in play. He couldn't remember how many points were scored if a ball hit a side post before being knocked into one of the wide pits in the grass, or when a ball was hurled into one of the three 'nests' that were suspended over the icy pitch. It was all a blur of terrifying, well-padded violence. After Dennis got a bloody nose from catching a spike to the face, Kai couldn't even watch any more.

His eye was drawn to the side of the pitch, where Dennis' Sarge stood wistfully, as if he wished he could be out there with the other Hounds. After Sergeant Clay had broken his leg in mid-game two years in a row, both teams ganged up on him, declaring he should stick to coaching.

Kai frowned as a tall, brown stranger approached the Sarge. The man had a military look about him, all handsome competence and shoulders beneath a soft blue turban. Like the Sarge, this man's face was hard-worn for someone who couldn't be near forty yet.

Sergeant Clay was startled to see the other man, clearly not a stranger to him. They exchanged a professional handshake and an awkward half-hug, then promptly started arguing with each other. Eventually, the Sarge stormed off, dragging his acquaintance with him. Friend or enemy? It was hard to tell.

"Is that a story?" Amira asked, leaning against Kai's shoulder without taking her own eyes off the game.

"You never know," Kai muttered.

One thing he had learned since coming to work at Castle Charming: everything was a story, but the most interesting ones never made it to the front page.

2

THE 'TEAM' IN STEAM

The first rookery match of the winter was a 1–1 draw. This in no way conveyed the sheer grind that the players put themselves through.

Dennis had the biggest target on his back: he was new blood, and had more muscle than most of the Hounds on Corporal Jack's team (except for Jack herself who was a force of freaking nature with excellent posture). Worst of all, he accidentally let slip in front of Prince Cyrus that he had played before.

Dennis was a local boy, raised in the mountains behind the little city that sprawled around Castle Charming. He and his mates played rookery with balls so old that their leather spikes had hardened like steel, and genuine abandoned eagle's nests tied to trees with strips of bark.

Yeah, he should have kept that under wraps if he didn't want to have at least one Royal marking him every time he took a step on the pitch. Serena of Argyll, a glamorous socialite every other day of the year, embraced rookery with the determination of a small angry dragon. She dogged his steps, blocking him whenever he tried to pass the ball.

Princess Camilla only played for a few minutes, to give the newspapers a chance to capture her action in monochrome as much as anything. She didn't have the same level of shoving and thumping skills as her brothers, but she had a good turn of speed. Obviously she had been doing something other than painting on walls and sighing sadly during the years she was hidden from view.

The big surprise was Ziggy. Their newest recruit was nervous at first, but her fighting instincts kicked in the second Prince Chase tried to trip her. She shifted her weight and flipped him into one of the side pits, which earned a penalty to the Royals, and a standing ovation to the Hounds. Even Chase was still grinning about it when they fished him out.

Dennis claimed the assist on the Hounds' only goal after passing to Jack in a messy scramble that got the ball in the nest and saved them from total humiliation.

Still, he managed to play the whole 90 minutes without gazing longingly at Kai, who was rugged up under scarves and coat in the stands. For Dennis, that was the most important victory of all.

BEING A ROYAL HOUND, personal bodyguard to the disgraceful teenage princes of Castle Charming, had led to many indignities and uncomfortable crossing-of-boundaries in the few months since Dennis accepted the position.

He was the last of this year's official cadets still standing: Dante quit the Hounds a week ago, when he caught Prince Chase on his knees in a coat cupboard, paying his respects to a young lady who turned out to be Dante's girlfriend.

Then there was Ziggy, who hadn't started out as one of this year's recruits, but was offered the position by Camilla and the princes when she needed to hide in a hurry. Dennis was glad there were two permanent positions available at the end of the season, so he didn't have to compete with Zig to keep his job.

He wasn't sure he could beat her.

She was a Royal herself until a couple of months ago, so Ziggy didn't blink at the weird informality between the royal teenagers and the young people hired to protect them. Dennis had learned a lot from her — including a masterful poker face, and an ability to go with the flow no matter what idiotic idea a prince pitched at them. (In turn, he would give her a quiet signal of warning whenever her inner princess began to show.)

Was he really the only one who felt this was weird? Sharing a sauna with the royal family as they recovered from the beating that both teams had given each other on the rookery pitch today… that was a blurring of boundaries that would horrify Dennis' own family.

There wasn't much about his current life that wouldn't horrify his family.

"Hey man, I think I can see my boot print on your butt," said Chase, peering at Dennis' bruised hip with pride.

"You wish," muttered Dennis, hitching his towel up more to cover the bruise. "That one was friendly fire." He gave Zig a dirty look.

On the other side of the sauna, Ziggy sat with Princess Camilla, Corporal Jack and Serena of Argyll, taking in the steam and admiring each other's bruises. No one — except those in on the scheme — recognised her as the same Princess Ziyi who had appeared in the flurry of husband-seeking debutantes when the season opened a few months ago. Zig's hair was short now, making her look boyish and several years younger. She smiled more genuinely now, relieved to be out of the princess business.

Dennis understood. This was something he and Zig had in

common. Being a Hound was so much better than anything they had left behind, even when they had to put up with the Royals treating them like friends instead of armed babysitters.

"Good game today," said Serena, wandering over from her end of the sauna, wearing a towel that had been designed to wrap around a much smaller person. She leaned over Dennis as if he wasn't even there, giving Prince Chase a high five. As she pulled back, she dropped a lazy wink in Dennis' direction, and let her towel slip further.

This sort of thing happened a lot. He had tried wearing his Book of Parnassus sash once or twice on duty. He'd hoped an expression of piety would provide sufficient excuse for not taking up the more enthusiastic ladies of the court on their not-so-subtle attempts to add another Royal Hound notch to their… Garter belts? Bed posts? All of the above.

Anyway, that was a disaster. Being a devout worshipper of the mountain gods only made Dennis more enticing to a certain kind of bored aristo lady, because now he was viewed as a challenge.

He could put them off by telling the truth, that he was really only interested in men (and one soulful-eyed newspaper reporter in particular), but he wasn't ready to share that information. Both princes and many of their friends were blissfully careless about such things — Dennis had followed Prince Chase into enough clubs to know that he was equally attracted to men as women, for a start — but they could afford to be.

In any case, the thing Dennis had for Kai was hopeless. Better to never acknowledge it.

"Where are we celebrating tonight?" asked Gawain, bumping shoulders with Prince Cyrus. "The Blue Dragon? Or further afield?"

Further afield meant sneaking out beyond the bounds of

the princes' curfew, to the outer city or beyond. It meant disobeying the rules laid out for the Royal Hounds by the king himself.

Sarge always said, 'princes gonna prince'. Unofficial policy was that it was better for the Hounds to join them on their stupid drunken adventures than to remind them it wasn't allowed, and risk them sneaking out on their own.

Fergus, another of the Hounds, groaned beside Dennis. "Guess I'm not reading a story to my kid tonight," he muttered, quietly enough that only Dennis could hear.

According to Jack and the older Hounds, this was the time of year that the princes usually ran completely off the rails, rebelling against the social expectations of the season. They had been behaving suspiciously well lately, as if Camilla's presence gave them more of a reason to consider their responsibilities.

The two princes exchanged a look.

"Nah," said Chase after a moment. "Got a lot on tomorrow. Best have an early night."

"Yeah, early night," Cyrus agreed.

Their friends chirped and harassed them, but the two princes stood firm that they wouldn't be partying.

"You've been good for weeks," Serena pouted. "You're no fun anymore, Chase."

"Maybe I'm growing up," said Prince Chase.

"Maybe you're trying to impress someone," she shot back. "I wonder who?"

"Maybe we just want to ensure that we beat the Hounds at the next match," declared Cyrus.

"You'll need more than a good night's sleep for that," Dennis said automatically, and the sauna erupted into teasing and laughter. The refusal of the princes to go out with their friends was dropped. For now.

As they headed out of the steam room, Dennis exchanged a look with Corporal Jack. The princes of Castle Charming were up to something, and it was their job to figure out what, before it turned into a full-bore disaster.

3

LOOK AT MY SHOES

Kai inhaled the scent of the ink. It wrapped around his lungs, and drew him in. He could taste the history in the ink, the words it had touched, the pens it had brushed against. As he breathed out, he remembered the first quill pen he had ever held as a child. He pictured every detail of it, every flare of feather, every scratch and line.

When he opened his eyes, he saw a perfect illustration of that quill appear for a moment on his forearm, before it exploded in a spreading patch of spilled black ink.

"Good," said Princess Camilla, using her own magic to clear off the failed tattoo.

"It doesn't feel like a win," Kai grumbled.

"You can't expect to be perfect straight away." She gave him a stern look, like she was an elderly aunt instead of a wild-eyed, magical princess almost exactly his age. "I had eight failed ink blots all over my legs before I even learned the charm to undo magical tattoos. Count yourself lucky you have a fabulous magical tutor like me."

"So lucky," he sighed.

Somewhere, a door flung open. "Camilla!" called an angry voice.

The princess looked tense. "Oh, stars. What does he want now?"

Kai half expected one of her brothers to march in. They often assumed they had the right to fill any space in the castle that they liked, even their sister's private workroom.

This was worse than that. This was the king.

King Iolchas was a narrow-boned, elegant man with dark hair and bright blue eyes — he looked very like his daughter, only thirty years older and carrying the weight of the kingdom on his shoulders. Kai shrank back into his seat as the king marched into the workshop, his burning charisma and fury filling the room like an entirely different kind of magic.

"Who is this?" the king demanded, eyes burning into Kai. "One of those reporters who has been sniffing around the castle?" Well. He wasn't wrong.

"This is Kai, my apprentice," Camilla said, standing up to assert her dignity in the face of this invasion. "You said I could keep practicing magic."

The king faltered, his initial reason for anger floating away in the face of this new problem. "You shouldn't be alone with a man."

"Oh, please," Camilla scoffed. "My brothers have a co-ed steam room, and Chase is openly bisexual. If you don't object to them hanging around with half-naked friends of all genders, you can't start applying random societal ideas of conformity to me."

King Iolchas looked puzzled, as he often did when his daughter spoke. "Never mind that," he said, dismissing Kai's presence as irrelevant. "I want to talk to you about the shoes."

"By all means," said Camilla, blinking at him. "The shoes."

"I know I said I would foot the bill for your new wardrobe, but this bill from the shoemakers is ridiculous."

"Is it?" said Camilla.

Her father waved a sheet of paper at her. "Sixty pairs of satin dancing slippers. Sixty! Not even a professional ballerina goes through that many shoes. You'd better make them last the season. Our household budget does not extend to unnecessary frippery."

"That… seems reasonable," said Camilla. "Anything else, Father?"

"Be at lunch to sit between me and the duchesses," he snapped. "If I never have to have another conversation about herbal remedies it will be too soon." The King of Charming turned around and marched out of the workroom.

Camilla's face slid from the polite, formal expression that her father inspired. She practically threw herself at Kai, eyes bright, arms winding around his neck. "Kai! You're a detective."

"Reporter," he corrected. "Could you not sit on my lap, your father is going to get completely the wrong idea…"

"I need you to help me solve a mystery."

He sighed, giving into the inevitable. "What do you need?"

"Kai," she said in an excited whisper. "Look at my shoes."

He looked. As usual, her thick leather work boots stuck out from under her long skirts. They were battered and solid, and familiar. "Okay?"

"Do you know how many pairs of satin dancing slippers I actually own, Kai? Not counting the pair I borrowed from Ziggy when I pretended I was the Midnight Princess the other month."

"Um," said Kai. "Sixty?"

"Two, Kai. I have two pairs of dancing slippers, one pair

of fluffy slippers, and my work boots. So." She raised her eyebrows at him expectantly.

It sank in. "Who is ordering dance slippers on your father's account?"

"Who is ordering dance slippers?" she agreed. "And where did all those shoes go?"

4

SATIN AND ROSES

Chase danced.

He had no idea where he was; did not remember his usual routine of sneaking out of the castle, ditching his Hounds (or charming them into joining him), scaling a wall or two to be free.

But he was here now, and he danced.

The music was rain and thunder around him, pressure that melted into his skin, flexed into his muscles, sang inside his head.

He caught the arm of a pretty girl, who laughed at him, but let him dance with her, against her, their bodies sliding and grinding to the thick, drugging beat of the music.

Chase danced, and he knew he shouldn't be here, but it tasted so good…

He could see his brother out of the corner of his eye, surrounded by willing dance partners, and if Cyrus had condescended to be here it must be all right. It must be a good choice.

The girl in Chase's arms tilted her head up as if to say

something, but when she opened her mouth, flowers fell out from between her lips like she was drowning in roses.

A dream. That explained a lot.

If this was a dream, then nothing he did had consequence.

Chase pulled her closer, and danced until his feet burned.

HIS TONGUE TASTED like dust and dried leaves. As he awoke in his bed, Chase spat out a mouthful of what turned out to be gritty sprigs of mint and laurel. Huh.

Somewhere, a door slammed, reverberating through his head like a knife vibrating between his eyeballs. "Stop. Noise."

Corporal Jack, mighty and terrifying, strode towards him. She wore her uniform, the perfect red hearts and black spades displayed against the bright white fabric of her tabard. "Where the hell did you go last night?" she demanded.

Ugh, Jax, why?

"Early night," Chase managed, wiping his mouth. Leaves. Had he been sleepwalking? Why would he eat mouthfuls of garden in the middle of the night?

Jack was so angry she was shaking. "We had a deal, Chase. You promised you would take a Hound with you every time, even if you were going to do something monumentally stupid — *especially* if you were going to do something stupid! How did you even get out without us spotting you?"

Chase's feet were surprisingly painful, even for the day after a hard game of rookery. "Don't know what," he started, then pulled back the bedcovers to see that his feet were sore and swollen, blistered along the heels. Bleeding in places. Scraps of what must have once been a pair of silken dancing shoes clung to the reddened flesh. "Damn."

Jack laughed at him, a harsh and furious sound. "But no, you had an early night," she said, heavy with sarcasm.

"Go away." He didn't have time for this — for explaining things to her, when he could not think of a single rational word. Jax had always been his friend. Long before she was Hound to his Prince, when they were kids growing up in the castle not caring about the boundaries that were expected between king's son and cook's daughter, she had always been on his side. She was more of a sister to him than Camilla, with her art and isolation.

But he could not listen to her now; could not stand being lectured to, not with his heart beating so hard in his chest with panic. *What did I do? Where did I go?*

Blackout drunk was nothing new, but Chase had been good lately. He had been behaving himself.

"Shut up," he said again. "Stop talking."

"Chase," said Jack, her voice lower and more concerned. "What's wrong?"

Sympathy was worse than fury. Chase flipped the covers back over his feet and gave her his coldest look. "Who do you think you are? I don't answer to you, Hound."

Jack's eyes narrowed, and for a moment he thought she might hit him. "My apologies, Your Highness," she said after a moment. "I forgot my place."

"Don't let it happen again," he snapped in as vicious a tone as he could manage, and he did not look at her for the entire time it took for Jack to walk away, closing the bedroom door behind her.

Chase winced, examining his feet again. Parts of the shoe were actually mashed into his foot. He peeled the scraps away and got out of bed, hobbling his way across the floor.

Cyrus had an adjoining suite, but usually barred the door because *oh no, you couldn't have your trashy, party-loving brother disturb your beauty sleep when you had running and push-ups to do and raw egg smoothie concoctions to inhale.*

Today, the door was unbarred.

Chase went through without knocking. He wasn't expecting Cyrus to be there, certainly wasn't expecting him to be still asleep. But there he was, that head of tousled hair sticking out from under the covers. Not even a girl with him, to justify the fact that for the first time in the history of the world, Older Twin By Five Minutes had slept in later than Younger And Handsomer Twin.

"Oi," said Chase, bouncing on his brother's bed for good measure, and not only because it was a relief to take his weight off his feet again. "Cy. Where the frig did we go last night? Must have been good."

His brother made a grumbling noise.

"Seriously. Wake up. Hounds are on the warpath. Don't you have some laps to swim before breakfast?" Chase leaned in, and flicked his brother on the ear. "Wake uuuuup."

Prince Cyrus of Charming muttered something indescribably rude, swatted at his brother with an open hand, and then leaned over the side of his bed to vomit a cascade of rose petals all over the carpet.

5

FRONT PAGE SHOES

K ai loved the clippings archives at the *Charming Herald*. Layers and layers of old paper, filed away under dates and themes. Decades of ink, whispering to him.

He was going to have to get one of Camilla's magical tattoos sooner rather than later. His yearning towards ink was getting stronger. At this rate he would end up in here late one night, licking old broadsheets.

"You're keeping something from me!" snapped a voice, loud in the muffled room of history and silence.

"Aargh!" Kai jumped, scattering a folder of clippings to the floor. "You startled me."

"I meant to." Amira stalked towards him, her eyes narrowed. "Look, baby boy has to grow up and fly out of the nest, I get that, but you've been ducking me for weeks and sneaking off to work on this secret project of yours."

"I've been keeping up with my assignments," Kai said defensively. He'd just turned in 400 words on the opening of a new ribbon store in town, and a puff piece about the local fire watch's tally of rescued kittens. He had been more than dutiful when it came to the scut work that the paper expected a rookie reporter to produce.

"Have you even told Bors what you're working on?" she asked. "You're supposed to run everything past editorial."

Kai hesitated. "It's not even anything yet. I mean, I'm not sure. Camilla asked me to —"

Amira glowered at him. "Is it a story or isn't it? Because I can't help thinking that your friendship with Camilla and those criminally attractive Hounds up at the castle is compromising your ability to report for this newspaper."

"I'm not compromised," Kai said hotly, willing himself not to blush.

"Let me see what you're researching." She knelt down and scooped up the clippings. "Fairy sightings? Really?"

"I told you it wasn't anything yet."

"I remember this one." She pulled out one article. "Marina Tyche, she was Head Gossip back when I started. Interviewed this shoemaker about how fairies kept producing new stock for him — made him famous. Then when he was super rich, she quit newspapers to marry him. I think she runs a shoe empire across five kingdoms now. Why were you researching her?"

Kai stared at the ground.

Amira tapped her own chin with a quill. "Okay, forget your mysterious project. I want to talk about Princess Camilla. Over the last several weeks, she has refused to appear at any of the public events scheduled with the king. Rumour has it they're not on speaking terms. With Yule bearing down upon us, it's getting more and more noticeable. Do you know what happened there?"

"I can't," Kai said helplessly. "I hear and see stuff I shouldn't because Camilla trusts me. She's teaching me magic in her spare time. I can't gossip about her."

"Then you are going to have to choose," Amira said

sharply. "Because if you know the truth and you're not willing to put it on the front page of a newspaper, then what are you doing here, Kai? Why am I wasting my time with you?"

This was getting rapidly out of control. But Amira was his friend. He was sure he could trust her. "It's not a story," Kai insisted. "Off the record, yeah? The king is upset about the shoe bill at the castle. He's blaming Camilla, but there are way too many shoes for any one person to go through anyway, and she suspects there's something magical at work. With the shoes. I was looking for precedent about shoe-related curses… but there's nothing. So. Probably a prank or something. Why are you… smiling like that?"

"Not a story?" said Amira. "Kai. Sweetheart. That is *so* a story."

Oh, gods. What had he done? "Off the record," Kai repeated weakly.

"Yeah," said Amira, patting his hand. "That's not a thing."

STORM IN A SHOESHOP

Castle observers have noticed a chilly drop in temperature over the last month, which has nothing to do with the snowy weather bearing down on us just in time for the festive season. Princess Camilla and His Majesty are feuding about… shoe leather?

While our Royals entertain the masses with winter parades, lantern concerts and rookery, behind closed doors they are fighting over the bills, including an extravagant order of satin dancing shoes which went missing long before the bill was paid.

Sources from Charming's most prestigious shoe emporium, Elfin Soles, confirm that the order for the shoes came from within the castle, but would not name the household member who authorised the invoice in the name of the king.

If Princess Camilla is dancing her nights away, no one can confirm where or how she manages it — castle security is at an all-time high, and as our regular subscribers know, the Charming Royals aren't usually this discreet about their partying. But what of our usual Princes Gone Wild, their Royal Highnesses Chase and Cyrus? According to several castle insiders, they have been spending their nights in like good little boys. Wonders will never cease!

Article by Kai Foster.

KAI USUALLY LET himself into the Castle Charming gardens via a small gatehouse, near the isolated tower that Princess Camilla used as a workshop. Camilla warded the gate with an ink scribble that only responded to her — and now Kai — which was how she came and went discreetly in the days before she came out as a Royal.

Today, Kai's palm grazed against the warding symbol, and it did not respond. His magic flared against the ink: he could feel it inside him, but it did not release the lock. He stood there for a moment like an idiot, wondering what error he had made. Wards were simple magic, and he usually didn't have much trouble with them.

When the gate opened, it was because Dennis was on the

other side of it, resplendent in his formal tabard, looking unimpressed.

"Uh, hi," Kai managed.

"Yeah, that's not going to work," Dennis said flatly, nodding to the ink symbol on the gate. "Her Highness changed the wards."

Kai's heart sank. He had hoped Camilla would give him a chance to explain himself. He knew she would be angry, but… "Look, I know I screwed up."

Dennis' face was a wall of awful. Kai hadn't realised how much he liked that smile until now, when it was missing. (That was a lie, Dennis' smile was the Eighth Wonder of the World.)

"You wrote a story about the princess' personal business," Dennis said quietly. "You broke her trust."

"I didn't write that story, I swear."

"Your byline is on it!"

Yeah, Amira had screwed Kai twice over with that little move. She had also taught him a valuable lesson about newspaper ethics versus friendship, but he wasn't thanking her any time soon. Her exact words, when he waved the paper in her face and demanded an explanation were, "It's for the best, kid, you'll thank me some day." Frustrating in a million different ways.

"Amira thinks I'm compromised by having friends in the castle," Kai muttered now.

"Don't think that's going to be a problem anymore," said Dennis, and closed the gate in Kai's face.

6

LET NOTHING YOU DISMAY

K ai was terrible at drinking his sorrows. After swallowing two glasses of something the bartender helpfully referred to as rotgut, he felt sweaty and miserable. The inside of his mouth was trying to eat its way directly through to his stomach.

He tried a beer after that, but it didn't help the situation, and he was pretty sure the bartender would laugh at him if he ordered lemon water to wash the taste away.

Getting drunk alone was *boring*. It concentrated his mind down to two things: Dennis was disappointed with him, and Camilla… was probably also disappointed.

Amira was right. Having friends in the castle was a terrible idea. Good thing he'd ruined that forever.

The tight ball of misery in his stomach was not getting any smaller. Kai sagged back against the corner of the booth, his eyes half closed. The bar, like everything else in the city, was decorated for Yule: green boughs of holly and evergreen hanging from the rafters, along with bright candles and paper lanterns. All very festive. It reminded him that he had promised his mother he would visit her for the holidays this year, which meant several days of enduring her disapproval at his new life here in Charming: of his choice to return to the kingdom she had avoided for his whole childhood, only to 'waste' his education on a newspaper job. That was something to look forward to.

Kai would allow himself to feel completely terrible for just a little longer, and then he would go back to his digs and sleep until the world was better. It was good to have a plan.

The word 'shoes' caught his ears. Then, a moment later, 'dance slippers.' He glanced up and around, only to see two men at a table nearby, bent over what looked like his article (Amira's article, not his article at all) in the *Charming Herald*.

He frowned at the backs of their heads. They looked familiar.

"Can't be a coincidence," muttered one. "It's happening again, and this isn't glass slippers and marriage market material. You know where they're going."

"My duty is to protect these kids," the other growled, and Kai recognised him now. That was Sergeant Clay of the Royal Hounds. Dennis' Sarge. The other was the tall, dark stranger that Kai had seen at the first rookery match, weeks ago. He had a close-cropped black beard, and the bearing of a soldier.

"You have a duty to Illyria," growled the stranger. "Have you forgotten her?"

"I can't get tangled up in all this godmother bullshit, not again," said Sarge.

"If I'm right, none of your precious kids are safe. *They've* found a way in."

Kai thoughts were blurry, and he had missed half of what they were saying, which didn't matter so much now, because they had dropped into hushed whispers. Sarge stood up, shaking his head, and walked out without looking back. His bearded friend stayed, knocking back the rest of his drink before he also headed out.

Kai followed him. He didn't mean to. But this was his story, damn it — he might not have written it yet, but he had researched it and gotten into trouble for it, so it was his. Amira had filled her copy with questions, not answers: Kai needed to find those answers. Even if he shared them privately with Camilla as a peace offering instead of inking them on to the front page. Assuming she ever spoke to him again.

(Kai would not, *would not* think of that look on Dennis' face as he kicked him out of the castle… he knew he had lost so much more than the princess' trust, but he couldn't allow himself to dwell on that, or he would curl up into ball of pain, no use to anyone).

The street outside was dark except for the twists of red and gold that hung from every street lamp. More Yule tidings. It was snowing, but not proper snow — it wasn't cold enough to stick, though the floating flakes made the air plenty cold enough for someone wearing a coat that was three winters old.

Sergeant Clay was nowhere in sight, but Kai could see the other soldier trudging down the street ahead, hands shoved in the pocket of his own coat, trimmed with military braid and brass buttons.

Kai hesitated, and began to walk in that direction, slowly enough that he wouldn't call attention to himself. Another figure slipped out of the shadows ahead of him, clearly also tailing the soldier.

In a couple of quick steps, he caught up to her. "We'll look less suspicious if we walk together," he said in a low voice.

Ziggy glared at him. "I'm not supposed to be talking to you," she hissed back.

"Want to argue about it now?"

"No, but only because I came without gloves," she huffed, and promptly stuck her hand into his pocket.

Kai let his arm settle around her shoulders, something he had never done with anyone before. So this was awkward. "Why are you following him?"

"Why are you?" she shot back with a whisper. "Jack's worried about the Sarge. He's not his usual cranky self, and it all started when this old friend of his came to town. All we know is that he's from Palomarr, where Sarge fought in the war years ago. Going to print that in the morning news, are you?"

"They were talking about dancing slippers in the pub," Kai whispered back. "I think my story — damn it, Amira's story. It shook them up. They know something. And I can't help thinking…"

"I can't believe you're still working on that story after Princess Camilla kicked you out, haven't you learned anything? I've never seen Dennis so —"

"Fairies," Kai snapped at her. "It has to do with fairies, sound familiar?" *Godmother bullshit*. That was what Sarge had said. It reminded Kai of something from months ago, an odd detail that had never fully made sense to him, an angry shout about bluebells on the night he and Dennis met Ziggy and Camilla and their lives started to ravel together.

Castle Charming was a fairy tale kingdom. There were stories about fairies and their magic under every other toadstool. That was something Kai's foster mother had always hated about this place, though she never admitted it was the reason they had lived abroad for so long.

Kai only knew one person who had ever had a real-life fairy godmother granting wishes for her, and that person was currently using his pocket as a hand-warmer.

Their mark disappeared around the corner ahead. Kai and

Ziggy hurried their steps, still arguing, and swung around that same corner, only to crash headlong into… well.

It was him. The soldier. A scraped-thin beard, blazing eyes set into a deep brown face with cheekbones to die for, and two arms folded across his very solid chest.

"Oh, cr… Crumbs," said Ziggy.

"Did you know?" said the soldier. "Sound carries excellently in cold streets when it's snowing. Are either of you bread-brains remotely experienced at undercover work?"

Kai sighed. "Obviously not. Also, I've been drinking."

Ziggy gave him an impatient look.

"Come on," said the soldier. "I want a word with you two. Let's get in somewhere warm."

7

OLD SOLDIERS

Jack would shout at her, Ziyi was certain. Jack would not approve of her returning with this soldier to his tiny room in a cheap tavern in Rackham Street. Sure, she wasn't alone, but Jack was ropable about Kai Foster and his newspaper ethics already, so his presence wasn't likely to reassure her.

Dennis wouldn't shout, but Dennis had been moping tragically around the Doghouse for days since the dancing shoes story went to print, so he wasn't unbiased.

Kai scowled, his pretty mouth drawn down in suspicion as he stared at the soldier lighting the fire in the grate, which warmed the room. The soldier lit two lanterns, one on the mantel and another in the centre of the wonky table in the middle of the room.

"My name is Saladin Teh," said the soldier. "But you knew that already, if you've been following me."

"I didn't know that," Ziyi volunteered. "All the Hounds had managed to gather was that you were one of Sarge's old comrades from the war in Palomarr."

The man's mouth twitched at that. "As we're sharing information, I haven't the least idea who either of you are. A Hound, and a…"

"He's the gutter press," Ziyi said sourly.

"I'm a friend," Kai grumbled, elbowing her.

"Oh, are you really?"

"I almost feel I don't need to be here for this interrogation," said Saladin Teh. "You, girl. You're one of Clay's Hounds. Shouldn't you be trailing him through the snow instead of me?"

"I know better than to ask him any direct questions," she snorted. "Questions drive him to drink."

The soldier nodded. "He wouldn't listen to me. He didn't want to. He gave up on our mission long ago. But I think something very dangerous is happening in that castle of yours. Something to do with dancing slippers, and princes."

"You think the princes are the ones wearing out the shoes?" Kai interrupted.

"I do," said Saladin.

His eyes were wise and kind, Ziyi thought. Dark like earth and wine. But he looked sad, and that was saying something considering she had spent the last several days working shifts with a broken-hearted Dennis. She shouldn't trust Saladin Teh. Jack had given her a mission: to find out how dangerous this man was to their Sarge. That was all that mattered.

"Go on, then," she said abruptly. "Dancing slippers and princes, you said?"

"And bluebells and clover," said the soldier.

Ziyi sucked in a breath. Kai was looking at her strangely. She didn't want him to know what she was thinking, didn't want her deepest secrets printed on the front page of the *Charming Herald*.

But that was unfair. Kai had known her story for months

and it was a good one: it would have given him plenty of column inches. He'd never breathed a word of how and why she came to this kingdom.

"Clover and bluebells," she repeated. Relenting, she explained to Kai. "My fairy godmother, the one who… you know. Tried to glass slipper me into marrying one of the princes. She used bluebells as a — it was her magic, I suppose. That's how I was supposed to summon her. Miss Clover."

"No," said the soldier. "That's not her name. At least, it wasn't once."

The door slammed open, bringing a gust of cold air that almost guttered the lanterns. "Fine," growled Sarge, standing there in the doorway with his face pinked from the winter air. "I walked four frigging blocks arguing with you in my head, but you're right, you're always bloody right, we have to talk to the boys and find out if Illyria's really the one behind all this." He huffed, realising that Saladin was not alone. "You're kidnapping my Hounds, now?"

"I was going to offer them cocoa," said Saladin mildly.

Ziyi leaped to attention. "Sorry, Sarge, I was just…"

"Yeah, yeah," Sarge said tiredly, pulling off his cap and shoving it in the pocket of his coat. "Doing Jack's dirty work. I might have known she was up to something when she went a whole two days without nagging me about my health or my drinking." He gave Kai a long, measured look. "Now you, you're a surprise. Not very popular around my neck of the woods right now."

Kai looked faintly terrified. "No, sir," he muttered.

Saladin sputtered with laughter at that. "Sir," he said. "Gods, Clay. How young are these kids?"

"Shut the hell up," said Sarge, his face flaming red. "You're not my captain any more, I don't have to take this."

"It's so sweet the way they look up to you. Such a figure of authority."

"Ha!"

They stared at each other for a moment, and for the first time Ziyi believed that this man was no threat to Sarge. They had the kind of friendship that ran so deep that you never had to question it.

She didn't have friends like that. Not yet, though she thought perhaps, as the months went on, she might earn something like that with her Hounds, with Jack and Dennis in particular. Loyalty and history.

"So," she invited the two old soldiers. "Are we really going to have cocoa? Because I want some. And then you can tell us a story about bluebells and clover."

~

IT WAS AFTER MIDNIGHT. Dennis was on night sentry duty outside the bedroom doors of the Princes Charming. It wasn't a usual security detail. But everyone was worried about the princes right now.

Everyone except the king, who remained convinced that Princess Camilla was the one behind the Great Winter Shoe Purchase.

Corporal Jack had asked Dennis to keep an eye on this corridor as a personal favour to her. She was planning to be outside in the snow, watching the windows. All bloody night.

"You really think this is necessary?" he checked with her, but only once, because Jack knew what she was doing when it came to calculated risk.

"Something's wrong with our boys," she sighed. "The likeliest explanation is that they're sneaking out somewhere they shouldn't. We can't protect them blind. We need more information."

She wasn't the only one who worried. Shortly after midnight, a barefoot princess made her way along the corridor to Dennis. Camilla was wearing a loose smock and silken trousers 'rescued' from Ziggy's former trousseau. The trousers were short on Camilla, hitting her mid-calf. They whispered as she walked.

Her hair was shorter than when Dennis had first met this strange, magical princess so consumed by sadness and art that she rarely stuck her nose outside her garden tower. But seeing her like this, in the dimly lit corridor, it struck him all over again how much she looked like Kai Foster.

How was it that no one else — except Jack, he was sure — had noticed? They had the same damned nose. They pulled the same scrunched-up facial expression when they were concentrating. Even their sarcasm hit the same dry notes.

Dennis didn't know for 100% certain that Kai was the long-lost prince — Camilla's twin, the one whose disappearance broke this royal family into pieces more than fifteen years ago. It could be a coincidence. Maybe he was some cousin from the wrong side of the blankets. But once their startling similarity had first made itself clear to him, he couldn't unsee it.

You idiot, had been his first thought when he saw that bloody newspaper headline, screaming out that Kai had chosen his job over his friendships at the castle — when he saw the stung, frozen expression on Princess Camilla's face as she took in the betrayal. *You don't even know what you just gave up.*

"Cadet," Camilla said now, oddly formal as she addressed him.

"Your Highness," said Dennis, matching her formality with his own.

"I need to see my brothers."

He hesitated. "It's late."

"They'll survive."

"I'm not sure…"

"I wasn't asking, Hound," she said, her voice trembling. "No one is going to blame you for this. A royal whim. So stand aside, and let me royal."

He made a vague gesture to Prince Chase's door, and followed her inside.

The windows were closed. There was no sign of disturbance. The prince's bed was empty.

"Damn it, damn it," said Camilla, and ran to the other suite. Cyrus' room was also unoccupied. "How did they get past you?"

"They didn't," Dennis insisted. He went to the window. "Jack's still out there. They didn't use windows or doors." He could see his corporal's silhouette there in the courtyard, standing to attention in her furs and cloak. He pushed open the window and signalled to her. Reacting instantly, Jack disappeared back into the castle at a run. "Is there any other way out of these suites? They don't have —"

"What, secret passages? I'll kill them if they do and they never told me." Camilla stormed across the suite, pulling Chase's pillows aside and hurling them across the room. "What the hell is going on here?" She went to the wardrobe and yanked on the door.

Dance slippers tumbled past her and on to the floor: many of them bright and new and ready to wear; others torn and broken, handfuls of fragments in silk and shoe leather.

"We have to inform the king," Dennis choked.

"No," said Camilla, blazing with fury. "Not until morning. This isn't new, Dennis. It's not the first time." She picked up a handful of shoe scraps. "If they're not back by morning to explain themselves, we'll tell Father then."

Jack pounded into the room. "What's wrong?" She took in the scene: the shoes on the floor, the empty bed, the lack of princes. "I'm going to murder them both."

"Get in line," snarled Princess Camilla.

8

____

BLUEBELLS AND CLOVER

The boy's name was Foxglove, and he was beautiful. He laughed as he led Chase through the club, his pale skin flashing pink and green and blue. Where were those lights even coming from? Foxglove pressed drink after drink into Chase's hand as the night went on, and they all tasted so sweet, like oranges in summer and pomegranates at Yule.

Foxglove's kisses tasted of wine and promises, like something that Chase had been looking for all his life.

"Why are you running?" another boy cried after him. "Don't leave, Chase!"

He spun around, and he wasn't in the club of the flashing lights and sweet drinks any more, he was in a field far from the castle, and that little boy over there with silver eyes and white-gold hair, that was his brother.

The brother he had been allowed to keep.

"Chase, don't run!" Cyrus called out. "Slow down!"

"No!" Chase hollered behind him. "You run faster! Keep up, old man!"

His brother was five minutes older; neither of them ever let the other forget that.

Chase ran through a maze of hedges that slapped and bit at his face. He ran until his lungs hurt and he was ready to hurl.

"Wake up," said another voice. "Chase. You're scaring us."

There was a low, sexy chuckle from above him. Chase looked up to where his beautiful dance partner, the boy with purple eyes, lay sprawled on top of the maze hedge like a cat sunning himself. "I'm not sure where you think you're going, prince," said Foxglove. "This place doesn't have a way out."

"Everywhere has a way out," said Chase, already doubting himself.

"Not once they've tasted a Pomegranate-Seed Paradise. Such an unforgiving cocktail."

Chase ignored Foxglove, plunging on through the maze. *Everywhere has a way out.*
Everywhere has a way out.

HE OPENED HIS EYES, and his bedroom was full of people. Jax, kneeling on the edge of his bed, reared back as if he had hit her.

"Your Highness," said another voice, sounding shaky. Chase turned and saw Dennis, the Hound cadet, by the window. He looked exhausted and miserable.

Ziggy was here too — they called her Ziggy now she was a cadet too, and Chase was damned if he could even remember what name she went by during her princess phase. Sergeant Clay, his arms folded, standing beside a dark-skinned soldier Chase had never seen before.

When he saw that the prince was awake, Sarge spun around without speaking, and went through the connecting door to Cyrus' suite. His soldier friend followed him.

"Where were you?" Jax demanded fiercely.

"Don't know what you're talking about, sweetheart," Chase muttered. "Dreaming, that's all."

"You weren't here," she insisted. "We got here hours ago, you weren't here, Chase. Your bed was *empty*. Cyrus' too. But when dawn came, we turned around and there you were. Back in bed like you'd never been gone."

Chase frowned at her. It was far too early in the morning for games. "So?"

"So, that was three hours ago. We couldn't wake you at all. Cyrus is still…" she caught herself. "Do you feel like you've been drugged? Is it some kind of spell?"

This place doesn't actually have a way out.

"I didn't go anywhere," Chase repeated, shoving back the covers.

He was fully dressed, except for his feet which were… raw, blistered. Covered in the ruins of yet another pair of dance slippers. He never remembered putting the damned things on, though he had got rather good at hiding the evidence the next morning.

Jax stared at his feet.

"Cyrus will tell you," Chase snapped, getting up and hobbling across the room. "I'm fine. Everything is normal. Don't…"

In the doorway to Cyrus' room, he stopped, because Camilla and Sergeant Clay were bent over the bed. Cyrus was unconscious.

Camilla looked up, her eyes catching Chase's. She looked furious, and frightened. "What did you two do?" she hissed.

"I —" said Chase. It wasn't often that he was lost for words.

I ran away, and he couldn't catch me.

∼

DENNIS HUNG BACK as everyone crowded around Prince Cyrus' bed, trying to wake him up and interrogate Prince Chase all at the same time.

He had spent the night trying to keep Princess Camilla calm as she awaited the return (so she hoped) of her missing brothers. Corporal Jack went to find Sarge and returned not only with him, but also with Ziggy and Sergeant Clay's long-lost best soldier friend. And Kai, of all people.

They had all been so busy arguing about what to do if the princes never came back, not one of them noticed the exact moment when they did in fact reappear in their beds.

That was suspicious, right? That meant magic.

This was way above Dennis' pay grade. Sergeant Clay was here now, and Jack, and two fully conscious members of the royal family. Plenty of people outranked him. His job was to wait until one of them told him what to do.

But in the meantime…

He crossed the room to Kai, who stood by the door, miserable and out of place, like he was hoping no one would notice him at all. Dennis made eye contact and then a gesture to make it clear he wanted to talk, privately.

"I know I shouldn't be here," Kai said in a low voice as they stepped back into Prince Chase's suite, where things were quiet.

"Damn right you shouldn't," Dennis hissed. "I swear, if I see one thing that happened here tonight in the *Charming Herald*…"

"I wouldn't," Kai protested.

Dennis gave him a sceptical look, because come on. He had. He did.

"I didn't write that article," Kai said, not for the first time. "I promised Camilla — I mean, Her Highness, that I would help her find out what was happening with those dancing shoes. And yeah, I was stupid to tell Amira about it. I learned my lesson. I swear, Dennis, all I want to do now is help."

Dennis took a deep breath. "Okay," he said finally. "I believe you."

Kai hesitated, and then ventured a small smile that did not help Dennis' crush situation at all. "You do?"

"You still have to leave. As soon as they stop arguing, they'll be bringing the king in on this," by stone and sky, Dennis hoped that task of informing His Majesty would not be given to him, "and you seriously need to be elsewhere when that happens."

Kai nodded, surprising him. "You're right. I don't want to make things worse for everybody."

They stood there, looking at each other for a long moment.

"*Go*," said Dennis.

"Um," said Kai. "Okay. Let me know if —" He turned quickly, tripping over his feet as he went.

Only he couldn't go, because the door would not budge.

"Let me," said Dennis, and lending a shoulder to the effort. The door shifted an inch or so, but there was some kind of massive obstruction pressing back against them.

Kai slid his fingers through the crack they were able to make, and came back with a broken piece of grass wound around his finger. "That's not good."

"The window," said Dennis. They hurried to it together, pulling back the velvet curtains. Earlier, when Prince Chase first awoke, there had been the silvery fingers of dawn casting beams of light through the cracks in the curtain. It should be bright by now, well and truly morning.

Kai pushed up the window, revealing a springy wall of greenery with tufts of white and blue flowers here and there, blocking the view entirely.

"The castle is surrounded," said Dennis, feeling sick.

"These rooms," said Kai hoarsely. "It's not just the castle. It's these rooms that are surrounded." He plunged his hands into the greenery, tearing off handfuls and pressing them against Dennis' chest to show him. "Bluebells," he said. "Bluebells and clover."

"I'm not sure where you think you're going, prince. This place doesn't have a way out."

9

CALLING MASTER FOXGLOVE

Prince Cyrus would not wake up, and that was the least of their problems.

Kai had never thought of himself as claustrophobic. Growing up, he and his foster mother stayed in all kinds of tiny rooms, some of them no larger than cupboards. He had spent many a pleasant hour surrounded by books and quill and ink inside actual cupboards, which were convenient bolt holes. Kai had learned from an early age to stay out of the way when Mother was teaching the other children, the rich ones she was paid to educate.

But there was something about knowing they could not escape that made the walls of these fancy royal suites press in around him, more confining than any cupboard had ever been.

Things were still awkward between him and Dennis. Camilla hadn't even made eye contact with him yet. Kai would give anything to be out of here, to be away from everyone. It was too soon to pretend he was back in the gang.

Except, of course, *right here* was where they were finally learning the story behind all this magic and madness, and Kai always wanted to be where the story was. Jack had interrupted them, back at the soldier's digs, before Saladin and Sergeant Clay warmed up to telling their own story. Kai and Zig hadn't even got their hot chocolate.

Right now, Prince Chase sat on the bed beside his still-sleeping brother, refusing to budge. Corporal Jack stood at his side as if she was still playing bodyguard, though Kai wasn't fooled. Her proximity to Chase was about wanting to comfort her friend without either of them admitting it.

Princess Camilla sat at the foot of the bed, arms hugged around her knees, her face grave. Kai's attention was drawn as always to the tangled, twisting ink tattoos that wound around her from wrist to elbow. The ink tugged at him, but he wasn't stupid enough to confuse that with intimacy. He was not forgiven.

Ziggy and Dennis knelt on the ground near Sergeant Clay, who had commandeered one of the chairs. Saladin stood near him, more comfortable on his feet than in a chair. Both men had a look about them: they wished to be anywhere but here. Being trapped in this room, unable to act, was the worst situation either of them could imagine.

Kai knew the feeling.

The greenery outside the windows and doors had to be fairy magic. There was nothing that any of them could do against that.

"Her name was Illyria," said the Sarge, sounding gutted. "She was the younger sister of one of our platoon — Barnaby. After he died, she was like a sister to all of us. We promised to look out for her, to keep her safe."

"We did not know about the fairy godmother curse until it was too late," said Saladin in a low voice.

Everyone in the room shifted uncomfortably. Ziggy met no one's eyes.

Kai had read a lot about fairy sightings and stories in the

Charming Herald archives. It was not an area of research he had paid attention to before — his foster mother disapproved of such stories, and pointedly left them out of his education. Perhaps that was why she was so unhappy about him moving here, to Charming.

It was clear from his research that Ziggy, who had a fairy godmother of her own, had been lucky to get away with not losing her soul, or her freedom. Magic always came with a price.

"Godmothers grant wishes," said the Sarge heavily. "Small ones at first, to get you hooked. Then more epic, life-changing wishes, until the bill is too high for any human to pay. Illyria's was a creature called Bluebell. We didn't notice what she was doing at first. She spent her wishes on a new pair of boots, a meal to share, a sunny day when it should have been thick rain and fog. We didn't know how deep she had gone until we fought a battle and — it was as if the enemy could not touch us. Any of us. Every weapon whistled over our heads. The entire platoon."

"How did she pay for it?" Dennis asked. He blushed hotly when everyone looked at him. "What? I was born around here, same as the rest of you. I know how fairy stories work."

"Too true," said Saladin. "Illyria went into grave debt. By the time we realised what was happening, she had already sold herself in hock to Bluebell and that other world. One morning she was gone, leaving nothing behind but a patch of bluebells growing out of her sleeping sack."

"She came back once or twice," grunted the Sarge. "Always looking to give us something. To grant wishes. That's when we figured out that she had become one of them. A fairy godmother. And she was calling herself…"

"Clover," said Ziggy steadily. "Miss Clover. My fairy godmother. It's her, isn't it?"

"I thought so, back when we first collected you," said the

Sarge. "That business with the Midnight Princess — it had her mark all over it."

"Well, then," said Ziggy, standing up, her chin lifting as if she was a princess all over again. "There's an obvious solution to our predicament. I can summon her to us now."

"No way," said Kai and Dennis, leaping to their feet at the same time, speaking in unison. They glared at each other.

"Weren't you listening?" Dennis accused. "There's always a price, Zig. Ask for too many favours and you'll end up like her."

"What choice do we have?" Ziggy snapped at them both, eyes blazing. "I'm a Hound now. My job is to protect the royal family with my life. That doesn't go away because the threat is something other than a knife or a crossbow bolt."

In his sleep, Prince Cyrus coughed for a moment. Chase turned to him in a panic. "Turn him on his side."

"What?" said Camilla, but Jack reacted instantly, helping Chase to turn his brother over. Cyrus' mouth fell slightly open, and something fell out of it.

"Is that a berry?" Kai blurted out.

Camilla glared at him which, yes, was worse than ignoring him.

"It's a pomegranate seed," said the Sarge, sounding like he wanted to punch something.

Saladin came alert. "Your Highness, do you think you and your brother… ate or drank anything, while in the fairy realm?"

Prince Chase's face went blank.

Kai didn't need his fairy research to know how bad this could be. It was laid out in every ballad sung in every tavern.

"Ziggy," said Chase in a low voice. "Do it."

Kai felt a burst of anger at that — was Prince Cyrus's safety more important than hers? But of course, they all thought that way. This was a fairy tale kingdom, and the Royals took precedence.

Ziggy snatched up a candle from the mantel and went to the window, grabbing handfuls of bluebells and clover to press into the wax. "Someone light this for me?"

There was a matchbook near the grate. Before Kai could reach for it, Saladin was at Ziggy's side with a tinderbox from his belt. "Do not be reckless," the soldier said in a low rasp.

"Don't get your hopes up," Ziggy said as she lit the makeshift candle. "Last time I did this, she didn't even answer. Instead I got…"

"A far superior replacement," broke in a mocking voice, right behind Kai.

He spun around, to stare directly at what could only be a fairy gentleman. He had seen him before, briefly.

"Master Foxglove," said Ziggy.

The fairy was young and devastatingly beautiful, with dark floppy hair and twinkling violet eyes. He wore an assortment of clothes that looked as if they belonged to another era, or several periods of history, like some errant time traveller. His doublet was ragged but embroidered with dainty skill; he wore bangles and baubles around his bare ankles that made a shimmering sound as he crossed the room.

"You," said Prince Chase in a shaky voice, staring at the stranger. "I danced with you."

"And it was unforgettable," purred Foxglove, circling around the various people in the room, on his way to the window, where Ziggy stood frozen, watching him. He did not get that far; Chase did not allow it.

"What have you done with my brother, fairy swine?" the prince howled, and threw himself at the fairy, punching him in the face.

Foxglove glowed with a fierce light. He looked ugly now,

all gnarled and twisted in his fury. "Why don't you go find out?" he shrieked back at the prince.

Kai saw Dennis moving, and Jack too, trying to get to Chase in time, but it was as if time itself slowed down to prevent them reaching him…

The room filled with bright, blinding blue light, and Kai was lost to it. They were all lost.

10

DANCING WITH THE STARS

Ziyi awoke, and found herself sheathed in a ballgown: her worst nightmare, basically. Ballgowns, along with glass slippers and pumpkin carriages, were high on the list of everything she did not miss about being a princess.

If only she had managed to rid her new life of princes, too.

The gown was blue and sprigged with fresh bluebells, because someone down here had a sense of humour.

Ziyi's only consolation was that she was not dancing.

She stood, barefoot and ballgown'd, inside an ice palace so pretty in detail that it might have been a wedding cake. Gold and silver branches made a false forest, surrounding a marble dance floor. Bright glass baubles dripped from those branches like jewels. The sky was alight with constellations of bobbing flames attached to no visible candelabra.

It was beautiful. It was breathtaking. It was supremely awful.

Around her, she saw her friends and companions of Castle Charming, dancing with all the enthusiasm of wooden dolls.

This was exactly the kind of — what had Sarge called it?

— *bluebell bullshit* she had expected. It looked like an illustration out of a storybook, and there was nothing real about it.

Ziyi's fist tightened on the candle she held, with bluebells and clover pressed into the still-warm wax near the wick that no longer burned. Was this the reason that her mind still worked, when everyone else had been swallowed up by fairy enchantment?

She held the candle up to her face, inhaling the last of its scent in one big breath, and the scene before her changed.

THIS WAS STILL the realm of Faerie. Her friends were dancing, but it was no longer anything that resembled a storybook illustration. Ziyi was trapped in a cavern full of shifting, grinding bodies. The music was loud and frenetic. Lights flashed bursts of colour in the darkness, showing ripped clothing, bare limbs and dance moves that certainly didn't belong in a respectable establishment.

There were elbows everywhere.

Ziyi pushed her way through the crowd, avoiding said elbows, many of which were at the exact height to hit her in the face.

There was Prince Chase, dancing intimately with Master Foxglove as if he had no memory of his previous anger. Corporal Jack, hair wild and eyes blank, danced up on Saladin Teh as if he were not old enough to be her father.

The atmosphere was steamy and breathless and wicked.

At the edge of the cavern, two young men pressed against each other, as if it was all that either of them had ever wanted. Dennis and Kai. They were as mesmerised as everyone else, but there was a warmth as they gazed at each other; almost enough to make a person regret that, at some point, this enchantment had to end.

She shoved her way through fairies and friends alike to reach a dusty, misshapen slab of stone which served this cavernous club as a bar. Vessels hung from it, twinkling in the coloured lights: glasses and flower buds or acorn cups.

Sarge was here, slumped across the bar with some vile cocktail set before him.

"Don't drink that," Ziyi said sharply, pushing it out of his reach.

Sarge sighed. This place had clearly broken him… or broken him further, since he hadn't exactly started the day with a full mental tea set. "I'm thirsty, Zig love," he muttered.

"You'll be stuck here forever. Don't you read fairy tales?"

"It's what I deserve. Spent my whole life paying for what happened sixteen years ago."

Ziyi hesitated. Was he enchanted like the others or merely lost in his own wounds? How could she tell? "The war in Palomarr started *fourteen* years ago."

"Wasn't talking about the war." Sarge laid his head down on the counter.

"The truth is," said another voice: lilting and female. "You signed up to that war expecting to die. All of you. The whole platoon. You weren't there to make amends for past mistakes, you were there to sacrifice yourselves. Believe me, I've had a lot of time to think about it."

Ziyi turned, and looked into the eyes of her fairy godmother.

"Hello, precious," said Miss Clover. "It's been a long time. You must be doing well." She laid a hand on the nape of Sarge's neck. He began to snore softly. "This one, though. This one is still a work in progress." She kissed the crown of his head.

"Don't touch him," said Ziyi, her voice shaking. "Don't touch any of them. You don't have that right."

When Ziyi first met Clover, she had thought her warm

and pretty. She still remembered the sight of the fairy in a crumpled silk tunic, kneeling beside the dragon statues in the Garden of Wives. Clover was nothing like the other women in Ziyi's life: her sisters, her stepmothers, her tutors. There was no formality about Clover, no careful artifice. She represented escape.

Now, knowing everything she did about this fairy, Ziyi saw no warmth or prettiness. Miss Clover's expression was hard like stone; she reminded Ziyi of the warriors who visited the Garden of Wives every season, to test whether the Emperor's daughters could perform the skills necessary to protect their virtues and those of their sisters. If they were capable of marching to war, when war came.

"This man was mine before you were even born," hissed Miss Clover. "Castle Charming was my home as a child. Who are you to claim these people?"

Ziyi wondered what would happen if you punched a fairy in the face, and then she remembered that Chase had done exactly that. It hadn't helped anyone. "I am a Royal Hound," she said. "These humans, all these humans, are under my protection. You can't have them."

Clover's eyes lit up with an unholy light, and now she was warmth and prettiness all the way to the bone. "Fight me for them," she breathed.

What have I done? thought Ziyi helplessly, but she didn't say that aloud. What she said was: "I will."

11

KISS AND TELL

Kissing boys was not something that Dennis' family had ever acknowledged as a possibility for him.

He had three brothers, raised on mountain air and goat milk. All four of them were strong and broad and good workers. They knew from an early age what was expected of them: to learn a trade, serve the mountain gods, bring money home every month, and eventually to find a sturdy and respectable young woman to add to their ever-growing family.

Sisters married out into other families, unless they stayed unmarried at home to look after the elders. Brothers brought girls home.

By the time he was thirteen, Dennis was an uncle twice over and had long figured out that he had no interest in Maisie the butcher's daughter, or Sadie the roofer's daughter, despite every attempt of the village to hurl them in his general direction.

He wanted Will the blacksmith's son, who kissed like he was trying to win a fight, and was quick to invent chores that could only be accomplished by the two of them, alone, out of the sight of prying eyes.

They were sixteen when they were finally caught: the worst day of Dennis' life.

His father didn't shout or bluster. The same could not be said of Will's father, who threatened to brand them for their shame. Dennis thought afterwards they probably could have stopped him, had Will's father reached for the iron instead of cuffing his son with his open hand, but that did not make their fear less real.

Dennis' father did not speak of it again. No one spoke of it: not his mother, or his brothers. Not Will, who was betrothed to Maisie within a fortnight, and behaved every bit as if he was pleased about it.

Silence blanketed the village like a fall of snow.

When word came up the mountain pass that the castle was looking for guard recruits, Dennis packed a bag and left without even realising he had made a decision. His family let him go without a word of protest, even though his brother Marten had never heard the end of it when he and his wife settled twelve miles away.

Dennis worked hard. He sent money home each month. He visited every other holy day, with gifts for his niblings. He earned a nod of pride from his father when he brought the news that he had won a coveted spot as a cadet to the Royal Hounds.

And every visit, without fail, his mother or grandmother or a sister or a sister-in-law asked him if he had met a nice girl yet.

KISSING KAI WAS nothing like kissing Will. It was no battle between them, but a slow warmth that built as their mouths came together and apart. Dennis curled a hand around Kai's hip, pressed him again the wall of the cavern, and ignored everything around them: the music, the magic, the strange flashing lights.

He had wanted this for so long. He forgot every reason he ever had for thinking this was a terrible idea.

When they drew apart, Kai blinked up at him, beautifully dishevelled. "We're, uh, in a cave," he said.

"Yeah," said Dennis.

Kai frowned. "Were we kidnapped by fairies?"

"We definitely were kidnapped by fairies." Whatever wild enchantment had caught them both up was wearing off. So maybe Dennis shouldn't be pressing his entire body quite as intimately up against Kai. He shifted his weight back on his heels.

Kai's wrists came up, wrapping around Dennis' neck, not letting him move an inch. "Also, you kissed me."

Dennis grinned, wanting to huff out his relief. He hadn't ruined anything. He leaned in, letting his forehead rest against Kai's for a moment. "I did that, yeah."

"Do it again."

KAI'S first crush was a girl so far out of his reach that he might as well have set his sights on a goddess, or a priestess. Lady Ashlyn of Trebor was the niece of a countess, and her family had been layering accomplishments upon her since she was a child: they intended her to marry a prince.

Not a Charming prince, of course; her family would never have stood for Chase and Cyrus' wild shenanigans. But there were other kingdoms, and other potential princes to ensnare.

Kai didn't care that Lady Ashlyn could speak four languages, that she embroidered and played piano and danced in twelve different cultural styles.

She was pretty, and she was kind, and she made jokes about obscure classical poets: that was enough for him. He nursed his crush for two years, until Lady Ashlyn's younger cousins came of an age to no longer need a governess, and it was time for Mother to move on to another family, three kingdoms away.

Kai's second crush was a stable lad at the house of the otherwise awful Meddow family. They didn't stay long in that household, as Mother had little patience for those who hired governesses and tutors but refused to invest in books and paper for their children.

Still, they stayed long enough for Kai to earn his first kiss, in a musty hayloft.

There were other crushes, and other kisses, but none had spun him around quite as much as those two, not until Dennis.

Mother did not seem to mind that Kai liked boys as much as girls; more boys than girls really, if you counted up his crushes and kisses and divided them by gender.

When Kai applied for the job in Charming, it was the first time Mother had ever disapproved of something he did. This came as a shock to both of them. Over several weeks she dragged out every dissuasion and discouragement technique at her disposal, but he had watched her use them on children his whole life, and they had little impact on him. He was eighteen, and it was time he started making his own decisions.

Kai came to Charming. He became a reporter. And — he had to admit this to himself if no one else — he was falling in love.

IT FELT like love right now, with Dennis warm and heavy

against his chest, pressing him into the wall. Kissing the breath out of him.

"Kidnapped by fairies," Kai said again, next time they surfaced for air.

"Ugh, yes," said Dennis. "We should probably do something about that." He eased back. Kai might have minded the loss of his heat and touch if Dennis hadn't promptly threaded their fingers together. "Don't want you getting lost," he added in a mumble, as if he had never held another boy's hand before.

"Okay," another voice broke into their conversation. Ziggy stood at a respectable distance, the only other person in this light-dazed, music-drenched cavern who was not swaying hypnotically to the pulse of sound and magic. "Not that this isn't adorable — believe me, I am tabling the conversation about how adorable this is for another time — but right now? We have princes to save."

12

DRINK ME

Miss Clover stood at the bar, pouring together a sweet and decadent concoction from ice and violets and moonlight. "You want my magic after all," she teased.

"No," said Ziyi, working to make her voice as commanding as possible. Sarge was unconscious on his bar stool. The other humans were caught up in the dance. All she had was herself and her boys — Kai and Dennis, standing on either side of her small shoulders, lending her their strength. She was pretty sure they were holding hands behind her back, but she wasn't going to call them on it. "I don't want your magic, Clover. I want to free the princes from your spell."

Clover tilted her head to one side. Her dark curls seemed to grow darker and curlier, all around her shoulders. Her eyes glowed, and her hands moved faster, faster as she mixed the drink with leaves and lemon, grasses and spring water. A spiral straw. A paper umbrella. "Oh, darling," she said. "It's the same thing. The only way you're getting out of here is by wishing for it really hard."

"You can't," Dennis blurted out. "Ziggy. That's what she

wants. If you use her wishes you'll end up like her. Stuck here."

"It has trap written all over it," Kai agreed.

Ziyi did not take her eyes off Miss Clover. "How many wishes do I get? How many is too many?"

Clover laughed, a broken and tragic sound. "That's the big question, isn't it? In stories it's always three. But wishes don't weigh the same as each other. The bigger the wish, the faster you fall."

"So," said Kai. "If Zig sticks to small wishes, will she be safe?"

"You can't be serious," said Dennis. "It's not worth the risk."

"Of course it's worth the risk," Ziyi hissed back at him. "The princes are our *duty*, Dennis. Who else is going to save them?"

Kai stepped forward, interested in the challenge. "What counts as a small wish? What makes wishes small?"

"Oh, you're full of questions," said Clover.

"I'm a quill, it comes with the territory."

She sniffed and turned away from him. "You smell of ink. Awful stuff. It gets under the fingernails and into the blood-stream. A filthy, clumsy sort of magic."

"Tell us about your magic," said Kai, sounding smooth for once instead of awkward and shy. "What makes a wish small, or big?"

"The more specific it is, the tighter you wrap it in words, the smaller the magic," admitted Clover. "World peace is enormous — that's a wish that would swallow you whole, first time out. You'd never come back from that one. Saving the lives of an entire platoon without specifying how or why," she added, with a touch of bitterness. "Too big. Too many ways for the magic to think for itself."

"So wishing everyone free all at once? Not that I'm wishing that," Ziyi clarified.

Clover raised her eyebrows. "That's big. Not world peace big. But I wouldn't risk it, if I were you."

"You're being awfully helpful," Dennis growled, on Ziyi's other side.

"That's what a fairy godmother does," Clover said sharply. "We help."

"All right," said Kai, sounding flustered, which might or might not have had something to do with whose hand he was holding. "We need to make a list of possible wishes, grade them on size, make a chart of some sort…"

"I wish Corporal Jack free of the dance enchantment," Ziyi said without hesitation, her gaze locked with Miss Clover.

Clover smiled widely. "You can have that one for free," she said. "After a round of drinks."

"WHAT," said Jack, her dark hair still scattered with rose petals and fern-fronds, her pupils blown wide from the music (or the magic), "the *hell* is going on?"

"This is the part where we save everyone," said Ziyi, clinging to Jack's shoulder. Jack had so many muscles. She was the greatest.

Jack leaned down. "Are you drunk, Ziggy?"

"It's part of the plan!" Ziyi said indignantly. "Shh. Don't tell anyone the plan."

She took Jack's hand and led her to the bar, where Kai and Dennis were most of the way through the drinks that Clover had poured for them: a Midsummer Peaseblossom and a Titania's Ass, respectively.

Ziyi herself had consumed an entire glass goblet full of a

swirling liquid that was either green or purple and somehow both at once. Clover called it a Bilious Fae, insisting that it was the exact colour of a fairy about to throw up.

It didn't taste sickening. It was soft and meadow-sweet and it made Ziyi feel like rainbows ran from the tips of her fingers all the way up to her hairline.

"What are you doing?" Jack demanded. "You can't eat and drink anything in fairyland, or you get stuck here. What are you, *new*?"

Ziyi wanted to straighten out the little crinkle between Jack's eyes, but had exactly enough sobriety left in her to keep her hands to herself. "Miss Clover says that's an old wives' tale."

"That's sexist," Dennis objected from where he was sprawled comfortably over the bar. "Old *person's* tale."

"Old toadstool tale," said Kai, who was sprawled comfortably over Dennis. The two of them snickered together.

Jack threw up her hands. "Miss Clover is lying to you, obviously!"

Their bartender smiled sweetly. "I can't lie. Fairies aren't allowed to. Well known fact. We can be as tricksy as we like, but if we tell an outright untruth, our magic unravels and we go all... *human*, ugh, it's a horrible mess."

"That could also be a lie," Jack said between gritted teeth.

Ziyi patted her arm. It was that or squeeze her bicep admiringly, and that might distract them from the main business. "If it is, too late. We drank the things!"

"We drank the things!" Kai and Dennis proclaimed in unison, and drained their cups dry.

"We need you to help save the princes," said Ziyi. "That's why I woke you up from the spell. You know them best. Can't use too many wishes, so we have to talk them into saving themselves."

Jack gave them all her most furious face. "Those princes couldn't save their way out of a wet paper bag!"

PRINCE CHASE WAS fourteen years old when he first thought about ending it all. It was only for a minute or two, up on the tallest turret of Castle Charming, staring down at the snowy courtyard below.

Would it be better to do it in summer, without the snow to cushion him as he fell?

He snapped himself out of it by digging his fingernails into his palms until he drew blood. When he was steady again, when he felt like he could be trusted with moving, he saw his brother: a tiny speck running laps of the shovelled-clear rookery pitch.

For the first time, he wondered whether Cyrus was trying to kill himself too.

"This is stupid," he huffed a few minutes later, down on the ground and trying to keep up with his brother's jogging gait. "Why are you working so hard at this? What's the point?"

"First rookery match this Saturday," said fourteen-year-old Cyrus, red-faced but not even out of breath. "Father will be watching."

Maybe it was the soreness in his palms, or the dizziness from what he had thought about up on the turrets, but Chase lost it.

"No, he won't!" he yelled. "He won't come. He won't watch. There is nothing you can do to impress him. It doesn't make a blind bit of difference. We could set ourselves on fire in the forecourt and he would just stare into the distance and mutter 'boys will be boys'. He doesn't care about us! He doesn't care about anything," he added in a smaller voice.

They both knew where their father's heart was. It was locked inside a glass coffin in a tower with their mother. It was out in the world, yearning after the child that had been lost. Chase and Cyrus and even their little sister Cami could never get close to it.

Cyrus stopped running. He leaned over, breathing hard, stretching by habit. "Maybe I'm doing this for me," he said. "I like being strong. I like having challenges to meet. I'm fine."

Chase stared at his brother and thought the words, *I'm not fine*. "Serena's invited us to a party," he blurted. "Over at Fortinbras. Do you reckon we can sneak three horses out without anyone noticing?"

Cyrus took a deep swallow of chill winter air, and stood up straight. Already, his incessant training was having an effect on his shoulders, his legs. He and Chase weren't identical any more.

Perhaps that was the point.

"Fine," Cyrus huffed. "We'll go to a party. But nothing crazy. We have a game coming up."

"Nothing crazy," Chase promised.

He was fourteen years old, and he needed to think about something, anything other than how long it might take to fall from the highest turret to the courtyard below.

A party was a start.

~

NOW IT WAS NOW. He was nearly twenty, only a few months from the big birthday that would change everything and nothing. Chase danced harder than he had ever danced before. His feet were slick with blood. The satin shoes had fallen off him in pieces.

Foxglove was in his arms, grinding and enticing. The

music was loud and frantic in his head. His mouth tasted like rose petals and acorns.

I'm never going home, Chase thought, and he didn't even mind all that much. It was winter. Home was a cold castle, frosted balconies, ice underfoot, slippery wet grass on the rookery pitch.

Home was people staring all the time, long silences over dinner, the endless debutantes being flung at him, like picking a bride would solve any of his problems, like having a girlfriend would make him steadier, easier to manage. Home was headlines in the *Charming Herald*: Princes Gone Wild.

Like it mattered, any of it. Cyrus was the one who had to be king someday. Chase was the spare. Unnecessary. He could fade away and no one would even notice.

He wasn't dancing with Foxglove now. It was Corporal Jack in his arms, his Jax, all broad shoulders and unimpressed face. She was talking. It was probably a lecture. He didn't need to listen.

"Stay and dance," he murmured, hands sliding over her hips, bringing her closer. "Dance with me, Jax."

She growled at him, but came into his arms more readily than he had expected, her face mashing into his cheek. Too late, he realised she was doing this so she could talk directly into his ear.

"The only way out is for you to want to leave. You have to say the words. Ziggy wasted one of her stupid wishes to give you that exit, but she can't *make* you take it. Not without the wish getting too big. You have to want to leave, Chase, and you have to say it out loud. Got it?"

Chase liked her here, pressing against him. This made more sense than anything else. She made him feel warm. She always had. "Marry me," he breathed into the side of her neck.

Jack made a distressed noise. "Are you kidding me right now?"

"We're so good together. You're the only one who calls me on my bullshit. We'd be great."

She pulled back, her face all squinched up in shock and unhappiness. "Chase," was all she said.

"Don't say no right away," he urged. The thought actually excited him. "You'd make a kickass princess."

"I'm not a Royal. And I'm a lesbian. *Which you know already.*"

That gave him pause for only a minute or two. "We don't have to have sex."

"Thanks for clearing that up," she said sarcastically. "Chase. If you weren't drugged out of your skull on fairy music right now I would punch you so hard."

He leaned into her, his head resting on her shoulder. "I don't want to go home."

Jack pinched him in the side. "That is the exact opposite of what I need you to be saying right now. You are such a disaster of a person."

"If you marry me, I'll do everything you say," he mumbled.

"Chase," she said, and there was worry in her voice now. "Stay awake."

"Don't want to," he sighed.

Never go home.

Never.

Go.

13

TRUTH OR DARE

K ai's feet felt heavy and clumsy, thanks to the fairy cocktail Clover had mixed for him. Still, he had a job to do, and he wasn't going to let his people down. Not again.

He found Princess Camilla dancing in the middle of the mob, her dress torn and her feet streaked with blood. Unlike her brothers, she wasn't even wearing shoes. Her work boots would probably have come in handy.

Kai stepped between Camilla and the fairy swain dancing up on her.

"This is my princess," said the creature rudely.

"Shove off," said Kai.

"Oh, it's you," said Camilla, her face twisted in confusion. "Are we home yet?"

"Not yet," said Kai. He put his hands politely on her waist. "I need you to do something for me."

Her eyes darkened. They looked almost black, like ink, instead of the usual blue. "I'm not happy with you, Kai."

"I know, and I'm sorry."

"I trusted you. And you wrote that stupid story…"

"Trust me again, just for now. Be as mad as you like when

we're home," which meant Castle Charming, of course. Her home, not his. "But right now, trust me. Please. It's my job to get you out of here."

"Do the tattoo charm," she said abruptly.

For a moment he thought he had misheard her, under the bright lights and intense, pounding music. "Excuse me?"

"I'll trust you if you trust yourself, Kai. It's an easy charm, for someone with your magic. The ink laid out the welcome mat for you. It's not exactly playing hard to get. But you don't believe you can do it. How am I supposed to believe you can get us home?"

Kai stared at her. They didn't have time for this. And yet…

He considered her lessons, over the last few months. The ink had summoned him to her tower, and he had always followed where it led before. None of the exercises that Camilla gave him ever worked unless she was there, encouraging him, with her thoughtful gaze and confident air.

I'll trust you if you trust yourself.

He called the ink to him, and felt it settle in his skin.

"Oh," said Camilla, breathing her surprise. She brushed her fingertips over his upper arm, where the new tattoo was displayed. "That's not a quill."

"It's not a quill," he agreed, dizzy with his accomplishment. The black ink depicted a pattern of stonework, and turrets, wrapping around his bicep.

Camilla's tower. The safest place he knew, the place where his new friendships had been sealed. Where he was learning, finally, to understand the magic that had confused him all of his life.

She smiled, an oddly familiar smile. "What's the plan?"

"Ziggy negotiated a wish. It's… complicated, but it has to be, to get us out without using too much magic. You have to want to go home. And you have to say something true. Not a… it doesn't have to be a secret. Just something true that you don't commonly speak aloud. Truth is a currency with the fairies. They don't want to let us go, your brothers most of all, so we have to pay our way out."

Camilla quirked an eyebrow. "What's your truth, Kai Foster?"

He hadn't thought about that. "Um. Dennis kissed me. It was part of the spell and then… it wasn't."

She practically glowed at him, taking his hand in hers. "About time! He was three times more furious than I was, when that article came out. I figured there had to be feelings going on."

"I didn't write it," Kai blurted out, not wanting her to believe that for a minute longer.

"Honestly? I didn't even mind that much," she shrugged. "It stung, but people have been writing about me like that my whole life. More so, since I came out of hiding."

"I wouldn't do that, not behind your back," he said earnestly. "Um. Is that your truth?"

"I shouldn't think so. Let's try this." Camilla squeezed his hand harder, and her face went very serious. "My twin brother's name was Camden. I barely remember him, but I remember having him there beside me. I remember not being alone. They never talk about it. I don't think I've heard his name spoken aloud in Castle Charming for… over a decade. When I was a child, I used to wish that he had never existed at all. Better that than this awful hole in our lives where he used to be. There. That's my truth. And I have never wanted to go home more in my entire *life*."

The cavern wavered around them, and suddenly the air smelled different, of plaster and wool and tea, ordinary castle smells. The two of them were back in Prince Chase's bed chamber. There was no wild greenery pressing up against the window. It was still morning. They were free.

Camilla's triumphant smile fell off her face, and she whipped around. "Kai? Where's everyone else?"

"My job was to bring you," he said, feeling awkward. He hadn't considered the possibility that they would be the first ones to make it out. Or the only ones?

Camilla burned with fury. "*Where are my brothers?*"

~

WHEN SHE GOT up this morning — or was that two mornings ago? This had been the world's longest night — Ziyi had not imagined she would end up dancing with Prince Cyrus. Again.

Dancing with Prince Cyrus was high on the list of things she had planned never to do again.

Being a Hound, with her hair cropped short and her uniform, it was easy to pretend that she was not the princess from a foreign kingdom who had tried to trap him into marriage with a fairy tale, only a few months ago.

"You have to say something true, Your Highness," she told him. "And you have to want to go home."

Cyrus looked exhausted, and sad. "I think my brother hates me," he said. "I know my father doesn't see me. And… I don't want to be king." He closed his eyes, and held her closer as they danced. "The other part, though. That's going to be tough."

Ziyi gave him a friendly squeeze. "Want it anyway," she ordered him.

~

DENNIS SHOOK SARGE AWAKE. "Time to get out of here," he told him gently.

"Yeah, sounds fair," muttered Sarge, his eyes still glazed

over. He allowed Dennis to help him stand. "Back to the castle?"

"Back to the castle." Dennis draped a friendly arm around Sarge, to keep him upright. Together, they staggered across the dance floor, to find Sarge's friend Saladin. "I have a boyfriend," he told his boss. The walls entirely failed to fall down on top of them. No mountains exploded. The gods stayed silent.

"Yeah?" said Sarge. "He a criminal?"

"No!" said Dennis.

"You're doing better than Jack's dating history, then."

"That's concerning."

Sarge slapped him on the back so hard that they both almost fell over. "Let me know if anyone gives you shit about it."

"Thanks?"

They found Saladin slumped against a wall at the far side of the cavern, covered in drunken fairies who giggled and nipped at his skin.

"Sorry to break up the party," said Sarge, kicking his friend in the foot. "Up and at 'em, soldier."

"You have to say something true, something not usually spoken out loud," said Dennis. "And you have to want to get home."

Sarge stared bleakly down at Saladin. "I was on duty the night that the baby prince was stolen."

Saladin met his gaze, unflinching. "As was I."

"Afterwards… I signed up for the war in Palomarr, knowing I would probably die there. And I welcomed it."

"And I," said Saladin. He looked up, past Sarge's shoulder, to where Miss Clover the fairy godmother was standing, her eyes dark and troubled, her hair strewn with glitter and rose petals. "Is that enough truth for you, Illyria?"

"I hate you both," said the fairy, and blew her nose on a

large dock leaf. "That's what I wanted to hear. From both of you." She narrowed her eyes at Dennis. "She knew that, didn't she? Your Ziyi. When she made the constraints of the wish."

"She's smart," said Dennis, his chest swelling with pride.

"Fine," snapped the fairy godmother. "Screw you all. Go home to your happy human lives and cups of tea and boring sense of duty."

"I came all this way to find you," said Saladin steadily, his eyes on her. "After all these years. What makes you think I want to go home?"

Sarge flailed an arm. "Come on mate, you don't mean that."

Dennis thought otherwise. There had been a lot of truth-telling tonight. He could spot the signs.

"Shut up," said Miss Clover furiously. "Go home, Saladin."

"How many wishes do I have to make before you let me stay?" asked the soldier.

They stared at each other. Sarge opened his mouth to say something else —

But in the second it took him to do that, Miss Clover sent them home. Sarge stumbled on the carpet of Prince Chase's bedchamber. Dennis reached out to catch him, to stop him falling, but Sarge pushed him away and hit the nearest wall. He looked ill.

Camilla put her hand to her mouth in surprise, and imme-diately looked disappointed that it was them. Dennis only had eyes for Kai, who lurched away from Camilla's side and enfolded him in the best hug he had experienced in years. Possibly ever.

Boyfriend. That was a thing.

The adjoining door opened and Prince Cyrus stepped in

from his own room, Ziggy at his side. "I didn't want to come home hard enough," he protested.

"Apparently you did," Ziggy shot back.

Camilla gasped and threw herself at her brother, hugging him. "Where's Chase? Did he get back?"

Dennis looked around, troubled. "He was with Jack."

"Weren't you supposed to bring Saladin out too?" Kai whispered, darting a look at Sarge, who looked like he was about to start tearing down the walls.

"Long story," said Dennis. "He stayed."

"So, not a very long story?"

"That depends on how far back you start."

CHASE FOUND himself on the turrets of the tallest tower of Castle Charming, looking out at the rookery pitch. Cold air stung his face. Snow was on its way.

That was one good thing about the land of Faerie. They had excellent central heating.

He shuffled forward, watching his feet as they neared the edge. "I didn't want to come home," he muttered. "Why did it even work? I was supposed to *want* it."

"You don't always get what you want," said a sharp voice. Jack. "Why are we up here?"

"I like it here. The view."

"Chase," she said, and that was wrong. His Jax should never sound so soft and sympathetic. "Can we go inside now? The others will be worried."

A fleck of snow danced down on the breeze, near enough to his mouth that Chase tried to lick it, and failed. He swayed a little, on the edge of the tower.

"Chase," she said more urgently.

"I got it, Jax. I'm good." His feet were cold. He could still feel things, apparently. They were going to hurt like hell, when he warmed up. "Can I be the one to explain to Dad how we all barely survived a mystical magical fairy adventure?"

"No."

"Can I tell reporters from the *Herald*? It'll make a nice change for them, to get the quotes all tidy from a proper interview."

Jack sighed heavily. "No."

He let her take his hand, and lead him towards the steps. "Marriage is definitely off the table, then?"

"I swear, Chase. I will push you off this tower if I have to."

Chase laughed, and it wasn't an entirely horrible sound. "Nah," he said. "Not today."

14

PITCH PERFECT

"I thought I'd find you here," said Amira.

Kai quirked an eyebrow at her, and said nothing. He was back on the rookery beat. It was Saturday morning, the pitch was freshly shovelled after the night's extra heavy snowfall, and his boyfriend was playing sport. Where else was he likely to be?

Amira huffed and sat next to him, wrapped in about three coats, and as many scarves. "This not talking to me thing is getting old."

Kai agreed, but he wasn't the one owing apologies.

"Fine," she snapped. "I crossed a boundary. I told myself that I was teaching you an important lesson about needing to be ruthless in our job but the truth is… it was a story and I wanted it. I took it. The end. *Also*, I was totally going to put my byline to it but Bors figured out I nicked the story from you and put your name on it to teach me a lesson."

She wasn't going to apologise, clearly. Kai shrugged.

"That story you filed yesterday," Amira went on. "About the Hounds and how they tracked down the fairies responsible for the shoe prank and banished them from the castle?

That was a good piece. I mean, clearly a bullshit cover-up of some kind, but you covered your butt with all those direct sources and quotes. Also, your writing isn't bad."

"Thanks," said Kai.

The Hounds emerged from their locker room, armoured up and ready for the game. The Royals took a little longer, straggling out. The princes had not yet made an appearance.

Kai barely noticed, because Dennis was there in his rookery armour and spiked helmet, all golden and pink like something out of a nursery rhyme about heroes and mountain gods. When he saw Kai watching him, Dennis went pinker about the face, and tipped a wink in his direction.

"O.M.G.," Amira whispered. "We have to be friends again, so I can catch up on this major piece of gossip. Kai. How can you even stand not telling me everything?"

"I'll think about it," said Kai, smiling to himself.

THE WORLD WAS DEFINITELY ENDING, because this was the second time in the history of Castle Charming that Chase was up and dressed before his brother. Pushing down any rose petal-related anxieties, because the Hounds had sworn black and blue that the castle was fairy-free these days, he barrelled into Cyrus's room to wake him up.

"Rise and shine, big bro. Time to rook our little hearts out. Big game. Fresh snowfall last night, so bonus potential frostbite? Arse out of bed, pronto!"

Cyrus grunted and opened his eyes. He looked like shit. He'd been quiet all week. He hadn't bothered to come to any of the trainings. Barely left his room. Meanwhile, Chase felt energised, ready to face the world for once instead of running away from it.

"Give it up," Cyrus groaned. "You don't have to pretend,

Chase. I know you hate rookery. And I'm not going to any more fucking parties with you any time soon, so. Deal over. Be free. You do you."

Chase stared down at his brother, stricken. "You don't want me to play." Was Cyrus ill? Was he a changeling?

"I don't even want *me* to play," said Cyrus, smacking his pillow over his own face. "Why bother?"

"Shut up. Get your gear on. Now." Chase didn't know what the hell was going on, but he was fixing this. He pulled his brother's pillow away and threw it across the room.

Cyrus didn't even look pissed off. "Chase," he said flatly.

"I don't hate it," Chase blurted. Maybe speaking the truth was addictive, like everything else that felt good. "Playing rookery with you is high on the extremely short list of things I don't hate about living in this castle. So. Don't let me down."

Cyrus stared at Chase for a long time. And then he got his arse out of bed.

DENNIS HELPED Jack adjust her straps.

"Think you can stop swooning over your boy long enough to play a full match?" she asked in her usual deadpan voice.

"Are you kidding?" said Dennis. "Have you seen him? You're going to get five minutes of my attention at a time, tops." It still felt strange, talking about this out loud, with his friends, with his sergeant and corporal. Like it was completely normal.

Nothing to hide.

He was trying not to dwell on how much lying he was going to have to do, when he went home for his next visit. In the meantime, the truth felt pretty great.

He darted a glance at Kai, and they exchanged giddy smiles. Even with the entire pitch between them, it felt like they were the only ones here.

"What did I do to deserve this?" Jack sighed.

Dennis frowned, turned back to her. There was a matter he had been meaning to raise with her. The one thing they never, ever talked about. "Jack."

"No. Whatever you're about to say, no."

"We have to tell them. I can't keep something this big from Kai, not now."

Jack looked horrified. "No," she whispered fiercely. "We don't have any proof. If we say anything and we're wrong, it will *wreck* them."

She was right about the lack of proof. All they had was a feeling. They didn't know anything about Kai and the Charming family that literally any other person who saw them together could not guess.

If Kai was Camilla's long-lost twin, if he was really a Prince Charming, he had a right to know. Jack was thinking about her people — about the Royals and the castle, but all Dennis could think about was Kai and how he wanted to blurt out the truth every time he saw his stupid, beautiful face.

"We have to get proof," he said in a low voice.

"Fine," Jack said impatiently. "You're right. But not today."

Chase and Cyrus turned up late, earning cheers and boos from the crowd. They were seized upon by their team, with mocking slaps and hair ruffles.

"Not today," Dennis promised. "But soon."

~

THE ROYALS WERE two points up, and Ziggy was limping when they broke for halftime. She grabbed a handful of orange slices and took them with her to where Sarge leaned against the benches, watching the game. For once, he didn't look like he was longing to play.

"How are you holding up, kid?" he asked her.

"Did you see how I tripped the Countess of Argyll and didn't even get a penalty?" she said proudly.

"Yep, you're definitely getting the hang of the game." He smiled, but it didn't reach his eyes.

She handed him an orange slice. "How are you doing?" He hadn't spoken about Saladin and Miss Clover, not since coming home. It was clear by now that Ziggy's fairy godmother had taken the soldier at his word and kept him.

"You know me, kid," said Sarge. "Job's never done. One day at a time. Shit like that."

"Duty gives you something to do," she said pointedly. "So you don't need to think about your troubles."

He bit savagely into the orange slice. "Don't need to welcome you to that club."

"If you ever wanted to talk to them, I mean. I could make another candle?"

Sarge sputtered orange juice over his hand. "No more wishes, cadet. I'm serious. Keep a lid on it. If there's one thing we don't need in this castle, it's more magic."

"No more wishes," she promised. "I'm done with all that. I actually like it here."

"Yeah," said Sarge, glancing around the snow-edged pitch, and up at the butter-yellow Castle Charming, looming over them all. "It's all right, as places go."

A whistle blew.

"Oi, Zig! Get your scrawny arse over here, we have Royals to flatten!" yelled Corporal Jack.

Ziggy grinned so hard, her face went warm all over. "Settle down!" she yelled back. "I know you can't win without me, but let's not make it too obvious!"

"Aww, big words from such a tiny Hound!" Prince Chase teased, as Ziggy ran back to her team.

Her team. Her castle. Her people. She knew now that she would do anything to protect them all.

Even if that meant holding on to a dried bluebell or two, for next time.

"Ready to go?" Dennis asked, shoving the spiky helmet down over her close-cropped hair.

"Yeah," said Ziyi, sucking the juice out of one last orange slice, and spitting out the rind. "Yes. Absolutely. Bring it on."

CHARM OR DARE

AN INTERLUDE

THINGS ARE ABOUT TO GET SPIN-TERESTING!
CHARM or DARE
Tansy Rayner Roberts

1

———————

A VERY BAD IDEA

Drinking games were never a good idea. Drinking games that involved the princes of Castle Charming, their royal friends, many cursed objects and the steam room, went so far past the concept of 'bad idea' that there was nothing on the other side but darkness, hangovers and regrets.

On the other hand, as far as Corporal Jack of the Royal Hounds was concerned, allowing such a thing to happen without her present to stop it getting out of hand was unthinkable.

You couldn't stop the princes from making bad choices, but you could have their backs. And, if necessary, hold back their hair.

"A drinking game," Cadet Dennis repeated, unconvinced. He had only been a Hound since autumn — there was snow still on the ground, so it wasn't two seasons yet — but he knew a bad idea when he heard one.

Jack liked that about him.

"It will be fun," she lied to his face.

"Since when are you about fun?"

Jack narrowed her eyes at him. "It will be fine," she corrected. "Bring your boyfriend."

"Kai's not my…" Dennis paused, and an utterly goofy expression took over his face. "He's my boyfriend."

"I noticed," Jack said patiently. "Bring him along." Kai Foster had, despite a few mistakes along the way, proved to be trustworthy when it came to protecting the Royals of Castle Charming. Since Jack's entire life revolved around protecting the Royals of Castle Charming, Kai was all right in her book.

"Hang on," Dennis frowned. "What kind of drinking game are we talking about?"

"They invented it themselves," said Jack. "It involves spinning bottles, playing cards, magic beans, truths, dares, kissing and, uh. Other complications. Best to lean into it rather than wrap your head around the rules. Chase always cheats to get what he thinks is the most interesting outcome."

Dennis nodded. "I think I'd better not invite Kai," he said firmly.

Jack considered what she knew about Dennis' boyfriend, which was technically not much. Except… well, she had a strong suspicion that Kai was not what he seemed to be, and that he himself had no idea of this.

"Good call," she said shortly. "Because he's a quill."

"It might make the others uncomfortable, having a newspaper reporter in the game," Dennis agreed.

What neither of them said aloud was this: there is no good way to break the news to your boyfriend that he might be a long-lost prince, but during a drinking game involving truths, dares, magic beans and kissing, you were bound to stumble across some truly *terrible* ways to break the news.

"Bring Ziggy instead," said Jack casually, as if she didn't care one way or another. "It'll be good for both of you to get to know the Royals in a more informal setting."

"Mm," said Dennis. "That's a better idea."

"No," she corrected. "Be under no illusions. The better idea would be to hide in our beds and pretend we don't know this game is happening until it's all over and the fires have been put out by someone else."

"You'd never let that happen," he said warmly.

Yeah, Jack was getting pretty fond of Dennis. He had figured out Castle Charming much faster than most cadets.

Like Jack, Dennis had a talent for spotting princes with terrible ideas from a distance, and he knew how to brace himself for the worst.

He'd go far in this job, with that attitude.

2

SPINNING BOTTLES

Everyone knew Prince Chase was in this for the kissing. It wasn't as if he was short on offers: as an eligible, handsome prince just shy of turning twenty, with gleaming silver eyes, golden hair and a habit of bathing regularly, he could easily drown in kisses, by exerting very little effort.

This was part of what made him so insufferable. Jack had no idea why she still liked him, after all these years. But he had grown on her. Like mould. There was no shaking him now.

She had a horrible feeling he might be her best friend.

Every member of tonight's game — except the royal siblings and the newcomers, had made out with Prince Chase on multiple occasions already.

Jack was in the minority, having only kissed him twice before: once when they were twelve, and she was looking for confirmation that she was indeed only attracted to girls, then again when they were fifteen and this specific game was in its early stages of development.

Jack's first kiss with Chase had confirmed that her interest was specifically girl-directed, though not for want of enthusiastic skill on his part. She had learned a lot from him.

"Let's get started," he said now, sliding the bottle back and forth in his fingers as the rest of the party crowd were slow to settle.

"Easy, tiger," laughed Serena, Countess of Argyll, who practically licked her lips when Dennis and Ziggy arrived in casual clothes, the two of them for once not sporting their official Royal Hounds tabards. "Anyone would think you'd never been kissed before."

"It's not only about kissing," lied Chase, rolling his eyes. "Have some respect for the Game, Serena. The Game is all."

"Kissing is optional," Cyrus assured everyone, which was not entirely a lie but also not a whole truth.

"We have some newbies here tonight," said Chase with a pleased smirk. "Of course, that's one of the rules…"

"Never the same combination of people," Cyrus added with a sigh.

Jack glanced around. Most of this crew were veterans of the Game: Serena of Argyll and Gawain of Gaheris, two of the princes' favourite cousins, distantly related enough that they did not object to kissing the local Royals or each other. Bree, Serena's lady's maid who was good for a laugh and, Jack happened to know from personal experience, extremely flexible.

Gawain had brought along one of his mates from the Academy, a posh boarding school from which he had recently graduated (both princes attended the same school a few years back; Chase was expelled after two semesters, and Cyrus after three).

This particular young aristo was called Hercules. Jack thought at first that he was new to the Game, but then she recalled a summer party in a gazebo several years ago, featuring a wet and awkward kiss from a younger, shorter and skinnier version of the same young man. Apparently he spent the intervening years packing on muscle like his life depended on it.

Dennis and Ziggy were new, and a visiting princess called Laurana of Thalm had also been invited — this was a wild card choice from Prince Cyrus, who usually avoided the girls who arrived at Castle Charming in the hope of landing a husband. Laurana had proven herself to be a good sort in an incident at a recent formal tea party, when she threw a plate of sandwiches at Prince Chase for making an unsavoury remark.

"What are the rules?" Princess Laurana asked now, craning her long neck around the loose circle of players, as if mentally judging everyone's net worth.

Jack noticed that Ziggy shrank into Dennis' side at the sight of Princess Laurana, trying to avoid catching her eye. There was a story there.

The Game was all about secrets spilling out, messily, all over the carpet. Perhaps Jack should have warned Ziggy off as well as Kai.

But if she did that, her chances of kissing Ziggy dwindled to zero and… Jack hated to admit how much kissing Ziggy had been on her mind lately.

This was a useful game for getting kisses out of the way, so that you didn't have to wonder about them for long, or let a lack of them distract you from more important matters.

"The Rules!" Chase announced cheerfully. "First round, we spin the bottle. You offer your opponent two of the following options: Kiss, Truth or Dare. They choose, you devise your fiendish question or challenge — or accept a kiss. If they acquit themselves honourably, you drink; if they fail or quit, they drink. Second round adds wild cards, third round adds magic beans and more drinking."

Cyrus poured cups of a concoction called Princely Punch,

which tasted different every time they played, mixed up from whatever alcohol they had scrounged.

"Seems simple enough," said Laurana of Thalm.

No one laughed at her. She would learn.

"Spin!" cried Chase with delight, letting go of the bottle in mid air. Filled as it was with magic beans, it hovered two feet from the floor. He tapped it wildly, and it spun with a rattling sound.

The first hour was mostly kissing, gentle dares, and truths of minor significance. The party were more interested in warming up than in inspiring regrets.

That would change.

Jack kissed Cyrus (painless) and Serena (always a pleasure).

The most awkward moment of the first round was when Laurana of Thalm challenged Ziggy to Dare or Truth. Ziggy froze for a moment, then finished her cup of Princely Punch rather than choose. Laurana's curiosity increased, her eyebrows drawing together like knives.

Chase managed to kiss nearly everyone, in a blur of bottle spins that had Jack wondering how he had managed to rig the game this time around. Gawain and Serena both provided modest kisses on request. Bree the lady's maid was overly enthusiastic; no one was drunk enough yet for that not to be awkward. There was also a moment of discomfort when Gawain's friend Hercules realised that having a male opponent did not mean you got a free pass from kissing, a new rule that had been established in recent years. He shrugged and went with it, kissing Prince Chase with a gusto that guaranteed he would be invited back in future.

When Chase's spin landed on Jack, he offered Dare or Truth, the first time all night he had not offered a Kiss. Was he finally done with flirting with her? She could only hope.

Jack raised her eyebrows at him. "Truth." Chase's dares were legendary; only a newbie would risk it.

"Who in this room do you most want to kiss?" asked the prince with a teasing light in his eye.

Jack was tempted to say a deadpan "You," but there were magic beans in that bottle, and she wasn't idiot enough to lie. She drank, causing a burst of cheers and teasing to explode around her.

She did not look at Ziggy for a full ten minutes after the bottle spun on.

3

PLAYING CARDS

"Second round!" Prince Chase declared. He now wore a lopsided paper crown he had been dared to construct out of pages torn from an outdated copy of An Instructional Manual Of Noble Manners by An Honourable Aristocrat. Both princes had a particular loathing for this book, which an over-zealous tutor had once used to punish them both.

The way they spoke about it, Jack always assumed they were beaten with a copy, but she eventually learned that the tutor in question had forced them to memorise huge tracts of it, which to this day they had not managed to burn, blitz or booze out of their brains.

Ensuring that part of The Dread Manual was sacrificed to a dare during the game was one of the Four Key Rule Amendments. Until all Amendments were enacted, the game did not end.

Jack had an awful feeling that no one actually remembered what the Fourth Key Rule Amendment was, but that was a problem for later in the evening.

"No more spinning bottles?" pouted Ziggy, who loosened

up considerably after her second cup of Princely Punch, and had a particular fascination for the magic beans.

"Oh, we still spin the bottle," Cyrus assured her. "We're not animals."

"Release the playing cards!" Chase declared with a flourish.

Princess Camilla had the honour of opening the box of charmed playing cards.

Doubly charmed, Jack liked to think, because the amount of personal charm that the princes expended on convincing a local witch's apprentice to magically charm their doctored playing cards for the purposes of a silly game was… excessive.

Everyone hooted and hollered as the cards flipped themselves out of the box, spinning and twirling in a wild mid-air shuffle before landing neatly in a stack beneath the floating bottle.

"Hearts are wild, diamonds are safe, spades are kissable and clubs are dangerous," declared Cyrus as his brother Chase leaned in and tapped the stack of cards imperiously.

The top cards whipped out one at a time, attaching themselves face out to each person's chest.

Those with diamonds peeled them off and returned them to the discard pile with obvious relief. Gawain and Serena had the 7 and 9 of spades respectively and exchanged a brief kiss to get rid of them.

Ziggy had a spade too, but Cyrus leaned over and explained you didn't have to rid yourself of a card right away — any kiss that came up would remove it.

Jack wondered if his helpfulness counted as him volunteering to take the kiss off Ziggy's hands, but the cadet nodded and thanked him and did nothing with her card, for now.

Chase, Dennis and Laurana all had hearts cards — wild

meant that in future they could swap a truth for a dare or a kiss, or any combination they liked. Wild were useful cards to have.

Jack was the only one with a club sticking to the middle of her chest. *Dangerous*. They weren't too hard to get rid of — you took dares until you did something the Game deemed suitably dangerous. It was getting to that part of the evening in any case; danger was inevitable.

But Jack had managed somehow to pull the Ace of Clubs, which triggered the Second Rule Amendment. Drawing an Ace meant the magic beans came out early.

Chase bounced with excitement, tapping the spinning bottle as it hung in the air waiting for the game to go on. "Gonna drink instead?" he asked, eyes bright.

Jack rolled her eyes at him. "I eat danger for breakfast," she sighed. This was the sort of thing that made him laugh like a hyena and what the hell. It was a party.

She put the bean in her mouth, chewed and swallowed. *Instant regrets*.

4

MAGIC BEANS

E ating a magic bean was like nothing else. They were
sweet and nutty and chock full of randomised peril.
Jack felt the effects of this one twist her stomach almost
immediately.

(Kids, don't experiment with magic beans at home.)

Common effects of magic bean consumption were mild
but amusing: you might float three inches off the floor for the
rest of the evening, or sing like a canary every time you tried
to say something (which at least meant no more truth questions). Your hair might turn pink. At worst, a boil might
appear on your nose, or your mouth might fill with ginger-
bread, because the witch's apprentice who charmed these
particular beans had issues with how her people were
portrayed in popular children's stories.

None of these things happened to Jack. It occurred to her
as she chewed that she had never eaten a purple magic bean
before, nor seen anyone else do it.

The tower spun around her and the floor lurched up in a
dizzy wave. She thought she was going to be sick…

She blinked, and the world was different.

Everyone was on their feet around her, so big and stompy and human and loud. Jack, who prided herself on being the most valiant person she knew, turned tail and fled.

She squeezed through the barely-open crack in the door, leaped down the stairs on all fours, and finally found refuge in another room, a quiet out of the way nook full of throw pillows and comforting smells.

It also had a large mirror on top of a bureau. Jack calculated the distance and leapt — to the chair, to the drawer, to the top of the bureau — and executed a series of clever jumps to reach it.

Only there, balanced on four perfect paws in order to stare into the mirror, did she realise the truth.

She was a cat.

She was a *cat*.

She was going to kill Prince Chase of Charming.

Because *she was a cat*.

5

TRUTHS

Jack took refuge underneath an armchair. It felt safe. The chair slightly muffled the sound of footsteps pounding around the tower. People were moving around, looking for her, presumably.

She did not want to be found.

Maybe it was a cat thing, but the thought of being seen right now was unbearable.

Jack heard voices right outside her door, and her whole body tensed, only slightly calming down when she recognised one of those voices as belonging to Ziggy.

Ziggy was her person.

No one must ever know that she had thought such a thing.

"…did you even follow me," Ziggy was saying. "You don't care a bean about Jack."

"I thought we should talk," said another woman in a smooth, elegant voice that made Jack's hackles literally rise. Princess Laurana of Thalm. The party's wild card. "You must know that I recognised you."

"No one else has," Ziggy muttered resentfully.

"It's not like you made much of an effort, darling. You

don't wear makeup any more, you cut your hair short and you changed one syllable of your name. That's *literally* all you did to change your identity."

"No one looks twice at me in a Hounds uniform," Ziggy snapped.

"Are you kidding me? This castle is full of sexually frustrated princesses, away from home for the first time. Believe me, they look at the Hounds. Besides, we spent a whole carriage ride together our first day. I'm not a *complete* empty-head."

"I don't have time for this," said Ziggy. "I have to find Jack." She slammed open the door to the safe room where Jack was — no, not cowering. Some other word meaning a sensible retreat. In any case, when the two women came inside the room, Jack sensibly retreated so far under the chair that she felt the skirting board squash up against her tail.

She had a tail now. She was going to lie on Chase's face until he suffocated on cat hair.

"I'm not going to give you away," Laurana said.

"Why should I trust you? What's in it for you?"

"What's in it for you?" Laurana shot back. "Maybe I just want to know why you'd do it."

"Really?" said Ziggy. "You have no idea why a royal princess might hide away and change her identity just — to avoid — one more humiliating — meat market of a dance — or a supper — or *whatever*." Her speech was punctuated by a flurry as she hurled cushions around the room.

"Some of us don't have that luxury," Laurana said furiously. "Some of us have a family at home depending on a half-decent marriage to save their whole damned kingdom."

"Ha, you want my help, I suppose? The inside story on the Princes of Charming?"

"Maybe. I don't know. I *liked* you," huffed Laurana. "In

the carriage, that first day when we arrived. The others were such…"

"Ninnies," said Ziggy reluctantly, as if she was smiling.

"Yes! So silly and vapid and hopeful. But you were like me, all snarky and competitive and… you saw through the bullshit. I wanted to be friends with you."

"You did?"

"Also, your cat is under that chair."

"JACK!" Ziggy practically hurled the chair across the room.

Jack froze on her haunches, calculating how many limbs she would have to scratch to get out of here, to be free of this horrendous situation.

Laurana passed Ziggy a quilt from a different chair and Ziggy approached slowly, quilt outstretched. "Come on, Jack. Let us help you. We need you back in human shape so you can properly murder Prince Chase."

Jack could not resist a slight purr at that. Ziggy got her. Ziggy was her person.

No!

Caught unawares by the traitorous behaviour of her person, she found herself snatched up and bundled in… the softest quilt… she'd ever…

Prrrrrrrrrrrrrrrrrrrr.

Being a cat was so embarrassing.

6

REGRETS

"Welcome back," said a soft voice that pulled Jack out of her slumber.

"Ugh," she said, stretching out her — naked —

"We have some clothes for you," said a rather less soft voice.

Jack's eyes snapped open, and she was human again. Human, and wrapped in an all-too small quilt. "I hate this game," she moaned.

"And yet you invited me," said Ziggy, handing her a shirt — Jack's own shirt — and holding a cup of water just within reach.

Jack pulled the shirt on over her top half and then glared fiercely across at Laurana of Thalm who apparently had custody of her underthings and trousers.

Laurana passed them over quickly, pretending not to be intimidated.

"Is the game over?" Jack asked, once she was fully dressed. She combed her hair with her fingers and tried to regain what was left of her dignity.

Ziggy still had the 10 of Spades pinned to her chest. Jack tried not to stare at it. (*Spades are kissable*)

Bree and Countess Serena appeared in the doorway at that moment. Bree was carrying Jack's boots.

"The boys and Princess Camilla are still playing," Serena informed them. "We left on the Third Amendment Girl Technicality."

"Ah," said Jack, taking her boots with some relief. She felt just vulnerable enough not to want to return to the party room in her socked feet.

Chase had thought he was being so snarky when he put in the Third Amendment of the rules, which allowed female members of the game to leave play for as long as they deemed necessary, if one of them left the room first. It came in remarkably useful, and not only for finding the nearest bathroom facilities in pairs.

Jack was not used to having female friends, but she appreciated the solidarity as she returned to the party with Serena and Bree leading the way, Ziggy at her side, and Laurana of Thalm at her back.

Chase opened his mouth to say something as Jack made her re-entrance, but Cyrus shoved the spinning bottle at him just in time, distracting him.

Chase spun merrily, and the bottle slowed to point at… Ziggy.

"Kiss or dare," said Chase, waggling his eyebrows at her suggestively.

Jack resigned herself to the inevitable kiss between them. Ziggy still had to get that Spade off her chest, after all.

But Ziggy narrowed her eyes and said 'dare' in a voice that was all challenge.

Jack had never liked her more.

7

DARES

"Okay," said Chase, his voice slurred and his eyes merry. "Cadet Ziggy, I dare you to pat Jack on the head and call her a good kitty."

It was as if the magic beans had frozen everyone in the room to the spot.

Even Cyrus looked afraid.

Jack turned very slowly, and gave Chase her most murderous expression.

He barely flinched, which had to mean he was very drunk indeed. No excuse.

Ziggy stood with great deliberation and crossed the circle towards Jack. She crouched near her, eyes fixed on Jack as if this was going to be a kiss, not a head pat.

She leaned in and whispered directly into Jack's ear: "You will be avenged." Then, loud enough for everyone to hear, she added: "Good kitty," and patted Jack's head.

The tension broke when everyone laughed, but Jack didn't care any more. She was warm all over.

Ziggy reached out for the bottle, and spun it. She only

broke her gaze with Jack to see where it was pointing. "Gareth," she said sweetly. "Truth or dare?"

"Dare," said Gareth immediately.

"Please sit behind Prince Chase and cover his mouth with your hand for the rest of the game."

Chase protested with a squawk, but no one was on his side right now. Gareth sat himself comfortably behind his cousin, covering his mouth with a large hand.

Ziggy squeezed into the circle to sit next to Jack, and looked pleased with herself.

All bets were off, after that. The direction of the game had clearly shifted towards 'make Chase suffer as we have all suffered.' Every truth and dare was designed somehow to punish him for taking things too far.

Jack was feeling positively drunk on friendship.

Finally Princess Camilla entered the fray by daring Laurana of Thalm, with a wicked smile, to: "Kiss everyone in the game... whose mouth is available."

Chase moaned in disappointment as Laurana made her way around the circle, taking and giving her kisses. He looked dolefully at Jack, over the top of Gareth's hand.

Jack's cheeks were still twitching with the sensation of whiskers, and she had no sympathy.

8

———

KISSING

Laurana of Thalm's kiss was thoughtful and pleasant. Jack had no objections to it at all. She managed somehow to not even be eaten up with jealousy when Laurana moved on to Ziggy, kissing her with a thoroughness that she hadn't quite demonstrated with everyone else.

Ziggy looked dazed, when she came up for air. The 'kissable' 10 of Spades peeled itself off her chest and fluttered to the floor.

The game went on.

The *drinking* went on, for everyone except Chase, who had never managed to sober up during one of his games before. First time for everything.

Everything went a bit… sideways, upside down and lopsided.

Jack lost some time.

Everyone else lost a whole bunch of inhibitions.

At one point, Jack found herself in a cluttered broom cupboard, making out like whoa with Serena, Countess of Argyll.

Some time later, she was in the same broom cupboard, but

with Serena's lady's maid Bree, and the two of them (who had been in this position on more than one occasion, not always because a game had put them there) came very close to doing a whole lot more than kissing.

Jack put a stop to it in the last moment. "Too drunk," she protested. "Better not."

"So honourable," said Bree, sliding her hands back out of Jack's shirt and starting to button it up again. "I do like that about you." She kissed Jack on the nose, and led her out of the cupboard with their hands tangled together, to be cheered on by the rest of the crowd.

Jack and Ziggy had still not managed to exchange a kiss.

Jack was not sure she had ever been this drunk in her life.

The game rolled on.

At one point — and this was a highlight — Jack's bottle spun to Chase, and she offered him the choice of Kiss, or Dare.

Resigned now to being muffled by Gawain's hand, Chase said something that sounded distinctly like "Kiff."

Cyrus cupped his ear. "Sounded like dare to me," he smirked.

"Dare!" everyone cried in delight.

9

GAME OVER

The Game did not end as such, which happened three times out of five. Jack was correct that no one remembered the Fourth and Final Amendment, which meant there was no real way to draw a close to the proceedings.

Eventually, as they crawled past the wee hours and into the disgraceful ones, the players slumped on their floor cushions, losing energy and impetus. Some played on. Some took a pause, which turned into a nap.

Eventually, the bottle stopped spinning.

Jack awoke mid-morning, when the sunlight swept over her face. She was curled up on a pile of cushions with a very cuddly Laurana of Thalm, and Ziggy folded up against her on the other side.

There were worse ways to wake up.

Chase lay staring at the ceiling, his head nestled against the sleeping form of Gareth. "I haven't even got a hangover," he complained.

"Poor baby," said Jack unsympathetically. "Also, you're welcome."

She was pretty sure the only reason *she* didn't have a hangover was because there was still far too much of everything in her system. "One of these days," she sighed as she went to check on the sleeping players, one by one. "This Game of yours is going to kill someone, Chase."

"And what a way to go," he said with a contented sigh.

They had all survived this round, at least. Jack shook Cyrus awake, and between them they co-ordinated getting everyone back to their rooms with a minimum of disturbance.

Jack sent Ziggy and Gareth to help Dennis, who had got sneakily much more drunk than anyone suspected. Everyone else cleared out in twos and threes.

"I don't actually need an escort," Laurana of Thalm said as Jack walked her 'home' to the wing of Castle Charming reserved for visiting princesses.

"I wanted to check in on you," said Jack steadily. "There aren't many people who know Ziggy's secret." This was getting to be a lie, really. The list of people who knew Ziggy's secret was dangerously long. "You're not going to do anything with that information, are you?"

"I do know what it's like to be desperate," said Laurana, her mouth going into a thin line. "I'm not a complete bitch."

"That doesn't mean we can trust you."

"Well, I say you can. And I'm an excellent judge of character."

They walked in silence along the portrait gallery of sad, angry and blank-faced former kings and queens of Charming, a shortcut to the residential wing.

"About your situation…" Jack began awkwardly.

Laurana laughed. "This isn't a job offer is it, Corporal Jack?"

"No," said Jack in horror, overtaken by a vision of a row of runaway princesses, all waiting for basic Hound training. "Ziggy is an exception," she said fervently.

"Ziggy," said Laurana disapprovingly. "She barely even bothered to change her *name*."

"What I was going to say," Jack went on. "If you're, uh, in the market for a husband. I wouldn't put your hopes on either of the Princes Charming. They'll do anything they can to avoid picking a bride, mostly because their father is piling the pressure on for them to do it, and that only makes them drag their heels harder. Even if they do, uh…" Jack already felt like a traitor for saying this much, and she couldn't think of a diplomatic way of saying: "Anyone who marries either of those lads will take on more baggage than a single human person should have to deal with." So she said exactly that, aloud.

It was a night of Truths, after all, along with the Dares and the Kissing.

Laurana's face made it clear this was not new information. "I wouldn't have travelled all this way if I had more viable options," she said pointedly.

"Well," said Jack. "About that. Did you know that Gawain of Gaheris — while not a prince — is second son of one of the richest duchies of the Riverlands?"

"Interesting," said Laurana. "Second son, you say?"

"He gets along very well with his brother the heir, he has a pretty spectacular independent inheritance coming to him when he's 25, and he's remarkably unfucked up, for an aristo."

"I thought he had something going on with the Countess of Argyll?" Laurana asked after a thoughtful pause.

Jack resisted the urge to laugh maniacally. "Serena's not the settling down kind, and they were childhood friends, so. I don't think there's anything longterm going on there."

She had never dabbled in matchmaking before. Was she still drunk, or was she brilliant at this?

"Thank you for your advice," said Laurana, stopping in

front of a door. "This is me." She held out a hand, and Jack clasped it, for a moment. "Perhaps I can offer you some romantic advice in exchange, one of these days."

Jack scoffed. "Sure. You do that."

Laurana had a small smile on her face when she closed the door behind her.

JACK FOUND DENNIS' boyfriend Kai hovering around the dorm building behind the Doghouse, headquarters of the Royal Hounds. "He won't be awake for hours," she assured the lad, clapping him on the back. "Assuming he even made it to his bed."

"I figured," said Kai with a reluctant smile. "I kind of want to see how much of a state he's in, though. If that's okay?"

"Knock yourself out," shrugged Jack, letting him follow her up to the dorm.

It was a huge room filled with narrow beds in rows. Most Hounds claimed a specific spot for themselves, though there was a certain… informality sometimes, when it came to claiming a bunk.

Jack found Ziggy and Dennis sprawled out on the floor between his bunk and hers, leaning against each other, snoring.

"Oh wow," said Kai, impressed at the tragic heap they made.

"Such a mess, but they're ours," said Jack sleepily. "'Scuse me, still wasted." She toppled into the nearest bunk, and was asleep almost as soon as her head hit the pillow.

In her dream, she was a cat again, curled up on Ziggy's lap and purring.

Cats didn't care whether they got to kiss certain people or not. Cats had it all sorted out.

Maybe she should have stayed a cat.

LET SLEEPING PRINCES LIE

SPRING

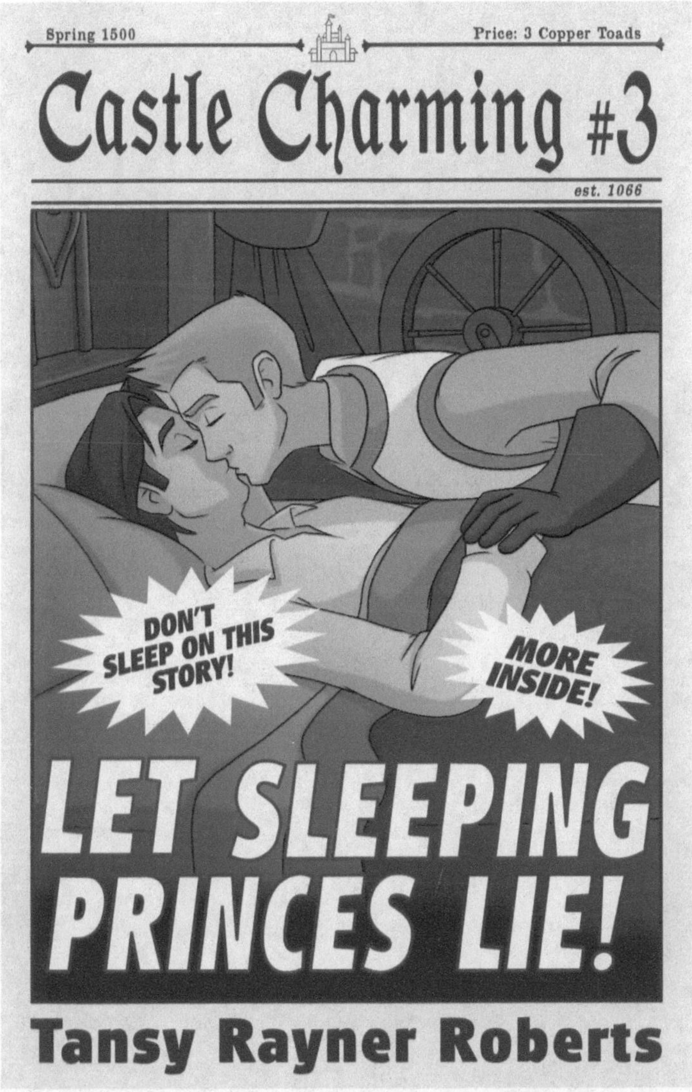

Castle Charming #3

Tansy Rayner Roberts

1

CHARMING DREAMING

Kai dreamed of ink.

He pricked his finger with a quill and the ink poured out of him like blood, gushing over his arms, soaking his clothes. He spat it out of his mouth, wiped it from his eyes.

He waded across the floor of his tiny bedsit, opened the door and watched the ink wash down the stairs, out into the night.

Of course, he followed it. He was a quill, and you always went where the story led you.

The ink splashed a messy path along the cobbles, through the streets of the city. It wound and poured its way up to the butter-yellow stones of Castle Charming.

Still Kai followed it, through the front gates, up into the castle itself. The ink drenched the priceless carpets, washed up the walls to destroy paintings that had been there for hundreds of years. All of the Castle Charming ancestors, splashed black and forever stained.

The ink led Kai up the stairs, along corridors, through a

door that had definitely been locked and barred a few minutes ago.

Princess Camilla lay still on a four-poster bed, her skin pale like marble, her eyes closed. Her dark hair splashed out on the pillows like ink, framing her face which had always felt so familiar.

They were part of something, Kai and Camilla. She worked with ink. Their magic was intertwined. He had so much to learn from her.

Was she even breathing?

There were spinning wheels, of all things, lined up around her bed, running threads of flax and gold and silk from one to the other, like some enormous web of machinery. The ink crept under and around the tangled threads, making for the bed.

Kai picked up a spinning wheel and hurled it aside, then another, then another, to reach the princess. His limbs were heavy and slow; he was too late to save her. The ink swamped Camilla, dragging her down into its blackness, leaving nothing but a gaping hole in the centre of the bed, surrounded by silken sheets and embroidered throw pillows.

He was too late, and his hand was still bleeding.

"SHH," said a low voice. "Bad dream, babe?"

Kai awoke to warmth, to the comforting bulk of Dennis, naked and wrapped around him in the too-narrow bed. "Ink," he whispered. It wasn't the first time he had experienced that dream. The spinning wheels were new, though.

"Ugh, that again," muttered his boyfriend, shifting against Kai, pressing his lips softly to the back of his neck. "Want me to make you forget all about it?"

Kai groaned softly, which was all the encouragement that

Dennis needed. He raised himself on his strong arms, rolling on top of Kai and kissing his way down, his mouth making a hot trail from chest to stomach and lower, to the crease of Kai's hip.

"You're the best," said Kai, the unsettling images of the dream already fading.

"I know," said Dennis with a smirk, and took him into his mouth.

Heat and pleasure washed over Kai, his skull bumping roughly against the headboard.

HE STARTLED AWAKE A MOMENT LATER, still hard and wanting, alone in his narrow bed, several streets away from the castle where his boyfriend spent his nights.

Damn. He'd had that dream before, too. Usually it lasted a little longer.

At least he was no longer seeing spinning wheels when he closed his eyes.

2

THE FIRST RULE OF SPINNING WHEELS

Kai didn't see the spinning wheels coming.

Then, suddenly, they were everywhere.

At the offices of the Charming Herald, he walked in on his work friend (less of a friend these days) Amira Chaudry having a knockdown, drag out fight with one of their editors.

"No more spinning wheel headlines!" Bors yelled at her. "Don't even try it. Are you looking to get this newspaper closed down by the Royals?"

"It's spring, no one wants to read about anything else right now!" Amira hollered, clutching a dummy front cover that did indeed proclaim SPINNING WHEEL CRISIS? "We can't stick our heads in the sand over this one. Readers are hungry for it."

"Superstition isn't news," Bors said between gritted teeth. "Get me a story we can publish without being arrested for treason, or find some other newspaper willing to put up with your diva tantrums."

He marched to his office, slamming the door. Amira caught Kai's eye and pulled a frustrated face before remembering that they didn't do that any more. So she huffed out, taking her spinning wheel headline with her.

He'd ask Dennis, Kai decided. His boyfriend (never got tired of that word!) had been working at Castle Charming for a year before Kai came to town. He knew a lot more about the weird local quirks while still being enough of an outsider that he didn't mind spilling the gossip.

Also, it was an excuse to see Dennis which… Kai didn't even need anymore. *Score.*

He kept himself busy editing all the errors that the proof-readers had added to his story about the upcoming tulip festival. There wasn't much point in dropping by Castle Charming until evening when Dennis would be off duty.

When Kai was a kid, his foster mother told him the story of a duke's son who bought a yellow horse and then, wherever he went, saw yellow horses and thought it was some kind of sign from the gods. "Humans are made to recognise patterns," she said, her hands embroidering as she sat by his bedside. "We're stupid about them."

Most of Mother's stories came down to people being stupid about something.

Still, Kai wasn't imagining this pattern. There were spinning wheels everywhere today.

He almost bumped into two of them on his way out of the office. A couple of large, burly lads were on their way somewhere in a hurry, each with an awkwardly-shaped wooden contraption slung across his muscled shoulders. Definitely spinning wheels. One still had a long strand of freshly-spun yarn trailing from it, tangled around the weft.

"Our Ange is gonna be mighty pissed we burned these," one of the lads grunted to the other.

"Nahhh," said the other. "Gotta be done, mate. It's like, a law, innit? Gotta burn spinning wheels in springtime."

Kai watched them make their way along the street. He

pulled out the small box-monochrome he carried slung from his belt these days, and snapped a picture of the odd pair. Smoke and the stench of silver puffed out of the box as it captured the image.

He saw more people carrying spinning wheels on his way up to the castle, as well as a small huddle of girls arguing about whether drop spindles counted. Some of the spinning wheels didn't even look real, made for the occasion (badly) from cheap wood or thick slabs of parchment and glue.

It wasn't until Kai reached the first gate of the castle that he saw the flowers — bundles and bundles of them, scattered before the walls, along with cards emblazoned with the words NEVER FORGET — and he realised what was going on.

Spring. It must have been spring when the royal baby was stolen, all those years ago. There was a spinning wheel in that story, wasn't there? Queen Ella even now lay in a sleeping curse, because of… something like that. Kai had never really paid attention to the ballads, even after he got to know Camilla and her brothers, the royal siblings left behind when the baby prince was stolen. It seemed awkward to check out the poetry about their family's tragic loss.

There were no spinning wheels here, among the bouquets and the cards. Only sadness.

"IT'S SPINNING WHEEL SEASON," said Sarge in his usual no-nonsense bark, at the morning meeting of the Royal Hounds. "And you all know what that means…"

Dennis put his hand up. "I don't know what that means, Sarge."

"Neither do I, Sarge," added Ziggy, the other new recruit.

"I think we'd all like to hear you explain it, Sarge," put in

Corporal Jack, who enjoyed being a little shit when she could get away with it.

Sarge sighed the sigh of the unjustly put-upon. "Right," he grumbled. "Fine. Gossip network not doing its job? YOU DON'T NEED TO KNOW WHY," he added in a sudden bellow. "All you need to know is that our charges — His Majesty, Their Highnesses — are not to go anywhere near a bloody spinning wheel. Not even a picture of a spinning wheel. You see one, you put your body between them and it. And you burn that fucker to the ground."

"I'm more confused than ever," Ziggy murmured.

Dennis nodded. Castle Charming was often confusing to him. He had been raised in the mountains, and ran away from the limited options and small minds of his community there.

He welcomed the more complex social and political inter-actions of the castle and surrounding city. There was hustle and bustle here, and a lad could kiss another lad without the world coming to an end.

But there were times when castle crap made no blooming sense, and this was clearly one of those times.

He risked putting up his hand again. "Can you clarify the risk factors of spinning wheels in relation to the royal family?"

Sarge gave him a filthy look. "Been reading those Law Enforcement Journals again, pup?"

Dennis shrugged. He liked to know things. He wanted to make corporal some day and Jack had told him that meant prepping for a proper exam.

"The risk factor," Sarge said clearly. "Is that if one of you Hounds lets a member of the royal family get within five metres of a bloody spinning wheel, I will punch you in the nuts. How's that for clarity, Cadet Dennis?"

"It's all very clear now, Sarge," said Dennis in a choked voice.

3

ROYAL COPING MECHANISMS 101

Prince Chase of Charming did not deal well with the first month of spring. Like, at all. He and his brother Cyrus had a longstanding tradition. When the bouquets started building up outside the gates, and the annual spinning wheel bonfires stank the air up with smoke, the two of them had license to do whatever the hell they wanted.

For Chase that meant drinking, dancing and meaningless sex, replacing rough hangovers and even rougher bed companions with more drinking and dancing and meaningless sex until the weather was warmer, and the entire country stopped being so goddamn sad about what had happened to his family all those years ago.

He wasn't 100% sure what Cyrus did for that month, though he suspected it involved a lot more running, weights training and obsessively monitoring his food intake than usual.

Not this year, though. This year, Chase had made a promise to his sister.

Sisters were the worst.

Camilla turned up at his door, her cropped dark hair

concealed by a cotton beanie. She wore soft trousers and a shirt that clearly had not been designed with princesses in mind, cut short over her shoulders to show off the spiralling ink that patterned her arms. "Morning, sweets," she said with a wicked grin.

Chase glared at her. Sunrise was never part of his spring survival plan, unless he was seeing it from the wrong end when he dragged himself home from a seedy nightclub three towns over. "I hate everything," he informed her.

"Healthy choices," teased Camilla.

Chase had to admit, she'd been doing well. Over the last six months, Camilla went from a virtual recluse hiding in her tower to — well, a sister who took an interest in whether or not her older brothers were being self-destructive this week.

It had to be an improvement, right?

"Healthy choices," he muttered resentfully.

She made a few impatient jogging motions. "It's going to be *fun*."

"Don't lie to me."

"It's going to be *not terrible*."

"You're overselling it, Cami."

"It's going to be DREADFUL," she said with relish. "Let's get started."

SINCE THE DANCING Shoes incident (and assorted drunken scandals), Chase was not allowed out of the castle without at least one interfering shadow. As he and his sister made their way to the grassy oval that no longer served as a rookery pitch (he missed winter already), today's shadow unfolded from the wall, making herself known.

"What are you two up to?" asked Corporal Jack: Chase's best friend, greatest critic and all-time nemesis.

"Jogging," Chase informed her.

Jack laughed, throwing her whole head into it. "No, seriously."

"Jogging!" Camilla confirmed in a crow of delight.

"Oh." The Royal Hound took the princess at her word, which was super annoying, because she never believed a thing that came out of Chase's mouth. "Well, then. This I've got to see."

"Why did you believe her and not me?" Chase pouted.

"Because I've met you," said Jack. Heartless and unfair.

"We'll be exercising very hard," he told her sternly. "Feel free to try to keep up."

It wasn't much of a threat. Jack had thighs like tree trunks, and her fitness level made even Cyrus look like he wasn't trying very hard.

"Healthy choices," Camilla reminded Chase, rapping him on the side of the head with her knuckles.

Yes, jogging. There would be time to plot vengeance against Corporal Jack later.

"Let's go," he said crisply.

CYRUS HAD CLEARLY BEEN RUNNING laps of the oval since before sunrise, because he was a maniac. As his brother and sister approached, he slowed to a light jog. "Joining me?"

"No need to look so happy about it," Chase sulked.

"We're not going to try to keep up with you," Camilla assured Cyrus. "Just some fun, light exercise to start the day. Every day," she added with a firm look at Chase, who was certain he hadn't agreed to that.

Oh, wait. Yes he had. Damn it.

"Fun," Cyrus repeated, as if the idea of exercising without

turning it into an intense, body-breaking challenge was completely bizarre.

Chase had no idea why *he* was the brother everyone worried about. Cyrus was clearly long past breaking point.

"I don't know about the rest of you," said Chase. "But I came here to jog."

~

JOGGING WAS *THE WORST*. Chase had assumed he was reasonably fit, coming off a tough winter of rookery and clubbing. He hadn't been out as much since the whole Fairy Kidnapping incident, but still. He had muscle tone. His body did most of the things he wanted it to unless he was three vodkas in.

After running four laps of the oval today, Chase learned some new things about himself. He learned that his muscle tone was basically porridge, grass was so boring he wanted to scream, and lungs were flammable.

He wasn't going to admit defeat. Camilla was still smiling.

They had attracted an audience of Royal Hounds and assorted castle hangers-on, who arrived in twos and threes, many of them carrying cups of coffee or breakfast rolls.

Apparently, Prince Chase of Charming was the morning entertainment.

Five laps. That was respectable, yes? He could stop after five laps. But there went Camilla, pounding on for her sixth, with Cyrus overtaking her. Chase glared at both of their backs.

"I have juice," Jack called out, which made the decision for him.

Chase slowed, stretching out his back and breathing deeply before accepting the cup of squeezed oranges and lemons that Jack passed him. He would never admit that he was grateful for the excuse to stop, but Jack was a good friend. Hardly a nemesis at all.

"You do realise you're talking out loud," she said, amused.

He leaned his sweaty face on her shoulder, wiping his hair on her bright red and white tabard. "I hate everything. But I do like juice."

"It's good for you," said Jack, patting him absently, like he was a dog.

If only she was into men, Chase would marry the hell out of this woman, peasant origins bedamned.

Jack's body stiffened, and for a moment he thought he had said that out loud too (not that his desires to marry her would be a surprise to literally anyone).

"What's that on the pitch?" she said instead.

Chase turned, but before he could focus his eyesight, the Hounds around them started shouting, waving their hands. Some of them ran on to the pitch.

Cyrus reached out and slammed into Camilla with his arm, knocking her back before she could collide with…

The object.

Who was Chase kidding?

He knew what it was.

Everyone knew what it was.

"Is that… a spinning wheel?" asked the new puppy, Blondy McMuscles. (Dennis, Chase knew his name was Dennis, but even in a crisis he was always going to be an arsehole.)

"How did that get out there?" asked the other new puppy, Ziggy McUsedToBeAPrincessFace.

Jack hung on to Chase's shirt like she thought he might dash out after his siblings, which was a stunning overestimation of his bravery. "Get that thing out of here!" she bellowed at the Hounds on the pitch. "Burn it."

Cyrus ushered Camilla back to the group, circling widely around the incongruous spinning wheel that had appeared on the grass before them.

"It's a silly superstition," she was arguing. "Someone's trying to scare us, that's all."

"That was magic," Corporal Jack retorted, all business now. "Someone enchanted a spinning wheel to appear directly in the your path. We have to consider this an Official Attempt."

Chase tugged at Jack to release him from her grip. She did so, looking startled, as if she didn't realise she had two handfuls of his shirt. "Does that mean no more sunrise jogging?" he asked hopefully.

"Worse than that," said Jack, looking grim. "It means we have to report this incident to His Majesty."

YOU SPIN ME RIGHT ROUND, BABY

Kai had been looking forward to seeing Dennis all day, but he wasn't expecting to be grabbed the second he set foot inside the castle, and hustled up a tower staircase until they emerged, both breathing hard, in a little room that looked like a private library.

"Wow," said Kai. "Um. Good to see you too."

"Sorry," said Dennis, as if only now realising that he had forgotten to say a proper hello. He leaned in, his large hands framing Kai's face, and kissed him thoroughly. "Things have been bonkers here. There was an attempt on the Royals this morning."

"What kind of attempt?" Kai asked, drawing back, though being kissed by Dennis was entirely his favourite thing in the world. Digging into an interesting story was his second favourite thing. "An assassination attempt?"

"Maybe," said Dennis, looking cagey. "I can't really talk about it."

This was still a source of tension between them, that Kai worked for a newspaper, and Dennis was constantly brimming over with private knowledge about the lives of his employers. It didn't help that they were both — if not friends, then *friendly* with the younger generation of Royals.

"It's fine," said Kai. "I mean, you don't have to tell me. Obviously."

Dennis kissed him again, but was clearly distracted. His heartbeat was thudding way too fiercely for a little light snogging.

"Hey," said Kai, pushing some space between them. "What's freaking you out?"

Dennis stared at him, glazed-over and panicky. "Um. I have to — I mean, I wasn't not not going to tell you, but I think now it might be. Essential. To tell you."

"Off the record?" said Kai, trying to lighten the mood with a joke.

Dennis reached out and brushed his large hand against Kai's flopping fringe, which apparently he had a bit of a thing for. "Okay," he said, breathing deeply. "Don't freak out, but…"

The library door burst open and Hurricane Camilla whirled in, carrying a stack of leather-bound journals and almost flattening Kai with the pressure of her magic.

Camilla was the most magical person that Kai had ever met. He had a modest amount of power himself, but Camilla's magic was… loud.

She had magical tattoos across most of her body, each representing a new spell she had learned, or a level of magic she had achieved during the 'princess in the tower' period of seclusion which lasted most of her teen years.

Whenever she was nearby, Kai could feel her, not only in the one imperfect magical tattoo he had managed to spell on to himself since he started studying magic with Camilla, but also in the old inky birthmark in the small of his back; in his blood, in his skin.

Even with his hot Hound boyfriend right here in his arms, it was hard to notice anything else when she was in the room.

"Sorry for interrupting!" Camilla called out, whipping past them both to dump her armful of books on to a large polished table. "Kai, I'm glad you're here, I could do with some help."

"Help," Dennis said flatly, putting a respectable space between himself and Kai. He was glaring at Camilla. What?

"Yes," she said, not looking at either of them, flicking open several books and whirling their pages without actually touching them. "I want to set up a protection spell for my brothers. You can help me, Kai."

"For your brothers," said Dennis and again, there was that odd, flat tone. "Because they're the ones in danger." Kai had never seen Dennis this close to being rude to one of the Royals. He tried asking what was going on with his eyebrows but his boyfriend avoided his gaze.

"He has a point," Kai said after a moment, giving Dennis a reassuring squeeze on his arm before going over to join Camilla at the books. "Why only protect your brothers? If the spinning wheels are… a genuine threat, aren't you a target too?"

Camilla tilted her head at him, as if she had never thought of that.

"I mean," said Kai, feeling super awkward about this. "Isn't that how your mother…"

Camilla's face went from confused to chilly. "It won't take a moment," she said. "Ten minutes, tops. It's a simple spell."

"Okay," said Kai. "I'll help."

~

DENNIS HAD no idea what to do with this information. It was weird, right? Knowing what he knew about Kai.

Part of him was relieved that Princess Camilla had interrupted his clumsy attempt to finally spill the beans, though the rest of him was grumpy at her for being so concerned about her older brothers only.

How could she not know?

It got even more uncomfortable when Ziggy arrived, delivering Prince Cyrus to be his sister's guinea pig for the spell. Dennis was pretty sure Ziggy shared his suspicion about the Thing, the Thing they never talked about, because they didn't know for sure. (He'd seen her looking at Jack when Jack was looking at Kai, and Jack *definitely* knew the same thing that Dennis didn't know for sure.)

Time was running out. It couldn't stay some Big Awkward Secret that only some of the younger Hounds shared. Not if the princes were in danger from this spinning wheel curse.

All three princes.

How could Kai not have noticed he was a dead ringer for the princess, who was almost certainly his twin sister? How could he not know it was only his dark hair and floppy fringe that made his similarity to the princes even slightly tricky to spot?

What would Dennis have said to Kai, if he hadn't been interrupted right now? *"So, uh, try to avoid spinning wheels this month, in case you're a secret long-lost prince. Sorry, babe."*

"What are you doing?" Kai asked suddenly.

Dennis pulled himself away from Ziggy's attempts to discuss their shared Awkward Secret via silence and eyebrows.

Camilla looked caught out. "The spell might have some backwash," she said quickly.

"How much longer is this going to take?" Cyrus drawled.

Kai backed away from both Royals. "I'm not new at this, Camilla. You taught me enough to know when someone is trying to put a spell on me without my permission. The question is why?"

Camilla hesitated.

Ziggy made a small noise, staring at the princess.

She knew, Dennis realised finally. He wasn't sure whether to be angry or relieved. He wasn't imagining it. Princess Camilla *knew* that Kai was her long-lost twin brother, and she was trying to protect him without telling him the truth.

"You should stay," he blurted out. If Camilla's spell could protect Kai from some kind of awful curse, he was all for it.

Kai turned and stared at Dennis. "What?"

"You trust Camilla, don't you? Let her do this."

"I'm going to do push ups until you need me again," said Prince Cyrus, and started doing exactly that. Kai had to step over him to head out of the room.

"You're all being weird right now," he snapped, looking furious. "So if no one wants to explain the weirdness?"

Dennis could not think of what to say.

Camilla bit her lip. "It's complicated," was all she said.

Kai rolled his eyes. "Let me know when you've figured it out." He slammed his way out of the room.

It was on the tip of Dennis' tongue to apologise because this was his job, he was a Royal Hound, and his boyfriend had just snapped at the princess…

Instead he said "How long have you known?" and there was no way he could prevent that from sounding like an accusation.

"How long have you?" Camilla bit back, then relented, pulling a hand through her short, curly dark hair. "The first day he walked into the tower. How does anyone else not see it? Are they all blind?"

"I know, right?" said Dennis with a wave of relief. He wasn't imagining it.

(Oh, hell. He was dating a long-lost prince.)

Prince Cyrus rolled on to his back and started stretching his triceps. "What am I missing here?"

KAI HAD TRUST ISSUES. He knew he had trust issues. But Camilla's magic usually felt so safe, and he couldn't shake how wrong it had felt today, her spell creeping on him, trying to do something to him without his consent.

Worse was how Dennis hadn't seen anything wrong with that.

This wasn't the first time that Kai felt like there was some massive joke going on, and everyone else was in on it.

He didn't want to be in this castle right now. He had to cool down, before he picked a fight with his otherwise adorable boyfriend over… nothing, right? It had to be nothing.

Were there this many stairs when Kai and Dennis came up this way earlier? Maybe not, they'd been too busy teasing and kissing each other to notice.

Kai whirled around yet another curve in the staircase and came face to face with a spinning wheel on the widest step.

Prince Chase, coming up the stairs at the same time, reared back as he also saw it. "Damn it. They've been turning up all day," he grumbled.

"Camilla said it's a curse on your family," said Kai. He had long since dropped the Your Highness greetings around Camilla and her brothers, unless one of them was behaving especially snooty.

Prince Chase arched his eyebrows, obviously remembering all over again that Kai was a quill. "Is this on the record?"

Kai rolled his eyes, officially sick of everyone who lived in this castle. "I mean, will it be a problem if *I* move it out of your way?"

Chase shrugged. "It's a Royals-only curse. Avoid the needle, though, just in case your distant ancestor was a king or queen."

Ha. Kai reached out to move the wheel aside, but hesitated as he felt a roil of magic emanating from it. This magic wasn't familiar, like Camilla's ink or his own gentle echo of her power. It tasted sour in the back of his throat.

There was a yell from the balcony above the staircase. Camilla must have followed him. That was the last thing Kai needed.

"Kai, no! Chase, don't let him." She sounded very high up, and far away.

"My sister's crazy again," sighed Chase. "Must be Thursday."

The wood was warm under Kai's hands, and he couldn't taste magic in it any more. He moved it aside easily, so the prince could walk past.

"Cheers," said Chase. And then, in a different voice, "Shit."

Kai could hear Camilla clattering above, and heard a shout from Dennis, but he was distracted by the sudden forest of spinning wheels that sprang up, all around them on the staircase. Six of them. Twelve. Eighteen.

"Stand very still," he said to the prince.

"No," said Chase sarcastically. "I never would have —— Cami, don't come any closer!" he yelled up the stairwell.

Camilla's voice echoed down to them. "Kai, be careful."

"Oh, *charming*," Chase yelled up. "No worrying about me? I'm only your favourite brother!"

There was a hum in Kai's head. If the spinning wheels weren't magic, something else was. He felt the ink heat up on his skin. "What kind of curse *is* this?"

"The kind that's trying to ruin my life," complained Chase. He was backed against one of the curved walls, unable to move an inch without touching a spinning wheel.

Kai's vision tunnelled down into a narrow channel. He couldn't even see the prince any more. "I had a dream like this," he said faintly.

"You — dreamed this?" said Chase. There was something odd about his voice.

Everyone was being so strange today.

"There was only one way out," Kai said. The air was warm around him, and everything felt strange. "It's okay," he added. "I know what to do."

"Hey," warned Chase, but it was too late.

Kai reached out, and grasped the nearest spinning wheel securely, the safe end with no sharp parts. Even as he did so, the object flickered in his arms, and he found himself holding the other side entirely. The side with the sharp needle, even now digging into the palm of his hand.

A tiny burst of pain. A drop of blood, falling.

And then they disappeared, the spinning wheels, one after another, with a soft popping sound.

Chase gazed at him. "How did you do that?" he demanded.

Everything was warm, and swirling. "I think I'm going to throw up," said Kai, and he dropped like a stone.

5

KISS THE QUILL

Prince Chase had spent his whole life taking Hounds for
granted. They guarded him, babysat him, and saved him
from the worst consequences of his terrible behaviour. They
mopped his brow when he was sick, and refused to marry him
even when he made a most persuasive case for it… (Those
last two were specific to Corporal Jack rather than Hounds in
general.)

Never had a Hound run at him like this, howling and
murderous. Not even Sarge on a bad day.

Cadet Dennis glowed with anger, like an avenging
golden-haired ogre, all muscle and smiting. He powered
down the stairs towards Chase as if he honestly meant to kill
him, but came to a stumbling halt when he saw the crumpled
figure of Kai on the stairs.

"He did it to himself," Chase said hastily. "I didn't ask
him to rescue me, that's not his job. It's *yours*," he added with
a sour note, but Cadet Dennis didn't notice the sting.

Cyrus clattered down next, with Jax who was clearly not
even trying to save Chase from her violent co-worker.
Camilla and Cadet Ziggy followed them, crowding into the

stairwell which had only a minute earlier been crammed with enchanted spinning wheels.

Dennis went to his knees with a wounded sound, cradling Kai's head in his lap. "How?" he started to say.

"That's what I want to know," snapped Chase. "It's *our* family curse. Since when do the spinning wheels go after civilians?"

"Oh," said Jack, looking gutted. "Damn."

Camilla closed her eyes, just for a moment, and when she opened them again she looked guilty as hell. So, she knew what was going on. Everyone seemed to, except Chase and his brother.

"What the hell is going on?" It was Cyrus who asked that, every bit as impatient as Chase. As the elder brother, of course, *his* question was treated more seriously.

"Can we take him to your room?" Camilla asked Cyrus with a sob in her throat. "Please. I'll explain it all then, but we have to get him out of sight. I don't know if we want Father to know about this. Not yet, anyway."

Dennis moved in one swift movement, gathering the fallen quill in his arms. My, the muscles on that one. "You knew all along," he accused Camilla in the kind of voice that Hounds (not counting Jax) never used in the presence of Royals: full of pep and insolence.

"I've been teaching him magic for half a year," said Camilla, tossing her head. "He has the same magic as me. I'm not stupid. Of course I knew."

The Hounds followed Dennis and Camilla up the stairs again, in an oddly solemn procession. Chase grabbed Cyrus' arm before they followed. "I think *I'm* stupid," he said urgently. "What the hell is going on?"

Cyrus looked like death warmed up, which meant he had figured it out too, the bastard. "It can't be," he said in a shaky voice. "Right here, all this time?"

"I HATE YOU ALL," Chase decided, ten minutes later when he had his explanation. "This baby quill has been in this city for half a year or more. You all guessed he was our long-lost brother and you failed to mention it?"

He wasn't looking at the Hound currently curled around his boyfriend's unconscious body on the bed. He was looking at Jack.

Chase didn't care about the others. He cared that his closest friend, one of the people he trusted most in the world — had kept this from him.

He should have known. His father had always disapproved of his children making friends with the help. He warned them time and again that when you were a Royal, you could not rely on anyone but family.

Given how badly his father had let them all down over the last… forever, Chase had taken that advice with a pinch of salt. If he hadn't already been head over heels in friendship with the sharp, sarcastic Hound who cleaned up all his messes and didn't pull her punches like everyone else, he would have befriended her to *spite* the King.

"I didn't know," Jack snapped defensively and then, seeing something of Chase's current betrayal in his face, calmed her voice. "It was a guess — a suspicion. We hadn't figured out how to ask him about it yet, let alone the rest of you."

"Apparently you didn't have to," said Cyrus, and his own searing gaze of accusation locked on to their sister.

"I thought we had plenty of time," Camilla said defensively. "Spinning wheels haven't done this to us before. I mean, apart from the obvious."

"Can we just," broke in Dennis. "I mean. Can we move

past the part where everyone blames everyone else? How do we *fix* him?"

Chase stared at the Hound. Had he not been paying attention? "I thought you knew," he said coldly. "This is the spinning wheel curse. It doesn't get fixed."

DENNIS WAS HAVING the worst day. Much earlier, he'd stood at Corporal Jack's side as she explained to the king about the magically appearing spinning wheel on the pitch that morning. Dennis witnessed the awkwardness of the scene as King Iolchas lost his temper. He raged and ranted at the uselessness of the Hounds until spittle flew from his mouth.

Now this. It didn't feel real. Kai looked peacefully asleep — his cheeks still had colour in them. His eyelids fluttered as if he was having a pleasant dream.

Prince Chase's words made no sense. Of course this could be fixed. Kai was going to be fine.

Ziggy nudged closer, clearly taking his side against the wall of Royals so wrapped up in whether Kai might be their lost sibling that they didn't actually see him as a person. "In the fairy tales," she said quietly. "A spinning wheel curse was broken by a kiss. Isn't that right?"

Dennis stared at her suddenly, wild with hope. But then — that was worse. He liked Kai so much. But was it love? Epic, curse-shattering, magic-dissolving true love? That was a lot of pressure on a relationship that was only a few months old.

"You're forgetting one detail," said Prince Chase, his voice like acid. "In the stories, the kiss only worked after a hundred years."

Dennis turned his blank gaze to the prince, as the pieces fell into place. Queen Ella, the mother of the Royals, had been asleep in a tower under this same curse for years. If there was a fix for this, if love was the only ingredient necessary, surely they would have found it by now, and released the queen from her cursed slumber?

"I have to try, right?" he whispered.

"Of course you do," said a distant voice that sounded a lot like Princess Camilla.

Slowly, Dennis leaned in and brushed his mouth lightly over the lips of his sleeping boyfriend, in the gentlest of kisses.

He waited.

Kai breathed in, and out.

And that was it.

He did not wake up.

6

SOMEWHERE OVER THE RAINBOW

K ai picked himself up, dusted himself off, and stared around his surroundings. "So," he said aloud. "This is where spinning wheels come to die."

It was a long, formal room. Somewhere in the castle? That made sense, though it was clearly a space that hadn't been used in years. Dusty, spider-webbed portraits glared at him from the walls, and a long banquet table (not far off the regulation size of a rookery pitch) stretched out into the distance.

There were spinning wheels everywhere. They piled up and over the table, on the chairs, underneath, and they were heaped on the carpet as well. Teetering towers of abandoned spinning wheels blocked off the windows, allowing only a little stained glass light to sneak into the dark, dusty room.

Kai couldn't remember how he got here, which was the first thing to worry about. The other was that he could not see a door.

There was ink here. He could feel it nearby, the magic rising in him to meet it.

His tattoo — still the only magical tattoo he had managed

to cast upon himself to date despite Camilla's patient teaching — felt warm on the skin of his upper arm.

It wasn't just ink and magic he could feel here, in this weird room. It was *familiar* ink and magic.

Kai set off marching to the far end of the long, thin room, and it was as if it narrowed and lengthened with every stride, so that he could never quite reach the other end of the table. He tried running, but that was too difficult with all the spinning wheels to climb over or dodge around.

He yelled, but heard nothing but echoes.

Be calm. You're stuck in some walled up part of Castle Charming, but it's not the end of the world. Someone will find you. Dennis will find you.

Sure, he might arrest you for trespassing like the snoopy newspaper reporter you are, but right now an arrest sounds awesome.

Kai walked slower now. He wasn't any closer to the far end of the long room, though he was certainly a good distance from where he had started. Wasn't he?

He looked back only once, and his vision tunnelled sharply. Something was wrong. Had he been drugged or bespelled? This was clearly some kind of trap.

Perhaps it was not a room at all.

Kai's tattoo was hot, like he was running a fever. He paused to run his fingers under his sleeve, prodding it for pain. There was none, only a heat that reacted to his fingertips, sparking against him.

The sharp lines of the tattoo were visible through his white shirt. He could see the stonework of Camilla's tower, and the jagged shape of the turrets, as if they were drawn thicker than before.

Ink, that was what he needed.

He followed the tug of his tattoo, and it drew him towards

one of the arched windows, pushing aside several antique spinning wheels and raising a cloud of dust as he did so.

There was light here, through patterns of blue and gold glass, and an inkwell sitting right there on the ledge, on top of a bound journal, with a battered, well-used nib pen.

This. He could do this. Camilla had taught him a spell to write for help. It was a simple process, even he could not mess it up.

He opened the journal to find a blank page, and instead saw a page of beautiful handwriting that felt strangely familiar:

>*Day 1.*
>>*I'm trapped here.*
>>*If you're reading this, you're trapped too.*

7

SOMETIMES, WITCHES

This was the worst slumber party ever.

Ziyi grew up in a walled wing full of her father the Emperor's wives, sisters and children. Piling into each other's rooms and whispering secrets away from the ears of their many mothers was a normal night for Ziyi and her siblings.

If something terrible happened, like a death or illness in the family, she and her closest sisters and cousins would cling together in piles, taking comfort in each other's presence.

This was not that.

The three Royals sat at a distance from each other, spiky and irritable. They were not quite clustered around the bed where Kai (what even was the lost prince's name?) lay asleep, one of his hand loosely clasped in that of a dazed and miserable Dennis.

Every now and then, Camilla or Cyrus or Chase would peer at the sleeping young man, as if searching for something, and then look away quickly.

Ziyi had not always connected with her siblings, and very few of them understood her hunger to get away from home… but she missed them now, fiercely.

"Was it fairies or witches?" she asked, and tensed up as all three Royals turned ferocious expressions on her. "It's always fairies or witches in the stories," she mumbled, embarrassed. She usually tried to slide under their notice, hoping they had forgotten that they knew her biggest secret.

"Fairies," snapped Cyrus, at the same time that Chase said:

"A witch, right?"

They both stared at each other.

Interesting.

"It was a witch," Chase said again. "Purple cloak, crown of thorns. How do you not know this?"

"Witches don't wear crowns of thorns, it was clearly a fairy…"

"She marched right into the naming ceremony of Cami and Cam."

"It was our parents' wedding, not a naming day," Cyrus argued. "The spinning wheel curse on the eve of…"

"No way!"

Camilla cleared her throat. "Actually," she said in a very calm voice. "It was your third birthday. In the summer. A witch — definitely a witch, not a fairy — cursed Father to lose all his happiness when a spinning wheel stole the one he loved most. When the next spring came around, our brother was taken from us. Camden and I were a year and a half old. Sixteen years ago this month. Mother was gone before we turned two."

"You weren't even —" Cyrus started to say, clearly still in an argumentative mood.

Camilla lifted one hand imperiously. "If you think I haven't taken a very thorough survey from every staff member and guard who worked for Castle Charming back then, you don't know me at all. The other version of the story, the one where Mother was cursed to fall asleep if her heart broke? That one's more popular, but it didn't start circulating until years later."

They all stared at their sleeping brother. No one was arguing that he was their brother.

Dennis glared at them all. Clearly he had issues with anyone who was only interested in Kai now that he was cursed, unconscious and possibly royal.

Ziyi really wanted to get out of this room, but she couldn't think of a way to do that without abandoning Dennis. She looked meaningfully at Corporal Jack, who didn't notice.

"Are you saying Camden was Father's favourite?" Chase said petulantly.

Jack rolled her eyes.

Cyrus cuffed his brother. "Idiot. Father's curse wasn't about us kids. Mother was the one that he loved best, and the spinning wheels took her." He frowned down at Kai. "I always thought she did it deliberately," he added. "No one ever said, but… I mean, I don't remember much from back then, but I remember how sad she was, and then she was asleep and no one could wake her up. Years later when I thought back on it, I assumed she *let* the spinning wheel prick her, because she couldn't get over losing Camden."

"Or she wanted to protect the rest of us," Camilla said sharply. "If she let the curse fall on her, it meant we were safe from it. After losing one…"

"How heroic of her," Chase sneered. "Leaving us with our dear father all these years. Perhaps she couldn't stand any of us, couldn't wait to escape."

That silenced the others for an awkward moment or two. "What I mean is," Cyrus started again. "The spinning wheels are feral this year. Like they are trying to trap us. What if a similar thing happened that year? What if Mother was chased down like we were, like —" He paused, obviously trying to remember Kai's current name. "Camden."

"His name is Kai," Dennis snapped.

"What does it matter why she left us?" Chase insisted, turning on his brother. "What does it matter if spinning wheels fall out of the sky?"

"We might want to stop it happening again!"

"I don't see why," Chase muttered. "We're probably safe for another sixteen years…"

"Kai's eighteen," said Dennis suddenly. "He — he moved to Charming when he turned eighteen."

"Someone lied to him," said Camilla. "He's seventeen and a half, believe me. He's my twin."

Dennis looked wrecked. Never mind escaping herself, Ziyi wanted to get *him* out of here. She'd never felt so protective of someone in her life. But he wouldn't leave Kai, of course he wouldn't. Not now. He wouldn't want to risk losing what claim he had over him.

Leave him alone with the Royals and they would take complete possession.

"I think we need to ask for help," Ziyi said, surprising herself by taking charge. "I mean, we can't just sit back and assume everything is hopeless. We should ask for advice. You might have been children last time this happened, but you're not now. So. We need to talk to a witch."

"There are several working in the city," Jack mused. "Sarge was saying the other day that half a dozen new witches had registered for their city license this year, which is unusually high."

"Oh," said Ziyi, catching on fast. "A witch new to the city isn't a suspect for the original curse."

"Exactly," said Jack. "Unless Your Highness's survey named the one responsible for the curse?"

Camilla hesitated, and shook her head. "No one knew

who she was. I don't think anyone ever found out. I… when I was twelve, I broke into the old Hound records, from before the Sarge ran it all. There was a brief description of the incident, but no mention of the witch's identity."

"What if it was a fairy disguised as a witch?" pressed Chase.

Cyrus shoved his brother. "Not everything is about fairies, numbnuts. We were cursed by magic dancing shoes *one time* and you see fairies around every corner." He nodded to Corporal Jack. "Find us a witch. Gathering advice is a good idea. I don't think we can hide this from Father for long, but I'd like to talk to the Sarge about it first — the whole business with the spinning wheels today already sent Father spiralling. I don't think we should spring a long-lost son on him just yet."

"You're assuming he remembers how many he had in the first place," said Chase sourly.

"We should take Kai to the Tower," said Camilla. It's safer. And I… I want him to be near Mother."

Dennis' head came up at that. "I'll help you," he said fiercely. "I can carry him."

"We'll see about that witch, then," said Ziyi, catching Jack's eye. This time the corporal was exactly on her wavelength.

They fled away from the room full of feelings, down and out of Castle Charming. The air was cool for spring, and Ziyi could finally breathe again. "So," she said after a moment. "We're going to check the registry for witches?"

"Nope," said Jack steadily. "I already know which witch to consult."

8

MONSTERS UNDER THE BED

Kai was growing certain that this wasn't an abandoned part of Castle Charming.

He escaped the endless dining room via a hidden staircase, but now the stairs kept going up and up, and the slitted windows he passed never offered a view. Every time he tried to look out of one of them, he grew dizzy until he stopped trying.

Sometimes, when he allowed himself to rest, he thought he heard footsteps. Not just feet. Big, heavy boots, running this way and that. Soldier's boots.

A guard, perhaps? A Hound?

It kept him moving, the thought that Dennis might be around here somewhere, trying to rescue him. It seemed in character.

After 2845 steps (yes, he counted them, and what was with the odd number anyway, architects were terrible people who made terrible choices), Kai stumbled into a new, impossibly large room.

It was a library of sorts, though the books all had that chilly, Only Here For Decoration look about them that reminded Kai of the sort of houses he grew up around, dragged from post to post by his mother. She was a governess in high demand because of her reputation for strictness and excellence in grammar, which meant fancy aristos who never used their libraries liked to hire her away from their friends.

She moved jobs a lot.

Kai remembered once putting a hand on a particularly beautiful volume of illustrated poetry in one of those libraries, only to discover that the 'book' was a polished mahogany box on a shelf of similarly beautiful, empty boxes. No pages, all for show.

He wasn't entirely sure that this *was* a library, now he came to look closer. Despite the beautiful walls of embell-ished books on shelves, there was also a bed.

Not any old bed. This was a masterpiece of sleep engi-neering. It had a sturdy structure of elegant metal spirals, and several fluffy layers of cushioning. It had lace draperies, embroidered coverlets, white velvet roses and so many throw cushions that a dozen princesses could have the pillow fight to end all pillow fights.

If it was made of glass, this bed would look exactly like the monstrosity back home currently housing the sleeping Queen Ella, Camilla's cursed mother. But this bed looked so comfortable it almost made him want to cry.

There was something underneath it. As Kai approached, he heard a low, snuffling sound. He picked up a large silver candelabra on his way to investigate, and the thing was almost so heavy he had to put it down again. Still, he gritted his teeth and persevered. He didn't have a handsome Hound to rescue him right now, so if there was something in this strange place with him, he had to be prepared for it not to be friendly.

"All the better to thump you with," he muttered optimisti-cally to himself.

The snuffling stopped. Kai took another step closer, and another. Perhaps if he lifted the draped lace just a little, he might be able to see…

It happened almost too fast for him to react — something scaly and hairy and bright blue snapped at his feet. There was a crashing sound, and a whoosh, and someone was standing in front of him, wearing an antiquated, faded version of the hearts-and-spades tabard that Dennis wore every day. A person, Kai realised as he stumbled backwards. A person with a sword.

The sword was enormous, and she brought it down with a thump, slicing the bed in two and coming up with a bright sticky blue liquid all over the blade. She turned on him, snarling, and Kai was so startled by the bright silver tea-tray strapped to her bosom that he couldn't react to anything else.

"RUN," she thundered, and he ran.

She caught up with him on the stairs, slamming the door behind them and locking it with a bright brass key from a ring she kept on her belt. She smeared her sword briefly above the doorknob, marking it with blue slime (blood?) and then gestured impatiently at Kai. "Up."

"Why up?" he asked, already scrambling to obey.

"Person with the sword doesn't have to answer stupid questions," she barked.

Fair enough, really.

He hurried up the stairs with the swordswoman behind him, automatically counting as he climbed. 56. 112. 224. They passed more doors, each locked and smeared with different bright colours. Some of the marks looked older than others.

The woman with the sword was behind him all the way. "Here!" she said finally and gave him a solid push in the back. The stairs opened up into a tower room that must be right at the top of wherever they were. The windows were larger than any Kai had seen in this building so far, but there was still too much cloud cover to provide a view.

"Where are we?" he asked, already starting to construct the story in his head. The woman had rescued him from a creature. They were trapped in an isolated castle. "Are we far from Charming? How do I get home?"

This was going to make an excellent piece for his newspaper, if he ever made it back to his job.

She snorted. "You really are fresh meat, aren't you?"

"What's that supposed to mean?"

The woman went to a table covered in alarming weapons, and began to clean her sword thoroughly with a cloth. Kai took the opportunity to look at her. She was an older woman, perhaps mid-forties. Hair hung in a long golden rope down her back, tied off with straps of leather to make sure not a single strand escaped to distract her from the fight. Her armour was improvised from two silver tea trays, the hacked-up remains of a wicker chair, and several belts. She had long scars on the backs of her arms and the side of her neck, and a nasty scab on one side of her face that suggested she had run into more than one snapping creature recently.

"What was that thing?" Kai asked.

His rescuer glared at him. "It was a monster under a bed. What more do you need to know?"

The door banged, and she whirled around quickly, but relaxed as a young man threw himself into the room with them.

He was another makeshift warrior, only his chest padding was wood, from the look of it. He had a Jasmine Empire look about him, with a long black ponytail and bare, muscled arms featuring flowered tattoos which Kai knew immediately were not magical at all. "L!" the young man shouted, then looked relieved to see his companion in one piece. "We've lost the library?"

"Blue," she said shortly, and indicated Kai. "We have a visitor."

The young warrior gave Kai a once-over which lingered only a little. "You don't look like you can fight," he said finally.

"Sorry?" Kai managed.

To his surprise, the young warrior grinned at him. "I bet she didn't even do the introductions," he said, holding out a hand to shake. "I'm Zed. Cursed here, like you, I expect. This is L." He nodded towards the woman. "Welcome to the war."

9

GONE TO SEE A WITCH ABOUT A SPINNING WHEEL

Corporal Jack had long legs and perfect posture: even without trying, her stride was mighty. Ziyi was shorter and more compact which meant she had to scurry like a rabbit to keep up. It was only mildly humiliating.

"Where are we going?" she asked breathlessly. "Which witch?"

"Oh, I have a particular one in mind," said Jack. "An expert in curses and fairy tales, and she moved to the city recently."

"So, not a suspect," said Ziyi, remembering what they had discussed earlier.

"Mmm."

"Do you think Kai's going to be all right?"

"I don't know, Zig," Jack said flatly.

They didn't talk much after that, which was worse because it meant Ziyi's head was full of thoughts. She had always known that the Royals were wounded over the lost prince. It seemed like knowing he was alive wasn't making any of them feel any better.

Which only served to remind her that her own scheme for

running away and avoiding her family's plans for her future meant that no one back home knew whether she was alive or dead.

It was… possible that she had not allowed herself to admit how awful that was until now.

"I feel sick," she muttered.

"No time for hurling," said Jack, making a sharp turn down a dark alley. "We're here."

Between an apothecary and a bookshop was a narrow door with no window, and a small card placed discreetly above the knocker. It read: Miss Ms Willemeena Birch, Glamour Lessons by Prior Appointment.

"She's not even a full-time witch?" Ziyi complained. "What kind of glamour does she teach? Spells for removing boils?"

"Glamour is a kind of magic. Illusion stuff. Chase said that there was a trend the season before last among the ladies on the marriage market — they all bought spells to make themselves more attractive."

"Trying so hard to bag a prince, how embarrassing for them," said Ziyi, with only a hint of irony. It wasn't so long ago that bagging a prince had been her own game plan. Thank goodness she had given up on it.

"Joke was on them, most of the spells involved almonds or hawthorn, and Chase and Cyrus are allergic to both those things. Every time a visiting princess covered up her spots, a prince came out in them."

"So sad I missed that season. Sounds like a riot." Ziyi tapped her foot. "She's not answering. Is it too late at night for the glamour business to be open?"

Jack knocked again. "It's never too late for glamour, Ziggy."

It wasn't even a shock any more, to hear her friends call her Ziggy. Just another reminder that she had cut all ties with home. Most days, she didn't feel like the same person who had been a Princess of Xix. Most days, she was happy about that. But the horrible scene with the Royals left Ziyi feeling bereft and homesick.

The door opened, and the witch peered out at them. She had a buttoned-up, schoolmarmish look about her, all tight bun and crescent spectacles. She looked disapproving.

"Is this even the right house —" Ziyi started to say, but Jack nudged her with her mighty elbow. A nudge from Jack was equivalent to a blow from someone else. Ziyi kept her mouth shut.

"Well? I don't have all night," said the frowning witch. "You both look rather old to be prospective pupils, and rather young to have children of your own. What do you want?"

"We need a spinning wheel expert," said Jack.

The witch tilted her head and looked unimpressed. "Throw a stone in this city and you'll find one."

"No, a real expert," Jack clarified. "We need someone who knows about fairy tale curses, and spinning wheels. There's been an incident up at the castle."

The witch gave them both a chilly, superior gaze. "Victims?"

"One of the princes," said Jack. Which was not untrue, probably.

"Wait," said Ziyi. "Are we even allowed to tell people —" Jack stepped on her foot. Gently, but still. Ziyi shut up.

"I'll get my coat," said the witch.

JACK LED Ms Birch to the front entrance of the castle, crossing the drawbridge. Ziyi was startled at first before realising that at this time of night, this was actually less likely to cause attention than heading in by the back way, which meant passing the stables where the Hounds had their head-quarters.

Their discretion was all for naught. They were halfway up the third central staircase on their way to the wing where the princes lived, when a familiar voice barked the words "Corporal Jacquelina Maree Hufflebundt!" across a landing.

Ziyi froze automatically. She was trained to be terrified of the sound of their Sarge in a bad mood. And yet... "I have so many questions," she murmured.

Jack gave her an annoyed look before turning around. "That's not my name, Sarge."

"I don't have time to learn names," he said dismissively, bearing down on their guest. "Meena."

The witch gave him a haughty look. "Clay," she said politely.

"Sooo many questions," Ziyi whispered.

"Oh," said Jack, sounding surprised. "Do you know each other, Sarge?"

"I know you're a better detective than you're pretending to be right now," their boss said, giving her the filthiest of looks. "Why is this person on castle grounds after hours, Corporal?"

"I was brought to consult on a spinning wheel curse," said Ms Birch.

"Well, you took your time getting here," Sarge said sarcastically.

"A *new* incident, Clay."

That got to him. His eyes darted to Jack. "Which Royal, Corporal?"

"The one who didn't know enough to see it coming," she replied sharply.

Jack was angry at the Sarge, Ziyi realised. Furious. Ziyi hadn't realised at first, because Jack always looked like that.

Jack had guessed the secret. Had everyone around them

done the same, apart from the princes themselves? Had the adults guessed? Had they just let everyone go on like this, knowing that Kai's existence would explode messily over everyone sooner or later? Ziyi was pretty sure that Dennis would have agonised a lot less over his suspicions if he knew more people would not be surprised by the idea that Kai Foster the quill from the Charming Herald was actually the Lost Prince Camden.

Ziyi was starting to see why Jack was so angry. They had been left out to *dry*.

Sarge made a strangled noise and headed for the princes' wing. Jack let Ms Birch go ahead of her, and brought up the rear with Ziyi.

"Who is this witch?" Ziyi hissed to her corporal. "Why did you pick her? What's going on?"

"Ms Willemeena Birch moved back to Charming less than a month ago," Jack said in an undertone. "But she used to live here, back in the day. Her registration was a renewal… she let it lapse in the same year that the baby prince went missing."

"But the whole point of picking a new witch was to find one who *wasn't* a suspect in the original curse," Ziyi said in horror.

"That was your assumption, and a bad one," said Jack, as if her reasoning should be obvious. "You don't solve a crime by avoiding an obvious suspect."

MS WILLEMEENA BIRCH swept into Prince Cyrus' bedchamber like she owned the place. She barely hesitated when she saw the figure of Kai laid out on the bed. She went to his side, briskly checking his breath and pulse; pinching his cheek to see how it coloured.

Sarge leaned against a wall, glaring at them all. Cyrus and Chase avoided his gaze like naughty schoolboys.

"Who's this?" asked Camilla suspiciously. She moved towards Dennis, who was still slumped in a chair beside Kai, and put her hand on his shoulder as if to support him. Dennis gave her a startled look.

"Someone who knows more about curses than you," said Ms Birch. "Any chance of a cup of tea, dear?"

"I'm the Princess Royal," said Camilla.

"Then a cup of tea is within your powers, I should think. Two sugars."

Camilla huffed and didn't move an inch.

"How many spinning wheels?" Ms Birch asked in a businesslike manner, after further examinations of the sleeping young man.

"It only takes one," said Chase.

Ms Birch gave him a cool, measuring glare which went on and on.

The prince looked away first, and then pouted defensively around the room as if he thought everyone might mock him for losing the battle of wills. "We were surrounded by dozens of them on the stairwell," he muttered. "They vanished after one spinning wheel pricked him."

"I see," said Ms Birch, and went back to her examination.

"Can you fix him?" asked Dennis quietly.

Everyone stared at him except Ms Birch who didn't bother. "Oh yes," she sighed. "Easy as pie. And I suppose I'll revive the queen while I'm at it."

"Watch your mouth," snapped Sarge.

The witch turned her glare on him. "You're the one who let this happen, Sergeant Clay. Do you have any idea who this young man is?"

"I'm catching on quickly, Meena," he said in a measured

voice. "Enough to figure out I should be arresting you, not letting you play curse doctor."

The witch turned back to Kai, and Ziyi saw that her hands were trembling.

Dennis saw it too, and for some reason that, more than anything else, woke him up out of the panic trance he had been in since Kai fell. "You're his foster mother, aren't you?" he said quietly. "He has a picture of you in his room."

"I am indeed," said Ms Birch, peering at Dennis. "Who exactly are you?"

"No one," he choked out and got to his feet, stumbling out of the room.

"Oh dear," said the witch, leaning over her unconscious son. "Could someone see if Kai's boyfriend is all right? I have my hands full at the moment."

"You're his foster mother," said Camilla slowly. "But that means…"

Ziyi felt the air change, crackling with energy.

"Your Highness…" Sarge said in a warning voice.

"You're the one who took him from us," Camilla said. It wasn't a question. Her voice was deeper and more melodious than usual, as if it was a spell and not a statement. She raised her hands, and black ink spiralled loosely off her skin, floating in loose shapes around her hands and wrists.

"In a manner of speaking," said the witch, not looking in her direction.

Camilla flicked her hands, and the ink whipped towards the witch, wrapping around her ankles and throwing her back against the wall.

The witch retained all of her poise and dignity, not even struggling in her bonds. "I suppose it counts as treason if I fight back."

"Let's just say yes," said the Sarge in a drawl.

Power whirled around Camilla. The whites of her eyes had turned black. "Why did you TAKE HIM FROM US?"

"Why does anyone do anything in Castle Charming?" Ms Willemeena Birch said with deadly calm. "I did it under orders from the king."

10

SNAKES IN A TOWER

Her name was L and his name was Zed. Together, they fought monsters.

The same monsters, apparently. Over and over.

Zed was the more cheerful and helpful of the two, which might be because L had been in this tower for ages, and Zed was something like the tenth cursed prince that the older woman had trained to fight the monsters. They did not discuss what had happened to the others, but L was clearly not in a mood to explain how this place worked all over again.

That left Zed to make the explanations. "They can't die," he told Kai as they ate a sustaining porridge of boiled peas, cooked over the small fireplace in the highest room in the tower full of monsters. "At least, they *can* die. We chop them up good and sticky. But they come back to life. Doors and locks slow them down, mostly. But some of them are shape-changers, and some of them are smart. We've pretty much burned this tower," he added to L. "Gonna have to find a new hideout for a while."

"We haven't been to the East Tower for a while," said L. "Most of the rooms there are locked and clear."

"The stairwell's not, though," said Zed, shuddering. "Snakes."

"I have a plan for that," said L, determined.

"Of course you do," said the young warrior, rolling his eyes at her. "She always has a plan which means me ending up with three different colours of monster ooze all over my face," he added to Kai.

"This one's easy," said L. "We go in, top to bottom. Slice all the snakes. Shove them in one of the free rooms before they have a chance to return to life. One clear tower." She nodded to them both. "Six hours. Don't spend all night swapping tragic origin stories."

She lay across the inside of the door like a heroic draught excluder, turning her backs on them both.

"Don't you want some, uh, mush?" asked Kai, looking at what was left of the pot Zed had cooked.

L tossed her long blonde braid over her shoulder. "The sooner the two of you give up pointless habits like that, the better off we'll be." She was silent after that, her shoulders relaxing. Kai wasn't sure if she was faking sleep, but it looked genuine — she was hardly the type of person to relax otherwise.

He glanced back at Zed and pulled a 'yikes' face. "Pointless habits like eating?" he whispered.

"Yeah," said Zed, looking uneasy. "We don't really need to, here."

"Are we —" Kai swallowed. "Are we dead?"

"Nah, nothing like that. It's more — you know fairyland?"

"Been there," Kai said flatly.

"Cool. Well, it's a bit like that. We're outside time. Don't need to eat or shit. Don't really need to be warm. The sky outside gets dark and light, but I don't think it has a regular schedule of day or night." Zed put the spoon back in the pot. "It's creepy. L's been here the longest so it's like she's given up. Doesn't care about anything but hunting the monsters."

"How long have you been here?" Kai asked.

The other young man shrugged. "Not sure. A few months? Time doesn't exactly leave us clues and I didn't think to count the sleeps, know what I mean?"

"Yeah, I think so." Kai had never wanted to feel as helpless again as he did when he and the others were snatched away to fairyland. This felt worse though, because it made no sense. "You're from Xix, aren't you?" he asked, hoping it wasn't racist to make that assumption from Zed's dark hair, light brown skin and finely shaped face.

"Yep," said Zed lightly, blowing on the embers of the fire. "My stepfather thinks I murdered his daughter, so he had me cursed by a witch. You?"

"Spinning wheels."

"Ugh," said Zed. "Spinning wheels are the worst. Lost a friend to spinning wheels once. It was thorns with me. Big-ass thorn bushes that hunted me down as I ran." He gave Kai a measuring look. "L said you mentioned Charming. That the kingdom you're from?"

"That's right."

"Hang on, I know this one. Had to memorise all the family trees when my mother married into a royal house. Are you Cyrus or Chase?"

Kai coughed on the last of his bean mush. "What? I'm not a prince."

"Right," said Zed sarcastically. "Because spinning wheels just go around spiking random members of the public." At Kai's blank face, he pressed the point further. "It's kind of a royalty-only deal."

"Not in my case," Kai said flatly. He was starting to

remember details of his last moments awake now, which was new. "I think Prince Chase was there when it happened. With the spinning wheels. They must have got me by accident. They were definitely going after him."

"Royalty only," said Zed in a sing-song voice. "I count because of marriage, not birth, but witch curses don't make mistakes, dude. They're super elitist."

"I'm not royal," Kai snapped. "I'm a quill."

Zed waggled his eyebrows at him. "Well, hold the front page, baby. You're also a prince."

KAI DIDN'T KNOW what to make of any of this, but he knew he didn't like it. He slept badly, staring at the ceiling of the tower room and watching the dark clouds swirl against the windows.

He wondered what Dennis was doing. Did he know Kai was missing? Was he worried? What had happened to Chase? They were surrounded by spinning wheels on that staircase, so why wasn't Chase in here too?

Kai refused to dwell any further on Zed's assertion that he was a prince. It was too ridiculous for words. He had a feeling the other man was flirting with him, and if so this was the weirdest attempt at a seduction Kai had ever seen.

THE NEXT DAY, if day and night meant anything here, they took the East Tower. Kai managed to find a sword he could lift, on one of the decorative walls in the endless dining room below. Zed gave him a whole ten minutes of instruction on how to use it, while L sniffed and said "Stay out of our way, boy."

Everything after that was — snakes and yelling and splattered gore in *so many colours*. The snakes went down easily enough but there were dozens of them, hundreds maybe, and cutting their heads off didn't prevent them from slithering up the walls and dripping goop on you.

"Do you do this sort of thing all the time?" Kai panted, wiping blue slime from the side of his face. "Like, every single day? Or did I get lucky?"

"Well, it's not snakes every single day," Zed considered. He had a wild grin on his face, like he was having fun. It was concerning.

There was a shout from above, where L tore through the snakes like they were butter.

"My lady calls," said Zed. He winked at Kai. "Kiss for luck?"

Kai backed up a step. "I have a boyfriend."

"Too bad," Zed shrugged, not sounding especially disappointed. "If I stay alive long enough, this tower is bound to send me someone single."

He took the stairs at a run, and the sound of fierce snake battle echoed down to Kai, who came up more slowly. By the time he reached L and Zed, they were wiping off their blades and done for the day.

"Pick a door," L said, sounding exhausted but satisfied. "The higher ones are more easily defensible but honestly, it doesn't matter."

"Ones with furniture are good," said Zed. "I wouldn't mind sleeping in a proper bed for once."

"You're still soft," said L, shaking her head. "It's going to get you killed."

"Aww, keep up all that caring talk and I'm going to have to hug you," Zed teased. "She sounds mean," he added, turning to Kai. "But she's way nicer than my real mother, so."

"Does one of the rooms have a bath?" Kai asked longingly. The smell of snakes was worse on the inside than the outside.

L rolled her eyes. "Pointless habits," she muttered, and marched up some more stairs. She was covered in at least six different colours of snake innards, with several gobs of flesh stuck to her clothes and hair as well as the bright slime.

"Is she… was that a joke?" Kai whispered.

"Maybe," said Zed, sounding impressed. "It's been quite a day."

~

THE ROOM they chose was some kind of bedroom suite, with fancy if flimsy furniture and a bed wide enough to play Rookery on. L and Zed sprawled all over the soft furnishings, not caring about getting snake slime on the fabrics.

A little while later, Kai realised why this was so. The muck on his clothes and skin dried and crumbled, powdering away as if it had never been there. He couldn't even see traces of it in the pale eggshell-coloured carpet.

"Yeah I'll admit that bathing is a pointless habit around here," said Zed from where he was stretched out across the enormous bed. "But don't tell her she's right," he added in a hoarse, meant-to-be-heard whisper.

L sat upright on a chintz sofa, clearly ready to fight again if she had to. "You were cursed in Charming," she said, eyeing Kai. "In town for the matchmaking season? Or are you one of the local princes?"

"I asked him that already," volunteered Zed. "He's in denial."

"Why does everyone think I'm a prince?" Kai moaned. "I work at a newspaper. My mother is a governess. I don't…"

That caught L's attention. She leaned forward, her shoulders flexing dangerously. "When you say governess, do you mean actual governess, or do you mean a witch who uses the cover of a governess position to teach magic to children?"

"I don't — wait," said Kai, his mouth hanging open. "Actually that makes a lot of sense." It was as if he was seeing his childhood through a whole new lens. If his foster mother was a witch, then… she had gone to a great deal of trouble to hide it from him. He had always felt like there was some big secret he was missing out on. Could that be it? "How do you even know that?"

"Because I knew your mother," said L, her own mouth tightly pressed in. "I think perhaps our original introduction was incomplete."

"Have we met?" She looked familiar to him, in that strange sort of way that meant you only knew someone who looked like the person, not that person herself.

L gave him a sharp, impatient look which reminded him of Camilla when Kai kept messing up spells that she thought perfectly standard. "A long time ago," she said. "I'm Queen Ella of Charming."

"Kiss for luck?"

11

READ ALL ABOUT IT

"It's better this way," said Camilla, as she unwarded her tower and led the way inside.

Dennis, holding Kai's unconscious body in his arms, followed her in, though part of him just wanted to take off, smuggle Kai out of this damned city.

He knew the mountains well enough. Could survive out there for months if he had to. But… that wouldn't help. Much as he hated it, he needed to be here if he was going to find a cure for Kai.

Dennis refused to believe that the princes were right, that there was no cure. Kai was still warm in his arms. They'd battled magic before and beaten it.

"Better for who?" he asked when Camilla glanced back, seeking a response to her platitude.

"No one can set foot in here without me, unless they're related by blood," she explained. "And you'll be able to visit him more easily than if we kept him in the castle."

"As long as you give me permission, Your Highness," Dennis said cynically.

She gave him an impatient toss of her head. "For someone

who swore his body in service to our family, you don't seem to like us very much."

"I like you fine," he said shortly. He didn't trust them, though, especially with people they didn't see as important. "It's not my job to like you, it's my job to protect you," he added.

"Him too, now," Camilla said, her face softening as she looked at Kai.

"Always him," Dennis muttered. *Him before you, lady.*

THE PRINCESS HEADED up the stairs to the room where her mother was kept. Dennis followed her, still holding Kai in his arms.

Camilla stopped in the doorway, looking at the wide glass artwork of curlicues and spirals that served as a bed. "I suppose there's room for both of them," she said.

Was she kidding with this? "No," Dennis said sharply. "He's never even met her."

Camilla opened her mouth as if to argue the point, then shut it again. "Fine," she sighed. "Wait here. I have bed things upstairs from when I used to live here. I'll bring them down."

Left alone for a moment, Dennis moved to the only other piece of furniture in the room: a wide armchair, presumably used by the queen's children when they visited her. He sank into it, folding Kai's sleeping form over his lap, like it was any other day, like he was going to wake up any minute.

Queen Ella of Charming was beautiful, blonde and painted like something out of a storybook illustration. Her face was barely creased, though she had to be well into her forties. Did time slow, with the sleeping curse?

Dennis pressed his lips briefly to Kai's forehead. "Getting

you back," he whispered fiercely. "They didn't try hard enough. I will."

WHEN CAMILLA RETURNED FROM UPSTAIRS, she was lugging a bedroll and several pillows with her. She set up the bed quietly in the corner, and Dennis brought Kai over to lie down on the soft layers.

"We can arrange something more permanent," she said softly, "If…"

"That's not going to be necessary," he cut her off.

"Of course not," she said too quickly. "Not now Sarge has the witch who kidnapped him in custody. We'll get our answers. Finally."

Camilla stared down at her brother, as if trying to memorise his face. Dennis looked at her, at the black magical tattoos on her pale skin, and the close-cropped dark curls of her hair. She didn't look like anyone's idea of a princess, but Kai — so calm and handsome in his sleep, layered beneath purple and gold satin covers — looked more like a prince than ever.

"Do you think she was lying about your father's involvement?" he asked.

"I don't know," Camilla said softly.

"Is Kai safe?" he pressed. "You said those with a blood connection have access to this tower. The king has access to this tower."

Camilla gave him a quick look, as if her first instinct was to be startled that Dennis did not trust the king. Then she sighed. "You're right, of course. I'll take the king's sigil off the wards. He won't be able to enter the tower alone. Not without me, or one of my brothers. I'll reconsider once we have our answers but… you're right not to trust him."

"And will you put me on your wards?" Dennis asked. He had to ask.

Camilla hesitated.

"Trust," he said calmly, trying not to let his fury take over. "Yes, I can see that would be difficult for you."

"I will take care of him," Camilla insisted. "I will keep him safe. And you can visit him whenever you like." But she made no move to make her statement official, through her magic. He would have to ask permission every time.

Dennis looked down at Kai, hating this.

He still had to walk away. From Camilla, from Kai and the tower itself. It was the hardest thing he had ever done, knowing he was reliant on Camilla's kindness to let him back in.

Dennis needed answers and for that he had to leave Kai's side. For now.

WHAT DENNIS WANTED to do was to head straight for the Doghouse and convince the Sarge to let him sit in on his interrogation of Kai's foster mother, the witch. But that wasn't going to happen. Sarge had made it very clear that Dennis was to consider himself on leave from the Hounds until this was sorted out.

He had to trust that Corporal Jack and Ziggy would tell him what they could, afterwards. *Trust*. There was that word again.

Freed of today's duties, at least, Dennis headed into town, making straight for the offices of the Charming Herald.

Amira Chaudry was at her desk. A bold, attractive woman with bobbed dark hair, she had been Kai's friend and mentor for months, before she screwed him over for the sake of a cheap headline.

Dennis didn't trust Amira as far as he could throw her, but he couldn't afford to be choosy. He marched up to her desk and stood over her, glowering.

She glanced up. "Well hello, tall, blond and brooding. Your boyfriend's late to work."

"I need to know everything about spinning wheels and sleeping curses," Dennis said shortly.

Amira's eyes narrowed. "Where's Kai?"

Dennis leaned in. She wasn't the kind of woman to be intimidated by his bulk, but you used what tools you had to work with. "You have newspapers from other kingdoms, right? Does this happen anywhere else? Or is it just local?"

"I'm not at your beck and call," sniped Amira, but her eyes were watchful, challenging him. She was clearly not stupid, and knew something was up. "Newspapers are not a personalised service."

Dennis leaned in closer. "Help me and I promise you the exclusive to the biggest royal story this newspaper has ever broken," he said in a low whisper.

Amira blinked. "That's a big claim. Bigger than…"

"Bigger," he promised. "The biggest."

Amira glanced around briefly. "The archive room is on the third floor," she said quietly. "I'll meet you there in ten minutes. But you'd better not be lying to be about size, handsome. That would be unforgivable."

DENNIS PACED, waiting for her. When Amira blew in, it was with a stack of papers and a lot of questions. "Okay, so Kai has never been late to work once, he's revoltingly good, and I covered for him, but I need to know what the hell is going on and why his boyfriend is here asking questions about spinning wheels."

Dennis waited.

"And when you say *big* what exactly kind of royal story do you think you can blow the whistle on, because after the year we've had…"

"We have a lead on the lost prince," he interrupted her, since she was clearly not going to take a breath any time soon. "That's the story I'm offering you."

Amira stopped, momentarily silenced. "If that's true," she said slowly. "And they find out you told me, they will fire you so fast your boots won't touch the ground."

"I don't care about my job," Dennis said, which was a flat-out lie. Where would he go if the castle kicked him out? Home to the mountains? He needed to be near Kai, and being a Hound was the only way to be sure of that.

"Cool," said Amira. "I don't care about your job either. Let's get to the juicy part. Where is Prince Camden?"

There was that name again, the wrong name. Dennis flinched. "I need to know if anyone has ever broken a sleeping curse," he said doggedly. "Find that out for me, and I'll tell you."

"No," said Amira, folding her arms. "That's not how this works. We're in this together, or we're not. I've been trying to get my editor to publish a spinning wheel panic story for *weeks* and he won't budge, not without some new twist on the fairy tale. Give me my twist, and we have a deal. Why do you care so much about sleeping curses?"

"Because a spinning wheel got Kai," Dennis blurted. He didn't trust this woman — Kai didn't trust her any more. But she was good at what she did, and he needed someone with brains and resources. He was desperate and right now he felt very alone. He needed someone who was just as invested in solving this, even if it was for her own selfish ambition. "He's currently under a sleeping curse. In Princess Camilla's tower. With the queen."

Amira stared at him. "But spinning wheel curses are for Royals. Only and always. That's how the story goes."

"Yeah," said Dennis awkwardly. "That's the thing."

12

___

ABLUTIONS

"You're Queen Ella," Kai breathed.

L looked annoyed at how slow he was. "Clearly. Yes."

"The sleeping queen."

She indicated her very much unsleeping self. Battered but unbroken. Angry, in her makeshift armour and warrior braid. Tired.

Kai had seen her in her enchanted slumber, laid out like a porcelain doll in a glass bed. Of course he had not recognised her here. The sleeping queen was a perfect, magical, frozen image of a fairy tale. She didn't scowl or roll her eyes or stab giant snakes with a sword.

"We're all asleep," said Zed, in a 'duh' sort of voice. "That's the point. Spinning wheels and cursed thorn bushes, right? We're not really here."

"So, this is some kind of horrible nightmare castle full of monsters that's actually a literal nightmare?" said Kai, trying to wrap his head around it.

"Beautifully summed up," said Queen Ella in an acid voice. "You must be quite the writer."

"You've had a lot of princes through here," Kai said. "Like Zed."

"Princesses usually," said Queen Ella. *L.* "One elderly king, cursed by his three daughters, who did not last long. More princes in recent months. The spinning wheels are getting hungry."

"But why?"

Fairy tales were made up of patterns, and those stories often reflected real life events and history. Kai knew that. He also knew that some kingdoms — like Charming, damn it — were more susceptible to fairy tale events. Stories infused into reality instead of the other way around.

But stories didn't make sense when applied to the real world. Newspapers did their best to predict modern patterns, to tell real stories that reflected what was happening in the world. There was a rhythm to those stories, which often made Kai feel like he was writing the same piece that had appeared in the newspaper a year earlier, or ten years, or fifty.

There were always bake sales and shop openings. Lords and ladies announcing their betrothals. Runaway donkey. Man bites dog. Tragic house fire. Dragon sighting. Heroic stranger. Poor boy loses inheritance and marries a princess. Princess gifted magical gown by fairy. Giant pumpkins. Transforming mice.

"Fairies or witches," he blurted out, remembering something that he'd heard Dennis say once, or his Sarge, or Corporal Jack, probably. It sounded like Jack. "It's always fairies or witches, right?"

Queen Ella twisted up her mouth, and shook her head at him. "You're looking in the wrong place for your story," she chided. "Asking the wrong question. Typical."

Kai stood his ground. "What's the right question?"

She hefted her sword, then set it aside to search through their heap of other reclaimed weapons. "I heard slithering in the bathing chambers two floors down. I think they broke through the sigil on the door."

"More snakes?" asked Zed, watching them both like they were fascinating.

"Crocodiles, maybe," said Queen Ella. "Button your boots up high. Things may get wet."

IT WAS CROCODILES.

The bathroom was enormous, far too big to exist inside a tower. It was more like the public baths in the centre of the city of Charming than anything Kai had ever seen in his visits to the castle. One room led to another and another.

Only, instead of tiles and saucy murals, instead of concrete and sensible bamboo matting lining the paths around the hot and cold pools, every inch of this place was lined with mirrors.

This was uncomfortably revealing about the mentality of the person who made the decor choices, or the person who hired the decorator. (That raised an odd thought about who designed this whole nightmare castle in the first place, or did it spring up fully formed from the dreams of kings and queens?)

Revealing. That was the word. In all the reflections and half-reflections of this enormous crocodile infested swamp of a bathroom, Kai saw himself: wrecked and ragged, tense as hell.

He hated holding a sword, hated having to be constantly aware of the snapping danger at his feet.

Queen Ella strode past the tiled pools like she was used to having a thousand eyes on her. She carried an ancient spear in one hand, and a ceremonial axe in another. When the waters frothed and a tail or snapping jaw surfaced near her, she stabbed and flicked, marching onwards as blood spooled in a slow orbit around her latest corpse.

Kai wondered if you could read patterns of crocodile blood in the water like you could read your future in tea leaves, and then he wondered if he was hysterical.

Had this place broken him?

Zed was enjoying himself far too much, frenzied with energy and twitchy as hell. "There was this kid already here when I turned up," he said to Kai, as they headed through the steamy caldarium. "Prince Nathanial of Herondale. Sweet as hell, very loyal to his hometown girlfriend. He was always trying to figure out where we were, why this place was the way it was. Whose nightmare we were living in, and so on."

He paused in telling his story to explain the difference between steam bubbles in the pool, and the ones that meant there was a crocodile lurking beneath. Kai tried to listen but honestly, the bubbles looked exactly the same to him.

"He asked all the big questions," Zed went on. "Like you do. Why is it always Royals? Why do the stories latch on to us? What is it about crowns and castles that lures in a fairy tale like a hungry crocodile?"

"Did he find any answers?" Kai asked.

"Oh, nah," said Zed. "He died. We always die." There was a rush of water to his left and a thing rose up out of the steaming water… twice the size of the crocodiles Queen Ella had been spearing, it had a huge snapping jaw and a long silver horn jutting it out of its forehead like a freaking unicorn.

Zed rallied, forcing the thing back and swinging his sword around. He miscalculated the timing, and the monster pressed him back, into the water.

Kai leaped on the thing, his own heavy sword chopping down. Purple gunk sprayed out of its thick hide.

Bedraggled and bright-eyed, Zed came up out of the

water, sword plunging deep into the side of the monster. Together, he and Kai hacked at the thing, shoving it back and back until it sank once more into the deepest part of the pool, leaving only bubbles behind.

"There are no fairy tales about a creature like that!" Zed gasped, spitting out purple. "What even was that?"

Kai caught a glimpse of them, reflected against the walls. They looked like warriors. Wet, messy warriors. "Did it get you?" he asked urgently. "That horn looked sharp."

"I'm fine."

"The horn was red with blood," Kai argued, and tugged at Zed's shirt, where it stuck out between the two makeshift layers of armour. The shirt was sticky, not just wet.

"If you wanted to get my shirt off, you only had to ask," Zed teased, but the words slurred into a yelp. "Hands off. I'm fine. We heal fast here."

"You're sure."

Zed grinned stupidly at him. "Of course I'm sure."

Queen Ella strode back into the room, her spear dented and her own hair falling in wet tendrils. "You all right in here?"

"L!" Zed crowed. "Seriously. We saw a mutant narwhal crocodile. You and I, when we get out of here, we have to publish a bestiary. Full colour illustrations. A bestseller for sure."

"We're going to have to seal this up again," Ella said, frowning at the purple sticky mass floating on top of the water where the monster had disappeared.

Once again, she went ahead and left Zed and Kai to trail behind her. Zed made faces into the mirrors as they moved through the bathing chamber. "Too bad we can't chance a proper dip," he said. "But the creatures have fouled the water, I reckon. It did not smell like tincture of roses in there."

"What happens to the captives here who get killed?" Kai

asked him in an undertone. "Do you think they just… wake up back in the world? Like when you die in a dream?"

Zed gave him a disbelieving look. "If L thought that was even slightly likely to be true, she would have thrown herself to the monsters years ago."

"Isn't that what she's doing?" Kai said darkly.

Zed rolled his eyes at him. "You're too young and pretty to be so cynical."

"I'm pretty sure L would want to know about that wound of yours…"

"Shut up," Zed hissed. "I told you. Everything's fine. I'm fine. Don't fuss."

His smile was bright and convincing, but Kai saw something else in the fractured reflections.

Every version of Zed, except the real one putting on the brave face, looked haunted and scared.

13

SLEEPING WITH THE FISHES

Dennis did not know Amira Chaudry well, but his words had lit a fire under her.

Her eyes blazed with fury. "The age is wrong. The timing's... he can't be."

"And yet," Dennis said evenly.

Amira spun around, wrenching an enormous portfolio down off a shelf. She thumbed through sheafs of front pages featuring monochromes of Prince Chase and Prince Cyrus.

Her finger traced the outlines of their cheekbones and jawlines. She sucked in a shaky breath, and was so angry at herself she couldn't even speak for several minutes.

"How did I not see it before?" she muttered. "I am a goddamn professional."

"To be fair," said Dennis. "Even he didn't know." And yeah, he was never going to be able to say that without feeling a stab of guilt that he should have told Kai his suspicions weeks ago. Months ago. "Can you have this crisis on your own time? I need to hurry things along."

"I thought you were supposed to be the nice one," she grumbled. "And this *is* my time. Try to remember that." She picked up another sheaf of papers, and led the way through to…

"Is this a cupboard?"

"Hush, it's a large cupboard."

"Not very," he complained, having to duck and tilt sideways to get his entire shoulder width inside.

It was larger inside, but an odd shaped, triangular space. Dennis sat on the floor so he wouldn't have to stoop.

"No one ever comes in here," said Amira, closing the door behind her.

"Can't imagine why."

She lit a lantern, and it threw more light against the far wall, which had a map of the kingdoms pinned up on it, along with… well, a lot of pins. Dennis leaned in, fascinated. Charming was there, a bright blue blot of ink. There was a gleaming pearl pin sticking into the castle, with several threads tied to it, fanning out to other pins in other kingdoms.

"So it's not just spinning wheels, said Amira. "And it's not just Charming. Royal curses, sleeping princes and queens… this shit has been going on for a long time."

"Is there a pattern?" Dennis asked. "Like one every year, or—?"

"Not that organised. Sometimes there are several years without any incidents." She bit her lip. "Thing is, they don't all last as long as our Queen."

"You mean they wake up?"

"No." Her voice was flat. "They don't wake up."

Dennis felt cold all over. "Tell me."

"Okay, well this one —" she tapped a green pin from four kingdoms away. "Herondale. Their sixteen-year-old heir Nathanial was found by a river last spring, gazing at his own reflection. Frozen, or asleep. They took him back into the castle, argued for six weeks about whether to build him a glass coffin…"

"Why glass?" Dennis interrupted. "Queen Ella's bed is made of glass too. Why would they do that?"

Amira's eyebrows almost hit the ceiling. "Well, that's a juicy piece of inside information. Anyway, moving on. There's a theory — a superstition, I guess, that being surrounded by glass helps preserve the sleeping royals."

"So, uh, what happened to Nathanial of Herondale?" Dennis didn't actually want to know this.

"He drowned," said Amira.

"He — did someone drop him in the river?"

She rolled her eyes. "No, he *drowned*. They were still measuring him up for his shiny glass casket, getting all the parts ordered and made up specially, whatever. One day, he opened his eyes and water gushed out of his mouth, and he died."

"How does that —"

"Not just water. There were fish in it. Small lilies, like from an ornamental pool. They found a piece of some kind of tentacle in his lungs."

"That's —"

"Yeah."

Dennis couldn't speak for a few moments. He had been holding on to the idea that Kai was safe until they resolved this curse, not that he could die at any moment with fish in his lungs. "What else?" he asked in a harsh rasp.

"Okay, this is the most recent." Amira pointed to another pin, on the southern pass through the Riverlands. "It was first reported as a wild thorn outbreak — I wrote a few paragraphs on it back in winter. Then it turned out they were enchanted thorns. The locals cut through the layers and found a small travelling party inside. No identifying documents. That's when I got interested, so I got permission to go up there on a training exercise with interns, to investigate."

Dennis vaguely remembered that — or at least, he

remembered that Kai had refused to join Amira because they still weren't on speaking terms. "Did you find out who they were?"

"Yep. One of the men was a local guide who'd been hired a couple of kingdoms back. The others were from the Jasmine Empire. All but one of them woke up when removed from the thorns."

"That's a long way to come," said Dennis. Did Ziggy know something about this? Xix was big, but all nobles knew each other, didn't they? "The one who didn't wake up, was he royal?"

"Yep, Prince Zuo-lin of the Gunpowder Isle."

Xix, Dennis wanted to correct, but didn't.

Amira went on: "Disgraced prince of the royal house (by marriage), exiled for some reason I couldn't find out because my editor yanked our funding and called us home. I've tried tapping some of my long-distance sources by letter, but everyone's zipping their lips over it. Apparently there's a missing princess story in the mix too. I hate it when everyone values discretion, it makes my job so much harder."

So, it did tie in with Ziggy, his fellow Hound. Dennis knew she was a runaway princess from Xix — or 'the Gunpowder Isle of the Jasmine Empire' as outsiders usually called it — but he hadn't actually thought about that for a while. Of course they would send people to find her. Princesses weren't disposable.

"Were you able to interview the prince's people when they came to bring him home?" he asked. "Did they know where he was heading?"

Amira gave him an amused look, like she knew exactly what he was thinking. "No one came to get him. According to my sources, he's still there. His hired servants fled as soon as they woke up. The locals had to move him into the nearest town before they could clear the thorns from the road, but apparently more grew around him in the second-best bedroom at the inn."

"But if it's been months," said Dennis. "They could have sent a delegation from Xix. Easily by now."

"They could have," said Amira slowly. "But they didn't. Apparently when they exile a prince, they really exile him. But if you want to know where he was heading, look at the map."

Dennis didn't have to look. It was obvious. If he had been found on the southern pass in the Riverlands, then ex-Prince Zuo-lin of Xix had been making a steady journey directly between his former home, and Castle Charming.

"You should ask your new recruit if she knows him," said Amira.

Dennis startled. "You know about her?" He kicked himself for falling for a clear conversational trap but he was emotionally compromised right now.

"I know everything, Dennis," said Amira with a sharp smile. "About how you and Kai and the Royals made the Midnight Princess disappear. Contrary to opinion, I don't put every fact I learn into print."

"And this story?" He gave the map a weak wave. "I mean, the whole — the whole story. Royals being cursed to sleep across the entire country. The big picture."

"I've been trying to publish *that* story for three years," said Amira with a grimace. "My editor's a chicken. He thinks if I let this particular conspiracy flag fly, the king will shut us down."

Dennis blinked at that. "The Charming Herald has been saying shit about the royal family — about his sons, mostly — for nearly a decade. And your editor thinks talking about *sleeping curses* is the thing that will make the king shut you down?"

Amira gave him a knowing smile. "With instincts like that, we'll make a quill of you yet."

"I'm not doing this for your story," he grumbled. "I want Kai back, alive and safe."

"Well then," said Amira. "We're on the same page. Mostly."

14

THE WRONG QUESTION

Ziyi thought that Sarge looked more tired than usual. He had been interrogating the witch — Ms Birch — Kai's foster mother — on and off for hours and got nowhere with her.

Ziyi and Corporal Jack took turns sitting in with them, as it was standard to have a second Hound to witness anything said. The princes, Cyrus and Chase, insisted on being here too.

But the witch said nothing.

They had nothing to report when Princess Camilla returned from hiding Kai in her tower.

"Nothing?" she asked impatiently.

"Nothing," Chase ground out. "A colossal waste of time."

Sarge finally asked the princes to leave, in case the witch was more receptive to a smaller audience. Corporal Jack stayed with him, and that left Ziyi in the unenviable position of keeping an eye on the princes to make sure they didn't do anything stupid.

Camilla, at least, could be relied upon to do that job now she was here.

"I want to burn it to the ground," the princess said aloud.

Okay, maybe Ziyi had miscalculated who was the most sensible member of the family.

"The Doghouse?" frowned Chase. "I think the Sarge might object."

"The castle," said Camilla. "Don't you ever feel that the people of Charming would be better off without a royal family?"

"Save us from the revolutionaries in our midst," Cyrus said dryly.

"I mean it. If our father… if the *king* is the kind of man who would arrange his own baby son's kidnapping, then why should our family keep pretending that the people can trust us, that we have their best interests at heart?"

"We all know you would rather play with your paints and inks than be a princess," Chase muttered.

Camilla levelled a sharp expression at him. "Really? We're going to talk about my lack of commitment to being a royal? You and Cyrus have been disgracing the family name since you were old enough to fake your way into drinking clubs."

"Shut up, both of you," said Cyrus sharply.

Camilla opened her mouth to argue, but swallowed it quickly. "Oh, crap."

Ziyi hadn't seen them arrive. They didn't pop out of empty air or anything, they were simply there… six spinning wheels in a semi-circle around the arguing Royals.

She drew her baton. The needles gleamed at the end of each spinning wheel, long and sharp. Perhaps she could use her baton to move one of them aside… or should she go for the sword instead?

"Back up," she warned the three of them.

"Are you planning to fight them?" Chase asked in a choked sound that was almost a laugh. "Careful, we don't want to find out too late that you're secretly a…" he trailed off, clearly remembering a beat too late that yes, Ziyi was secretly a princess.

I left all that behind, she told the spinning wheels fiercely, knowing it didn't matter whether she felt like a princess or not. Kai had no idea he was a prince, and the spinning wheel took him anyway.

"Now," she snapped at the Royals, not taking her eyes off the spinning wheels. "Move it!"

They ran and after a few beats, Ziyi ran with them.

Inside the airy former stable that served the Royal Hounds as their headquarters — the Doghouse — Sarge looked up in surprise as they burst in. Ziyi slammed home the bolts, though what even was the point of that?

Magic spinning wheels laughed in the face of locks.

"What's going on?" asked Sarge, eyes on Ziyi. Clearly awaiting a sensible report.

It was Camilla who answered, marching towards Ms Birch. The witch sat calmly on a pile of upturned crates as if it was the most elegant sofa. "We're out of time. You need to tell us everything."

"I doubt your questions will be any more inspiring than those of the good sergeant," said Ms Birch, nose in the air.

"He's less likely to hit you," snapped Camilla.

"Your Highness," Sarge protested, which was not a 'no.'

Camilla stood over the witch, glowing with outrage. Literally glowing, Ziyi realised. The ink tattoos on Camilla's arms were brighter than usual, humming with power. "I want to know what its all about," Camilla demanded. "Not about taking Camden — you're clearly never going to tell us the truth about that. I want to know why it started. A witch cursed my father nearly seventeen years ago. Why? Who was she, and what did he do to earn her hate?"

Ms Birth smiled. "Finally, a question I can answer."

"Seriously, Meena?" the Sarge complained.

"What can I say, Clay? It took the princess to get to the heart of the issue."

"Pity that she's asking the wrong question." That voice didn't belong to any of them. It wasn't even familiar, unless… Ziyi felt a cold sensation creep up her spine as she turned, slowly.

A man in a long silk dressing gown stood at the door that Ziyi knew she had bolted shut. She knew that a king was entitled to go anywhere in his castle, but this was ridiculous.

"Your Majesty," said the Sarge, scrambling to attention. "I was…"

"Investigating me, Sergeant?" King Iolchas sounded amused, which was rare. Stony silence and the occasional burst of fury were the most common modes Ziyi had witnessed in the king, on the few occasions she came into his royal presence.

She was well aware that Hound duty schedules kept her out of the king's sight as much as possible, especially when she first joined as cadet, to make sure he did not catch on to her true identity. She had good friends in this castle, who wanted to protect her.

"We have a situation," Sarge said between gritted teeth. "There hasn't been time to put together a report…"

"By 'situation' do you mean the return of the woman who kidnapped my baby son?" asked the King. "Or do you mean a conspiracy between you all to conceal the fact that my son is here in this very castle?"

There was a long, startled silence, and then Prince Chase threw up his hands. "What the fuck?" he roared. "If you know everything, then how about you explain it to us? I am so sick of all the bloody secrets in this family."

"What did you do, Father?" It was Cyrus who spoke this time. Cyrus the quiet one, who spent more time worrying about how fast he could run a mile than he did about royal protocols. Of the siblings, he was the one more likely to be polite and deferential in the presence of his father — the one least likely to challenge King Iolchas to his face. "What did you do?" he asked now, his voice trembling. "How exactly did you bring this curse down on our family?"

King Iolchas smiled, a cruel twist of a smile. "What did I do to earn our curse? Why don't you ask the witch who cursed us?"

15

PRINCESSES HAVE MANY SKILLS

A silence followed the king's words.

No one moved, at first. When they did it was slight movements only, bodies tilting and eyes sliding towards the most obvious culprit. Ziyi had never in her life seen so many people all trying to observe without calling attention to themselves.

Ms Willemeena Birch sat in the midst of it all, untouched by their subtle accusations.

"No," said the king as if he was, for the first time in recorded history, enjoying himself. "Not her."

Camilla screamed. It was a short, sharp scream of frustration. Her eyes glowed as she advanced on her father. "Why do you do this?" she demanded of him. "Why play games with us like we are creatures to be wrangled and not your children?"

King Iolchas raised his eyebrows at her. "Think, Camilla," he drawled. "What exactly might have given me the idea that you are dangerous?"

It was as if time had stopped. Ziyi stepped a fraction away

from the royal tableaux, moving into the comforting, warm presence of Corporal Jack.

Everyone else was motionless. The princess stared at her father. The witch was unsurprised. Sarge looked like he couldn't decide who to arrest first.

Camilla did not stay still. Camilla was furious. She swayed on her feet, hands curling up into fists. "I was a baby when Cam was taken," she said shakily. "What are you…"

"Even then," said the king. "From the moment you were born, there was something dark inside you. A magic looking to escape. You pronounced the curse on our family on your elder brothers' third birthday: that we would lose the one we loved most."

"No," she breathed.

"I sacrificed Camden, sent him away with Ms Birch because he was closest to you. The one you loved most. The nursemaids believed you had been leeching his power, stealing his magic."

Camilla was pale as a statue, her dark hair and thickly-inked tattoos standing out in harsh relief against her skin.

The king was dark-haired too, with those bright blue eyes of his. He looked very like his daughter, though he held himself with more control.

"You took him away from me," she raged. "We mourned him. Did Mother know what you did, or did you make *her* think he was dead?"

"*You* cursed your mother," the king snapped.

Camilla gasped. "No!" She turned on her brothers, eyes glowing with power. Both of them flinched at her approach, but stood their ground. "You don't believe him, do you? You don't think I —"

"I don't believe a word that comes out of that man's mouth," said Prince Chase.

"But you flinched," she said helplessly. "You do think I'm dangerous."

"Cami," said Cyrus. "I'm sure there's an explanation." He moved to her, but this time it was Camilla who flinched back.

"Don't touch me," she hissed. "I can't be around any of you."

"Is it your family you don't trust, or yourself?" asked the king.

"Shut the hell up!" It was Cyrus, usually the calmer of the twins, who roared that at his father; Chase who reached out for their sister, but it was too late.

Camilla threw up her arms, and a whirl of magic spun around her for a moment, like a smear of ink in the air. When it faded, she was gone.

"I didn't know she could do that," Chase said with a yelp. "Did anyone know she could do that?"

Sarge stepped forward, and stood before his king. "Your Majesty."

"Sergeant Clay," said King Iolchas. "There is no need to trouble this good woman further. Her actions in taking and keeping my son were upon my orders. I would have preferred her not to allow him to return to this kingdom until his twentieth birthday…"

"Most kingdoms claim their majority at sixteen or seventeen," said Ms Birch quietly. "Prince Camden believed himself to be eighteen thanks to the ruse we created to hide his identity; there was little I could do to stop him."

"And I shall personally address her failure to keep him safe," the king continued. "But do not feel the need to keep her under arrest. She will answer none of your questions without my authority."

Sarge raised his eyes, staring directly into the face of his king, and then he reached up and removed his iron badge, the one that proclaimed him Sergeant at Arms.

Jack sucked in a breath as if she had been punched in the stomach. "Sarge," she hissed.

Ziyi put a hand on Jack's wrist, steadying her.

"Is that necessary, Sergeant?" asked the king, unmoved by the gesture.

"Every man and woman who served in this castle on the night that the baby prince was taken, carried the weight of failure with us for the rest of our lives," said Sarge, his voice steady. "We dealt with that burden, that *guilt,* in different ways. I was younger than your boys are now when it happened. We were all punished for the loss, but no punishment felt heavy enough. When you went to war in Palomarr, most of us signed up to fight for you. We felt like we owed you our lives because we let your son be taken. My friends died…"

"I am your king," said King Iolchas. "Some might say you owed me your lives anyway."

"You let us think we were responsible!" Sarge shouted. "You let us… you let the world think you were a victim of some terrible crime. But you just sent him away with Meena."

"For his own good…"

"I saw how your children mourned, even if you never let yourself," Sarge growled. "I saw how your *wife* mourned."

"Never speak of my wife!" thundered the king.

Sarge let his badge fall on to the dusty floor. "You're not my king," he said quietly, and walked across the Doghouse, unlatching the door.

There was no sign of spinning wheels outside now.

Ziyi wanted to say something, to call out to him, but what could she possibly say?

Sarge looked back once, and met Jack's gaze. "Take care of my Hounds," he said simply, and left.

16

THE HALL OF LOST PRINCES

Dennis had a plan. It wasn't a great plan; it wasn't even a good plan. But if saving Kai meant riding across country to rescue a prince from an enchanted thorn bush, then by the mountain gods, he was going to ride and rescue.

While Amira made the arrangements (including a fake story to pitch to her editor), he headed back up to the castle to look in on his sleeping boyfriend, and leave a message for the others. The last thing he wanted was to lose access to Kai because hadn't kept Princess Camilla (Kai's sister, he had to keep remembering that strange fact) in the loop.

His palm gave Dennis access through the wards on Camilla's tower, which surprised but pleased him. For now, she was letting him come and go as a family member.

The sound of breaking glass alerted him that he was not the only one awake in the tower. He leaped for the stairs, taking them two at a time, and burst into the sleeping chamber only to find…

Kai the same as ever, fast asleep on his pallet on the floor. Queen Ella still sleeping, though one post of her glass bed had shattered, with pieces strewn all over the floor as if someone had taken an axe to it.

Princess Camilla stood there, surrounded by a sea of glass, looking like someone had just told her magic wasn't real.

One crisis at a time.

"Stay still, don't move your feet," Dennis urged, and went for a broom to help clear up the glass while Camilla did indeed stand still. When he was done with the worst of it, Dennis wedged a chair under the bed to make sure it was still going to keep the queen stable, then helped the princess across the floor. She had a few cuts on her feet where the satin shoes (he remembered a time when she only wore giant work boots) had failed to protect her from the shrapnel.

She resisted only when he tried to take her from the room. "I can't leave him."

"What's wrong? Did you find something out?" To Dennis' horror, the princess burst into noisy tears, burying her face in his chest.

He knew how to do this. He had sisters and sisters-in-law. Female friends, though of late his female friends consisted of Ziggy and Jack, neither of whom had ever cry-hugged on him. He was well out of practice.

Still, this was a basic enough task. Pat the back, mutter something calming, wait for them to talk or not talk; make tea where possible.

"I have to give him back his magic," said Camilla in a muffled voice, wiping her messy face on his tabard. "Can you stay here while I do it? I don't want to hurt him."

"I can do that," said Dennis, though he had no idea what was going on.

~

KAI WOKE UP.

The three of them were sleeping in some kind of giant wardrobe tonight, surrounded by ballgowns and doublets that smelled of mothballs. He wasn't sure at first what had woken him, until he saw a movement in the darkness by the doorway.

"Come on," whispered Zed. "Don't wake Her Indoors. I have something to show you."

Kai moved carefully around the sleeping form of Queen Ella and crept out after Zed. "Where are we going?"

"Shh," was all he heard. Zed moved ahead of him, carrying some kind of lantern that sent strange shadows in fluttering shapes against the walls.

"It's not usually this dark," Kai observed.

"That's cursed nightmare castles for you. Minds of their own. In here. I knew it was close by."

Kai accidentally jostled against the other man as he stepped into the new room, a few doors down. He was startled at how clammy Zed's skin felt, hot like he had been sleeping under far too many covers. "Are you all right?"

"Don't fuss."

"It's not fussing to be concerned…"

"That's the definition of fussing, dude. Chill out."

"You don't sound like a prince," Kai muttered. "Why do none of the princes I meet actually behave like princes?"

"Never meet your heroes," Zed said sagely.

"My heroes include fourteen novelists and the inventor of the printing press, not spoiled rich boys in pointy hats…" Kai's words trailed off with a choking sound. He forgot what he was talking about, as Zed's lantern illuminated the truth of the room before him. "Where are we?"

"Oh, this is our tomb, basically," said Zed, sounding far too cheerful about it. "The hall of lost princes. And princesses. The occasional grand-duke. More of them towards the back. Don't knock any over, it would be hell to clean up all the smashed marble."

Kai stared.

The statues were life-sized and horribly pale, stacked up in rows like someone was planning an epic if morbid game of skittles. Kai had seen statues like this before, in the occasional nook and gallery of Castle Charming, but never so many all at once.

They were Royals, which was evident because every one of them wore some kind of crown, coronet or tiara. They were young, even taking the youthening effect of smooth marble into account. Baby faced princes and princesses, frozen in a moment of awkward elegance.

Many of them carried weapons, which looked at odds with their fancy formal outfits. One princess in the front row, with perfectly curled hair and a lace-draped bosom, had her hand curled around the handle of a lacrosse stick which had half a tentacle hanging from it, all rendered in stone detail.

The prince next to her held a ceremonial axe, but the carving made the axe look old and dented. It looked real.

"So, this is Nathanial," said Zed, laying a hand on the shoulder of the prince with the axe. "Old friend of mine. Well, recent friend. Recent brief friend. Before you, poor kid. L introduced me to a lot of these, the ones from before my time," he added. "The front two rows are her lot. Or maybe the front three rows? Anyway, that lady there is Aeryn of Torth," he said with some semblance of a formal bow. "Next to her is Prince Egbert of Seefrith, and the one with the bow and arrows next to him is Prince Hal, from some island I've never heard of."

"All dead," said Kai flatly.

"All dead. I'm not here yet, or L. The statues just… appear when one of us is killed by the castle."

"Why are you showing me this?"

Zed shrugged, looking uncomfortable. "No reason. Thought you should know as much as I do about how all this works."

"Oh my god, are you dying?"

"I'm fine."

Unable to resist, Kai leaned in and prodded a finger into Zed's chest, roughly where he thought the creature had stabbed him.

"Aughhh." Zed swayed back, slapping him away. "Don't."

"Heal faster here my arse. Were you lying about that?"

"I'm fine." It sounded less convincing every time he said it. "Look…"

"I don't want to hear it," Kai said suddenly, turning away.

"If something does happen to me, L's going to need you."

"You can't leave me here with her, she's terrifying," Kai snapped. "I think I'd rather team up with the monsters."

"Dude," said Zed, looking pained. "I think she's your mum."

A wave of dizziness came over Kai. He wasn't sure if it was shock at the stupidest thing he'd ever heard, or… something else. Black stars exploded in his vision.

"I have to," he muttered, and shuffled quickly to the open hallway, out of view of those chilling statues of dead Royals.

"Are you okay?" Zed asked, following closely.

Kai wasn't sure if he was about to swoon or throw up. "Don't fuss," he said, his voice cracking with irony.

He could smell ink. He wasn't sure how or where, but it was close. His tower tattoo hummed to life, sensing the source of its magic. His head felt like it was going to explode.

Ink blossomed on the nearest wall, spiralling out shapelessly as if someone had thrown a bottle and watched the contents smash against the surface. A face appeared in the spreading black smear, so familiar that at first Kai thought it was himself, reflected in a mirror. Then he recognised her.

"Bro," said Zed at his shoulder. "I didn't know you had a sister."

"That's not my sister, it's Camilla," Kai corrected, and then stopped talking, his tongue stuttering over the last syllable of her name. *Oh.*

"Is this the long-lost prince thing?" Zed asked sympathetically. "Awk-ward."

"Camilla," Kai breathed.

"Kai," she said, sounding miserable and exhilarated all at once. "I have something to tell you."

17

JUST WHAT CASTLE CHARMING
NEEDED: ANOTHER PRINCE

Nothing about this was okay. Dennis had lost his grip on this whole situation, and he wasn't sure that Camilla had much of a grip to start with.

He had many concerns about Camilla. She looked manic, her blue eyes fierce, and her hair wilder than usual. Not quite out of control, but well on the path to get there.

She tried to pour her magic into the sleeping Kai, but it bounced back harmlessly to her, as if he was incapable of accepting it while trapped in the sleeping curse. Finally in frustration, she threw her magic at the wall above Kai, black light streaming from her fingers, mouth and eyes.

Dennis had no idea how to stop her without losing a hand, or his life. She didn't look like she would respond well to a quiet word of caution.

He edged towards the door. He needed reinforcements. Jack, maybe, or Sarge (no, Sarge quit, think again). Maybe one of Camilla's brothers?

Then Kai's face appeared in the wall, looking like a ghost in an ink-splattered mirror, but unmistakably him. Awake. Alive.

"Kai," Dennis breathed.

He wanted to speak louder, to call Kai's attention to his presence, but Kai's attention was all on Camilla.

"Are you my sister?" Kai asked in a broken voice.

Camilla lifted her hand closer to him, continuing to stream magic into the ink blot on the wall, the window between her tower and whereever Kai was. "I think so," she whispered. "Yes."

"How?" Kai sounded so hurt. Dennis wanted to wrap his arms around him. "Why did no one tell me?"

"It's a long story." She hiccupped a laugh. "I'm so sorry. This is all my fault."

"No," Dennis said sharply. "That's not true. Don't do that."

Kai wavered in and out of sight, as if the magic couldn't quite hold him in place. "Dennis? Is that you?"

"Hey, babe." Dennis stepped closer, looming over Camilla's shoulder so Kai had a better chance of seeing him. "Missed you."

"You too," said Kai, lifting a hand and prodding at the magical window, which hissed and shimmered at his touch. "Camilla, this is amazing. Can you bring us home?"

"I'm not sure," Camilla said wildly. "I'm not — I don't know where you are."

"Nightmare castle," muttered a voice from somewhere behind Kai. "How hard is it to say Nightmare Castle Made of Nightmares?"

Dennis frowned. "Are there people there with you?" At least Kai hadn't been alone all this time.

"Three of us," said Kai. "Zed's wounded."

"You don't have to tell everyone," protested his unseen companion. "I told you I'm fine."

Camilla frowned, swaying a little on her feet as she struggled to keep the channel open between them. "Is — Kai, who's the third person?"

ZED THREW BACK his head and laughed humourlessly. His skin was sweaty. He sprawled with his back against the wall, a short distance from Kai and the magical ink blot window. "Of course you'd be able to find a way to call home," he mumbled to himself. "Stupid pretty boy chosen one."

Kai could not look away from the tunnelling shape of magic, from Camilla and Dennis. "Camilla, can you bring us through? All of us?"

His sister — *sister*, now there was a thought that didn't fit entirely in his head — looked troubled. "I don't know. No one's ever done this before."

"We're running out of time. Everyone dies here, Camilla." Everyone except L. Their mother. Against all the odds, she had stayed alive this long. He couldn't lose her now, before he even figured out what they meant to each other.

"I think I can open it wider, for a short time. But you'll have to be quick."

"There are three of us," Kai repeated. He would have to go to get L. Zed was in no position to do it. He was looking worse. Had there been some kind of slow poison in the wound? "Zed, come here a minute, look at this," he said lightly, as if there was no urgency in the world.

Zed, still pretending for his own part that there was nothing wrong, struggled to his feet and managed to fake a saunter in Kai's direction. "Anything for you, sweet prince."

"Try it now," Kai advised Camilla.

Her eyes widened, and he knew that she understood what he was asking. "I don't know if I can do it again."

"You can. I trust you. You'll find us. But for right now…"

"Hang on," said Zed, turning to him. "What are…"

"Do it," agreed Camilla.

"Wait, what?" yelled Dennis from very far away.

Kai pushed Zed as hard as he could, into the magical window. He felt Camilla — her magic, her power, her sadness — on the other side, reaching out to them both.

It would almost be easy, to hang on to Zed all the way, let the power suck them both through.

But Kai was not leaving Queen Ella behind, not if he could save her.

He let go.

DENNIS DIDN'T REALISE what was happening until it was too late. "What did you do?" he raged at Camilla.

She looked shocked, about ready to collapse on her feet.

The ink stain magic was gone. The whole room smelled of dry books and air that came from somewhere else, just for a moment.

And there: a hazy shape of a person, slumped against the embroidered coverlet of the sleeping Queen of Charming. A complete stranger. He was lithe and handsome, with cheek-bones to die for, and a strange mishmash of clothing including makeshift armour. He had a long, sweeping black ponytail.

You could see right through him. His skin was literally insubstantial.

"Hey," said the stranger, sitting up slowly and gazing through his own arm, fascinated to see his own translucency. "I'm Prince Zuo-lin of Xix. Has anyone seen my body?"

KAI RETURNED to the wardrobe where they had all been sleeping, not so long ago. If he and Zed had stayed put, would Camilla have been able to contact them here? Would they all be home already?

He hesitated over waking up L, but she stirred and snapped her eyes open the second he came near her. "Where's Zed?"

"Gone," Kai said honestly, and saw something broken cross over her face. "No, not — I mean yes, he was injured. But I think I sent him home."

"Home," she said abruptly, sitting up. "What do you mean?"

"My sister is a powerful witch." That much was true, apparently. "She opened a portal. I sent him through because, you know. His injury. I figured he was running out of time."

L did not blink at the revelation of the injury. "Good call. Can she try again?"

"I hope so. We need to stick together until she makes contact again."

L lifted one sarcastic eyebrow, making it clear that she wasn't the one who had been wandering around the castle. Kai deserved that eyebrow.

"There's something else," he said hesitantly.

"Really, there's more?"

"I think I'm your son."

"Camden, yes," said L, and waited expectantly. "Is there more?"

He felt a strange rushing sensation in his brain at her utter lack of surprise, or emotion. She had *felt* for Zed, at least. There was a brief flicker of emotion when she thought this place had killed him. What had all these years here done to her that she wasn't willing to show a single feeling about meeting a son she had not seen in sixteen years?

"Don't you have anything to say about that?" he tried helplessly.

L sighed. "If you're looking for some kind of maternal connection, I lost mine somewhere around the ninth and fourteenth dead protégé. Feelings will get you killed in here. They're…"

"Pointless habits," he sighed.

She gave him a look which might almost have been sympathetic. "I'm glad you saved Zed."

"I think I can save us too," Kai promised her.

L's face closed over. "We'll see. Don't get distracted, kid. If you really think your sister is coming for you, we have one job — keeping you alive until then."

"Both of us," Kai said doggedly. "She's coming for both of us."

"Sure," said L, as if humouring him. "Both of us."

18

KISS YOUR PRINCE

Z iyi ran, crashing headlong into the wards on the tower in the castle grounds. They tingled and stung at the palms of her hands. "Damn it," she said breathlessly.

"Here," said Cyrus, who had kept up with her pace easily. Jack and Chase were not far behind. The prince lay his hand over the wards, and the door clicked open. "Family only," he informed her.

"You don't have to let me in."

"Oh, we trust *you*," he said, steering Ziyi through the door.

Once Jack and Chase were inside, the princes sealed the wards again.

"Not that we don't trust our father or anything," said Chase sarcastically.

"But we don't trust him," Cyrus agreed. "Not with Camilla, not with any of us."

Jack looked troubled. "You don't think she's dangerous?"

"Maybe to herself," muttered Chase.

"We need to talk to her," said Cyrus. "About Camden,

about everything. But she'll listen to us. She knows we're on her side."

Jack looked unconvinced.

Ziyi heard a shout above them. "That's Dennis!" she said, and made for the stairs.

"Wait!" one of the princes called after her, but she ignored them. She barrelled up the several flights of stairs and burst through into the Queen's sleeping chamber, just in time to see…

"I'm Prince Zuo-lin of Xix," said the ghostly figure before her. "Has anyone seen my body?"

"Zuo-lin," Ziyi breathed.

His eyes went to her and his expression hardened, as much as possible in a face that had no substance to it. "Ziyi. You little bitch. You *are* alive."

"Of course I'm alive," she said, glaring at him. "What are you doing here? Where's your body?"

He threw his arms up dramatically. "That's what I was saying!"

Dennis, who looked like someone had hit him over the head with a rookery stick, cleared his throat. "Uh, I can answer that question. Your body's on the Southern Pass through the Riverlands."

"What, just lying about on the highway?" said Zuo-lin in distress.

"Ziggy, do you know this bloke?"

"He's my brother," Ziyi sighed. The princes and Jack had crowded into the room behind her, and it wasn't like it was news to any of them where she came from; who she really was.

Everyone in this room knew her secret.

"Stepbrother," Zuo-lin corrected sharply. "Oh and suspected murderer, let's not forget that. Where have you been? What are you *wearing*?"

"You don't get to complain about my uniform when you're wearing — what even is that, some kind of fake armour made from an old chair?" Ziyi paused, tilting her head. "Murderer?"

"They thought you were dead, you selfish cow! What did you *think* they would think? A weird note claiming you married a commoner and weren't coming home? No one believed that. I was the prime suspect because of that ridiculous plan to marry us off — they thought I'd do anything to get out of it, which FAIR ENOUGH REALLY."

"I'm amazed anyone thought you had the necessary attention span to pull off a long-distance assassination and cover-up. Besides, that whole marriage plot was your mother's idea in the first place!"

"THEY TRAWLED THE RIVERS FOR YOU!" he howled at her.

They stared in mutual silence for a moment.

"They really thought you killed me?" Ziyi said in a small voice.

Zuo-lin folded his arms. Translucency aside, he did look different to the spoiled prince she had known for years. His face was harder, his eyes hollow. He looked like someone who had worked and suffered and mourned. "They believed it enough that they exiled me," he said darkly. "So you could run away to a fairy tale kingdom and play at toy soldiers, by the looks of it."

"That wasn't the only reason." She'd never liked him. They'd never liked each other. But somehow, she wanted him to understand why she had escaped.

If he can forgive me, maybe the rest of them will too.

"And oh look, apparently I'm still a prince because even though I have no money, no title and no family any more, I'm still vulnerable to a curse of sleeping thorns. Hooray for the perks of royalty."

Ziyi sighed. "I'm sorry. I'm sure we can find your body. Dennis said…" She looked around. "Where's Dennis?"

"Oh, shit," said Prince Chase with feeling. "Where's Camilla?"

CAMILLA WAS IN TROUBLE. Dennis saw her slip out of the room in all the chaos of Ziyi's argument with the newest prince in the tower, and he chose to follow because he was pretty sure everyone in that room had at least some vested interest in keeping Kai alive and safe.

He wasn't so sure about Camilla. She muttered to herself, bumping into walls as she went, clearly not 100% there.

He followed her down through the kitchen and into the workroom where she had spent so many hours teaching Kai to master his magic. Dennis had barely spent any time here before; he never entirely felt welcome in this tower.

The intense friendship that built up so quickly between Camilla and Kai was important to both of them; Dennis had assumed for a long time that Camilla was as much in the dark as Kai about their true relationship.

"You knew he was your brother," he said now.

"Of course," said Camilla, running her hands over the black, wild paintings that adorned her walls: tattoo-like whorls of shadow and light forming patterns, mazes, monsters and… well, castle walls.

Now that he came to look at it, Dennis saw a coherence in the images that Camilla had painted here over the years, in the ink that connected her magic to Kai's. Towers and turrets, deep rooms, chaotic staircases leading nowhere. There were monsters on the walls: giant snakes, angry phoenixes, horns and wings and claws as if she had painted a lifetime's worth of nightmares here.

"Did you make these with magic?" he asked.

"They help me focus," said Camilla, her hands roaming the images as if she could read them through her fingertips. "I have to put the magic somewhere…" She paused, turned slowly to gaze at him, her eyes wide. "My father's an idiot."

"Okay," said Dennis, not sure where she was going with this.

"I can't have been stealing Kai's magic as a baby. That's ridiculous. I've always had too much of it. I was… I think perhaps I might have been trying to put magic *into* him."

Dennis tried to stay calm at the bewildering idea that this was somehow better. Camilla was smiling, and he wasn't sure why. "Is that helpful?" he tried.

"I've been putting all my excess magic here, for years," she said in delight. "I can take it back."

He opened his mouth to say something pointless like 'are you sure' then shut it again. Camilla clearly had a better idea than he did what was going on. "How can I help?"

Camilla pressed her fingertips against the spiralling ink painting of an enormous crocodile with a unicorn's horn. It burst free of painted waves as if about to spike something — possible the several snakes depicted on the wall next to it. "Tell me about my brother. I wasted all this time trying to teach him to control his magic, and I hardly know anything about him. Tell me why you love Kai."

Dennis sputtered at first because *love*, they weren't there yet, neither of them had said the words to each other.

Still.

"He's smarter than me," he blurted out. "I keep waiting for him to figure that out, but he doesn't seem to mind. He's funny and sharp and just really freaking beautiful. I can't believe he's mine, most days."

So yes. Love, apparently.

Camilla smiled at him, her eyes glowing and her mouth

twisting up wickedly. It was nothing at all like Kai's smile, which was a relief somehow. "Good," she said, and breathed in.

Every painted tattoo from the walls whirled for a moment and then flocked to her: peeling off the walls, slipping and sliding. Camilla inhaled them, patterns re-forming over her skin. Every inch of her was now decorated. Heat washed over Dennis as Camilla stalked towards him, placed hands on both sides of his face, and kissed his mouth.

Dennis hadn't kissed a girl since he was twelve and still figuring himself out; as an experience it wasn't any better now. His only consolation was that this was as far from romantic as any kiss was ever likely to be.

His own skin burned for a moment, as if he was standing outside at midsummer, and then the heat subsided.

Somewhere, a heavy door broke open with the hiss of magical wards dissolving. "Get your hands off my daughter, Hound," said the haughty voice of King Iolchas of Charming.

Dennis, whose hands were nowhere near anyone's daughter, pulled back from Camilla, staring at her.

She looked almost normal now, though there were still more tattoos than usual crammed on to her neck, arms and all visible skin except her face. "Go get him," she said with a warm, sisterly smile. "Kiss your prince awake."

"Stay exactly where you are," ordered the King. "What is the meaning of this? Did you think you could keep me out of my own tower?"

Dennis turned, stumbling over his own feet. The King was right there, with the witch Ms Birch at his side.

"Go," said Camilla. "I'll deal with this."

"You'll deal with nothing, young lady," said the King.

Camilla threw a cloud of bird-shaped shadows at him, in a burst of fury. "Stop telling me what to do!"

Dennis should stop this, should calm her down, should prevent some kind of irreparable royal family tragedy.

But Camilla's words burned through his thoughts.

Go get him. Kiss your prince awake.

As Ms Birch sliced through the shadow birds with some kind of broomstick weapon made out of light, and the King howled his rage at his daughter, Dennis ran for it.

He clattered up the tower steps and did not look back.

Go get him. Kiss your prince awake.

19

WAKING UP

L took point, her broadsword at the ready. Kai followed behind with a broken chair leg in one hand and Zed's old sword in the other, trying not to feel utterly useless.

This was a losing battle.

"I think I can smell dragons," the former Queen of Charming muttered in an undertone. "They must have got into the wainscoting again."

"How can anyone smell dragons?" Kai demanded. He reconsidered everything he thought he knew about dragons. "What *size* are these dragons?"

"This isn't your fairy tale," said L.

"I'm long past any illusion that it is," Kai snapped.

He didn't properly get to enjoy the fact that, for once, he had managed a half-decent comeback. The wainscoting was vibrating. The walls were vibrating. The floor ahead of them, a beautiful mosaic pattern of tiles that laid a path of ancient heroes and steeds, seemed to ripple.

Steam rolled out of the edges. A deep, awful smell of burnt rubbish and wet frog surrounded them.

"That's what dragons smell like," said L in a conversational tone.

"I regret asking," Kai told her.

The walls tore like newspaper pages, and a swarm of creatures burst free — tiny, stinking flying lizards, with lopsided wings and death in their eyes.

If these dragons ever swooped on a damsel, it would be to strip the flesh from her bones.

"What do we do?" Kai yelled, as L backed up so fast that she almost crashed into him.

"We run or we die," she spat. "This is how we lost Aeryn…"

There was a loud crunching sound, and time stopped.

Kai blinked. The stinking, buzzing swarm of dragons had been… flattened, by the look of it. An entire stone tower now blocked their path, having fallen through the ceiling above directly into the corridor. "That was… lucky?" he ventured.

L did not look relieved, but he never expected human responses from her. "That depends," she said warily. "Who threw that tower at us?"

Kai could hear other thumping sounds, more distantly. Echoes of stone falling, walls crumbling. "Um," he said. "How old is this castle?"

"Judging by the statues in that hall Zed promised not to show you," said L. "Several hundred years at least. Sucking in royals under sleeping curses. Throwing monsters at them."

"Has the warranty run out?" he asked.

The floor shook beneath their feet again.

"This isn't good," said L.

"Nothing around here is ever good!" exclaimed Kai. "Is it survivable?"

"I guess we'll find out," said his ever-reassuring birth mother.

DENNIS BURST into the tower room, interrupting what looked like an epic row between Ziggy and the Prince of Xix that Kai had chosen to save instead of himself.

There would be time to be bitter about that later.

Prince Chase whistled. "Got ink?" he said as he checked Dennis out.

Dennis felt his face, wondering what Camilla had done to him with that kiss. "Your father's downstairs."

"Damn," said Prince Cyrus, and then looked immediately like he wanted to apologise for mildly swearing in front of women. Zig and Jack both rolled their eyes at him.

"Your sister is fighting him. And uh, the witch. There's a lot of…" Dennis was distracted by the sight of Kai on his bed roll. "Did he just move?"

Kai's body twitched. Two small wounds burst open on his face, like someone had flicked his cheek with a sword.

"It's happening," said Prince Zuo-lin in a low voice. "If there's any plan to get that boy of yours home, I suggest you do it now."

Go get him. Kiss your prince awake.

"Camilla seems to think I can do it with a kiss," said Dennis awkwardly.

"Well?" demanded Prince Zuo-lin. "What are you waiting for?"

ZIYI HAD no idea what was going on, or why Dennis now had a black tattoo of some kind of sea serpent scrawled across his face, but her friend looked terrified.

"Dennis," she said firmly. "You're a Royal Hound. If the princess gave you a command, then do it."

There was a smashing sound from below, and what could have been an explosion.

"When you said Camilla was fighting our father," Chase said in alarm. "Did you mean with fists, or…"

Ziyi gave Dennis a push.

"What if I'm not enough?" he protested.

"Try harder," advised Corporal Jack, and her matching push almost sent him to the floor.

Dennis leaned over Kai, whose white shirt suddenly blossomed with blood down one arm. "Okay," he said shakily. "Kissing the prince. Here I go."

"WHAT'S EVEN HAPPENING?" Kai yelled as he and L raced down a wide staircase. It crumbled under their feet, one step at a time, and they only just made it to the carpeted room of endless table before the whole staircase collapsed in a cloud of dust.

"The castle's lost its power source," said L, huffing for breath. She leaped for the long table and ran along it, her heavy boots ringing on its surface. Kai clambered up after her and followed.

"What *is* its power source?"

"Camilla, I think."

Kai almost stumbled over his feet at that one. "But she was a baby when the curse got you. And you weren't the first… there have been Royals coming here for generations before you. Right?"

A chandelier fell, ahead of them, shattering crystals and candles and glass beads along the surface of the table.

"Under!" L commanded, and skidded off the side of the table.

Kai went with her, and the two of them crouched underneath the long stretch of polished mahogany. Even the underside of the table was polished. Who did that? "Should we crawl for it?" he asked, peering into the distance.

"Where would we go?" asked L. For the first time since he met her in this awful place, she sounded like she had no idea what she was doing.

Kai stared at her face. He couldn't think of her as a mother, not even as mother to the princes and princess of Castle Charming. She was a fairy tale character: a queen, a warrior. His own mother was a starchy governess who made a tsking sound when he did anything of which she disapproved.

"Tell me what you know," he begged. "We've got nothing but time."

L huffed out a laugh at that, and picked a piece of broken castle out of one of her golden braids. "It was all my fault," she said.

"How can that be true?"

"Let me finish. I was in a miserable life, and I was offered a way out. The stories always say it was a fairy godmother that made my story happen, but it was a witch. Not a very nice witch. She'd been watching over me my whole life, from next door to my father's home. She saw my miseries and misfortunes. And just as I was on the verge of giving up on everything, she gave me hope. Something that seemed small at first. A party and a dress."

"The Midnight Princess." Kai knew this story. He had reported on it the second time around, last autumn, when a foreign princess mimicked Queen Ella's story to win the hand of Prince Cyrus.

"I caught a prince. Married a king. And it was only when I was pregnant with my second pair of twins — you and your sister — that the witch told me her price."

There was a skittering sound to their left, and several small fanged boars lunged at them from under a nearby dresser. Kai and L moved in practiced symphony, hacking the creatures with their swords.

L didn't even bother to clean her blade. That was how dire this situation was.

"She had been chosen as a child to hold the magic that kept this place going, and she needed a replacement. I refused to let her near my babies, but she never intended to let me make a choice. She died within weeks of that meeting, and her magic… well. It had to go somewhere. I saw it in Camilla the day she was born. You had a little, but she had the worst of it. I was already numb with the fear of what this curse would do to you both. When you were stolen, I… was relieved for you, in a way."

Her voice hardened. "Then I learned that you were not stolen at all. His Majesty spirited you away with his… with that woman. For your safety. Without you to calm and balance her, Camilla's magic went wilder, out of control… so I went to the fairies for advice."

Kai winced. "The fairies."

"I was desperate," L said. "And they promised to help me. But before I could get back to the castle…" She shrugged, her face flat. "Spinning wheels."

"If this place is tied to Camilla's magic," said Kai softly. "It's falling apart now. What's happening out there in the world?"

"I suspect we'll never know," said L. "We won't be there for the end of the story."

They felt it a moment before it happened; a shudder of the whole castle. Then the carpet folded beneath them, buckling and twisting. They fell… and along with the pieces of stone and table and chandelier, they plunged into deep water.

Kai twisted and kicked, looking around for L, but it was chaos down here. A dark tentacle snapped at him from the depths, stinging his face once and then again. He punched it and kicked away, swimming upwards, but was dragged back down with a jerk when a vine, sharp as a blade, slashed his arm and then wrapped tightly around his wrist.

A shape like an alligator loomed in the bright water above him, then another, and another.

Something white drifted past his face and he thought it was a person at first, only to realise it was one of the marble statues, a prince who had died fighting the monsters right here in this nowhere place.

This was it, then. The nightmare was going to swallow him whole.

Kai closed his eyes and thought of what he had left behind. Of Dennis, grinning bashfully after the first time they kissed, in a fairy cavern cut off from the real world.

Dennis. Kai would never get a chance to say goodbye, to say he was sorry, to tell him that he —

A mouth pressed against his, hesitantly at first, then with greater confidence. Kai could not breathe, could not see, and yet here, underwater in the wreckage of a nightmare castle, someone had kissed him.

Someone was still kissing him.

Kai woke up.

20

VIABLE ALTERNATIVES TO
DROWNING

Dennis had never felt more stupid in his life, kissing his sleeping boyfriend in front of everyone. The heat in his face wasn't just a blush from the embarrassing situation; it was Camilla's magic.

His lips stung with heat as his mouth pressed warmly to Kai's, and perhaps it was his imagination but it felt for a moment as if Kai was kissing him back.

Dennis pulled back, wondering what he had done wrong, wishing it could be different, wishing…

Kai's eyes snapped open, and he caught Dennis' face between his hands, pulling him down to him.

There was a sound behind them, as if everyone exhaled at once.

"Finally," said Corporal Jack.

"The problem now is going to be how to get them to stop kissing," observed Ziggy.

Kai's face was wet where he pressed against Dennis, and not with tears. He pulled away with a gasp. "Ell."

"What?" said Dennis, so dizzy with happiness and relief

that nothing Kai said for the next week was going to make any sense to him.

Kai slid from under him, looking around wildly, and then threw himself on to the bed with the sleeping Queen Ella. With one of the glass legs missing, it creaked and tipped slightly from the additional weight.

Kai pressed fingers to the pulse of the Queen's wrist, and her neck. "Where's Camilla?" he yelled. "Get her here now."

It was Chase who made for the door first, his brother close at his heels. Jack went with them and after a moment, Ziggy too.

The ghost prince Zuo-lin, still lacking in bodily substance, drifted nearer to Kai. "What's wrong?" he asked urgently. "Why the rush?"

"The castle is gone," Kai said. "It's just water and rubble. We don't have time."

"So kiss her or give her a bonding mother son hug or something," ordered Zuo-lin. It seemed to Dennis as if the three of them — Kai and the sleeping queen and the ghost prince — were the only ones in the room. He didn't know whether to be scared or jealous but he sure as hell felt useless here.

"She doesn't even like me, Zed!" Kai yelled at the prince.

"So?" the prince yelled back. "You don't like *me* and you saved my life!"

"I like you fine!"

They stared at each other. Kai was panting as if he had been running — or fighting — or swimming. And it occurred to Dennis that he was never going to be able to share, really share, whatever had happened to Kai in that spinning wheel place. This wasn't like their other adventures at all.

Chase smashed back into the tower room, looking desperate. "Camilla's gone!" he yelled. "She turned the king into a fucking tree."

Dennis stared at him. "What about Kai's mother? The witch?" Maybe Ms Birch could be some use…

"THERE ARE TWO TREES IN THE KITCHEN, DENNIS," Chase shouted at him.

Kai looked up, distracted for a moment. "Camilla turned my mother into a —"

"Look," breathed Prince Zuo-lin of Xix and in that instant, Dennis couldn't hate him.

Queen Ella gave a slow, shuddering breath. Her lips parted, and water bubbled up between them.

"Turn her over!" ordered Zuo-lin, waving his arms uselessly as if he could turn Queen Ella's body with his mind alone.

Kai dug a knee into the sleeping queen's side and turned her so hard that she tipped, embroidered silk bedclothes and all, on to the floor. The bed creaked around them and finally broke, cracking right down the middle.

"Let me," begged Dennis, and Kai actually moved aside, letting him lean in and pound the queen on the back to clear her lungs and stomach of the water that erupted from her body.

"What the hell —" said Prince Cyrus, finding chaos as he returned to the tower room.

Prince Chase burst into tears.

Queen Ella reached out and gripped Dennis' arm in hers. She had a remarkably strong grip for someone who had been asleep for sixteen years. Slowly, he helped her to sit up, steadying her just as Ziggy and Jack piled into the room behind Cyrus, their eyes wide.

Kai hung back, staring at the queen. Everyone was staring at the queen and, by extension, Dennis.

She took a deep, shaky breath, and then another one. When she spoke, in a drowned-hoarse voice, the first thing the Queen of Charming said was: "Where is my daughter?"

Not one of them could answer her.

21

____

THE END OF THE STORY

In the chaos that followed, somehow Dennis found himself volunteering to escort the insubstantial Prince Zuo-lin of Xix to his own unconscious body in the hopes that they could revive him.

Dennis would do anything to put an expression on Kai's face other than the sort of baffled worry he had worn for most of the day as the remaining Royals orbited uncomfortably around each other. Also (Dennis didn't like to admit to this particular reason) he had a feeling that if he did not go, Kai would, and…

Dennis was in no way jealous of the time that Kai had spent in that other place with a handsome exiled prince, but there was no reason to sabotage himself.

Besides, Amira already had made all the plans.

~

"THIS IS UNEXPECTED," said Amira, when Dennis appeared at the hired carriage with a flirtatious, snarky ghost trailing behind him.

"After the day I've had it's not even weird," Dennis informed her.

Zuo-lin turned out to be an amiable travelling companion, cheerfully keeping Amira entertained on the road with anecdotes of his adventures in the nightmare castle, knowing full well she didn't believe half of what he said.

Dennis felt his stomach twist every time Zuo-lin 'call me Zed' and his tall tales mentioned Kai, or the woman he still referred to as L (because Amira was a reporter and Zuo-lin had, despite all evidence to the contrary, some discretion).

Every story reminded him that Kai had been in so much danger. Dennis had almost lost him, a dozen times over.

Snakes in a tower. Horned water-beasts.

When the carriage was only a few minutes away from the inn hosting the prince who had fallen victim to a curse of sleeping thorns, their resident ghost disappeared mid-sentence.

"You know I'm going to publish everything he told me," Amira remarked to Dennis.

"The royal family could probably do with some distracting nonsense in the press for a day or two," Dennis sighed. "Knock yourself out."

AT THE INN, Dennis paid the ticket price to get a glimpse of the sleeping prince, and promised himself he would ask the Royals to officially ban that particular business enterprise.

Assuming of course that any Royal was ever again caught under a sleeping curse. Perhaps the destruction of the nightmare castle meant the end of this fairy tale trope?

He knocked awkwardly on the door, and entered to find Prince Zuo-lin sitting on the edge of his bed, peeling dead thorn branches off his solid human body.

"So uh, that worked out then," said Dennis.

Zed gave him an exhausted look. "I need a bath and a change of clothes and a plan for what the hell to do with the rest of my life. Any ideas, bro?"

He looked so pathetic, Dennis couldn't dislike him. Not the man who had helped keep Kai alive all this time. "Stick around," he offered. "Cash in on your friendship with the royal family. Bag a rich socialite. They hang around Castle Charming all the time, hoping to marry a prince…"

Zed laughed hollowly. "Might have known you'd be the noble sort."

"Not my prince," Dennis said sharply. "No one else is allowed to marry him."

Oh. Where had that thought come from?

Zed smirked, and punched Dennis lightly on the shoulder as he passed him. "Did they charge tickets for me? Have they been selling locks of my beautiful hair?"

"I think you have reasonable grounds to demand a cut of the proceeds," Dennis told him.

"Let's see if they can scrounge up a free bath and beer, for a start," said Zed.

"Two beers," said Dennis, accepting the inevitable. "Don't be stingy. You're going to need all the friends you can get. Start with me."

CAMILLA WAS STILL MISSING. The Queen of Charming was awake, and the King of Charming was … yes, a tree in Camilla's kitchen, as apparently was Kai's foster mother.

Kai had no feelings left to deal with any of this. As Chase and Cyrus circled around their mother, trying to manage some kind of reunion (good luck on acquiring any maternal hugs, Kai thought uncharitably), he sat out on the tower steps as night darkened around them, thinking about spinning wheels.

No one talked of leaving the tower. No one was ready to explain any of this to a castle full of servants and relatives and random hangers on from the court. No one was ready to sleep, either. Not tonight.

Jack and Ziggy sat with Kai, squashing comfortably up against him, which was nice. It felt normal. He'd always thought they were more Dennis' friends than his own, but right now they felt very much on his side.

He couldn't think of himself as a Royal. Not yet.

"We need to get Sarge back," said Jack. "He'll know what to do."

Ziggy blew out a breath. "He never knows what to do."

"I just want someone to shout at me until I feel better," Jack muttered.

Kai knew the feeling.

"Oh," said a toneless voice behind them. "It's dark. I was hoping for a little sun after all these years."

L's way of speaking was oddly reassuring to Kai. She was no more queenly now than she had been in the nightmare castle: all brute force and sarcasm.

The princes clattered down the stairs with lanterns, climbing over Jack to stand on the grass and make eye contact with Kai.

"So, uh," said Chase.

Cyrus stuck his hand out, even more awkward than his brother, if that was possible. "We should reintroduce ourselves."

"I know who you are," said Kai, amused. "We've met."

"Yes but we haven't — you know."

"Yeah," said Kai. "I know. He shook Cyrus' hand because the alternative was even more awkward. "Any sign of Camilla?"

"Nope," said Chase, looking warily at Kai. "Look, I don't know what you…"

"I have no idea what I'm doing here," Kai interrupted. "I'm kind of hoping you'll help me out with that."

Chase laughed bitterly. "Sure. Because we're such experts in dealing with family crisis."

"Well," said Cyrus, elbowing him. "We kind of are."

"What are we going to tell people?" Chase said explosively. "I mean… what's the story?"

"Ah," said Kai, smiling a little more naturally. "If only you knew someone who was an expert in handling the press."

THE ROYALS WEREN'T any closer to a plan by the next morning, when Dennis returned with a restored Prince Zed (Kai couldn't think of him as Zuo-lin), Amira hot on his tail.

Kai was a startled to receive the warmest hug of his life when Amira saw him.

"I was worried about you, arse," she snuffled into his shoulder. "Can we be friends again?"

"Pretty sure I can't afford to have you as my enemy," said Kai, and hugged her back. He had missed her.

"If you don't let me write this story, I may die," she growled at him, drawing back only slightly from the hug.

"What?" he teased. "You think I'm going to let you have the byline?"

She punched him lightly, then cooed over the slash on his arm. "Oops, sorry. Do you need a bandage?"

"Didn't even feel it," he said truthfully.

Amira made a noise, a wheezing shrieking sort of gasp, and that was how Kai knew that she had spotted the woman in the old-fashioned nightgown, currently braiding her own hair as she sat with her sons on the step of the tower in the springtime morning sunshine.

"What the freaking heck," said Amira, enunciating each word. "That —" She turned around and punched Zed, who was awfully chummy with Dennis all of a sudden. "You didn't mention THAT PART OF THE STORY."

"Didn't I?" said Zed, rubbing his arm. "Must have forgotten."

"That is Queen Ella, right?" gasped Amira. "I mean…" She stared in stunned silence at the scene before her.

L caught sight of them, tied off her long braid, and walked across the lawn with the confident stride of a woman who had been fighting monsters daily for more than a decade. "Amira Chaudry?"

"Yes," squeaked Amira.

L glanced at Kai. "This is the one?"

"This is the one," Kai confirmed, barely holding back his smirk.

L looked her up and down. "You come highly recommended."

"I do?"

"Indeed. What we have here, Ms Chaudry, is a situation. A delicate situation."

Amira's mouth twisted up with disappointment. "And you want me to kill the story."

"On the contrary," said Queen Ella of Charming. "I want you to *sell* the story." She smiled a practiced political smile, which chilled Kai to the bone because it actually looked warm and inviting. "I'm offering you a job. Royal press secretary. How does that sound?"

Amira opened her mouth and no sound came out. Obviously the world was ending.

∼

"ARE YOU OKAY?" Dennis asked later when he found Kai in a nook of the garden, hiding from everyone.

Kai gasped out something that was not a laugh. "Not even slightly."

Dennis moved in behind him, wrapping his arms around his boyfriend's back and resting his chin on his shoulder. "Does this help?"

"Yes," breathed Kai.

There were things they had to say to each other, so many stories still to unpack and examine. But for now, this was enough.

"I'm glad you came back to me," muttered Dennis.

Kai let out a long, shuddering breath. "Nothing's going to change," he promised. "I mean, you know."

"The prince thing."

"Yeah."

And he meant it. Dennis knew that Kai meant it. Just as he also knew that it wasn't true.

"Sure," he agreed, kissing the side of Kai's neck, taking an equal share in the lie. "Don't worry about it, babe. Nothing's going to change."

DEAD QUEEN WALKING

SUMMER

Summer 1500
Price: 3 Copper Toads
Castle Charming #4
est. 1066
DEAD QUEEN WALKING!
SHE'S NO DEADBEAT!
Tansy Rayner Roberts

1

WALK AND TALK

Queen Ella of Charming did not sleep.

Dennis was not sure if anyone had noticed. He never heard anyone gossiping about her behind her back, in or around the castle. Fair enough, really. If there was a Royal you did not want to be caught out by, it was the queen.

In the city, that was different. The people of Charming were obsessed with their returned queen. They waved placards and threw confetti at her in the street. Half of the small businesses in town named themselves after her. She was beloved. She was a miracle. She was a sign that, somehow, their fortunes were changing.

King Iolchas had not been popular. Tragic figure or not, he had provided little encouragement for his people to love him over the last seventeen years. He had been taunted and maligned in the press, who blamed him for the wilder behaviour of his out-of-control elder sons, the scandalous Princes Cyrus and Chase of Charming.

His beautiful, absent queen, lost to a sleeping curse nearly two decades ago, was considered beyond reproach. If anything, King Iolchas had been tolerated for so long because the people still held to the romantic fairy tale of Queen Ella's rise and fall.

Now he was gone, his mysterious absence neatly buried beneath the distracting return of the queen, whole and healthy, ready to capture the hearts of the city.

Queen Ella was Charming's miracle. The kingdom could not get enough of her.

Dennis had noticed that she did not sleep. She barely ate and drank. She twitched at every surprising noise. She was armed, always, even if you couldn't see the weapon at first glance. This was not the gentle fairy tale queen who had fallen into an enchanted slumber seventeen years ago, at the prick of a spinning wheel needle.

No one talked about this. Not her staff, or her children. Dennis knew better than to be the first.

He knocked on the queen's bedchamber door, and waited.

"I hardly need the armed escort," Amira huffed beside him, tossing her dark bob of hair. The former quill with questionable scruples was enjoying her new role as royal press secretary. Given the run of the castle, she had already discovered enough secrets to fuel the Charming Herald and other gazettes for years — so clearly, this was a job for life. They could never let her return to writing for newspapers.

"I'm not here for you," Dennis muttered. "I'm the Hound on Her Majesty's personal detail today."

"Interesting," Amira said with a sly look. "You don't seem to end up on Prince Camden's detail all that often. Almost as if they're keeping you away from him deliberately."

Dennis knocked again, waiting for the queen's response. Queen Ella liked to make her staff hang around a few moments, as part of her ongoing pretence that she slept through the night and breakfasted like a normal person.

"You're not as funny as you think you are," Dennis told Amira. His relationship with Kai — recently revealed to be Prince Camden — was not exactly a secret, but they hadn't made a public announcement or anything. That was the sort of thing you had to think about, apparently, when your boyfriend turned out to be a long-lost Royal. Whoever did the rosters on behalf of the new Sarge was clearly aware of their connection.

"Please," Amira sniffed. "I'm hilarious."

The door swung open. Both Dennis and Amira straightened their backs. Queen Ella of Charming's presence encouraged good posture.

She wore one of what Dennis thought of as her queen costumes. At first look, it was your standard aristo gown, elegant if matronly. Pale cream with jewelled beading at the sleeves and collar. A silken belt falling in an ornamental swoop around her hips. An antique sapphire necklace, not too showy for before lunchtime. ("Oh yes, my day sapphires, in their modest silver setting, la what an ordinary person I am.")

Queen Ella even wore a little lipstick today, in a light shade, the same style that other married ladies of the local aristo collective preferred. It was all part of her disguise.

Dennis knew about the secrets layered within. The deep pockets that seamstresses added to every gown in the queen's new wardrobe. The hidden weapons — a number between three and six. The flat, sturdy boots concealed (just) beneath the long sweep of her skirt.

While she was lost in that enchanted sleep, Queen Ella had fought for her life in an endless war against imaginary monsters for almost as long as Dennis himself had been alive. You didn't recover from an experience like that straight away, picking up your life where you left off. If battle changed a person, then seventeen years of battle? It had to leave some damage.

This was another thing that no one ever talked about, inside or outside the castle.

As usual, the queen assessed Dennis in a brief glance, then ignored him entirely. "Talk," she ordered Amira as she strode out along the corridor. "It takes four minutes to get to the public gallery. What can you tell me on the way?"

Amira trotted along beside the taller queen, doing her best to look dignified as she tried to keep up. "Despite our best efforts to quash the rumours, you can expect questions about the whereabouts of King Iolchas and Princess Camilla. I have a few useful loudmouths stashed in the crowd to fill up as much time as possible with details about the Solstice Gala, but you'll have to be prepared…"

"Of course I'm prepared," said the queen.

"Princes Cyrus and Camden will attend you at the press conference…"

The queen's head whipped around like she was about to stab a manticore. That wasn't an image produced by Dennis' imagination. He had once heard a detailed anecdote illustrating exactly how good Queen Ella was at stabbing manticores. It wasn't a comfortable thing to hear about the mother of the man he loved.

Good thing that his common status made it very unlikely she would ever be his mother-in-law, eh?

"Does Prince Chase have something better to do?" Queen Ella demanded.

Amira stumbled only slightly on her high heels. "New policy. Last time all three princes appeared with you for a public statement, the monochromists had a field day with the pictures. Seeing the four of you united only reminds the public that, uh…"

"Two of our family members are missing," the queen said dryly. "Yes, I understand. Divide and confuse."

Amira continued to update the queen as they swept down the wide staircase together. Dennis followed, eyes checking windows and doors of the less defensible space. Amira's voice grew quieter as they got closer to the public gallery, and dropped into polite silence as they stepped into the private ante-room.

The princes had been here for a while. Prince Cyrus paced the small room, never one happy to sit still. Ziggy, the Royal Hound on his detail, glanced up and nodded a greeting at Dennis.

On the far side of the room, Kai played a game of chess with Corporal Fergus.

Relief washed over Dennis, as always. There was a constant tension in his stomach these days when he didn't have eyes on Kai. His boyfriend was a target now. Signing up as a Hound, to protect the Royals from outside attack (and their own worst personal choices), had seemed like a good career move once upon a time, before Dennis became invested at a personal level.

Now, his heart was on the line.

Fergus was a good sort. Dennis liked him well enough, but that didn't mean he trusted him — or literally anyone but himself — to keep Kai safe. He knew that meant he was the last person who should be doing this job. (Sarge would have figured it out by now, might have done more than shake up a few rosters to remove Dennis from this conflict of interest, but Sarge was gone.)

Kai glanced up from his game to notice the presence of his mother and his boyfriend. A full five seconds after they arrived — no situational awareness at all! Kai's spine straightened, because Queen Ella was there, but he still took the time to give Dennis a melting smile.

Dennis wouldn't be applying for other jobs, as long as this was something he could have, every day. They would have to prise him out of the Royal Hounds with some kind of crowbar.

"Let's get started," said the queen with an air of authority.

And the day properly began.

2

BLINDED BY THE MONOCHROMES

There were many terrible things about being a long-lost prince.

Kai knew he was an ungrateful sod, but really. What was the up side?

The clothes were uncomfortable. The rooms were chilly. The only member of his newly restored family who actually liked him was missing.

He didn't have to worry about making ends meet any more — no more worrying about the rent or a food budget — but on the other hand, he owned *nothing*. He didn't have a coin to his name, and never quite got up the nerve to ask if there was some kind of allowance with this thankless job he had never applied for.

Actually, he was pretty sure L — his mother, the long-lost Queen Ella — would block any attempt at financial independence on his part. She stared at him sometimes like she knew how much he wanted to run away from this place.

He was lucky to be allowed shoes.

On top of everything, there was Dennis — his lovely Hound, the boy who literally kissed Kai awake from an enchanted sleep. There was a distance between them now that no amount of stolen moments and private kisses or promises could make up for.

If Dennis wasn't here, Kai would not have lasted a month in Castle Charming after the horrible revelation about his true parentage.

THE SIZZLE and pop of the monochromes filled the air with a burnt magic sort of smell. Kai did his best to smile cheerfully out at the sea of reporters and other vultures who wanted a piece of him.

He understood the irony well enough. That was him, only a few months ago — he was the wet-behind-the-ears quill ready to write stories about the Royals and their dramas. Now, he *was* the story.

"You look like you're being led to your execution," drawled Prince Cyrus at his side.

It hadn't taken Kai long to realise why the elder Princes Charming — a few weeks short of their twentieth birthday — always looked so dead inside at public appearances, or why they worked so hard to lower the public's expectations of appropriate princely behaviour.

The monochromes snapped and popped, filling Kai's vision with bright white explosions. To his right, Queen Ella answered the intrusive questions of the reporters with her usual smooth politeness, relying on Amira to bat away anything that bordered on inappropriate. Today's topic was the upcoming gala to celebrate the birthday of Kai's elder brothers.

"Prince Camden!" cried one voice. Amira gave him the nod.

That was who he was now. Not Kai at all. *They'd taken his name.*

"Will your father the king be returning to Castle Charming in time for the Solstice Gala?" asked the quill. Kai didn't recognise him; not a face from the Herald, unless he was new blood brought in to fill the job openings left behind by Amira and himself.

"Will he be naming his heir at the Gala?" shouted another quill behind him.

"I —" Kai started to say. He knew the party line. Amira had drilled him on this extensively. He was to cite the king's important work abroad, and add something vague to suggest no one should even question whether the king would return for such an important family event, without actually saying outright that yes, King Iolchas would be in attendance.

He knew exactly what he should say, but the flashes of the monochromes had him dazzled. Suddenly it was all too much, too loud. Why was everyone looking at him? For a moment, he caught the eye of Dennis, who stood at the back of the room looking helpless and sympathetic.

Cyrus moved, hooking an arm around Kai's neck. "You know our father," he said smoothly. "Family is everything to him. If he loves me and Chase at all, he'll be here for our birthday."

THE QUEEN WAS FURIOUS, of course. She remained polished and perfect as long as they had an audience, but once they were back in the private ante-chamber, she let loose her fury on Prince Cyrus. "I know this is a joke to you, but this is about our survival as a family!"

"Not all of us surely," he bit back, eyes cold. "I don't

know why you keep up the pretence. Father's long gone, and you don't want to be here any more than the rest of us."

"And you," Queen Ella snarled, turning on Kai. "How hard is it to remember a few prepared lines?"

Kai stared at the floor, avoiding her gaze. He was so tired of pretending — pretending this Royal Family reunion bullshit was normal. That they could make something of this bizarre situation. "I think I liked you better when you were telling me how bad I was at fighting monsters," he said dully.

Cyrus snorted.

The queen did not soften — Kai did not think she was capable of that — but she at least stopped looking at him like he had failed to spear a winged gargoyle right in front of her. "Camden…"

"That's not my name," he said, and walked out.

He had tried so hard to be their missing puzzle piece, to fit in here as the lost prince. Queen Ella had stepped back into her old life with an effortless perfection. Why couldn't he do the same?

But Kai wasn't a missing puzzle piece. Nothing was complete. Prince Camden might have returned, but they lost Princess Camilla in the process. How was that a fair trade, to finally be reunited with a family he never knew about, just as his twin sister disappeared?

If Camilla was here, perhaps it would make sense. Or, at least, Kai would have someone at his side to explain it all as they went.

He didn't think about where he was going as he left the castle by a side door and headed out across the grass, but of course there was only one place. He heard a soft footfall behind him. Though he wanted fiercely for it to be Dennis following him, Kai knew it was Corporal Fergus, his shadow for the day.

"Don't mind me, mate," Fergus said in a quiet voice.

Kai nodded to show that he had heard. He liked Fergus, who treated him like a person rather than a prince most of the time. Still, it was galling that he couldn't even be trusted to walk across the gardens on his own.

When he reached the Tower, in the quiet wilderness corner of the grounds, he turned to give Fergus a pleading look.

The heavy-set corporal shrugged and took up residence on a tree stump. "Here if you need me," he said affably.

Kai laid his hand on the door, and the wards welcomed him inside.

Here at least, he could be alone — as alone as was possible, when the kitchen at the foot of the tower was full of two tangled, enchanted trees that had once been his birth father the king, and his foster mother the witch.

Kai avoided looking at them, like always. He stepped carefully over humped roots bulging their way up through the rippled, broken tiles of the kitchen floor. He headed to the studio beyond the curtain.

When Camilla was here, the walls of her studio were whorled and adorned with glorious black ink artwork. So many patterns and shapes and illustrations, each imbued with her magic.

The walls were empty now. Kai had tried to draw power from them, or to push his own magic into them, but he barely managed more than an ink splatter. Wherever Camilla had fled, after she transformed their parents, she took her magic — their magic? — with her.

Kai slumped against one of the walls, curling up with his arms around his knees. "I miss you," he whispered. "I wish you'd come home."

It was the first time he had admitted aloud that Castle Charming was home, and it filled him with nothing but dread.

3

PRINCE IN STABLE RELATIONSHIP
SHOCKER

Dennis hated Camilla's tower.

It was creepy. It was creepy even before his boyfriend was interred here in an enchanted sleep, before Princess Camilla filled her kitchen with twisted trees that used to be people.

It was extra creepy now. And worse somehow that Kai only hid out here when he was really miserable.

Kai hid out here a lot lately. It hurt, that this was something Dennis couldn't fix for him.

He found his boyfriend in the empty studio where Camilla used to do all her magic shit. For a moment his heart froze to see the crumpled figure in the corner, but no, it was okay, Kai was just asleep.

It sucked that Dennis now had a stress reaction whenever his boyfriend closed his eyes. On the rare occasions they got to spend the night together, he always had to restrain himself from prodding Kai awake every few hours, just to check that he could.

"Babe," he murmured now, one hand brushing Kai's shoulder. "Hey. It's time."

Kai's eyes snapped open — he always woke up like that these days, sharp and startled, like he expected to find himself in a room full of teeth and claws. "Already?"

"You had a nap."

"Ugh." Kai stood up, stretching his neck. "How was the queen after… you know?"

He always called her the queen, Dennis noticed. Never 'my mother'.

"The usual. Frosty. Amira calmed her down a bit. Then Cyrus riled her up. Then Chase arrived and both princes irritated her all through to lunchtime."

"Ha," said Kai dryly. "Whenever I feel the urge to apologise for being a brat, I remember who set the bar."

Dennis leaned into him. "You're not doing too badly. I would have run away to the mountains by now."

"Is that plan completely off the table?"

Dennis laughed, and took his boyfriend's hand.

THEY EMERGED from the tower together in the bright sunshine and headed through the grounds.

"No Corporal Fergus," Kai noted.

"Ziggy relieved him at noon, then went ahead without us." They had selected this time for the meeting because Ziggy was on Kai's protection detail, while Dennis had the afternoon off.

"A rare window of opportunity to be alone together and we're wasting it," Kai lamented.

Dennis rolled his eyes. "I mean, it depends what you mean by wasting…"

"Ha."

They had to cut through the ornamental orchard, to reach the grotto where they were supposed to meet the others.

Shady trees on a sunny afternoon meant plenty of opportunity for them to hide away where no one would spot them.

"I mean," said Dennis, drawing Kai into a thick cluster of peach trees, heavy with fruit. "We have a little while before they expect us for the meeting."

Kai grinned, already pressing up against him. "Better make good use of the time…"

They had about three minutes of slow, lazy kissing before they were interrupted. If Dennis had realised the time constraint, he would have gone to his knees immediately.

"Don't stop on my account," said an amused voice.

Dennis stilled. He could feel Kai roll his eyes, his lashes fluttering against Dennis' skin.

And yeah, this had to be handled carefully. Apparently you couldn't tell a prince to get stuffed, even a foreign one.

"Hello, Zed," said Kai in a long-suffering voice.

Prince Zuo-lin of Xix was beautiful, sharp, witty and heroically brave. A rare list of princely attributes for Castle Charming, where Kai's two elder brothers had spent years educating the kingdom to expect nothing more than drunk, disorderly, sports-mad and fashionably attired.

He had saved Kai's life, so Dennis couldn't hate him, but Prince 'Zed' Zuo-lin was on a mission to make that resolution difficult for him.

"I'm looking for my sister," the prince said now, with an entirely unnecessary swish of his long dark pony-tail. "Isn't she supposed to be with you?"

"What," said Kai, sounding unbearably fond. "Are you that much of a stickler for the rules? Going to turn us in for snogging without a chaperone?"

There was a flicker on Zed's expression, gone too quickly for Dennis to be sure it was there at all. "Nah," said the foreign prince with a grin. "But your Cadet Ziggy has to stop avoiding me. Pass it on, please? There's a mess back home, and she owes me a clean-up operation."

Kai nodded, and slid a hand into one of Dennis' pockets, pulling him a little closer. "Now if you don't mind? We have like ten minutes before someone else from the castle comes looking for one of us."

"Fine," said Zed, loping away. "Don't do anything I wouldn't do, lads."

Dennis waited a moment until he was sure they were alone again. "We have to be careful he doesn't follow us," he said in a low voice. "The last thing we want is someone nosing around when we're about to…"

"Ssh," murmured Kai, leaning in for another kiss. "It's okay. Zed's wrapped up in his own family drama right now."

"That doesn't mean we can trust him."

"It doesn't mean we can't."

More kissing. They couldn't manage a perfect day or even a perfect hour together, but they could have this. Today, it was enough.

4

ROYAL HOUNDS IN SECRET GROTTO CONSPIRACY

The biggest mistake Ziyi ever made in her whole life was trusting a fairy.

What was she thinking, back then? She wasn't a trusting person. She grew up in a family with so many half-siblings, step-siblings and smiling, politically-savvy stepmothers that she knew you could take nothing at face value.

It only took one weak moment, and all that court-hardened, knife-blade cynicism fell away…

Once upon a time, she trusted a fairy godmother, a creature called Miss Clover, to grant her wish and fix her life, and instead…

Well. Ziyi was not unhappy with the life she was now living — she was a Royal Hound, with friends and a sense of purpose. She never had to wear formal silks as long as she lived. Being a Hound was much, much better than being a princess.

Still, the good parts were in spite of the fairy's best efforts, not because of them. Right?

"You're thinking too loud," said Corporal Jack in the silence of the grotto, her voice echoing around the rocky walls of the artificial cave in the centre of the castle gardens.

"Sorry," said Ziyi automatically. Her eyes went to the altar they had set up, covered in flower crowns and sugar lumps, pretty rocks and candles. Everything you needed for a good old-fashioned fairy summoning. "It just feels like — this is the sort of bad idea you look back on and regret."

"Oh yeah," said Jack. She shifted slightly on the rock where she sat, in the casual clothes that made her look like even more of a badass than her uniform. "I spent the morning writing an 'I told you so' letter to my future self."

"Really?"

"Nope." Jack smiled wide, her teeth gleaming in the odd, distilled grotto light that reflected off the drippy meditation pool. "But I'm well aware we're nowhere near Good Decision Country."

It felt like a good moment between them, a warm moment. That was why Ziyi dropped her usual restraint to ask, "Is that why you didn't ask Sarge his opinion on this plan of ours?"

The warmth left Jack's face in an instant. She shifted on the rock, her whole muscular body going taut and defensive. "How do you know I didn't ask him?"

Ziyi rolled her eyes. "Because he's still in town pretending he's a bartender, and he hasn't raged up here to storm the castle and put us all in handcuffs."

The Sarge quitting his position in the Royal Hounds was a loss from which they were all still reeling. Ziyi knew that it had hurt Jack more than any of them. The Hounds dropped into the Crown and Peg regularly to show him they were all in one piece, and the Sarge always looked pleased to see them, letting that craggy face of his roll into a familiar grin. It was weird though, to not have him shouting at them and giving out work orders every day.

The new Sergeant of Arms in charge of the Royal Hounds, a blustery old guard long past retirement age, also shouted at them all the time, but it wasn't the same.

"He'd hate this plan," Jack agreed. "He'd put a stop to it quick smart. We can't let him do that. This isn't his job any more. It's ours."

Kai and Dennis joined them all in a rush, holding hands and trying to look like they hadn't spent the last half hour making out in various corners of the garden.

"Thanks for sparing the time," Jack said dryly.

"We're not even late," said Dennis, crowding in next to her and knocking his shoulder against hers.

"Had to ditch a prince," added Kai, brushing grass off his trousers.

Ziyi shook her head, smiling at him. "Didn't get very far with that, did you, Dennis?"

"Oy," Dennis laughed. "This one's *inside* the secret conspiracy." He tangled his fingers with Kai's again.

Ziyi regularly teased them both for their ridiculous heart-eyes and shmoop, but she might admit under torture that it was nice to see them together and relaxed. When Kai was on duty as Prince Camden, he sloped uncomfortably around the castle exuding polite misery. "Which of your brothers was getting nosy?" she asked.

It was Jack's idea to keep Chase and Cyrus out of their plan, and Ziyi agreed. The fewer people involved in what they were doing, the better.

"Not mine, yours," said Kai.

"Stepbrother," Ziyi said automatically. What was Zuo-lin up to now?

She knew what he wanted. Of course she did. He wanted her to come home with him and prove to the family she was still alive, so he wouldn't be the disgraced exile any longer. And she knew that he was right. She woke up in the middle of the night with her stomach twisting with guilt over what she had done to him.

She wasn't ready yet, though. There was a job to do here. Maybe after the mission she could let herself sit down with him, have a proper conversation instead of ducking and avoiding him every time he caught her eye…

"Well, now. What do we have here?"

Ziyi went cold all over. She blinked at the others in horror.

Jack moved quickly, tossing a cloak over the fairy altar. Kai and Dennis looked mortified, and well they should if they were so wrapped up in each other that they didn't notice they had been followed after all.

Prince Zuo-lin of Xix, Ziyi's stepbrother and nemesis, ducked his head as he stepped into the grotto, and smirked at them all. "Such a cosy little conspiracy," he noted. "Can anyone play?"

5

GODMOTHER, GODMOTHER

Kai felt like an idiot. How had he not noticed that they were being followed?

He had always liked Zed, but right now the former Prince of Xix looked less than friendly as he lounged in the middle of their secret grotto. His eyes sparkled, which might be the way that light bounced off the decorative crystal flowers dotted around the artificial cave, or might be… amusement?

"You shouldn't be here," said Dennis gruffly, beside Kai.

"No, I can see how everyone here is far more experienced than I with strange magical adventures," said Zed sharply. "Oh, wait." He gave Kai a look that was more reproachful than angry.

Kai actually felt Dennis' shoulder become more tense, where it was pressed against him. "This is a need-to-know project," Kai said firmly.

Zed's eyes flicked down to where Jack's cloak was heaped over the fairy bric-a-brac. "And does your mother need to know, or not? Approved this project, has she?"

Kai rolled his eyes. "See, this is why you don't get invited to things, Zed."

"Oh wow, sorry for being loyal to the queen who, by the way, is the boss of everyone in this room." Zed looked furious, but his eyes were locked on Kai like the rest of them didn't matter. He had barely even acknowledged Ziggy's presence. "After everything we went through together," Zed hissed. "The three of us. How can you not trust her?"

"Because she's not my mother," Kai snapped back. "My mother was transformed into a tree and the only person who can fix her is missing."

Zed's bright eyes narrowed. "You're looking for Princess Camilla?"

"So, we're going to go," said Jack, taking Ziggy's sleeve. "This is, uh. More awkward and personal than any of us signed up for."

"Don't go anywhere," said Dennis, his voice tight like he was trying not to sound annoyed. "We have to get this done, right?" He leaned forward, hand on Kai's sleeve, soothing him. "Babe."

"You're right," said Kai. He sighed. "Zed… stay if you want to. If this works out the way we hope, it won't even matter if you run off to tell Queen Ella straight after."

Zed hesitated. "She wants Princess Camilla back too. Why would she even be upset?"

"Exactly," said Kai, not feeling the need to add all the complex layers of thought and feeling (and yes, suspicion) that he had about their golden queen. "We're keeping this secret because the fewer people who know why Camilla ran off, the better. And I don't want to get anyone's hopes up if it doesn't work."

"Fine," said Zed, dropping to the floor of the grotto and folding his legs up in some complicated pose like he didn't have bones. "I'll stay for the show. Wow me."

Ziggy gave her stepbrother a filthy look. She nudged Jack who reluctantly drew back the cloak. They both leaned over the makeshift altar, tidying a few of the things and straightening the candle.

"Let's get started," said Kai, remembering belatedly that he was in charge here, if anyone was. He was the prince, so this had to be his responsibility. He was the only one the queen couldn't kick out of the castle.

It was beyond strange, the thought of performing any kind of magic without Camilla to show him the way. But he had to do this. He needed her back, so badly. Not only to transform his mother and the king back from being trees in the kitchen of Camilla's private tower. But because being here in the castle *as a prince* made so little sense without her here.

His twin. They hadn't even had a chance to figure out what that meant yet. Kai missed her — not only the friend who taught him magic and laughed him out of bad moods. He missed the possibility of what she was supposed to be.

It was always going to be awkward, thinking of Prince Chase and Prince Cyrus as his brothers. But Camilla… Kai could *see* her as his sister and he wanted that, more than anything.

He needed her here, so Castle Charming could start feeling like home. If it didn't… Kai had no idea how he could be expected to stay.

Ziggy took a deep breath, and lit a match.

"Wait," said Zed. "Why are you doing this part? Isn't our lovely Prince Camden the one with the magic?"

Ziggy glared at him, the match still burning in her fingers. "Kai has a different kind of magic. Fairies aren't fond of ink. I know what I'm doing."

"I never said you didn't."

"You literally just interrupted me to — ow!" Ziggy dropped the match. "Damn it."

"Fairy magic is about wishes," Kai explained to Zed. "And uh, Zig has the most experience with that."

"Really," said Zed, rolling the word around on his tongue. "What did you wish the fairies would do for you, little sister?"

"I wished them to turn you into a toad but they said you were halfway there already," she shot back.

Zed laughed, throwing back his head. His ponytail swished.

Dennis made a grumbling sound. "*Your* friend," he muttered, prodding Kai in the ribs.

"Zed, keep your mouth shut," Kai ordered the foreign prince. "We need to concentrate. Ziggy won't be able to ask the fairies for help if she's busy setting fire to your face, so…"

ZIYI WAS FURIOUS AT EVERYONE, furious at this whole situation, but most of all… yes, Kai was right. She pretty much did want to set fire to Zuo-lin's face. Instead, she lit another match. This time, she let the flame flicker over the wick of the bluebell candle until it caught.

She had bought the candle in the market earlier this week, because she threw out all her fairy summoning crap months ago, after that business with the dancing slippers. She had never planned to do this ever again, not after she learned the true risk of asking fairies for favours.

Her fairy godmother, Miss Clover, was a human once. A human who asked for wishes once too often, who tried to save everyone she loved… and was consumed by the bluebells and foxgloves and eerie fairy magic.

Ziyi wanted to help Kai and the others. They were her friends. She owed Camilla. If this could help…

One last time. She could ask one last time and hope this wasn't the one wish too many.

"Godmother, godmother," she began, then blinked as a new figure appeared, sprawling on the rocky ledge above Dennis and Kai's heads. "Oh. You."

It was Master Foxglove, all wicked smiles and sultry looks, his dark hair falling into his eyes. Honestly, he and Zuo-lin were as bad as each other.

"You know you missed me," drawled the fairy she hadn't invited.

"Where's Miss Clover?" Ziyi demanded.

"She's busy. You'll have to come to her if you want to chat."

Jack, Dennis, Kai and Zuo-lin all protested in one burst of noise. Ziyi held up a hand, silencing them. "It's sweet that you all care, but everyone can shut up right now." She got to her feet. "Take me to her." Carefully, she did not phrase it as a wish, or as a request.

Master Foxglove stretched out on the ledge, laughing at her with his eyes. "You may take one companion," he told her.

Ziyi knew that Kai was ready for this, that he expected to go, but she couldn't lead him back into fairyland. He wasn't some nosy reporter any more, he was one of the precious Princes Charming. It was her literal job to keep him safe.

She felt the warm line of Jack standing behind her, ready to offer her support. Of course it should be Jack. Ziyi trusted her more than anyone else in this place.

"Take me," Zuo-lin demanded, dropping his usual facade of death-defying jokes, crocodile anecdotes and sharp-tongued commentary. "*Ziyi-shensa.*"

Her eyes flew wide. "Don't call me that."

"This is adorable," said Master Foxglove, yawning broadly. "But, Midnight Princess, I didn't say you got to choose."

The grotto swam before Ziyi's eyes. The last thing she heard before it all went dark was Jack, shouting in pure outrage.

6

BURNING THE BLUEBELL CANDLE AT ONE END

Dennis reached Jack first, putting a friendly but firm arm around her to stop her from smashing the fairy altar to pieces. "Breathe," he told her, holding fast. He was pretty sure saying anything along the lines of "Calm down" would get him punched.

Jack shoved at him, and he let her. Bruises would heal, but they needed that bluebell candle to stay burning right now.

"He took her!" she roared.

"Ziggy will be fine," Kai assured them, staring at the space where Zuo-lin had been sitting. "They'll both be fine. They've done this before."

"Yeah we've all done our time being kidnapped by magical bullshit," Dennis growled. "Doesn't mean we have to like it."

"I'm more worried about Zed," said Kai. "Ziggy knows what not to say around fairies. His experience with magical kidnapping was… less nuanced."

"I don't care if the fairies eat him for breakfast," said Jack. "How long should we wait?"

Kai gazed at the burning bluebell candle, which reflected two bright burning dots against his eyes. "Given that we have no way of following them or contacting them… forever? As long as we have to? Until dinnertime?"

"That candle has about three hours in it," said Dennis before he could stop himself.

~

FAIRYLAND TASTED AMAZING. The air smelled of flowers and fresh grass and happiness. It tingled on Ziyi's tongue with a spark that made her whole body shiver with excitement.

If it wasn't for her fury at having her stepbrother along for the ride, she might almost be enjoying herself.

Master Foxglove played tour operator, helping both Royals of Xix into a boat made of a giant lotus blossom. He then paddled them down a silver river with enormous daisies floating in it like lily pads.

"Those are the dancing mountains," Master Foxglove said with an air of authority, waving into the distance. "That's the whispering forest, don't get lost in there, it's where we send all the willow-the-wisps who don't play nice with others. That's the bracken death trap valley…"

"He's messing with us," Zuo-lin said in a low voice, into Ziyi's ear.

"He can also hear you," she said, swatting Zuo-lin away.

Master Foxglove laughed, trailing his fingers in the silver water. "What? Everyone knows how dangerous fairyland is for mortals. And here you are. Completely at my mercy." The lotus boat bumped gently against the shore on the far side of the river. Master Foxglove made a fuss about leaping out first and helping them both to dry land.

Ziyi rolled her eyes at him, refusing to take his arm. She

stepped to shore on her own. "I'm not here for myself, you know."

"Because being selfless has protected so many mortals from fairy magic in the past," Foxglove said gravely, and then winked at her.

"I thought there'd be more monsters," said Zuo-lin, twitching at every rustle or cracking twig as they made their way through a birch forest with jewels hanging from every branch. "Something to fight."

Ziyi tried not to be impatient with him; he had spent months trapped in an enchanted simulacrum of a castle trying to murder him. Of course he was twitchy.

"Maybe later if you've been good," she said in a low voice.

Zuo-lin laughed in a sudden bark and then stared at her. "You made a joke."

"It happens."

"Not usually around me."

She shrugged. "We're in this together now."

"So sweet," said Master Foxglove, capering up ahead of them. "Fraternal togetherness, bound to doom you both."

Zuo-lin sighed. "I can fight him, right? At some point. Eventually?"

"I'm not going to stop you," said Ziyi.

DENNIS HAD no idea what to do. The bluebell candle was down to its last inch of wick. Jack refused to leave the grotto.

Eventually Kai admitted he had to go back to the castle to change for dinner. Dennis went with him as far as the castle kitchens and collected an empty lozenge tin from a confused cook, which he returned to the grotto.

"If you put the candle in the tin the wick will last longer," he told Jack, which wasn't a lie. He remembered his sisters trying to stretch every candle for as many minutes as possible because they had to work on some kind of trousseau embroidery through the night.

Jack nodded sombrely and let Dennis transfer the sticky, dripping mess of a nearly-used candle into the tin. The wick dipped a little and he almost lost the flame, but recovered it at the last moment.

"I don't know how much time it will buy us," he admitted to her. "Maybe another hour if we're really lucky?"

Jack nodded and stared at her feet. "I hate not being able to save her right now."

Dennis thought about Kai, lost to the enchanted sleep full of monsters… and now, swallowed up by castle ritual and hating every minute of it. "I know what you mean."

"DELIGHTED YOU COULD JOIN US," said Miss Clover, as Master Foxglove led Ziyi and Zuo-lin through a canopy of flowers to her bower of buttercups. The fairy godmother sat on a swing twined with leaves and flowers, her hair streaming behind her as she pushed back and forth like a metronome made of whimsy. "Do eat the fruit cake, it's divine."

"Don't eat anything," Ziyi told Zuo-lin.

"Obviously," he muttered back. "Also, have you noticed? There is no fruit cake."

There was fruit: a cornucopia of sticky rinds and dripping berries that stained the grassy lawn at the feet of the mortals and the fairies alike, but no cake.

"We have questions," said Ziyi.

Master Foxglove climbed on to the swing with Miss Clover and kissed her, his hands in her hair. "Did you hear our friend? She has questions."

Miss Clover giggled, a strange and brittle sound that didn't suit her at all. There was something very wrong here.

"How do we get past the game-playing?" Zuo-lin asked quietly.

"We'll have to wait it out," said Ziyi, losing confidence fast. This had all been a terrible mistake.

"How much time do we have?"

THE CANDLE WAS LIQUID NOW, a tiny flame floating on a quarter-inch of wick, in a sea of molten wax.

"We can't lose her," Jack said, staring at the wick as if she could keep it going by sheer force of will.

The flame went out.

7

THIS MAKES THINGS AWKWARD

It was dark in fairyland and nothing made sense. Ziyi was lost, untethered. Every time she took a step into the darkness, her stomach lurched badly.

Someone grabbed her hand and she swung around to hit with the hardest part of her hand, but he caught that too. "Ziyi, it's me."

"Is that supposed to make me feel better?" She did actually feel better at the sound of Zuo-lin's voice, but she resented it. "What happened?"

"I think the candle went out."

"That makes no sense. Why would the lights go out in all of fairyland because of one candle?"

His hand tightened on hers. "Ziyi… are you saying you can't see?"

She blinked furiously into the darkness. "Of course I can see. I can see the entire lack of light!"

Somewhere nearby, fairies giggled at her.

His hand loosened on hers. Scared, Ziyi grabbed out at him. "Don't leave me."

"I don't want to." Zuo-lin's voice was distracted. "But there's music."

"I can't hear any music."

"They want me to dance, Ziyi."

"Don't let go," she begged, hating herself for feeling so weak. "Don't dance, Zuo-lin. That's how they get you."

"I can't…"

There was a soft tapping sound, and she realised it was his foot.

"Don't join the dance," Ziyi said, squeezing his hands harder. "Zuo-lin. I need you."

A soft touch like a brotherly kiss brushed her temple. "I'll be back. Just one dance."

"No!"

And he was gone.

~

HERE THEY WERE AGAIN. Yet another awkward dinner where Kai sat at a table designed for twenty people, with his family of four.

Queen Ella was in attendance, but barely spoke. She pushed her soup around, and asked occasional questions about their day. It was excruciating.

Usually Zed was there to break some of the tension, but of course he was in fairyland, and Kai was only grateful that no one had questioned him about their guest's absence.

Chase and Cyrus were clearly in the middle of some kind of 'best behaviour bet,' because they smiled politely and lied happily about their day's activities. No one could possibly open as many local businesses, sponsor as many charities, or kiss as many babies as they claimed.

Kai narrowed his eyes at them both, not knowing if he

wanted to catch them out himself, or watch Queen Ella call them on their bullshit.

The new castle chamberlain entered the dining hall, looking nervous. There was always a new chamberlain, and they always looked nervous. Queen Ella had a habit of firing anyone who questioned the whereabouts of the King, or asked after Princess Camilla.

This chamberlain, who was called something like Percivale or Peregrin, was twenty-two years old and until yesterday had been a footman. He had bright red hair, and was clearly about two inches too tall for the official chamberlain's frock coat with pearl trim.

"Your Majesty," he said, stumbling over even the basic address. "I, uh — there's a delegation at the gates."

Queen Ella tilted her head, like she was wondering how he would look kneeling at a guillotine. "Boys. Have any of you invited guests that I should know about?"

"I mean," said Cyrus, and shrugged.

"Our guests usually shin up the drainpipe," said Chase, as if he had forgotten the 'pretend to be a perfect prince' game. "Easier to smuggle the booze in that way. More discreet."

"Where is the delegation from?" asked Kai.

They all stared at him, like they had forgotten he was there. Did he speak so rarely?

"Answer Prince Camden," ordered Queen Ella.

"They are a royal delegation from the Empire of Xix, Your Majesty," said Percival or Peregrine.

Kai met Chase's gaze and the two of them mouthed the same, very unprincely word together.

"Ah," said Queen Ella. "Not unexpected." She rose to her feet. "Let us greet the family of Prince Zuo-lin. Someone fetch him."

"I'll go," Kai said automatically.

She rolled her eyes at him. "You are not a footman, Camden. We have people for that."

"But do any of those people know where our Xixese friend is to be found?" asked Chase with a sly look at his newly rediscovered younger brother.

"ZUO-LIN!" Ziyi was lost in the darkness. Fairies were the worst, and fairy-dazzled stepbrothers were nearly as bad. "I'm going to eat your eyes when I see you next," she swore at him. It didn't help.

"Cadet Ziggy," said a hushed voice near her ear.

Ziyi jumped, her hand whirling around in a short jab that she pulled at the last moment. "Who is that?"

"My name is Master Iris." He continued to speak quietly, as if he wanted no one to hear. Still, there was a deepness to his voice, a melodious quality that she recognised.

"You're —" she started to say, remembering Saladin Teh, the Sarge's old friend. Of course. He was one of them now. A fairy. He had followed Miss Clover into this world months ago, and refused to give her up.

"I believe I told you my name," he said. "I am Master Iris now."

"They made you change it?"

"No one made me do anything."

"I can't see," she said wretchedly. "I can't — I think I've lost my path home."

"Have you eaten anything? Kissed anyone who belongs here?"

"No."

"Then it remains possible that you will find another path home. Keep it that way."

Ziyi felt something brush against her hand. She held

herself very still as the fairy formerly known as Saladin Teh pressed something very small into her palm. It felt like a nut, or a dried pea. "What —"

"I have given you nothing," he stated.

"Are fairies allowed to lie?"

"Fairies are allowed to do whatever they can get away with. You should know that by now."

She waited, but he said nothing more. After a long moment, she held up her palm, and for the first time in far too long, saw something other than darkness.

A tiny bead of light glowed in her palm, illuminating the rest of fairyland. She could see hanging fronds of tree branches around her, and the shifting shapes of people, dancing. Ziyi took a few steps, moving in the direction where her bead of light shone brightest, and then she saw him.

Zuo-lin, Exiled Prince of Xix, had never been a darling of the court back home. He was rude to those he should flatter, and had a sharp streak in what he chose to say to his step-mothers and sisters. She had seen a different side of him in recent months at Castle Charming, and she was now convinced that for some reason he had been playacting a cruel persona back home, especially around her.

She had no idea why a King's stepson would choose to alienate the court instead of cultivating allies with a few honeyed words, when honeyed words clearly came easily to him. But she had never asked, even now that she knew there was more to him than met the eye.

His one great social advantage back home was that he was an excellent dancer. Aristocratic men of the Empire were expected to excel at dancing and music just as aristocratic women were expected to learn the art of close combat and weaponcraft: all the better to be ornaments of the court. Zuo-lin, for all his barbed comments and veiled insults, was always much in demand at a ball. Ladies of the court were willing to overlook a great deal of rudeness for a dance partner who made them look fantastic, and knew the difference between a three-spin and a promenade twirl.

None of which explained why he was currently dancing like a deranged octopus with one too many arms.

Ziyi peered through the near-darkness at the utter spectacle her stepbrother was making of himself, surrounded by delighted and admiring fairy people of many apparent genders. She almost didn't want to stop him.

Then one fairy leaned in to brush their mouth to his. Ziyi threw herself forward with a yell, arrowing through bodies until she was there between Zuo-lin and the fairy attempting to claim a kiss.

"We need to go home!" she yelled in his face.

"You spoil all my fun," he yelled back, eyes glazed over. "This is the first magical otherworld where no one's trying to kill me!"

Ziyi looked around wildly, holding up her bead of light to see an ocean of unfriendly faces. Did fairies always have that many teeth? "I think you're drastically misreading this situation."

They had to return to Castle Charming, right now. Without asking for a wish or a favour from any more fairies. Ziyi did not want to spend the rest of her life as one of these fruit-eating, wild-dancing creatures. There was nothing about her interaction with Saladin Teh/Master Iris that made her think he was happy in his new life.

"We have to run," she begged Zuo-lin. "And no kissing."

Belonged here, she remembered suddenly. *No kissing anyone who belonged here.* What if you kissed someone who did not belong? Was that a loophole?

"Where do we even —" Zuo-lin started to complain at her, and she shut him up with…

Well. It was a kiss. Probably one of the least appealing

kisses of her life. He stared at her in shock, as she pulled her mouth back from him hastily.

Evening sunlight streamed through the window of a familiar corridor, high up in the castle. Human sunlight, human corridor. Home, for a given value of home. Castle Charming. It was late in the day, but not dark yet because summer.

Zuo-lin was still staring at her, now with more horror than shock. "Why would you —"

She wiped her mouth with the back of her hand. "Fairy rules don't always make sense. And they change, all the time. If you listen carefully, there's always a loophole." Ziyi still had the small glowing seed in her hand, and shoved it now in the pocket of her trousers.

"Did there have to be kissing?"

"I didn't enjoy it," she said grumpily.

"I should hope *not*."

"Here you are," said a voice, breaking into their argument.

Ziyi and Zuo-lin quickly stepped back even further from each other.

"Hey," said Ziyi, not meeting Dennis' gaze.

"We were worried. How did you get back?"

"Loophole," said Ziyi at the same time that Zuo-lin said: "Don't ask."

"Okay," said Dennis slowly. "Thing is, there's a situation downstairs. And we need you. Prince you, not… actually, both of you, come to think of it."

"Words," said Ziyi impatiently. "More words. Get on with it."

Dennis took a deep breath and went unexpectedly formal. "Prince Zuo-lin, your family have arrived at the castle. To visit you. Now I come to think of it, this probably is… a both of you situation." He gave Ziyi an apologetic smile.

Ziyi shared a horrified look with Zuo-lin. "Which family members?" she whispered.

"How many?" asked Zuo-lin, speaking over the top of her.

"Do they look angry?"

"Are they dressed in formal silks?"

"Are there any white flowers or very sharp swords in their retinue?"

Dennis held up both hands. "How about you both come and see for yourselves?"

No, Ziyi thought wildly. *No, no, no.*

"Yep," said Zuo-lin, bracing himself. "Come on, Ziyi-shensa. What's the worst that can happen?"

8

IMPERIAL FAMILY REUNION SHOCKER

Ziyi was almost brave enough for this. Almost.

With Dennis and Zuo-lin, she made her way to the Rose Parlour where the Queen of Charming was apparently entertaining three members of the Imperial House of Xix. It was only at the very last minute that Ziyi lost her nerve and ducked into one of the many hidden passages in the castle that she had made it her business to know about.

"Seriously?" Zuo-lin called out from somewhere. "You little coward!"

Ziyi ignored him, ignored her rising guilt, and ran for her life.

~

KAI HAD LEARNED in recent weeks that when four or more Royals were in one place together, there would be tea.

(Previously his experience was in combinations of only two or three known Royals at a time, which usually eventuated in sport, drinking games and/or the slaying of monsters.)

Chase pulled a vanishing act this time, but Cyrus was still

working on his Best Prince impersonation. Kai had not figured out how to do either of those things. Instead, he sat beside his eldest brother on an antique settee while Queen Ella directed the flow of tea and tiny cakes to their visitors.

There were three of them, all women. Kai memorised their beautiful, complex names with grim determination, but instantly forgot which of them belonged to which name, which was embarrassing for him. He was pretty sure one of them was Zed's mother. Perhaps they all were. They wore stiff, complicated gowns with sleeves of sculptured silk. He suspected there were weapons concealed beneath every artificial rose pinned to their wrists, shoulders and waists. So they were going to fit in fine around here.

The door of the Rose Parlour crashed open and Zed stood there, looking wrecked. His usually-sleek ponytail was all over the place, and his clothes were rumpled. He had flower petals scattered over one shoulder of his white linen shirt.

But hey, he wasn't trapped in fairyland any more, which was more than Kai had expected.

Dennis appeared in the doorway, a step or two behind Zed. "Prince Zuo-lin," he announced, since no one else was doing it.

"Ayma," breathed Zed.

"Zuo-lin-shensa," said one of the mothers of Xix, flinging out her arms so wildly that she almost took out the woman next to her with an enormous silk rose pinned to her sleeve along with a series of very sharp daggers and even sharper pearl brooches.

Zed flung himself into the lap of the woman, who burst into noisy tears.

Another of the mothers passed her a handkerchief with so much embroidery and beading on it that it was unlikely to be useful.

The third mother sipped her tea. "We are most grateful for

your message, Queen Ella, enabling this reunion with our son."

Kai glanced at the Queen in surprise. Ella was unmoved. "Family is important," she said serenely. "Parents and children should not be separated."

Cyrus coughed into his sleeve, muttering something to himself.

"I am glad you feel that way, Majesty," said the middle mother, her back straightening as if she was about to march to war. "Perhaps now you can assist us in finding our lost daughter."

WHEN ZIYI WAS SMALL, and she felt the world becoming too big and scary — whenever she became overwhelmed with the pressures of what it meant to be a princess — she retreated into her training. Of all the traditional feminine arts of Imperial wives and daughters, she preferred those which were physical: archery, horse riding, hand-to-hand combat, ornamental swordwork.

Today, on the roof of the castle as the sky darkened around her, she ran through sword drill after sword drill. Charming swords were solid and less nuanced than the blades of her home empire, but a sword was a sword.

Out here, she felt useful. She felt like Cadet Ziggy, Royal Hound.

Until someone came to find her.

If she thought at all about who might be sent to drag her back to the Rose Parlour, she might have hoped for Dennis, who she could wrap around her little finger, or Zuo-lin, who she could shout at until she was hoarse.

Instead it was Kai, the new Prince Camden. That was cheating, surely?

They were nearly friends, she thought, thanks to their shared custody of Dennis, though their friendship was hampered by the awkward prince thing. (And, unspoken, but Ziyi could now admit, the awkward princess thing.)

Kai had always been pretty, all floppy dark hair and soulful eyes, but in prince clothes he looked like *he* was the one who had recently stepped out of fairyland. Like he was an illustration in a children's book, not a real person.

"They know you're here," he said gravely.

Ziyi kept running through her sword drill. This allowed her to turn away from him without it counting as rude. "Who told them?"

"L, I think. The queen, I mean." Wow, he was really bad at that. Sooner or later, someone was going to notice that he never called her his mother.

"I suppose you're going to say that she means well," Ziyi said between gritted teeth. "That I should trust she has my best interests at heart."

Kai shrugged. "I would trust the queen without question if the castle was under attack," he admitted. "With anything else… I don't know."

Surprised, Ziyi swung around to face him, and lowered her sword.

Kai gave her a rueful grin. "Dennis doesn't trust her," he volunteered. "He won't badmouth her to me or anything, but I've picked up on what he doesn't say. He's a better judge of people than I am. If he's suspicious of what she's doing here, I have to be."

"So reassuring, Your Highness," said Ziyi.

"Here to be helpful."

"Do you know at least —" she wished she didn't care so much about this particular question. "Is one of the visitors Zuo-lin's mother?"

Kai scrunched up his face. "It kind of sounded like they all were?"

Oh, they were playing that game, were they? Magical happy families, closing ranks against outsiders. Everyone belonging to everyone. No way of knowing if the group was made up of the stepmothers who wished the worst for her, or the ones who had been kind. Ziyi took a deep breath, and sheathed her sword. "I suppose it's time to face the music."

"Hang on," Kai said as she started past him. "Did you learn anything from the trip to fairyland? To help us find Camilla."

Ziyi hesitated, but only for a moment. This was his quest more than it was hers. She dug the little seed out of her pocket. It looked more like a dried bean, no longer glowing with light. "There's this. Saladin Teh gave it to me — Master Iris, as he's known now. I don't know what use it is, but fairies don't give away anything casually."

Kai accepted the seed from her, turning it over in his hand. "Do we plant it?"

Ziyi shrugged. "I mean. What's the worst that could happen?"

THEY PASSED Prince Cyrus on their way to the Rose Parlour.

"Where are you off to?" Kai asked.

His elder brother gave a weak grin. "Making myself scarce. A lot of my friends have duchesses for mothers. And baronesses. Baronesses are almost as bad as duchesses."

"In what way?" Ziyi asked curiously. What did baronesses or duchesses have to do with anything?

"They all wear matchmaking hats. I know them when I

see them." He gave Kai a thunderous clap over the shoulder. "Good luck to you, little brother. Better you than me."

"That's not ominous at all," said Kai, watching the elder Prince Charming disappear into the distance.

Ziyi had a sinking feeling that their Prince Camden wasn't the only one who might be in the firing line, if match-making was on the cards.

Oh, gods. Had the queen or princes told her stepmothers about the Midnight Princess trick she played, last autumn? She was going to die of embarrassment.

"Here we are," said Kai a moment later, using his stiff Prince Camden voice as he ushered Ziyi into the Rose Parlour. She was still wearing her crumpled Royal Hound uniform. (She had considered ditching it but really, she had to assume that everything was out in the open now. What did it matter if they knew where she had been hiding?)

"Come on in, *Your Highness*," said Queen Ella, in a voice of icy politeness.

Ziyi stepped forward, her eyes lowered to the carpet. She could see silk slippers and formal flowers pinned to sleeves, but did not yet dare to look up into the faces of her visiting stepmothers (mothers, she should say mothers if that was what they were calling themselves, the last thing she could afford was to insult them now).

"Please excuse me," Kai said in a strangled voice. "Gardening emergency. Back later." He scarpered out of the door, abandoning Ziyi to her fate.

Furious at him, her head flew up, and she caught her first real look at the visitors.

"I believe no introductions are in order," said Queen Ella.

Ziyi could not quite believe what she was seeing: Zuo-lin, of course, sitting arm-in-arm with the fairy she knew as Master Foxglove. Holding his hand like they were intimately acquainted, practically in his lap. Beside Foxglove were more familiar faces: Miss Clover, and a fairy Ziyi had only even seen in passing, but knew instantly was Miss Bluebell. The one who cursed Clover to her fairy existence.

All three of them wore formal silk robes as if they were indeed members of the Imperial House of Xix. Every detail was perfect, except that all three of them smiled with warm, open affection.

"Ah," said Miss Clover, with an arch expression. "Good to see you, daughter. We have so much catching up to do."

9

SPIFFY

Dennis knew he shouldn't leave the Parlour of Awkward Family Reunions. He was on duty. On the other hand, Ziggy was the one technically on Kai's detail until bedtime, according to today's schedule, and she was busy being a princess.

Kai was out there without a Hound on his heels.

Dennis withdrew as discreetly as possible, and went looking for his boyfriend.

It was almost completely dark outside now. He found Kai in the castle grounds, heading for Camilla's tower. "Staying out of the family drama?" Dennis called out, not wanting to startle him.

Kai spun around anyway, looking guilty. "Um," he said.

Dennis eyed the clenched hand. "What's up?"

"I think," said Kai, and opened his hand. "I think it's a magic bean."

Dennis knew magic beans. The princes and princess had an inexhaustible supply of them, which they mostly used to spice up party games. Those beans were bright-coloured, like candied comfits, each containing a single act or effect of minor magic.

The small dried pulse in Kai's hand looked nothing like those. "From fairyland?" Dennis asked, leaning in to examine it.

"From fairyland," Kai confirmed. "Because this is our life now."

"Hey, storybook nonsense isn't confined to Royals," said Dennis. "Remind me to introduce you sometime to my sister and her talking cat." He prodded the bean tentatively. "Gonna plant it?"

"I mean," said Kai. "We have to. Right?"

"Moral imperative."

"It's the thing to do."

Dennis leaned in and kissed Kai quickly; a brief peck on the mouth. "Let's do it together. Then, when it all turns to shit, I'll tell them it was your fault. They're less likely to execute a prince."

"Good plan," said Kai. He went down on his knees, scrabbling at the lawn. "Here works, right?"

Dennis measured with his eye. "Not too close to the tower. Less likely to cause major structural damage if it goes all, you know."

"Giant beanstalk."

"Giant beanstalk." They'd both read that story as children. The giant. The goose that laid the golden eggs. The impossibly large green stalk that led directly to a castle in the clouds.

Kai dug the bean into a furrow he made with his fingers, and Dennis helped him scrape dirt back over it.

"And now?"

"Now we wait."

They waited at least five minutes.

"Happened overnight in the fairy tale," said Dennis.

"Fairy tales don't always get it right."

"And yet."

They both watched for another three minutes.

"Want to find a dark corner to make out in?" Kai asked eventually.

"Your Highness comes up with the best plans," Dennis grinned.

LATER, when Kai returned to his rooms, a tunic hit him in the face. "What —?" He snatched it out of the air and tossed it to one side, only to see a pair of trousers flying past him. "Amira, why are you in my wardrobe?"

There were many things that came with being a prince, including a shiny suite of rooms that were far too fancy for him, like he was squatting in a hotel room on someone else's tab.

The wardrobe, full of outfits he was uncomfortable even looking at, was about the size of the hired room he lived in when he first moved to the city of Charming to write for the newspapers. Kai mostly pretended the wardrobe wasn't there, cycling through the simplest of the tunics and trousers he could find.

Not tonight. Tonight, the royal press secretary was digging through his things, chucking around jackets and scarves so encrusted with fine beading and gold embroidery that they clanked when they hit the walls. "Why don't you have any green velvet shoes?" Amira demanded.

"Who even wears velvet shoes?" Kai sat on the bed. He had spent a few very pleasant hours with Dennis, and no giant beanstalks had broken into their private time. He wasn't ready to let go of the comfortable happiness that came from pretending they were two ordinary boys in love.

"Princes, Your Highness. Princes wear velvet shoes."

"Don't you start Your Highnessing me. If you pretend to respect me, I have no hope of a normal life."

They were friends, once, he and Amira. Work colleagues. Then they were enemies, briefly. And now they were… this. Somehow, Kai's official rise in status meant even more of Amira telling him what to do.

She stuck her head out of the wardrobe to give him a scornful expression. She wore a silver sailor's cap with a ruby brooch the size of a small egg right in the middle of her forehead. He hoped desperately that it did not belong to him. "You don't get to be normal any more, Highnessy McHighness. We both have a job to do, and mine is to get you all spiffy for the reception tomorrow."

"Isn't that below your pay grade?"

"Indeed it is, Royal Fancypants Lost Prince of the Realm but what the queen commands, I do."

Kai wrinkled his nose. "Queen Ella of Charming used the word 'spiffy'?"

"She said suitable. I'm translating."

"Didn't know you were fluent in Queen."

"One of my many skills." Amira emerged triumphantly with a forest green suit covered in gold frogging, a matching hat, and what looked like white knee socks with garters.

"Nope, no, nup," said Kai, and threw himself on the bed. "I'm a prince, that means I get to get drunk and run away, doesn't it? I've read newspapers, I know how this story goes."

Amira sighed. He closed his eyes and ignored her. He heard some rustling of fabrics, and then the bed dipped as she lay down next to him. "Kid. That's for bad princes. You're the good prince."

"Ugh." Kai knew he was being a brat. He'd never been allowed to be a brat before, not with the governess to out-intimidate all governesses as his mother, and growing up as a stranger in other people's rich houses. (His childhood, as it turned out, was a rehearsal for right now.) "Why do I have to be suitable?"

"I imagine it's to show off how hot you are as a marriage prospect," said Amira and then squawked in protest as Kai sat up so fast, he knocked her off the bed. "Oi!"

"Marriage prospect," Kai repeated. "Marriage prospect? Who exactly do they expect me to marry?"

DENNIS RETURNED to the Doghouse dorm late, happy and relaxed right up until he saw Ziggy standing miserably in front of their lockers. "What's wrong? Shouldn't you still be on duty for another hour?"

"I don't do that any more," she said, scooping the last of her things into a bag.

"Wait, what?"

"I'm not a Royal Hound, Dennis," she explained, looking miserable. "I'm a princess. And now they all know it."

"Your stepmothers," he breathed, understanding. "I mean. You didn't want to be away from your family forever, did you? Maybe this could be a good thing?" He didn't believe a word of it. He'd run away from his own family to be a Royal Hound, and he wouldn't trade back for a second.

"It's not even real," Ziggy wailed, and spun around quickly, pressing her face into his tabard-covered chest. Awkwardly, he patted her back.

"What's not real?"

"My —" she broke off, as if she literally could not say what was bothering her. "It doesn't matter. I have to go through this whole charade of putting on a frock and parading around like I'm hunting a husband all over again. It's so embarrassing!"

"We'll miss you," said Dennis. It was barely beginning to sink in that Ziggy wasn't one of them any more, that she had to go back to that world of aristo weddings and frocks. "This sucks. Have you told Jack?"

Zig lifted her head, something like fear on her face. "I can't. Dennis, she'll hate me."

"That's basically impossible. You have to tell her, Ziggy. She'll understand."

"Oh, she'll understand," Ziggy said sourly. "She's been friends with the princes most of her life. She knows what I'm in for."

"See?" Dennis urged her. He was a massive hypocrite, he knew. He wasn't over Kai's new change in status, and he wasn't sure he ever would be. "She'll have your back. We all will."

"It's not even real," Ziggy sighed again, and hauled her bag on to her shoulder. "But this wasn't real, either. It was a stupid dream, being a Royal Hound. A really brilliant dream. And now it's over."

10

——

BALLS

Technically, it wasn't a ball.

A royal ball required at least six weeks extensive party planning, menu testing, gold-dipped invitation cards, and three beautifully executed scandals. Plus new togs for everyone, and several hundred napkins folded into the shape of unicorns.

Prince Chase of Charming had once been subject to a two-hour lecture from his cousin Serena, Countess of Argyll, on exactly how much work went into planning a ball: from the servants who prepared the ballroom and served refreshments, to the gardeners who prepared the flowers, all the way to the designing and sewing and selecting of outfits and…

He didn't remember what he'd done to deserve the lecture, but he was duly chastened by it, and after that kept his sabotage of ball-related activities to a minimum. For him, a ball meant a hidden flask or three, at least an hour of hard drinking ahead of time with friends (if he was feeling cheerful), or alone in his room (if he wanted to get truly blitzed).

Chase never noticed what he wore for such occasions. The castle tailor had learned to fill the princes' wardrobes with beautiful clothes that could be mixed and matched at random, because honestly neither Chase nor Cyrus ever bothered to look at what they put on.

This was not a ball.

He knew it wasn't a ball, because it hadn't been on the schedule this week until the delegation from Xix landed on the castle doorstep yesterday, depriving the Royals of an excellent Hound and requiring some form of gathering involving formalwear and snacks.

This was a Castle Assembly, which looked a lot like a ball, but was able to be thrown together at the last minute. A supper room filled with unthemed goodies, ornamentation that spoke to splendour without extravagance, and no out-of-town guests except those who happened to be here at Castle Charming already.

Prince Chase was so blindsided by this entire event that he had failed to prepare for it in his usual manner which meant, against all the laws of probability, he was sober.

Sober.

Worse of all, summer should mean a respite from the matchmaking season, but this hadn't stopped the wave of eligible aristos who filled up every spare room in the castle, angling to catch the eye of a prince.

In two weeks, Cyrus and Chase would both come of age, and be officially named heirs to the kingdom… or would be disowned, which was honestly what Chase had always expected of this particular birthday before his sister transformed the king into a tree and ran away.

Now… who knew what would happen at the Royal Birthday Solstice Gala? Chase might end up the next King of Charming, or the heir apparent. That made him pure 100% debutante-bait, and not in the fun way.

As the assembly filled up with all manner of doe-eyed lovelies in their best frocks and suits, Corporal Jack appeared like a vision of freedom in a Royal Hounds tabard.

"Jax!" Chase greeted her with a desperate sort of glee. "Come stand next to me and frighten away anyone with a dance card. I'm going to be eaten alive out here and I forgot to get drunk."

She frowned at him, but stood at his side because she was the best of all possible Jacks. "Have you seen Ziggy? She's been removed from the duty roster and no one will explain why."

"Oh, fucknuckles," sighed Chase. "Please don't make me be the one to tell you. I'm not cut out for emotional conversations, and there's nothing here to drink but wine. Wine, Jack. That's practically a vegetable."

She turned on him, glowering. "Chase, if you don't let me in on whatever is going on, I will call you nothing but Your Highness for the rest of your natural life."

Chase swallowed. And then, very slowly, he pointed.

His mother had just entered the assembly, wearing a golden gown that reflected sunshine into every corner of the room. She wore a crown that glittered so hard that it was almost impossible to look directly at her.

Clever mummy. An outfit like that was perfect to disguise that she had at least four weapons on her at all times, and that she wasn't smiling. Trust her to find a way for a queen to be radiant without making the slightest effort towards traditional courtesy.

Behind Queen Ella came the delegation from the Jasmine Empire: three older women in silken robes that danced and fluttered around them with every breath of air. They wore pearls and jewelled brooches in their high hair arrangements. Each of them looked like a birthday cake that cost a million gold coins.

Then there was Prince Hero-Face, the monster-killer that

Queen Ella liked so much more than her own sons, if you counted how many conversations they shared in secret corners. Zuo-lin the Swaggerer, dark and handsome, dressed in a high-necked silk shirt covered in butterflies, with trousers cut obscenely tight.

Chase would never admit that his mouth went dry at the sight of the gorgeous bastard.

Beside Zuo-lin, wearing a distant smile perfected by a pretty girl who had been told her whole life not to scowl in public, was Princess Ziyi of Xix. No longer their rough and tumble Cadet Ziggy. She was dangerously eligible, Chase knew, though he could never consider taking up with her himself.

Not once he saw the devastated look on Jack's face.

"Oh, hell," said Chase. "You like her, don't you?"

He'd never seen his favourite person broken-hearted, and he did not enjoy seeing it now.

"Shut up," Jack said fiercely. "I'm worried for her, that's all. This isn't what she wants."

"And what about what you want, Jax my love?"

Corporal Jack looked furious for a moment, then unbearably sad. "I never get what I want. Why does it even matter?"

Damn it all, thought Prince Chase of Charming. So this was what sober felt like. He could not recommend it.

11

DANCE DANCE REBELLION

Kai's education had been eclectic at best, considering his foster mother was a governess. Always more interested in the children she was hired to teach (to teach magic, he had to remind himself, now that he knew that particular secret), she had never bothered him as long as he spent most of his day on some form of academics.

He learned to bury himself in spare corners of big houses, appearing to read something worthy, even when he was secretly perusing cheerful novels or week-old newspapers discarded by the family of the house.

Occasionally, his mother took an interest. Languages, she was very firm about. Geography, also. But she steered him away from history — from kings and queens, he realised in retrospect. And she made it very clear that he should have nothing whatsoever to do with even the most theoretical texts on magic.

One aspect of his education that she had been weirdly insistent about was dancing. No matter which house they stayed in, or how many children she had charge of, when dancing lessons came around, Kai was always included.

When it first started happening, he assumed it was to make up the male numbers. Then, when his mother insisted upon it even in a house with several brothers and only a single sister, he thought perhaps it was her way of letting him know, discreetly, that she didn't mind him dancing with people of either gender.

It had never occurred to him until now that she was preparing him for this possible future, back in his rightful place as a prince of Castle Charming.

Kai resented his foster mother for many things, but he could not imagine how much harder this transition would be if he was not able to lead his way through every fashionable dance of the last decade.

Kai danced.

HE DANCED WITH ZIGGY — no, with Princess Ziyi of Xix, who looked miserable beneath her pretty pearl cap and elegantly painted face. She flinched whenever one of the Imperial Mothers of Xix came within her line of sight.

"What's wrong?" he asked quietly. He had the feeling there was more going on here than he knew.

"Is it possible," Ziyi said in a whisper. "For magic to prevent secrets from being spoken aloud?"

"I don't know," he admitted. "I'm still so new at all this. Camilla would…" Her words caught up to him. "Does someone have a spell on you?"

She smiled sadly at him. "I'm so happy my mothers are here to see me dance with a prince." It was the least truthful thing he had ever heard her say.

"Can I help?" he asked urgently. "How can I —"

But Ziyi smiled harder, and the dance spun her away from him.

~

KAI DANCED WITH ZED, who pulled his usual flirtatious act, pressing a little too close, holding Kai's gaze a little too long.

Kai pushed away his discomfort to ask, "Is everything all right with your mothers?"

"I'm glad they're here," said Zed warmly, sounding a hundred times more honest than Ziyi had. There was no fear or wariness in his eyes. "Don't look now, but L and my Ayma are halfway to planning our wedding."

Kai recoiled. "Zed, you know I'm in love with someone else. That's never going to happen."

"We're princes," said Zed with a shrug. "I know you're new to all this, but our feelings are never taken into account, once the marriage machine starts grinding. You'll save your-self a lot of heartache if you stop fighting it now."

Was Zed under a spell, like Ziyi had hinted of herself? Or had he always been this much of a dick?

"I'm not going to marry you," Kai warned. 'There are plenty of Royals here. Pick another."

"We'll see," said Prince Zuo-lin of Xix, not sounding bothered by the rejection.

~

"IT MAY INTEREST YOU TO KNOW," said Laurana of Thalm, as she settled politely into Kai's formal embrace. "I'm not the slightest bit interested in marrying you."

"Good to know," said Kai. "Have we met?"

"Here and there." She waved a vague hand at him. "I'm on the verge of eloping with Gawain of Gaheris, if you must know. He might only have a minor title but he's devoted to me, his family has pots of money, and there's far less danger of being assassinated by one of the ladies desperate to nab you or your brothers."

"Excellent," said Kai. "Want to stay by my side for the rest of the evening and protect me from the horde?"

"Goodness, no." Laurana laughed cheerfully. "Poor thing. You look positively trapped."

The ink tattoo on Kai's shoulder twinged, and started to itch.

"Nope, I'm fine," said Kai. "Don't mind me. Congrats on your imminent elopement."

Elopement. Now there was an idea. He glanced past Laurana's elegant shoulder to meet Dennis' steady gaze from across the room. If they ran away and got married without the queen's permission, no one would be able to force him to be part of some royal alliance… no, wait. That was stupid. Wasn't it?

It was sure as hell not a great reason to get married.

Besides, Kai thought, as he exchanged further pleasantries with the delightfully unthreatening Laurana. If he was going to elope, he may as well go the whole hog and keep running until he wasn't a prince any more.

KAI DANCED with one of the Imperial Mothers of Xix. Her silk gown felt like stiff paper in his arms, and he was sure he felt something sharp pricking at him from one of her sleeves.

"Are you Ziyi's mother, or Zuo-lin's?" he asked politely.

"Neither," she said with a delicate smile that was oddly familiar. "Aunt. Stepmother. When we are among outsiders, we claim each other equally." She smelled of jasmine, and bluebells.

A sharp pain stabbed at Kai's head, as if his mind had brushed against a thought that he should stay far away from.

"Beautiful weather for this time of year," said the lady in his arms. Her smile widened, like she was about to bite him in half.

Is it possible, Ziyi had asked, *for magic to prevent secrets from being spoken aloud*? What did Ziyi know that she wasn't saying?

"It has been a temperate summer so far," Kai assured his dance partner, and kept dancing.

Camilla would know. Why wasn't she here?

The ink on his arm ached, as if the tattoo was new.

KAI WANTED to dance with Dennis, but that wasn't possible, not in this company. Not with everyone watching him so closely.

Besides, he didn't want to *dance* with Dennis. He wanted to drag him under the covers of the biggest bed he could find and hold him close, far away from everyone else.

He couldn't do this. He couldn't prince.

KAI DANCED WITH QUEEN ELLA. She smiled at him for the first time in weeks, like he was finally doing what was expected of him — or, perhaps, like she knew that the guests of the assembly would think it strange if she didn't pretend to enjoy her son's company.

"Chase, I think, for the Princess of Xix," she said as if they were halfway through a conversation. "Her dash of unconventionality will suit him. Help him accept the need to settle down."

Kai stared at her. Where was the warrior who sliced her way through monsters? "What are you talking about?"

"Well," said Queen Ella with a dip of her head as they spun slowly around the floor together. "Forgive me for the presumption, but I assumed you would prefer to be matched with her brother."

Kai stopped short, letting other couples stumble into them. "What is wrong with you?"

Queen Ella stepped back, a familiar fiery expression taking her over, just for a moment, before that icy neutrality returned. "How dare you?"

"How dare *you*?" he shot back. "Who do you think you are, talking about your children like we're pieces on a chessboard?"

"I am your queen," she said. "This is what queens do."

Kai was too angry to calm himself down. It was too late to be polite and smooth things over. He saw Dennis, standing frozen by the wall, and for once the sight of him wasn't remotely soothing. He saw Chase and Cyrus, staring as if they had not expected him to be the one to make a scene at this wretched party.

"Anyone could throw parties and talk bullshit about arranged marriages," Kai snapped at Queen Ella. His mother. The fairy tale, tragic figure. "Is this really what you came back for? To stand there and pretend you care about the monarchy? You and me coming back to them was supposed to *fix* this family. And you haven't even tried."

Queen Ella was pale, very pale. Shaking with anger. Too late, Kai remembered that she was always armed.

"I'm a queen," she said. "Not a miracle worker."

Kai stared at her. His hands were shaking. The ink on his arm burned hot, like the tattoo was trying to scorch its way off his skin. He had no idea what he was going to say next.

Luckily, he didn't have to, because that was when a giant beanstalk burst through the nearest window and slammed Queen Ella of Charming into a wall.

12
____

BEANFIGHT

The crowd gaped at the mess that the giant beanstalk had made of the room. It was a huge, swirling cord of green, thicker than a horse's belly. Branches and tendrils sprouted off the stalk, many of them flailing and unspooling with violent tendencies.

Servants scurried to pick up fallen cups. The beautiful guests gasped and jostled at each other. At least three footmen had fainted from shock.

Kai stared, unable to breathe. Unable, for a very short moment, to take in what had happened.

There was a hole in the wall where the beanstalk had punched its way directly through stone and mortar.

Dennis was there, with Jack at his side, hacking at the monstrous plant, right where it had slammed the Queen of Charming into a wall.

"Stop," Kai said, finding his voice. "Don't damage it."

They turned, staring at him.

"I'm *sorry*," said Prince Chase in disbelief. "That giant vegetable just totalled our mother, and you're worried about doing it harm?"

"That giant vegetable might be the only way to get our sister back," said Kai savagely.

"It's still wriggling," Dennis called out, taking a step back from the danger zone. "I think it might…" A bright green tendril burst out of the side of the beanstalk, knocking him to the floor.

Jack yelled in fury as two tendrils caught her by the arms, wrapping around her biceps and holding her fast.

"And now?" Chase demanded of Kai.

"Yeah, okay," said Kai reluctantly. "Kill the vegetable. It's not like we'll be able to climb it while it's still…" Twitching.

There were more screams of alarm as a lashing frond of greenery swung out at several young ladies in fancy frocks.

The beanstalk bucked and shuddered for a moment, then heaved itself up, smacking the ceiling and raining pieces of chandelier down upon all the guests.

Queen Ella of Charming climbed out from underneath the beanstalk, sword in hand, and a look of determined vengeance on her face. Her golden gown was ripped in several places. She had lost her shoe. Half her hair was falling down one shoulder. She looked more alive than she had since she was first awoken from her enchanted sleep.

"Finally," she snarled, and raised her sword. "Something I can *fight*."

WHEN IT WAS OVER, the beanstalk lay limp across the length of the assembly room. Most of the guests and servants had fled, including the Mothers of Xix.

The Royal Hounds remained, as did various members of Queen Ella's family, but their only job here was to witness her.

Dennis had never seen anything like this in his life. Beserker rage, that wasn't a new concept for him — a few of the lads in his mountain town had that tendency, and would always be packed off to serve in the army as soon as was deemed appropriate.

But this — Queen Ella was *terrifying*. She had beaten a giant beanstalk into the ground before their eyes. Even now it had stopped trying to attack them all she was still there, astride the wide green stalk like it was her mighty steed, hacking at its thick flesh with her sword.

Kai, who had been watching the fight with equal awe and horror, now stirred from beside Dennis, striding forward. "Stop it," he called out. "It's dead. You can't kill it more."

"Can't be sure," the queen muttered, drawing back her sword for another slash. The blade bit deeply into the green flesh, splattering her with viscous goo.

"**L, stop**," Kai demanded. It was a voice of command, the voice of a prince.

The queen whirled on him, her messy sword in the air for another strike. Dennis tensed, ready to throw himself between the two of them if he had to. Around the room, he saw other Hounds — including Ziyi in her fancy silk frock — doing the same. "You dare?" Queen Ella accused her son.

"We need to climb it, not chop it up," Kai said with quiet confidence. He spoke as if he was her equal — for the first time since the two of them returned to the castle, he sounded like he knew how to talk to the queen.

This tied Dennis' stomach in knots, and he wasn't sure why.

Now Prince Zuo-lin was stepping forward, shoulder to shoulder with Kai. "Listen to him, L."

Her face twisted up in fury. "Oh, *now* you two choose to team up? What have you summoned to my castle, Camden?"

Kai glanced around once, as if checking how secure the

room was. How many people there were to overhear him. "I want my sister back," he said quietly. "If I have to plant a hundred beanstalks, I won't hesitate."

Now it was Prince Cyrus who looked furious, marching forward to confront them all. Chase was a few steps behind him. "You had a plan to get Camilla back and you left us out of it?"

"I didn't know if it would work," Kai yelled back at him. "I still don't. And the rest of you have barely mentioned her name in months, forgive me for thinking you didn't give a —"

Cyrus punched him in the face.

Everything went red. Dennis lunged, furious at these spoiled princelings who thought they could go around doing whatever the hell they wanted. Something hard slammed into him from the side, and he shoved back automatically before realising it was Corporal Jack. She jabbed him in the chest with both fists, and then Princess Ziyi was there in front of them both. Dennis was on his knees, struggling to breathe.

"Stay down," Ziyi said in a fierce whisper. "This is between brothers."

Cyrus was on the ground, hand over his nose. Blood trickled from beneath his fingers. Kai — sweet, quiet Kai — stood over him, clearly handier in a fight than he had been before he spent all that time in Enchanted Sleep Monster-Fighting Boot Camp.

Chase had his hands up as if in surrender, laughing at both his brothers.

Prince Zuo-lin leaned intimately into Kai, peering at his face to check the damage.

Kai didn't even glance in Dennis' direction. Why should he? This was an important moment. All princes together.

"Got that out of your system?" Queen Ella said dryly.

"That depends on what happens next," said Kai, lifting his chin.

Dennis was so proud of him that it hurt.

"What happens next is a mission to climb a beanstalk and rescue my daughter," said the Queen of Charming, cleaning her sword on the nearest pearl-white tablecloth. "Any objections? No? Good."

KAI AND THE BEANSTALK

Dennis did not expect to be picked for the beanstalk mission, not now that the queen had taken the lead. Especially not once it became clear that she was allowing Kai to come with her.

Dennis wasn't even surprised that she chose Prince Zuolin too. They had been through a lot together. Queen Ella likely trusted those two at her back as much as she was capable of trusting anyone.

(He was not, would not be jealous).

But Dennis had no illusions that the queen had given up on the idea of match-making Kai. She was clearly keeping her options open, because Princess Ziyi was also invited on the mission. At which point, Jack invited herself along, and no one argued with her.

Perhaps Dennis should do the same: step forward and stand at Kai's shoulder, refusing to leave him. Something held him back. He had a lot more to lose than Jack did, from pissing off the queen.

"You will stand as regent until I return," the queen told Prince Cyrus, whose nose had finally stopped bleeding. "It's about time you got a taste of what your future might look like, if you are chosen as heir to Charming."

Cyrus looked stunned.

Chase muttered a question about how many brothers you had to punch before you got picked to be the favourite.

"Amira and Prince Chase will help you," announced Queen Ella.

The press secretary promptly climbed out from under an upturned supper table, tidying her hair and attempting to look professional.

"How kind of us," said Chase.

"Help me with what?" Cyrus blurted out. "More press conferences where we dodge questions about our missing family members and pose for monochromes?"

"They will help you get this mess cleaned up, placate the guests in the castle, entertain the delegation from Xix, and prepare all that is needed for the Solstice Gala," said Queen Ella clearly. "We will be back in time for that. Have no doubt."

"Right," said Cyrus, looking overwhelmed. "Is that all?"

THE QUEEN GAVE all members of the rescue mission twenty minutes to change into more suitable clothes and gather essential provisions. Kai, who owned no weapons and wouldn't have the first idea what provisions would even be useful, was ready in ten.

He was relieved when Dennis knocked on the door of his bedchamber. "I thought we wouldn't get a chance to say goodbye," said Kai, dragging him inside.

They kissed quickly, intensely.

"Better not be bloody goodbye," Dennis grumbled.

Kai held his gaze. "I should have made her bring you on the mission."

"Nah," said Dennis, sounding unconcerned. "It's for the best. Let her think the Ponytail has a chance of making an honest prince of you. Save that battle for when Camilla's back and you actually have an ally in this damned family."

"Exactly," said Kai, relieved that Dennis understood.

Queen Ella was a Wild Card, and right now, she thought she was in charge of this family.

As they headed out together, Dennis elbowed Kai in the chest. "Her face, though, when you stood up to her. That was a picture."

"Yeah," said Kai with a quick grin. "I didn't hate that. Weirdly, neither did she. Maybe I'll try it again."

THE MAGIC BEANSTALK had punched its way through the entire castle. It spiralled around the castle like a snake going in for a cuddle, before spiking directly upwards, past the fluffy clouds in the bright summer sky.

Luckily, Kai was not afraid of heights.

Amira summoned a press corps to see them off, which meant Kai's vision swam with the bright pops of light from the monochromes, and his ears buzzed with questions from the reporters, by the time they were finally ready to make the climb.

"The things the kid will do to catch up to our headlines," Chase joked, but his words caught in his throat.

Kai was startled at this evidence of emotion. His elder brothers had spent the last few months keeping their distance from him, and now they looked genuinely gutted to see him leave.

Cyrus hugged him, one of those exuberant all-body hugs

that Kai had previously only seen on the rookery field. "Bring her back," he whispered in Kai's ear.

THEY CLIMBED.

Queen Ella took point, with Zed at the back. Kai, Ziyi and Jack were roped between them, so that if one fell, the others would cling on for dear life and might have half a chance of hauling them back up.

Kai did not intend to fall.

It was a magic beanstalk, of course. While hardly commonplace, this was a known phenomenon in the history of Charming and other nearby kingdoms. Kai once wrote an essay on famous beanstalk quests of the fourteenth century, and his foster mother was so impressed with his use of footnotes that she awarded him a rare compliment.

He still remembered some of the case studies.

> *In 1342, a miller's three sons climbed a beanstalk to track down their errant cat, who ate most of their stash of magic beans, stole a pair of boots and set himself up running short cons across Gaheris and Argyll. When the cat's former masters tracked him down in his magical cloud castle, it turned out that the cat had kidnapped several princesses who were highly grateful to be rescued.*

> *In 1367, a goose girl in Splott attempted to remove a curse that had turned her brothers into ravens. She wove magic shirts from fibres sliced from a beanstalk,*

*but only rescued five of her six brothers
after the youngest raven ate one of the
shirts.*

*In 1371, fourteen different children named
Jack claimed they had a) sold a cow for
magic beans, b) climbed a beanstalk, and
c) stolen all manner of wealthy trinkets
from a giant. It later turned out that the
urchins all belonged to the same crime
ring, run by a disreputable storyteller with
a long beard. The storyteller later died
under mysterious circumstances, after
ingesting of the wrong kind of magic bean,
causing a beanstalk to grow directly out of
his oesophagus. (No children were charged
for his murder, and the official
investigation ruled that it was death by
fairy tale misadventure.)*

Kai had nightmares for years after reading that last story, and always avoided the recreational consumption of magic beans. There was a reason he hadn't been offended that time Dennis was invited to a Castle Charming drinking-game-and-magic-beans night without him.

Most beanstalk stories had several things in common: the stalks grew to giant size, they led to mysterious locations beyond the clouds, and they always caused more problems than they solved. Kai had never heard of one trying to kill anyone, as had happened here, but perhaps Queen Ella brought that tendency out in everyone.

Climbing a magical beanstalk wasn't especially hard, as long as you didn't look down. There were strong hand and foot-holds everywhere, exactly within reach.

What made Kai uncomfortable was that this particular beanstalk was sprouting. First it was flowers, all kinds of noxious blooms with stinky pollen, none of them remotely belonging to the same plant, let alone the same garden.

Now they were higher, though, it was beans. Beans everywhere. Beans of many colours, beans that sang and squiggled and sometimes leaned directly towards the climbers, as if luring them in.

"I wouldn't," Kai warned when he spotted Ziyi picking a few. She had ditched her princess costume for the mission, sticking to a plain tunic and trousers with many useful pockets.

"You never know when they'll come in handy," Ziyi said, ignoring his warning.

"Less talking, more climbing," ordered the Queen.

Upwards, upwards, upwards.

Kai had to hope this wasn't one of the beanstalks that came with a hungry giant at the top.

14

AT HOME WITH TEAM CHARMING

DAY ONE

Dennis was not sure what Queen Ella had expected her left-behind sons to contribute, but Prince Chase and Prince Cyrus interpreted her commands in their own special way, and spent the day in their rooms, avoiding the post-beanstalk clean up.

Dennis, rostered on Prince Chase's detail, spent the morning sitting in a corridor, playing cards with Corporal Fergus.

Amira was, in an entirely unsurprising fashion, handling everything that the queen had requested be done for the Solstice Gala without any involvement from the Princes Charming. She hired four interns to help her, including one whose only job was carrying around all the necessary spreadsheets for pulling off a Major Castle Happening.

"It'll be all right, you know," Fergus remarked. "With, you know." He mimed the climbing of a beanstalk with stunning accuracy. "I do improv classes," he added, when Dennis stared.

"I know it will be all right," Dennis muttered back, which was a lie. "I just hate, you know. Not being there."

"Never mind," said Fergus cheerfully. "Maybe something really dreadful will happen here while they're gone, and you'll be glad you were here to help deal with it."

Dennis stared again. "You're a comfort and a blessing."

"Glad I could help, mate."

DAY TWO

"You have to help me," demanded the voice of a prince. It didn't matter which prince, because it wasn't going to be the one he wanted.

Dennis pretended to still be asleep. It was morning. His morning off. New Sarge refused to give extra time off despite the extreme lack of Royals left in the castle to protect, but there was only much marching in formation and standing "usefully" on the turrets of the roof that even that red-faced blusterer could enforce.

Dennis wasn't sleeping so well these days. The fact that he had dropped off at all was a miracle. He did not need to deal with any prince he was not currently in love with this early in the morning, if he was not being paid for it.

Someone jumped on his bed, and smacked him on the chest. "*Hound,*" complained the whiny prince.

"I know you have manners," Dennis grunted, too tired to put on any facade of diplomacy. "I've seen them in action. Around other people."

Prince Chase loomed over him, thoroughly dishevelled and in still his pyjamas, which cost more than most people would spend on a pair of winter boots… if not four pairs of winter boots. "I need your help," he demanded imperiously.

"Is this how you wake Jack up? No wonder she gets a tension headache whenever you walk into a room."

"That's horribly accurate." Chase looked glum. "I miss her."

"Is that why you woke me up?"

"No!" The prince bounced again, genuinely fretful. "I need you to protect me."

"Check the duty roster…"

"Not *protect me*, protect me." Chase looked genuinely haunted. "I think Prince Zuo-lin's mother is trying to seduce me. And the other two, as well. They keep giving me these looks, and suggestive touches."

Dennis put a pillow over his face. "Doesn't seem like the sort of thing that would bother you."

"I know, right? They're very attractive, as older ladies go. But there's something — unsettling about their flirtations. It gives me a bad feeling and usually when I have a bad feeling, I run away from things and drink a lot."

"Do that, then," said Dennis from beneath his pillow.

"Normally I would lean into any inappropriate seduction," Chase continued, as if he hadn't heard Dennis. "To annoy my father. But he's not here. And, well… he would shout a lot and threaten to lock me up or whatever. But Mother… I think she'd murder me with one of her actual swords. It makes me want to be on my best behaviour. I don't like it. Besides, this is suspicious, right? Last I heard, the Imperial Mum Brigade wanted me to marry Zuo-lin or Ziyi. So what are they up to? And why all three of them? *Am I supposed to bed them all together*?"

Dennis huffed, and removed the pillow. "What exactly do you want me to do?"

"Investigate," hissed Chase. "That's what you do, right? I need you to find out why the Imperial Ladies of Xix are after me."

"Maybe they find you very attractive."

"Wow, you made that sound convincing."

Dennis rolled his eyes. "Like you don't know you're pretty."

Chase smirked. "La, sir."

"Almost as pretty as my boyfriend."

"Oh, right." Chase frowned. "I forgot about that. Look, it's simple. I want you to stick to me all day, and make sure I don't bed any attractive older ladies that throw themselves at me. Got it? Good."

There were times, Dennis mused, when he did not doubt at all that Chase was the son of Queen Ella.

DAY FOUR

Amira started complaining from the moment Dennis led her out of the castle. She kept complaining all the way along the path towards the rookery pitch. "I have so much to do, I don't know why you think this is remotely relevant to…"

"Take ten minutes, it's important," he told her.

She continued to huff and complain until they reached the slope overlooking the green field. Prince Cyrus was at his usual morning exercises, shirt off, muscles gleaming in the early sunshine.

The Imperial Mothers of Xix sat in the stands in their formal silks, unmoving as they watched the prince with a collective gaze that could only be described as 'hungry'. As Dennis and Amira approached, all three women turned their heads at the same time, staring them down.

"It's just…" Amira said, and faltered. "Really, they're from very far away, they're bound to have different social norms, and it's highly inappropriate to demonise them for their odd foreign quirks."

"One of them approached Prince Chase in the bath house yesterday," said Dennis evenly. "While naked. And he fled."

"So the situation resolved itself," Amira said weakly.

"Chase running away from someone who wants to seduce him is worrying, yes. Also, the kitchens reported that the entire castle stock of sugar went missing overnight."

"You can't blame our visitors for that…"

"Something *weird* is going on, Press Secretary Left In Charge Of Everything," Dennis insisted. "You must see it."

"Have you tried reporting to New Sarge… I mean, the Sergeant at Arms?"

"I've just finished doing the hour's worth of push ups he gave me for insolence."

"Right," said Amira. Her head tilted slightly as she took another moment to watch the shirtless, athletic prince running his laps. "Right. I'll, uh, take it under advisement."

DAY SIX

This time, Dennis' early morning rude awakening came from Corporal Sheedy, who was supposed to be on Prince Chase's detail. "Please come," she begged. "With Jack gone, no one else can get through to him."

Dennis ran from the Doghouse dorms, up through the castle, in pyjamas and bare feet. By the time he reached the corridor where Prince Chase and Prince Cyrus had their adjoining rooms, he could already hear the screams.

Prince Cyrus' door was propped open, and there were several Hounds clustered around the door, looking worried and embarrassed. Dennis elbowed his way past them.

Cyrus was nowhere in sight, but his bed was covered in rose petals. Prince Chase stood there with handfuls of the things, howling with fury.

What Dennis should have said was "Your Highness," but he knew what this meant, and his voice cracked slightly as he said, "Mate."

It had happened again. They had lost *another* one.

Chase whirled on Dennis, smacking him in the chest with both fists. Crumpled rose petals rained down on to the carpet. "I'm the last one," he said desperately. "*How can they all have left me here?*"

Fairies. Bloody fairies, all over again.

Before Dennis could even start to come up with a plan, there was a murmur from the corridor, and Prince Cyrus strode in, wearing his sweaty morning training clothes. "What's going on?" he asked sharply. "Why is all that flower shit on my bed?"

Chase made a strangled noise and threw himself at his brother. "I thought the bastard fairies had kidnapped you," he choked.

"Not this week," said Cyrus, sounding baffled. He patted his twin awkwardly on the back, and met Dennis' eyes. "Is someone screwing with us?"

Well, yes. That much was obvious.

DAY TEN

Ten days. How could it take ten days to climb a beanstalk and rescue a princess?

Every morning, between breakfast and his first shift, Dennis would go and stare at the damned thing, the giant green blight on the castle and their lives.

He would imagine climbing it, going to rescue Kai and the others.

Every morning, he did not do it. Because he had orders.

It was now less than a week until the Solstice Gala, and no one was talking about the fact that… well, the queen said they would be back by then. But what if she wasn't? What if none of them came back?

Dennis reported in for his afternoon shift with Prince

Chase, to find New Sarge shouting at Corporals Sheedy and Macnamara for losing said prince.

"Don't worry about it," said Dennis heavily. " You checked the roof, right? If he's not up there, I know where to find him."

He headed down the hill to the town that surrounded the castle, and let his feet guide him to the Crown and Peg, a tavern much like all the others except that their Sarge had funnelled his entire retirement savings into it, teaming up with a couple of old friends from the army.

Old friends other than those who had been magically transformed into fairies, Dennis had to hope.

It was a comfortable pub, just the right side of seedy, and the beer wasn't bad. It had unofficially become the place that the Hounds went on nights off, because they liked to be around Sarge, even if he was drawing beers and wiping tables instead of planning how to prevent the Royal Family from being murdered in their beds.

The Crown and Peg was also where Prince Chase came, whenever he dodged his detail and ran away. Dennis wasn't sure if it was a deliberate new habit, chosen to make it easy for Jack to find him, or because he too missed their gruff former Sergeant at Arms.

Still, there he was. Prince Charming. His artfully styled silver-blond hair slumped over the bar, and a tankard of Mild Peculiar in front of him.

"Pup," the Sarge greeted Dennis from behind the bar. "Took you long enough. This one's been here since breakfast."

"Knew he was in good hands," said Dennis. It was good to be here. Back at the castle, everyone kept looking to *him* for answers. He wasn't even a corporal yet. He sure wasn't Jack. But with her gone, and New Sarge refusing to listen to anyone, well.

Might be time to put in for a pay raise.

Dennis went to sit next to Prince Chase on a stool that was slightly sticky. "You can't keep doing this," he said. "You think Cyrus doesn't freak out about *you* when you go missing? At least tell someone where you're going."

Chase stared at the counter like it held the mysteries of the universe. "How long can it take?" he muttered. "To climb a freaking beanstalk?"

"I dunno," said Dennis in a low voice. "But in four days, if our people aren't back in time for that stupid fancy birthday party of yours, I reckon you and me are going to find out for ourselves."

Chase lifted his head and stared at Dennis, eyes bright, smile far more beautiful than he deserved. "Really? You and me?"

"Try and stop us," Dennis said fiercely.

"I suppose I'd better be sober for that," sighed Chase.

"I mean," said Dennis. "Couldn't hurt."

DAY 12

It was Cyrus who collared Dennis this time, and dragged him to Amira. She was pacing around her office like it might speed time up, or possibly slow it down.

"Two days to go," she repeated under her breath in a panicked tone. "Two days, two days. *Where are they?*"

"Why ask me?" Dennis said plaintively. "This is not my job."

"Whose job is it then?" asked Prince Cyrus.

That was a good question. Kai would be useful to have here right now. Even Queen Ella, with her air of authority. Dennis would cut off his arm to have Jack in this room, dealing with this bullshit.

But no. There was just him.

"Amira," Dennis said sharply. "Get over yourself. No one cares about the Solstice Gala."

She turned on him, eyes practically glowing with fury. "There are twelve dozen mushroom canapés that say otherwise, you absolute animal."

Dennis threw up his hands. "This is above my pay grade, mate," he told the prince.

"Amira," Prince Cyrus sighed. "Pull it together. We agreed we'd present our suspicions to the Sergeant at Arms today."

"Right," said Amira, almost tripping over her high heels as she stopped pacing. "Was that today? Right. Good."

"Which suspicions?" asked Dennis. There were so many suspicions to choose from.

"The castle has been infiltrated by fairies," Cyrus told him. "You know the signs as well as I do. Rose petals turning up in weird places. Sugar going missing. Shoes turned inside out. This morning, the fourth floor staircase transformed into a bluebell wood."

"Well, yeah," said Dennis blankly. Obviously the castle had been infiltrated by fairies. He'd reached that conclusion days ago. "What do you think New Sarge will do, shout at them and make them do pushups?"

THE SERGEANT at Arms was not going to shout at anyone.

When Dennis, Amira and Prince Cyrus found him, he was lying on his back in the Doghouse, one meaty hand still clenched around the duty roster clipboard, his mouth and throat filled with buttercups.

He had been dead for hours.

"Right," said Dennis. "The fairies have declared war on us. That's new and also, horrifying."

"I don't have enough spreadsheets or interns to deal with this," moaned Amira.

Prince Cyrus looked utterly helpless. "Whose job is it to fix this?"

Dennis patted him on the back. "Mate. You're the eldest son of a mostly missing royal family, you come of age in two days, and the queen made you regent in her absence. I'm pretty sure fixing this is *your* job."

15

ABROAD WITH TEAM BEANSTALK

Ziyi had tried to say the words dozens of times.

They're not my stepmothers.

Those are fairies pretending to be my stepmothers.

I don't know why I'm the only one who can see who they really are.

Every time she opened her mouth to explain it to someone, to yell or howl or whisper the words, they froze in her throat.

The fairies had a hold over her. It was different to the hold they had over Zuo-lin — he was convinced they were the genuine mothers. Queen Ella and the others, too. Many of her friends knew what Clover and Foxglove looked like, and none of them had jumped around saying 'I recognise those faces, aha!' They saw what the fairies wanted them to see.

Ziyi had not been able to warn a single one of them.

Even now, on this endless climb up the impossibly large beanstalk, so high above the castle, she couldn't get the words out. Even if she was the only one to hear them.

Imposters.

Magic.

The closest she had come to telling anyone the truth was Dennis, and clearly her attempt was too subtle for him to suspect something was up.

It's not real.

She hated being here, her hands seizing handfuls of the clammy plant to haul herself higher. She hated knowing that every step took her further away from whatever those fairies were up to at Castle Charming.

This is all my fault.

The fairies only took an interest in Castle Charming and its Royals after Ziyi made her stupid Midnight Princess wish, to catch herself a prince. She wished she could take it back. What was the point of this whole last year?

She almost wished it *was* the real Imperial Mothers back at the castle, ready to drag her home and marry her off to her stepbrother and be the obedient princess. At least she knew what that future might look like.

What were the fairies up to?

Ziyi climbed. Was it too much to hope that Princess Camilla could fix things? She had more magic than anyone Ziyi knew.

It was dangerous, to pin all her hopes on one person.

At least Zuo-lin was here. A few days ago, Ziyi would have been annoyed at them being paired on the same mission, but... whatever the fairies were doing at Castle Charming, at least he was safely away from them. For now.

They had been climbing for hours. It had to be hours, right? Ziyi's muscles were sore all over. Just as she was beginning to wonder how far up this thing went, the pressure of the rope ahead of her slackened a little. She looked up, and got a face full of cloud.

"Oof!"

Up close, clouds weren't white and fluffy. It was just like

being rained on in slow motion. Ziyi couldn't see Jack ahead
of her, except for one boot. "Jack?"

"I'm here, Zig," said the weary voice of her corporal.
"Just a bit further. You can do it."

Of course she could do it. She wasn't some child who
needed to be cheered on. Ziyi reached higher, and her hand
smacked stone instead of stalk.

She hauled herself up on to an impossible paved floor,
invisible because of the cloud that still hung low around
them. But solid. Real. As real as a stone floor in a magic
cloud on top of a beanstalk could possibly be.

Jack leaned down, helping Kai on to the stonework, then
stood there and watched Zuo-lin do it without offering him
the same helping hand.

Ziyi didn't blame her. Zuo-lin's flirting with Kai had gone
beyond a joke. They were all Team Dennis around here.

A shadow moved close to Ziyi in the cloud, and she held
in a yelp before realising it was Queen Ella. That could have
been embarrassing.

They divested themselves of their ropes and hooks quickly.

"We'll have to be quiet," said Queen Ella. "We don't
know what we're walking into. If Camilla is here, she may be
unstable."

"None of this was her fault," Kai snapped.

"I didn't say it was," the Queen replied.

"I —" said Ziyi, and then stopped.

"Something to say?" Zuo-lin asked, sounding (as always)
like he was making fun of her.

"Fairies have invaded Castle Charming," she said, startled
to hear the words actually come out of her mouth. "Oh. I
guess. We're far enough away that I can tell you now."

"Fairies have what?" demanded Jack, catching hold of
Ziyi's arm. "What are you talking about?"

"The delegation from Xix. It wasn't our mothers." Relief swept through her. Finally, she wasn't alone in this.

"Of course they were," Zuo-lin growled. "How can you…"

"It was Bluebell and Clover and Foxglove," Ziyi said quickly.

"Shit," said Kai.

"I'm sorry," said Queen Ella. "You know these fairies by *name*?"

"It's been kind of a busy year," said Kai.

"We have to get back," said Jack. "Three of them. Actually in the castle. And no one knows?"

"We will continue," said the queen. "We have come this far. If we are successful, we will be home in a matter of hours. We can deal with your… friends then."

"I don't think you realise how serious this is," said Kai. He sounded gutted. "How much damage they can…"

"You think because I was cursed by a witch, I don't understand the danger of fairies?" replied Queen Ella in a brittle voice. "One thing at a time. We must secure Camilla. Surely we have left the castle in safe hands?"

Sarge was gone. But Dennis was there, and Chase and Cyrus. They should recognise fairy trouble when they saw it. Ziyi didn't even know for certain that the fairies meant to hurt anyone. It could be just another game.

"They like to toy with us," she said finally, reluctantly. "We probably have time."

They moved along the stone floor, quickly and quietly. The cloud dissolved into clear air by the time they reached the far end of what turned out to be a huge stable, with empty stalls and straw strewn over stone pavers.

"At least the mighty steeds around here must be normal-sized and not, you know. Giant-sized," said Kai, who had clearly read a lot of similar fairy tales to the ones that Ziyi's tutor always tried to hide from her as a child. It wasn't done to read books that came from outside the Empire.

"Check," said Zuo-lin cheerfully. "No giants. Though those stalls are still bigger than any stables I've ever seen. They spoil their mighty steeds something rotten." He pushed open the door of the stable and stepped on to… well, more cloud.

This didn't behave like cloud, though. It was white and fluffy like you might see in a mural on a child's wall. When Ziyi stepped out next to her stepbrother, she thought it felt like walking on cushions.

"Oh, that's not right," muttered Jack, sticking close to Ziyi. They could all see each other better now that the cloud was staying under their feet. Kai still had a painfully bruised face from where his brother had hit him.

The cloud stretched wide in all directions. In the distance, there was a shape that looked almost like a rainbow but when you focused, was more like a castle.

There was no cover between here and there, unless you wanted to lie on your stomach and wriggle through the cloud. The only way to proceed was with your head held high, as obvious as a party of travellers approaching a castle could possibly be.

"Let's go," said Queen Ella, striding forth.

The rest of them followed, sharing looks of unease.

"The journey didn't take too long," Jack said in an undertone to Ziyi. "Hopefully we'll be back by supper —"

Her foot slipped on the cloud and she vanished, falling like a stone. It happened so quickly, Ziyi couldn't even scream. She choked instead, on her next breath, overwhelmed. *Jack*.

"Where did she go?" Kai demanded. He fell on his knees in the cloud, trying to scoop handfuls of it away so he could peer through it. "What the hell?"

"Keep going," said the queen. "If they're picking us off one by one we have to…"

"Who's *they*?" Ziyi screamed at her. She wasn't a Royal Hound any more, she was a princess, and that meant she could yell at a queen if she wanted to. (She didn't even care if she couldn't.)

"She could have…" said Zuo-lin, looking sick. "I mean. We're so far up."

Ziyi felt like she had been punched. She felt Kai's hand on her arm, and it was all she could do not to punch *him*.

"I can't see her," he said desperately.

"Looking in the wrong place," said a triumphant voice.

Ziyi whirled around, letting out a sob.

Corporal Jack rose up out of the clouds like a warrior maiden from a ballad, sitting astride a bright purple… well, it wasn't quite a horse. But it was a horse shape. Larger, and stranger, with two curling horns behind its ears and… oh, wings. Bright, fierce rainbow wings.

"You found the mighty steeds, then," said Zuo-lin, strangled laughter in his voice.

Ziyi couldn't stop staring at the vision that was Jack, untouched, her face full of humour and delight.

Oh, she thought, feeling numb as she slowly rose to her feet with her eyes on the woman astride the flying horse. *I'm in love with her*.

16

COLD IRON AND BLUEBELLS

Prince Cyrus stormed into the halls of Castle Charming, his boots ringing on the floors as he made his way up the stairs. He had never looked so much like his father. He looked like a king.

Dennis and Amira followed.

"To me," Dennis called down to Corporal Fergus and a couple of other Hounds loitering in the main entrance hall. They snapped to attention, marching in behind him like he was their leader.

(That was a thought for another day, which was not this day.)

"Where are the Imperial Mothers of Xix?" Cyrus demanded of a terrified footman on the first landing, who gripped his silver tray with white knuckles.

"Uh, they were taking tea in the library, Your Highness."

"Who's the chamberlain this week?"

"Still Persifleur, Your Highness."

"Get him. Now."

They waited on the landing for a moment or two. Dennis

ducked into a nearby parlour and emerged with two sturdy looking iron pokers.

"Cold iron," said Amira approvingly, taking one of them off him. "What, you think your boyfriend is the only one around here who reads the old ballads? This is Charming. We eat fairy tales for breakfast."

By the time Persifleur made it to the landing — a stammering redheaded youngster in an ill-fitting suit who had against all the odds stayed in the position for several weeks now, mostly because the queen wasn't here to fire him and no one else had the heart to do it — Corporal Fergus and the other Hounds had raided the rooms on this floor for more cold iron. They came up with several more pokers, a sharp letter opener and a spiky fire grate.

"Your H-Highness?" said the chamberlain, catching his breath in a wheeze.

"Persifleur," said Prince Cyrus. "We're evacuating the castle. Everyone — staff, guests, family, everyone. Spread the word. Anyone who is willing to fight fairies can meet us on the fifth floor armed with iron, or uh…"

"Salt?" suggested Dennis.

"Don't they like saucers of milk?" asked Amira.

"I'm not sure that can be weaponised."

"Iron or salt," said Prince Cyrus. "Everyone else needs to get out. Send them to the village, and spread the word. Our castle is under magical attack."

Persifleur nodded, his back straightening. "Got it, Your Highness."

Cyrus swung around. "Has anyone seen my brother Chase?"

There was a brief silence.

"Never mind, I'll just assume he's in the worst possible place and needs to be rescued."

The network of maids, footmen and other staff — with

their secret staircases, dumbwaiters and let's face it, hidden passages probably, worked fast when it came to spreading the word about anything in Castle Charming — which made for an efficient evacuation. As Cyrus and his people headed up the stairs, they met a stream of castle residents going the other way.

Not everyone left. Cyrus' makeshift army grew as they went. Gawain of Gaheris and Serena, Countess of Argyll, met them on the third floor with armfuls of rookery equipment and armour. Several Hounds joined them there, along with a couple of very determined-looking princesses.

Dennis was pretty sure that the ladies in question were aiming to impress Prince Cyrus with their grit, but he'd take it. They needed all the help they could get.

No one had seen Chase.

The flight of stairs between the fourth and fifth floor was still a bluebell wood. The steps were made of logs, and a chorus of crickets rose up as Cyrus started upwards. Dennis could hear owls in the distance.

The air smelled sweeter than any wood that he had ever known. It was like honeyed wine and memories.

"Keep alert," snapped Cyrus.

More Hounds awaited them at the top of the stairs, armoured and serious. Dennis nodded to them all.

The landing was carpeted in clover. Beyond, on either side of the library door, stalks of foxgloves waved gaily as if brushed by a summer breeze.

"They're not being subtle any more," Cyrus said to Dennis. "That means I don't have to be polite."

Amira scoffed. "Let's not pretend you ever had a handle on polite, Your Highness."

"Let's show these bastards whose castle this is." Cyrus kicked in the door to the library.

Dennis had spent a bit of time in the Castle Charming

library over the last few months. It had been one of Kai's favourite hiding spots, when the whole Royalness of his situation got too intense. Normally it was a quiet room, all echoing bookshelves, green leather furniture, and the occasional discreet decanter of brandy.

Today, it was not that.

Grass grew up the walls. Buttercups sprang freely from the ceiling. A babbling brook ran up the side of a bookcase full of poetry, complete with frogs and dragonflies.

On a mound of flower-strewn earth, lay a silver-blond prince with his eyes closed, as if he was sleeping.

Cyrus let out a pained sound.

The Imperial Mothers of Xix, still dressed in their formal silks, turned as one and smiled with sharp teeth at the new prince.

"You're interrupting our tea," said one of them. She leaned down, and kissed the unconscious Prince Chase on the mouth. "Delicious."

"Get the hell out of my castle," roared Prince Cyrus.

Dennis stepped forward to stand beside him, gripping the handle of the iron poker. "Bluebell," he said sharply. "Foxglove. Clover." There was a power in names, and as the prince had noted, these three were not being subtle.

The illusion of the Imperial Mothers of Xix fell away, revealing three beautiful creatures in colourful, wispy clothes. Dennis recognised two of the three — Ziyi's Miss Clover, and that smarmy Master Foxglove. The other had to be Bluebell, the fairy godmother who turned Clover into what she was now.

"I thought you granted wishes," Dennis said, outraged on behalf of the castle. "What are you even doing right now?"

"Wishes are how we get under your skin," said Master Foxglove, trailing a hand over Prince Chase's limp arm. "But we always come back to feed eventually."

"My brother is not on the menu," said Cyrus.

All three of the fairies laughed.

"Child," said Bluebell. "Your entire castle is our feast. And we're ready for dessert."

17

FLYING HORSES ACTUALLY

Ziyi did not have time to process her newly realised love for Jack or the sudden arrival of a purple flying horse before the clouds rippled beneath their feet.

"Firm ground," said Kai quickly. "Let's find some."

Jack, majestic on the back of her steed, shaded her eyes against the sun, which was bright up here when your head wasn't literally in the clouds. "I'm not sure how solid that castle is," she reported. "It rippled just now, when the clouds did."

"I believe I would also like a mighty steed with wings," Zuo-lin said fervently.

"Get your own," said Jack. She smiled down at Ziyi. "You can share with me, though. You're about the size of a kitten."

Ziyi wanted to go home to Castle Charming so she could scream into a pillow and feel all her feelings. No time for that now. Hoping she didn't look like nineteen different kinds of idiot, she reached up an arm and let Jack pull her on to the horse behind her.

Queen Ella led the way on foot, her hand on her hilt. She

looked as if she would prefer to proceed with her sword blade bared, but was trying to be diplomatic.

The two princes followed the queen, equally wary. The three of them moved like a unit of Hounds, always aware of each other's position.

Jack and Ziyi brought up the rear on horseback.

"Are there a lot of flying horses underneath the clouds?" Ziyi asked in a whisper. She could not forget that moment when she had thought Jack was lost.

"Also cupcakes," said Jack.

"You're kidding."

Jack gave Ziyi a withering look over one shoulder. "Yes, about the cupcakes. There are a few dozen of these beauties flapping around down there, though. Luckily this one decided she liked me."

Up close, the castle looked less like a sparkling rainbow and more like a fortress. Its walls were mirrored. The advancing party saw themselves reflected in its surface.

"Creepy," muttered Zuo-lin. Kai stood on his foot.

There wasn't a front door so much as a raised portcullis. Queen Ella, wary as ever, was the first to step over the threshold. As she did, a wash of black liquid poured over her feet.

Blood was Ziyi's first, panicked thought. Her second, more rational thought was: *ink*.

In that same moment, Kai cried out, clutching his upper arm as if in pain. "Camilla!" he shouted, and dashed directly into the mysterious castle, dodging his mother as she tried to stop him.

"Damn it," said Jack in frustration. "Peony's wingspan is too wide to bring her into the castle."

"You called your flying horse Peony?" Ziyi blurted out.

"She feels like a Peony," said Jack, ducking her head in embarrassment. "Come on. Time to get our boots mucky."

KAI COULD FEEL CAMILLA HERE, inside the sky castle, and he knew that she was hurting.

As he splashed through the ink that puddled on the floors in every room, he could feel her presence and her magic. *Our magic.*

This castle was built around a central atrium, open to the sky at the very top of what looked like an excessively tall tower. Kai stared up at the spiral staircase that ran around the walls of the tower. The steps were wet with ink. Greenery grew there, swirling plants wrapped around the thin silver bannisters on both sides of the staircase. Familiar plants. More beanstalks.

The steps were slippery with ink, but that didn't stop Kai hurrying up them, as fast as he could go.

"Camilla!" he yelled up, and heard a faint echo bouncing back to him.

"*Ka-ka-kai…*"

Good enough for him.

THE SOUR SMELL of wet ink was everywhere. Ziyi was choking on it. It made the air inside the castle thick and warm.

They made it as far as the central atrium. They could see Kai, already several spirals of staircase ahead of them, making his way up the walls.

"Stay here," Queen Ella commanded the rest of them, and began her own slippery march upwards. "We do not want my daughter to feel under attack."

"Maybe you should stay then," Ziyi muttered.

"I heard that!" the Queen of Charming called down to them, but did not halt her climb.

"Changed your mind about marrying a prince now you've met the mother-in-law?" Jack said lightly.

Ziyi met her gaze, trying not to laugh. "Something like that."

There was a muffled sound from Zuo-lin. Annoyed at the interruption, Ziyi looked over at him. "Are you — don't eat the beans! They're covered in ink."

"I wasn't eating them." He had a smear of ink near his mouth, though. Ziyi did not trust him an inch. Zuo-lin held out a handful of glossy black beans he had picked. "These don't have ink on them. They're just black."

"So?"

"So, I thought you knew the stories. Magic beans come in many colours. Black are the rarest of them all…"

"Not up here," remarked Jack, looking up. Whether it was the ink cascade or something else, every bean on these stalks was glossy, bright black.

"Black magic beans show your loved ones," said Zuo-lin, sticking his hand under Ziyi's nose. "Look!"

She looked. The beans were mesmerising, as if made of shadows. Something moved inside one of them. And then…

Ziyi saw her mother. Not her real mother, who died years ago, but the stepmother who had always been kindest to her. Yeboni, a stern, formal woman, stood in one of her favourite ornamental gardens, a tea glass in one hand.

Around her, the irises danced in the breeze. The image shifted, and another mother — Tasharian, mother of Zuo-lin — joined Yeboni. They sipped their tea and talked quietly together. An ordinary evening at the imperial palace.

"They never left," said Zuo-lin, sounding broken. "They never came looking for me, did they, any of them? I know you're worried about the fairies and the castle, but… I was so relieved that they had forgiven me. It wasn't real."

"They must not know I'm alive," Ziyi said with a wave of guilt. "I'll tell them. I promise."

He pulled his handful of beans away, his face crumpled. "Whatever. Don't do me any favours."

"For what it's worth," she shot at him. "They didn't come looking for me, either. They were quick to believe you killed me, but couldn't imagine I might have been unhappy enough to leave of my own accord?"

Jack let out a groan.

Ziyi whirled around. "Are you all right?"

Jack was staring at her own magic bean, held between finger and thumb. "How long have we been gone?" she asked hoarsely.

Ziyi frowned. "We just started climbing today…"

Jack tilted the bean to show her. Ziyi stared, watching Dennis and Prince Cyrus arguing over the dead body of what looked like New Sarge. Then the image shifted and she saw the castle staff gathering weapons, marching up within their own walls. She saw a bluebell wood indoors, and Prince Chase lying very still…

"We've been gone less than a day," Ziyi insisted. "Haven't we?"

"We have to get back," Jack said grimly. "Now."

18

PITCHFORKS AT NOON

Dennis had never fought in a battle before, not a real one. He knew some of the older Hounds and other castle guards were veterans of the war. Sarge — their real Sarge — had been younger than him when he marched away with the army.

If he had stopped to think about the possibility of fighting a proper battle to protect the Royals, Dennis would never have imagined something like this.

He ducked and weaved as the giant flowers bore down upon him, hissing through stamens like angry dragon tongues. To his left, he saw Cyrus battling a wild tangle of vines and brambles. To his right, Amira threw angry blows with an iron poker against a waterfall with a face.

They were losing. Not just the battle. They were losing the castle. Castle Charming itself, transformed into a fairy nightmare, had turned against them.

They were losing.

Dennis slashed the heads off two enormous tulips and turned to the Prince. "We have to fall back."

"No surrender," said Cyrus with gritted teeth.

"These people, *your people,* are all going to die. At the hands of fairies, so they'll be mocked and tortured first."

This entire battle was an elegantly constructed piece of mockery. Still lethal.

"Not if you bring reinforcements to us," said Cyrus. He lunged past Dennis, his sword whistling past his ear as he stabbed an enormous bumblebee.

"I'm not leaving you," said Dennis.

"Reinforcements," snapped Cyrus with all the confidence of a king. "From the town. Reinforcements and Sarge."

Sarge. Who had battled the fairies long before everyone else.

"You see," said Cyrus, reading the relief on Dennis' face. "It's the right call. Go now, fast. Before this escalates further. Bring the whole town if you have to. And their ironwork."

And Sarge.

Dennis turned and ran. The moss and buttercups rose up to stop him, but he leaped over the obstacles and kept running. Down stairs after stairs.

The fairy magic had spread. There was moss on the second floor. Even by the time he reached the ground floor, he could see tufts of grass growing up through the marble tiles.

Out. Sarge. Reinforcements.

Two sculpted conifers lunged at him as he made it out the front doors, and Dennis only just got out by the skin of his teeth.

Out. Sarge. Reinforcements.

~

DENNIS KEPT RUNNING, down the front steps of the castle, and along the road that led to the town. Reinforcements met him halfway there.

A mob with burning torches and pitchforks had never looked so beautiful. Leading the group of iron-armed townies, he saw Persifleur the footman, and Sarge himself, with a sword in one hand and an iron tankard in the other.

Dennis skidded to a halt in front of them.

"Fairies?" Sarge asked.

"Fairies," Dennis confirmed.

"Let's go, then," said Sarge, with a savage grin. "Always wanted to storm a castle."

For the first time in hours, Dennis felt a spark of hope.

19

GOT INK

K ai climbed the staircase, higher and higher. He could feel the dark pull of Camilla's magic surrounding him, drawing him towards her. He wanted to call out her name but his throat rasped when he opened his mouth, as if even the dust in the air wanted him to stay quiet.

His feet splashed where they hit the ink-drenched steps.

The black beans became more obvious as he climbed. They held images: flickering pictures designed to distract him.

He saw the tree in the kitchen back at Charming, the one that had once been his foster mother before she got in Camilla's way.

He saw his birth mother, Queen Ella of Charming, reflected in the surface of a bean… like him, she was climbing this staircase. A waste of a vision, that one. She was only a few flights behind him.

He saw Dennis, exhausted and scared, fighting off what looked like living, giant flowers in what used to be the library of Castle Charming.

Kai couldn't stop, couldn't let himself worry about the man he loved, not right now.

He had a sister to save.

Camilla.

FINALLY, he reached the top of the staircase, where it opened on to a balcony surrounding the atrium below. The ink was gushing faster here, at ankle-height. It soaked into his trousers, above his boots.

There was magic everywhere, thick like a fog around him. He breathed it into his lungs. "Camilla?"

"I'm here."

Something unfurled inside him as he recognised her voice. He sloshed on through the ink to a doorway, and beyond.

This was another room, small and cozy, with a huge arched window looking out over the cloudscape.

Camilla was there, seated in a comfortable armchair, her bare feet tucked up to keep them out of the ink that still poured across the floor. Kai couldn't see where the ink was coming from, but he didn't stop to investigate. He was so pleased to see his sister, finally.

Her hair was still short, curling around her ears. She was paler than usual, possibly because she'd been stuck in here for so long. Too thin beneath her cheerful smock and skirt, the kind of clothes she used to wear for painting and magic study, not princessing. She had some of her tattoos back, winding around her arms and spreading across the line of her collar bone. Some of the tattoo designs were different, as if she had taken time to rearrange them on her skin. She kept her face turned away from him, not prepared to meet his gaze.

"Are you all right?" Kai asked.

Camilla laughed distantly. "I turned our parents into *trees*."

"Not all of them." It was the first thing that he thought to say, and he regretted it instantly. At least her second laugh was more genuine. "You can fix it. If you come back. No one blames you."

"Oh really? So that isn't our mother climbing the staircase behind you with a big sword, ready to finish me off?"

Camilla waved a hand at the far wall, where a mass of beanstalks twisted into a complex pattern. Beans, fat and shiny and black, hung from the spiralling tendrils. Kai saw a tiny image of their mother, climbing, reflected in several of the beans. Then a flash of Dennis, running for his life.

Kai tore his gaze away reluctantly. "L's not here to do you any harm."

Camilla's smile was sad. "Killing monsters is her specialty."

"You're not a monster," he assured her. "We just need to figure all this out."

"Not everything can be fixed, Kai." Camilla finally tilted her face towards him and he saw her eyes: black from edge to edge. "Too much magic, not enough person. That's always been my problem."

"Bullshit," said another voice. Queen Ella stood in the doorway, one hand on her sword hilt. Her face was set, and steady, showing no emotion. She looked like a warrior who had travelled a long way to perform a thankless task. She did not look like she was here to rescue anyone.

Without even thinking about it, Kai took a step to place himself between his sister and his mother.

Queen Ella's mouth quirked up into something that was not entirely a smile. "Which of us are you protecting?"

"I don't want either of you to do something that can't be taken back," he said. "We came here to bring Camilla home."

"We came here to save her," Ella corrected. "That's not the same thing." She took another step, her boots moving heavily through the thick ink.

"I didn't ask to be rescued," Camilla said, from behind Kai. "I'm doing fine here. I have it under control."

Ella stomped, deliberately. Ink splashed up around her boot. "Yes, you're doing a bang-up job." Her face softened, a little. "Trust me, princess. Spending decades of your life stuck in a magical world that doesn't exist is not the solution to anyone's problems."

Camilla lifted her chin. For the first time, Kai realised how similar their faces were. His mother and his sister. "Who said anything about decades? I've barely been here a week, and I'm doing great. I'll be ready to go home in no time."

Ella laughed coldly. "You think home will still be there? You think there will be a Camilla-shaped space waiting for you? They will mourn you and move on. Going home to them will be nothing but an embarrassment for everyone."

Too close to the bone. Kai cleared his throat. "Camilla. You've been gone for months."

"I just got here," his sister said, her whole body vibrating with frustration. "A little longer and I'll be ready…"

"Ready to get home and meet your great-grandnieces? I think time moves differently here." Kai considered the visions he had seen in the magic beans. "And they're in trouble without us."

Camilla stood up from her chair. The ink swirled up, wrapping around her wrists and ankles, as if she didn't trust herself to hold back otherwise. "I can't bring all this magic back to the castle. To the real world. It's too much for one person."

"You're right," Queen Ella agreed, and her hand finally slipped away from the hilt of her sword. "You should leave it here. With me."

"WHAT?" Kai and Camilla shouted in unison, turning on her.

"You want my magic?" Camilla snarled.

Kai was furious too. "Have you been waiting for a chance to sacrifice yourself so you don't have to even try to fit back into your old life?" he demanded of their mother.

"That's not fair," said Queen Ella, her face like stone. "You both have lives back there in Charming. I should have protected you as babies, stopped that witch from passing her power to you, Camilla. Kept you from being kidnapped, Camden. Kai," she added, reluctantly acknowledging the name he used now. "This is something I can do to make up for all that."

"Or we could find another way," Kai said bitterly. "And you could make it up to us by being our mother. Stop acting like you died, back in that spinning wheel place. *Live*."

Queen Ella looked miserable. "I don't know how."

"I don't know how to live without my magic," Camilla said crossly. "And I don't intend to, by the way."

"Cyrus and Chase will never forgive me if I come back home without either of you, so where does that leave us?" Kai asked.

There was a splashing sound outside, and then Corporal Jack strode into the room, drawing to a halt at Queen Ella's side. The Prince and Princess of Xix followed her. They were all splattered with ink, and exhausted.

"We have to get home," Jack said in a voice of authority. "It's all-out war between our people and the fairies, and Castle Charming is losing."

Every drop of ink in the room drew towards Camilla, forming a spinning moat around her feet. "I can't take this into battle," she protested. "I'll end up destroying the whole castle."

Jack shrugged. "Give half your magic to Kai. Come on, let's move."

Camilla blinked. "I've *tried*. When we were babies. When we did lessons together. And when he was in the spinning wheel place. Every time I try to give him my magic, it fails."

"Have you tried asking him to take it instead of pushing it at him on the sly?" Jack suggested.

Everyone stared at her.

The corporal rolled her eyes. "*Royals*. You always think it's fine to stand around making decisions for other people. It's not hard to ask first."

Kai turned to face Camilla. She blinked, her eyes looking normal for a moment, then they returned to being creepy black orbs. "Camden," she said, sounding broken. "Kai. Do you want half my magic?"

"No," he said immediately. He heard Ziyi snort behind him, and almost laughed. "I mean, no. I don't want it. At all. But I'll carry it if you need me to."

His sister smiled sadly. "You'll probably regret this."

"I mean, probably," Kai agreed. "But I do not want to be the last member of this family left alive. So we'd better rescue them all, yeah?"

"Sounds like a plan," said Camilla of Charming.

"I didn't ask to be rescued."

20

GO BIG OR GO HOME

Ziyi's flying horse was called Persephone. She didn't choose the name. As soon as she climbed on to the back of the majestic steed with a soft violet hide and broad rainbow-coloured wings, the name Persephone fell directly into her brain.

Jack kept giving her smug looks. The whole Peony business didn't seem so silly now.

If only the smugness made Ziyi want to kiss her less. Alas.

"Mine's called Gilbatrar," said Zuo-lin, who had managed to choose a flying horse with a tail that flicked and swished almost as much as his own hair.

"No one asked," Ziyi muttered, sneaking a look at Kai.

Kai looked so different, since Camilla's magic flowed into him, filling his skin. He held himself like he might explode at any moment, and yet he seemed taller, more confident too. For want of a better word, he looked properly royal, instead of his default expression of 'uncomfortable.'

He looked like he had spent his childhood being drilled on press galleries and responsibility and deportment.

At least his eyes were normal — and Camilla's, too, now she had siphoned some of her magic off into her brother. Where Kai's shirt was torn, Ziyi could see black tattoos spiralling up his arm, from wrist to shoulder.

The twins walked in symmetry, each movement reflecting the other, in a way that could only be described as eerie. Chase and Cyrus never walked like that — the older twins were always aware of each other when they shared a room, but they made an effort to demonstrate their differences to the world. Cyrus flexed; Chase slouched.

Princess Camilla and Prince Camden moved like they had been a team their whole lives. They mounted their chosen flying horses, and sank their fingers into the manes in an identical movement.

Kai looked surprised for a moment. "Zakhariah?" he said. "Where did that name even come from?" His mighty steed whinnied and flapped its wings like a trapped moth ready to launch itself at a lantern.

"Mine's called Peanut," said Camilla, and the twins exchanged a strange, private grin. "We should get moving," she added. "I'm pretty sure this place built itself from my magic when I needed a hiding place. Now we're leaving…"

Ziyi thought of the cloud disappearing underneath Jack's feet, and shivered. "Wait a moment," she said aloud. "Are the flying horses real, or also made from your magic?"

Camilla gave her a wavering smile. "How about you not ask that question again until we're safely back at Castle Charming?" she suggested.

The scenery rippled around them.

Queen Ella rode out from behind the dream castle, astride a flying horse that was 100% rainbows. Its wingspan spread out majestically, and when the sunshine hit the horse exactly right, a thousand other rainbows refracted out from it in flecks of dancing light.

"Mine is called Basic Transport," she said calmly. "Let's ride."

THE TRIP HOME was a lot faster than the trip there, which was probably for the best given that Ziyi was convinced the flying horses were about to disappear out from under them at any moment.

They spiralled out from the cloud and beanstalk like falling petals; like the air dancers from the poetic sagas that Ziyi used to listen to when her grandmothers started reciting old verse; like twirling chestnut husks falling from a tree.

It should not be far to Castle Charming. Not from here to there. Not with a single rope of a beanstalk guiding their way. And yet...

The closer they got to the base of the beanstalk, the less it looked like Castle Charming was even there any more. It had become something else. A wide green mass, like a tangled forest left to sleep for a hundred years.

Their flying horses touched down on the castle lawns. Each mighty steed, one after the other, vanished like a soap bubble pricked with a fingernail. Everyone stared up at the green tangle that used to be a castle. It was a maze of thorns and spiky trees, green fronds hiding every yellow brick from their sight. Old thorns. Old branches. Overgrown. Forgotten.

"How long were we gone?" Jack asked in horror.

The twins, Kai and Camilla, turned identical blue-eyed gazes on her. The air around them tingled with magic.

"Less than a month," Kai said after a moment. "This isn't natural growth."

"No," said Queen Ella grimly. "It's the fairies. They won the battle. And we missed it." She drew her sword, approaching the overgrown castle.

"I mean," said Zuo-lin, coughing discreetly. "There's a door?"

Queen Ella blinked, and nodded. Sword bared, she marched around the perimeter of the castle. The rest of them followed.

Eventually they made their way around to the front entrance of the castle. Like everything else, it was now clogged and covered with thick, green branches and leaves. But that wasn't all that they found.

"Dennis," gasped Kai, sounding properly human for the first time since he accepted half of his twin sister's magic. He ran forward, dragging at handfuls of vine and thick, thorny twigs that cut his hands. The greenery fell away, revealing pale grey granite speckled with moss. Not the buttery yellow stone of the castle. This was a carved statue.

Many statues, Ziyi realised, looking at how the green vines bled out from the entrance, down the castle steps and across the turning circle for carriages, all the way down the road to the town. There were so many statues caught up in the fronds and thorny tendrils along the way, clumped together in marching order, exactly like they had come to save the castle.

Kai had his hands pressed against the stone face of his boyfriend. It was clearly Dennis. It was also, quite clearly, a statue.

"Sarge," Jack choked, striding forward to clear away the matted roots and leaves covering the figure beside Dennis. This was indeed a statue of their Sarge, the original Sergeant Clay. Here to rescue everyone.

Ziyi was not going to cry. Princesses did not cry. Not in the face of disappointment, tragedy or assassination. Not if the only home they had ever felt comfortable in was gone forever.

"We can —" Camilla began to say.

Too late. Kai had already gone in for the kiss.

As his mouth touched the statue of Dennis, there was a surge of magic in the air around them. Ziyi's ears popped, as she had been needing since she first began her descent on the flying horse.

(Persephone. With everything else going on around them, was it appropriate to feel even slightly sad that her flying horse was a figment of some other princess's imagination?)

"Don't use too much," Camilla warned Kai, far too late. "It can be hard to control at first…"

As if the world was breathing out, all at once, all the statues came to life. Dennis' skin pinked out of the grey granite. Beside him, the Sarge coughed and dropped some kind of farming tool on to the steps.

The coiling, twisting mass of plants turned black and sizzled as they fell away from the people.

Kai and Dennis were still kissing, arms wrapped around each other. That might go on for some time. Ziyi wasn't going to begrudge them that.

Sarge staggered away from the melting plant goo and lowered himself to sit on a step, head in hands. "I mean," he muttered. "Any battle you can walk away from…"

Queen Ella approached him. "It might be easier to walk away if you stayed on your feet," she said in a chilly tone.

He tipped his head back, and gave her a tired smile. "I don't work for your family any more, Your Majesty."

"Yet here you are, soldier." She held out a comradely arm, and he allowed her to pull him to his feet. At which point, to the embarrassment of everyone in the immediate vicinity, Corporal Jack threw her arms around Sarge and hugged him with far more emotion than anyone had ever seen her display in public.

No, Ziyi was *not* going to cry.

Sarge patted Jack awkwardly on the back. "We're not done yet, kid."

The queen raised her chin at him. "Ready to take the castle? Successfully, this time."

Sarge looked down at his fallen weapon. The wooden handle of the implement looked fragile, like it had aged centuries. The metal fork part of the tool was red with rust. "Even iron has its limits," he said thoughtfully. "They came at us so fast…"

"Don't worry," said Camilla, her eyes flashing black. "We can fight magic with magic this time around."

"Yep," said Sarge, giving her a wary look. "That has put all of my worries to rest."

Kai pulled away from Dennis. "Camilla and I should go in alone."

"Yeah, not happening," said Dennis in disbelief.

"Not in a million years," Ziyi added. She met Dennis' eyes and nodded. She was a Hound where it counted. Keeping the Royals alive was their duty, always.

"You can't fight the fairies," Camilla insisted, eyes on her mother. "None of you can. Kai and I can get this done. *Fairies hate ink*, and our magic is… well, whatever it is, it can do some damage to them."

"And what do you expect us to do in the meantime?" Ella said scornfully. "Weave cloth and bake cakes?"

"All perfectly valid tasks," said her daughter. "Give them a try."

They glared at each other.

Dennis stepped around his boyfriend, flexing his hand around the hilt of his own sword. He gave an experimental hack at the thorns covering the entrance to Castle Charming. He took out a good chunk of spiky greenery, which fell to one side, but did little to clear the way.

"Those of you with magic," he said with a meaningful look at Kai, "Could probably ink splatter your way all the way through to the fifth floor, which was Fairy Central last I looked. But you'd burn out a hell of a lot of power getting there. We can cut a path through for you."

"And give the fairies more people to use against us," said Kai. "The more of you in there, the more hostages there are."

"No," said Queen Ella, her eyes on Dennis. "The Hound is right. Those of us with weapons and fighting skills can clear the path. As we free the survivors inside, the team gets them out."

Dennis nodded respectfully. "Works for me."

Kai started to protest, but was met with matching glares from his mother and boyfriend, and nodded reluctantly. "Fine." Even the seriousness of the situation couldn't conceal his quiet delight that the two of them had teamed up against him.

"Sure," said Sarge, looking back at the mass of scared people who were until recently an angry mob and, more recently, a collection of statues. "What's the worst that could happen?"

"I could make a wish." Ziyi hadn't meant to say it aloud. But now, everyone was looking at her. "I could make a wish," she added. "And then another wish. As many wishes as it takes."

"You know where that leads, Cadet," said Sarge, his voice shaky. He had a longer and more troubled history with the fairies than the rest of them.

"Yes," Ziyi said, more confident now. "If I wish too much, I pay the cost. I become one of them. And they get a win. Do you really think we can beat them without giving up something? Maybe one battle, or another, but you need the whole castle back. You need the fairies gone for good. You can't scare them away, or force them away. They have to *want* to leave."

Kai threw up his hands. "What is it about this kingdom that makes everyone so eager to sacrifice their lives?"

"Fairy tales," said Ziyi. She was smiling. Making this decision was easy. She had started all this, back when she first arrived in Charming. She thought she could act like a character in a story, and get everything she ever wanted. Now, she knew better. "Royal propaganda, fed to children. Eternal friendship. All that stuff."

Queen Ella moved forward, regarding Ziyi as if she was a particularly dangerous snake. "You don't want this."

"I do," said Ziyi. "I love your castle, Your Majesty. I love everyone in it, even my dick of a brother."

"Hey," protested Zuo-lin.

"I want everyone in Castle Charming to be safe and well," said Ziyi. "I want the fairies to leave us alone, for good. I want everything to be okay, and happy. It's a lot to want. But I don't just want it. *I wish it.*"

FAIRIES ALWAYS LISTEN TO WISHES, in fairy tales. They always grant them, one way or another. Sometimes, they don't even count the cost…

At first.

Eventually, once the wishes get big enough, the fairies call in the debt. With interest.

The first rule of fairy tales is: never wish anything out loud. Especially if there's magic in the air.

You never know when some random, cruel creature will choose to give you everything you ask for.

One way or another.

21

HAPPILY EVER AFTER

There was once a little girl called Ella, who had a cruel stepmother and a loving but distant father. From a young age, Ella was good at two things: sharpening knives, and telling people what to do.

One day, an old woman came to their shop. Ella was the only one working that day, as her father was away selling his award-wining knives in another kingdom, and her stepmother was at yet another tea party.

The old woman gave Ella a block of wood and told her she needed a knife that was not made out of iron. Ella sharpened the wood, and painted it in lacquer, and sharpened it again, and eventually she made the sharpest, wickedest wooden knife that she had ever seen.

"Not sharp enough," said the old woman.

Ella tried again, filing down the edge of the knife and polishing it until it shone.

"Not sharp enough," said the old woman.

Ella worked through the night and eventually the knife was so thin, and so sharp, that it cut its way through three rods of iron. The old woman was pleased, and paid for the knife with three copper coins that smelled like blood and bluebells.

As she left, she offered Ella a wish. "Anything you want," she said. "Just for you. Something to make you happy."

Ella thought about her long hours in her shop, and her father's many absences. Her stepmother's cruelty and disinterest. "I want a family," she said. "I want to be loved, and never bossed around. I want to be the one who tells everyone what to do."

"Those are all fine things to want," said the old woman, who was of course a fairy. "But none of them are wishes." She left Ella with a bluebell candle and told her to light it when she knew what to wish for.

A MONTH LATER, the Prince of Charming rode through Ella's village. He was young and handsome, and looking for a wife. His father the king was only willing to cede the throne to him once he had a queen at his side.

There was to be a ball to decide the matter.

Ella looked at her hands, calloused and sore from all her hard work, not only making the knives when her father was gone, but cleaning the house and doing every chore that her stepmother demanded of her. She looked at her ragged work-dress and the boots with soles so paper-thin that she could feel every cobble when she walked through the village.

She thought about being a queen.

When the night of the ball came, she made her wish.

I wish he would choose me.

ELLA DID NOT WISH for a party and a dress, though those

things were very much in the front of her mind when she lit the bluebell candle.

She did not wish for the mice in the wainscoting to be transformed into footmen, or the pumpkin in the cellar to be transformed into a carriage so iconic it would set the fashions for royal transportation in the decades that followed.

She did not wish for glass slippers that hugged her feet so softly it felt like they were made of fur.

She got all these things, and more, when she made her wish. A desire she imagined to be quite small and personal was, as it turned out, an enormous wish.

She became the Midnight Princess for one night. Soon after, she became the Queen of Charming.

GOOD FORTUNE FOLLOWED. The king and queen had twins, darling silver-eyed boys. Then the second pair of twins: the dark-haired prince and princess.

No witches ever came close to hurting their happiness.

No magic stained their lives.

No baby was stolen.

No spindle pricked a finger.

No war was fought in Palomarr.

THE TREND of scandalmongering newspapers and snapping monochrome magic never came to the kingdom of Charming. There was little entertainment to be made out of good fortune, ever after.

All was well.

All was happy.

All was, as it had ever been, the perfect fairy tale.

22

HAPPY BIRTHDAY, PRINCES CHARMING!

As birthday parties went, this Solstice Gala was swish. There wasn't much for a Royal Hound like Dennis to contribute beyond standing around looking pretty, and being prepared for anything.

Prince Chase and Prince Cyrus were on their best behaviour, which meant plenty of flirting with the younger guests while avoiding the well wishes of their parents' pompous, older friends. Basically, they were doing their job.

Dennis was pretty sure that some of the princes' friends had spiked the punch enough to enhance the general merriment, but he wasn't bothered about it. They deserved to cut loose from time to time, and they never took it too far.

Really, this was a dream job.

Princess Camilla swept past in the arms of a foreign prince; one of many here in the hopes of catching her eye. This particular foreign prince, Something Something of Xix, had a sparkling smile and a swishy pony tail. Dennis had no objection to him romancing the princess.

(Earlier in the evening, the same Prince of Xix seemed far more interested in Princess Camilla's twin, Prince Camden.

Dennis managed to conceal his inappropriate jealousy. After all, he had always known that his crush on the youngest of the princes would come to nothing. This party was Arranged Marriage Central, and a Hound from Mt Nowhere wasn't on anyone's list of Most Eligible.)

The big excitement of the day was the impending announcement about which of the elder Princes Charming would be officially named the heir. Prince Cyrus, older than his brother by a few minutes, had shown killer strategy by securing the witty and charming Laurana of Thalm as his betrothed. Chase, never one to back down from a challenge, had announced his own engagement only a week ago, to his cousin Serena, Countess of Argyll.

By all accounts, the King and Queen of Charming adored both of their clever, beautiful prospective daughters-in-law equally.

Neither prince had put a foot wrong PR-wise in months.

It was going to go down to the wire as to which of them was considered the best possible future king.

Dennis wasn't worried. There was never much in the way of drama around here. They'd sort it out, as they always did.

Corporal Jack approached him, from the side of the room. Was it shift change already? She looked serious, her body language tense.

"Something wrong?" Dennis asked her. As she reached his side he realised, she wasn't just tense. She was miserable. Devastated. He'd never seen her so… "Jack. What is it?"

She set her shoulders back, as if preparing to be disappointed. "Dennis. Do you remember what happened to Ziggy?"

Reality shifted around him, and he stared at her in dawning horror.

"Oh. *Shit*."

JACK HAD SPENT most of her life in the pocket of the Castle Charming Royals. Even before she took on the job of a Royal Hound, she was always trailing after the Princes Charming, protecting them from harm.

There was an argument to be made that Prince Chase was her best friend.

She had seen this family through misery and torment, through unhealthy life choices and drunken parties.

She had once genuinely thought it impossible that Chase and his brother Cyrus would survive to adulthood.

When Camilla did her vanishing act last spring, Jack had thought it highly probable that no one would ever see the princess again.

And if anyone had ever asked Jack what she would sacrifice to see those ridiculous, spoilt, unreasonably pretty royal teenagers happy and reunited in a whole, loving family, the answer was: a lot.

After Ziggy (Princess Ziyi, another bloody princess *of course* this was Jack's life) made her wish and the world irrevocably changed into a perfect Happily Ever After (if that was what you wanted to call it), Jack experienced about ten minutes of blissful ignorance.

Her life barely changed. Here she was, still a Royal Hound, protecting the family of Castle Charming. As it should be.

But those cheerful, laughing princes with their relaxed shoulders and apparently no hidden booze flasks, they were not her lads. The king and queen, all golden and shiny, without worries or weapons? They were not Jack's rulers.

It was wrong. Her whole body screamed out to her that it was wrong.

And then Prince Zuo-lin of Xix danced past her in a haze

of jasmine perfume, strong enough to make Jack sneeze. When she opened her eyes, she remembered.

Ziyi, freaking out and full of regrets, after her failed attempt to pull off the Midnight Princess routine, so many months ago.

Cadet Ziggy, wild-eyed and valiant as she played her first game of rookery last winter.

Zig, Jack's partner and friend. Always reliable, devastating with a sword in her hand, beautiful when laughing at Dennis' jokes. A true Hound.

Ziyi, a princess once more, wishing for a happy ending no one else had asked for.

Damn it all. If Ziyi was what Jack had to sacrifice, then it wasn't fair. None of this was fair.

Ever since her mam told her that to live in the castle, she would have to pick a job and be better at it than anyone else, Jack's entire life had revolved around duty. She gave up sleep and peace of mind and any sense of a private life, to do her job. To keep the Royals safe.

Looking around this happy, perfect Solstice Gala, she knew that it would be selfish, to burst their bubble. To wreck this pretty dream that Ziyi had somehow managed to build for them out of fairy magic.

But damn it, Jack was overdue for some selfishness.

"IT'S NOT REAL," she informed Dennis, after they withdrew to an upstairs supper room for some privacy. No one was in here yet, just tables and tables of food ready to serve when the guests were bored with the ballroom. "The castle was wrecked. The people — she didn't just tidy up after us. She changed our history into some flawless storybook version."

Dennis nodded, looking as grim as she had ever seen him.

"I can remember both versions if I hold them carefully in my head. Camden — Kai. He had tattoos all down his arms, last we saw him. Camilla too. Her Highness, I mean."

"They never had magic in this world," said Jack. She was desperately relieved that Dennis had his memories back too, now she had jolted him with the truth. Did that mean they hadn't lost their old world entirely? Was this an illusion or a brand history going back decades? "But what's happened to Ziyi?"

"You know what happened to her," said Dennis gravely. "That was a big wish. The biggest she could come up with on the spot. There's no way they didn't get her. She's one of them now. That's how they turn humans into fairies."

Jack knew that. Of course she knew that. But hearing it come out of Dennis' mouth still felt like a punch to the gut. "If we undo this…"

"Then we'll be back where we started. Fairies invading the castle."

"At least we can fight that."

"Can we? I was a statue, Jack. They never even let us get as far as the castle. I can still feel the coldness that came from *being transformed into stone*."

"What are you saying?" she challenged him, her voice rising. "You're just going to give up on Kai? Ignore the prince you love and just carry on like none of that ever happened?"

"I don't know," Dennis snapped back.

There was a soft clicking sound as a door closed. Prince Camden — Kai, stood looking at them, the supper room door firmly closed behind him. How long had he been there?

Kai was perhaps the most transformed. His hair was all swoosh, like he'd allowed years of royal hairdressers to have their way with him. He had a poised elegance about him, and a guarded look on his face. He was wearing jewels — emeralds at his throat and buttons and cuffs, like he had never even thought about how much they cost.

Dennis stared at him like a drowning man, watching a rescue ship approach.

"I've never seen either of you leave a formal event while you were on duty," Prince Camden — certainly not Kai — said in a clipped voice. "Must be quite the catastrophe."

"Nothing we can't handle, Your Highness," said Dennis.

Prince Camden raised his sculpted eyebrows. "Sounded to me like you were discussing your love life."

"Ugh," groaned Jack. "Just kiss already." Oh. She had said that out loud.

"I beg your pardon?" said Prince Camden, startled.

Dennis' face flamed red.

"Don't mind me," said Jack, dodging for the door. "Dennis, escort the prince back to the Gala. I have an idea. See you later."

"You can't just —" Dennis called after her.

Oh, but she could.

NO MATTER what reality you were in, some things never changed. Jack found Sarge at the Doghouse, poring over the security plans for the Solstice Gala while he drank the blackest, grimiest coffee known to gods or cooks.

"You're supposed to be on duty," he grunted at her.

"It's an emergency," said Jack. "You trust me, right?"

"Usually," Sarge said, his eyes thoughtful. "What's up, kid?"

"I need a candle. A bluebell candle. For summoning fairies. You know about that stuff, right?"

He laughed in an odd sort of bark. "What makes you think I know anything about fairies?"

"Because of what happened to you in Palomarr. During the war."

The Sarge blinked, and Jack realised her mistake too late. "What war?"

"Crap," she said miserably. "Of course. Everyone's history changed."

"Jack. You need a holiday?"

"No," she said in frustration. "I need to find a *fairy*."

Sarge shrugged, looking less bothered than he should about his favourite corporal cracking up in front of his eyes. "I mean, I hear they live at the bottom of gardens?"

IT WAS TOO much to hope that the grotto still had their old fairy summoning kit. It was empty, as if no one had ever used it as a secret meeting place. Jack stood over the pool and shouted herself hoarse, calling for Foxglove and Bluebell and even Clover, despite her suspicion that Clover might now be alive and well and a human person with a real name who never broke Sarge's heart by wishing too many times.

If Ziyi was a fairy now, she would have another name. She might not even know who Jack was.

That made her heart hurt.

It made her want to punch things.

How many flowers did she even know the name of? Surely the fairies ran out eventually and had to start calling themselves things like Dock Leaf and Random Pond Pebble.

A memory struck her, of Ziyi teaching her to pronounce 'Xix' properly, because it bugged her, the way that everyone in the castle got it slightly wrong.

"Still, I'd rather be from Xeeeex than have them going around calling us the Gunpowder Isle or the Jasmine Empire," she had confessed, wrinkling her nose. "The jasmine you have here isn't even like the flower we have back home. It smells the same, though. Like funerals and sadness. Men who wanted to marry me always wore it on their coats, which made it very easy to stay single."

One thing Jack knew about fairies was that they had weird senses of humour.

"Jasmine," she said aloud, in a voice that wavered in a thoroughly embarrassing way. "Miss Jasmine. Are you there?"

"Oh, Jack," said a familiar voice, sounding disappointed.

Jack whirled around. It was Ziyi, perched up on the ledge overlooking the grotto. Her hair swung in long braids beneath a spiky veil of twisted white flowers, and she had a look on her face — calculated disinterest, like she was trying to decide which leg to pull off a spider.

A fairy. It was all true. Ziyi was a fairy.

23

HOW TO WRECK A FAIRY TALE

Ziyi was beautiful. She had always been beautiful. But there was a coldness about her now. Even when she had gone into full formal silks princess mode at the Castle Assembly weeks ago, she still looked human. No longer.

Jack was angry, and for once she wasn't going to bottle it up behind a flat expression and crossed arms. "Don't you 'oh Jack' me," she said hotly. "What the hell did you think you were doing?"

"Saving you," said the fairy named Jasmine, rolling her eyes. "Obviously. You're welcome."

"You can't go around saving people like *this*," said Jack. "Not by changing them so hard that they become completely different people. You didn't ask us."

"So you're the only one allowed to go around protecting people?"

"Is this what you call protection? Taking away everyone's free will?" Was this really what Ziyi had in mind when she made her wish?

"Who cares?" said the fairy. "I'm better than I was.

Everyone's better. Only you could be this pissed off about a Happily Ever After."

Jack shook her head. "I liked you the way you were. Grumpy and stubborn and sometimes kind of selfish. But brilliant, and brave. I liked all those things about you, whether you were Ziyi or Ziggy. I don't know who you are now."

Miss Jasmine gave her a bleak, soulless smile. "It's sweet, Jack, that you liked her. But it's too late now. The deed is done. The story's over." She spread her arms wide. "Welcome to the fairy tale ending."

THE WALK from the supper room back to the ballroom was one of the awkwardest of Dennis' life, and that was saying something. He didn't know how to act around Prince Camden now, with two versions of him in his head: the confident prince he had always protected, and the bright-eyed quill who fell in with the royal family by accident… and fell into Dennis' arms, the first time they were kidnapped by fairies.

"There's something you aren't telling me," said Prince Camden, as they came down the stairs. "Am I really not worthy of your trust?"

Dennis gave him a startled look. That expression on his face, the warmth in it, was so familiar. But he couldn't afford to start thinking of this man as his Kai. That was a quick way to being fired for sexual harassment in the workplace. "I don't know where to start," he said honestly.

"Is someone in danger?" Prince Camden pressed. "Someone in my family? I've never seen Jack so rattled."

"Me neither," Dennis admitted. He hesitated. They were close to the main doors now. It would be easy enough to avoid the prince, once they were back in the midst of the gala.

(Part of Dennis wanted to hang on, to keep the conversation going as long as he could, no matter how uncomfortable it made him. How often would he have Prince Camden's full attention centred on him, in the future?) "Are you happy, Your Highness?"

Now it was Prince Camden's turn to look startled. "Happy," he repeated, as if it was a concept he never had to think about. "We live in Charming. Everyone knows that this is the happiest kingdom in the world."

Dennis sighed. "Of course it is," he muttered. "I didn't ask if your kingdom was happy, mate. I asked about you."

Prince Camden lowered his ridiculously long, dark lashes. "Why wouldn't I be happy?"

Dennis shrugged. "Maybe because you're still trying to avoid the question? I dunno, don't mind me. Wishful thinking, I guess."

A small, private smile appeared on Prince Camden's face. It didn't seem like an expression that Kai Foster would ever have worn. "Wishful thinking? What exactly are you wishing for, Hound?"

"That's a good bloody question," said Dennis, and pushed open the doors. Princes couldn't be expected to do that sort of thing.

The ballroom was in chaos. Both young men gaped at the madness.

There were screams and shouts of alarm. Furniture was overturned. Swooning had occurred. Prince Chase and Prince Cyrus crowded around the thrones, both of them shouting and waving their hands.

Queen Ella of Charming stood behind the throne of her husband King Iolchas, a sword at his neck. "Stay back, or I'll slit his throat!" she screamed into the crowd. "I don't want to hear it. All of you shut up, unless you can explain why my husband is not a tree."

"Mother!" called Prince Camden, stepping forward.

Dennis grabbed his arm, hauling him back. "Not you," he grunted, then raised his hand. "Your Majesty? I can answer some questions."

Queen Ella gave him a fierce expression. "Approach, Hound."

Dennis walked forward, keeping his hands where she could see them. As he walked past the other Princes Charming, Cyrus murmured, "Just keep her talking."

"Don't do anything stupid," Dennis said quickly, and stepped past them. Now he was directly facing the thrones on their fancy dais, because kings and queens didn't slum it at ground level like everyone else.

It really sucked that Dennis was in love with a prince, and worked in a castle, because he was genuinely starting to hate the entire concept of royalty.

"What do you know?" Queen Ella demanded.

"You're right," said Dennis aloud. "Your husband is totally supposed to be a tree — sorry, Your Majesty."

King Iolchas blinked furiously at him.

"Did you do this?" the queen demanded. The sword trembled in her hand — this happy fairy tale version of Queen Ella was less battle-ready than her previous counterpart, despite her memory returning. "Did you — is this some kind of bizarre revenge because you're not allowed to marry my son?"

Even in a world so far removed from the reality Dennis thought of as home, that one stung. The queen had never admitted before that she saw no future for him and Kai. Clearly she had been thinking it all along. The crowd around them buzzed with shocked delight at this new scandal, even more exciting than the business with the sword and their king's threatened life.

"If your son ever decides to marry me," Dennis said,

looking directly at her. It was important right now that he not see whatever expression was on the face of Prince Camden. "I'd like to see you try to stop us. But no, this wasn't me. I'm just the unlucky sod with memories of both places. You too, I suppose?"

Queen Ella stared at him as if she could hardly believe it. "It was all true? The monsters? The dead children? All the lost years…"

"All of it," he confirmed.

"Which world is real?"

Now, that was a question.

"Not sure," said Dennis. "Why don't you take that sword away from the king's neck so we can figure it out?"

Queen Ella hesitated, and lowered the sword.

Her husband pulled away from her, whirling around with fury on his face. "Of all the stupid —" he made a choking sound, staring at his hand.

Everyone was staring.

His hand was green. Roots exploded from his wrist, and from his legs, burrowing into the polished tiles of the floor.

Flower petals began to fall from the ceiling. Roses at first, then bluebells. Foxgloves. Buttercups. Clover. The air smelled of warm jasmine.

Panicking, Dennis turned to Prince Camden. "We have to get all the Royals out of here now. The fairies are coming."

Prince — Kai — Camden gave him the oddest look. "Did I forget you kissing me?" he asked in something like wonder.

Oh hell, of all the timing. "Survive this, and I'll kiss you again," said Dennis desperately.

Kai smiled that beautiful smile of his. "Promise?"

The doors to the ballroom burst open. Literally burst. Wood fragments and bronze fixings went everywhere, and light streamed in like molten honey. The crowd screamed, and cowered back against the walls.

Dennis held his ground. What else was there to do? Kai stood near him, close enough to hold his hand. (Maybe later)

Figures moved through the broken doorway, shaped of light and rainbows and flowers. Dancing, beautiful people who were certainly not human. They weren't armed, either. Not that a fairy needed weapons to mess you up.

They were dancing.

Slowly, as if in a trance, the humans began to dance, too. There was no music. No laughter. No clinking of cake forks and champagne glasses. Just the slow, rhythmic, hypnotic movements of a fairy dance.

"Are you seeing this?" Dennis asked Kai.

Kai — no, Prince Camden still, get a grip — gave him another smile, this one with far less warmth. "The queen is coming," he said. "Kneel to the queen."

"What?"

"The queen is coming," said Prince Cyrus as he danced past them, with Laurana in his arms.

"Kneel to the queen," advised Laurana with a smile so false it dripped with sugar.

Queen Ella stepped off the throne dais, avoiding her tree-again husband, and headed for Dennis' side, her sword held loosely in one hand. "What the hell are they —" she said.

Prince Chase and Serena walked hand-in-hand towards the broken doorway. "The queen is coming. Kneel to the queen."

They did not mean this queen. Dennis saw the realisation in her eyes.

"Fairy bullshit," Queen Ella snarled.

"When is it anything else?" Dennis was tired, so tired.

Every human in the ballroom, except for Queen Ella and Dennis, went to their knees. "Kneel to the Summer Queen," they all said in unison.

A woman walked through the golden haze of light. She

didn't look like a queen, Summer or otherwise. She looked completely ordinary, except for a trail of beanstalk running around one wrist, and roses wrapped around the other. She had also looked completely ordinary last time Dennis met her.

"YOU," howled Queen Ella, utterly incensed.

"Hello, Ella," said Willemeena Birch: witch, occasional governess, and former foster mother (some might say kidnapper) of Prince Camden of Charming. "I'm the Summer Queen of the Fairies. Time to grant some wishes."

Before Dennis could think of stopping her, Queen Ella lurched forward, and punched the Summer Queen of the Fairies in the throat.

24

LAST QUEEN STANDING

It was not a pretty fight. Dennis had seen this sort of thing happen before, when a spar turned personal. Then messy. Then bloody. He'd never seen it between queens, but the principle was much the same.

Ella had fury and human grit on her side. The Summer Queen fought like a human woman, all slaps and scratches, but every time Queen Ella got a blow in, the Summer Queen's face shadowed into something that was magic, alien and awful.

Dennis had spent the last few months hating Queen Ella. Now he only hoped she could hold her own against… well. Kai's other mother.

IT WASN'T MAGIC that brought Kai's memories back completely. It wasn't Camilla, or his brothers. It wasn't even Dennis, the man he loved, would always love, in every world.

It was the sight of his mother — of both Kai's mothers — brawling like fishwives in the marketplace.

A wave of shock and embarrassment hit him in the solar plexus. Kai looked wildly around. His Majesty was a tree again, rooted into the throne dais. His arms had twisted into branches, and his mouth was frozen in a silent scream. Kai's family members were watching the fight with a little too much enjoyment.

Dennis was by his side.

"Two sets of memories," Kai said, trying the idea out on his tongue.

His boyfriend's head whipped around, and his face softened. "Thank the gods," he said. "This Prince Camden thing was *killing me*."

"I'm him too," said Kai. It was a strange thing, to have two versions of his life side by side. Two different kinds of happiness.

"You remember me, though?" Dennis asked eagerly.

Kai reached out, took his hand, and brushed a kiss across his knuckles. "I hope so. Otherwise Prince Camden has an extremely vivid imagination."

His mother — foster mother — the only mother he had ever known was here. Not a tree any more, though roots trailed beneath her skirts. Willemeena Birch. She screamed in the face of Queen Ella, and drew back her hand to strike with something that looked more like a branch than a human limb.

Butterflies rose up, out of her hair and skirts, filling the air around her with unnatural splashes of colour.

Queen Ella rolled and took her out at the knees with a slash of her sword.

Bright red rose petals bled across the floor like pools of ink.

"How's your magic?" Dennis asked in a low voice.

"I don't know," Kai replied. He couldn't find it. Couldn't feel it. Across the ballroom, he saw Camilla, her arms bared in a ballgown. Not a tattoo in sight. "What happened to Ziyi?"

~

IN THE GARDEN GROTTO, Jack stared at Miss Jasmine. At the inhuman creature wearing Ziyi's face. "I don't believe you're really gone," she said.

"It doesn't matter what you believe," said Jasmine-not-Ziyi.

Jack shrugged. "I live in a fairy tale kingdom. We all learned from an early age that stories can screw you up, whether you believe in them or not. But believing in them *helps*."

Jasmine gave her a secret, dancing smile which hurt somehow, far worse than the disdain. "Why don't you wish it all better?"

~

PRINCE CHASE WAS PERFECTLY happy before his mother punched the strange lady in the throat.

He had a good life. He was content with what he had. A happy family. A fiancée who was a good friend, and wouldn't bore him. No complaints. But something niggled at him, as he stood watching his mother wrestling with a woman who was also half a tree. A small wrongness, like a loose thread in a tunic.

The return of his old life hit him like a castle in the face.

~

JACK HAD A PLAN. It wasn't a good plan. But it was hers. She dragged the protesting Miss Jasmine back to the castle by one skinny wrist. Ziyi, without her humanity, weighed about as much as a sandwich.

"Sod off back to fairyland if you're so bothered," Jack grunted, as Jasmine's complaints about being manhandled reached a particularly high pitch.

As Jack made it to the door of the ballroom, Prince Chase was coming out of the splintered doorway, looking frantic. When he saw her, he threw himself at her in the world's awkwardest hug. Their specialty. "We weren't even friends!" he complained loudly into her shoulder.

"You didn't need me," said Jack, patting his back. She was lucky, she supposed, not to remember much about this sugar-sweet reality Ziyi had built for them.

"What kind of idiot would not need you?" Chase muttered, releasing her from the hug. He glared at the fairy. "She's not even that cute."

"Watch it," Jack warned him. "She's my person. If we fix things, you two are gonna have to be friends."

"What exactly do you plan to fix?" Chase asked.

"Everything," Jack replied. "Right, petal?"

Miss Jasmine looked deeply offended. "I am *extremely* cute."

L HAD SPENT a lifetime fighting monsters.

Here, in the home that was no longer hers, she thought she was finally free of that burden.

But what else was she good for?

Since her return, she had felt completely out of place in Castle Charming, until…

Until she had a chance to fight a beanstalk.

And now.

Now she had a fairy queen to hack into pieces.

The witch who stole her baby.

The woman who conspired with her husband.

Rose petals pooled at their feet. Branches fell with every swipe of her sword. But still…

Still, the fairy queen — the Summer Queen — laughed in L's face, and held her off.

She couldn't do this alone.

"Mother!" yelled a voice.

Both queens whipped around, following the sound of Kai's voice. Her youngest son. Her long lost baby, all grown up.

He wasn't looking at L.

IT WAS A DELICATE BALANCE, holding two sets of memories in his head. Prince Camden — the version of himself that Kai could not help but think of as the *real* Prince Camden — was so free of anxiety. He walked through the world with confidence and privilege. He barely thought about consequences, social or otherwise.

Kai kind of hated him, that other Prince. The one who had everything going for him. What had he even done with his life? Played games, made friends, wore suits?

This version of Charming didn't even have newspapers.

He strode towards his foster mother, letting his frustrations and stresses uncoil from their hidden places inside him. "Mother," he said again, to the Summer Queen. The greatest liar that he had ever known. "*Where is my magic?*"

"You left it in that other world," said Willemeena Birch with a laugh. "The one that was wished away. There's nothing more powerful than a wish."

"I'm not so sure," said another voice. Corporal Jack strode into the ballroom, with Chase at her side. She had her fingers locked around the wrist of a dazzling fairy, all sparkle and flower petals.

Kai narrowed his eyes, looking again. "Ziyi."

"She made a wish," said Jack savagely. "And it didn't hold. Look at this mess!"

Around them, everyone was confused and muttering. The King of Charming remained rooted to the ground. Queen Ella wiped a trickle of blood from her mouth. Dennis, defiant, took Kai's hand again.

"Humans broke it," snarled the Summer Queen.

"Or your magic wasn't strong enough to manage such a big wish," Jack snapped back. "You broke the contract. So take it back, all of it. And give Ziyi back to us."

"The rules are the rules," said the Summer Queen. "We grant wishes, and we take our price."

"I know all about your price," said Queen Ella, blazing with fury. "I was a *child*. I wanted a handsome prince to notice me, and you gave him to me as a gift, and more. So much more than I had asked for. I trusted you. And when I came to you one more time, because my children were suffering from a witch's curse… you promised to help me."

"I did help you," said the Summer Queen sweetly. "I took your son. Without him, your daughter's ugly ink magic stabilised."

"And who sent a spinning wheel at me, to steal decades from my life and my family?" Queen Ella yelled.

The Summer Queen smiled. "Humans, so ungrateful."

"What will it take?" Kai asked.

Everyone stared at him. Dennis' hand clenched hard around his.

"What do you mean, dear?" his foster mother asked.

Kai had never seen her pretending to be nice before. She was always cutting and insulting to her employers. That was why they paid her so much money. Why had she kept up up the pretence for so long? Playing governess, being a whole pretend person, to raise him away from this kingdom. Why had she done it?

"What will it take, for your fairies to agree to leave Charming alone?" Kai asked. "To fix the mess you made here, all of it. All the lives you destroyed. What price would you charge to grant that wish?"

"Kai, no," Ella said sharply.

"Finally, you start asking smart questions," said the Summer Queen.

"Camden," said Chase in a shaking voice. "If you try to sacrifice yourself right now, I will get Cyrus to beat the shit out of you."

"Good to know," said Kai with a wavering smile.

Cyrus stepped forward from the crowd. "If she wants a sacrifice, she can take me."

"Not what I was hinting at," said Chase. "We all know I'm the biggest screw up in this family. I'm the one who can be spared."

"None of you can be spared," said Camilla. She stepped forward, and her bare arms blurred as if her magic was fighting to find its way back to her. "No one would even miss me…"

All of them exploded at each other, all at once.

"Are you kidding me right now?"

"Stop being such a —"

"SHUT UP," Queen Ella thundered. Everyone stopped arguing, and stared at her. She met Kai's gaze with an uncharacteristically gentle expression. "No sacrifices today," she said calmly. "We're not going to do that any more."

"Thank you," said Kai in relief. "I thought we were going to have to spray them with cold water."

All three of his siblings gave him identically unimpressed expressions. It was pretty great.

Kai stepped forward, facing off against his foster mother. The Summer Queen. "My sister turned you into a tree," he said. "And before that, you avoided this kingdom for what, sixteen years or so while you were raising me, far from here? Sure, you had your fairies causing trouble. But you don't seem that keen on this place. Why is that?"

The Summer Queen smiled a chilly smile. "It's a fairy tale kingdom," she said. "So many stories. So many happy endings. Fairies don't do well in places like this. Once you've all memorised the stories about the cold iron and the curse-breaking kisses and the salt, things get a little… uncomfortable for us. And then there's the ink. So much ink in all those newspapers."

"Fine," said Kai. "Sounds good. Find somewhere else to torment people who aren't as diligent with the bedtime stories."

Still smiling, she shook her head.

"What do you want?" he asked of her, frustrated beyond all belief. What more could they possibly give? "You wrecked our family. You turned love and loyalty into miserable fairy magic. You've taken your price from Charming."

"You haven't even started paying for it," she said.

"What do you want?" he asked again.

The Summer Queen said nothing.

Fairy tales were all about rules and codes and messages. The rule of three was a standard trope. "What do you want?" Kai asked for a third time.

The Summer Queen huffed out a sigh. "The Winter Hag owed me her magic. She promised it to me. And instead, when she was dying, she gave her gift to your sister instead. A stupid baby without the strength to keep it safe. Worst of all, she used ink in her protective sigils so I couldn't get near it. I have worked for decades to get back what she promised me."

Camilla made a small sound. "My magic? Ours," she added with a quick look at Kai. "Is that all you want? My mother would have given it to you the second she learned that I had it."

"Your mother couldn't give it to me," said the Summer Queen. "Only you can give it away. Only you can clean it so it will be pure, as it was before the Winter Hag's corruption."

"Oh," said Kai, feeling unsteady. "That's why you bothered with me. You made me love you, made me trust you. So that someday, when Camilla gave me half her magic, I'd give you mine."

"It's too late," broke in Camilla. "Whatever happened with that last wish, whatever happened when the world changed, my magic is gone."

Kai shook his head. "It has to be somewhere. That means our old world is out there somewhere too. The Summer Queen can undo Ziyi's wish, and bring it all back. But she won't, not until she's sure that I'll give the magic to her."

Clean. How did you clean magic? How could the Summer Queen trust him to give her the magic in a form she could touch?

But of course she trusted him. Until the last year of his life, his mother was the only constant in his world, the only person he had ever loved.

Did she have any idea how much that had changed for him, since he came to Castle Charming?

"You only have half, Kai," said Camilla. "We both have to give it to her. But if we promise…"

"No," said Ella and Kai sharply, at the same time.

"No more wishes, no more promises," Queen Ella continued. "No more putting *any* power into the hands of fairies, or words. It stops here."

Kai raised his eyebrows at the Summer Queen. "Mother knows best. Put the world back first, and then… you get to find out if we have a scrap of gratitude left. It's your only chance. We won't let you win, but maybe… if you choose kindness, no one has to lose today."

~

THE WORLD BLURRED. The wish unravelled. Reality shifted under their feet.

~

FOR A MOMENT, Kai felt his magic rushing back, and Camilla's with it. It would have been the easiest thing in the world, to let it fall back into his skin, and hers.

It would be equally easy to shift the magic, just enough, that it no longer took the form of ink. He could see how to do that, in this moment.

He could give his foster mother everything she had ever wanted from him.

Instead…

He did something else.

~

KAI KEPT SMILING at the Summer Queen. Slowly, he pushed up the sleeves of his shirt to show that his arms were bare.

"Where is it?" she shrieked at him. "All that magic. Where is it?"

"I'd like to know that too," said Camilla, staring at her own bare arms. "I can't feel it. Where did it go?"

"I made a wish," said Kai.

"WHAT?" Camilla said furiously. "What kind of wish?"

"It doesn't count if you don't say it out loud," snapped the Summer Queen.

"My mistake," said Kai. "Seems to have worked, though. The magic is safe and sound. My sister isn't holding it. Neither am I. I guess that means it's fair game to whoever gets there first."

"WHERE IS IT?" demanded the Summer Queen. Not his mother. Never, as it turned out, his mother.

"This is the world as it was before that wish, right?" Kai asked her, to be certain. "The one with all those the newspapers obsessed with Chase and Cyrus getting into trouble? The one where my mother slept for sixteen years, fighting monsters. The one with pumpkin coaches and war veterans and two different generations of Midnight Princess? The one from just before Ziyi made the wish." He could see green fronds covering the windows, but otherwise the ballroom looked much the same.

"Yes," the Summer Queen said impatiently. "*Where is my magic?*"

Kai leaned in and whispered something in her ear.

She gave a triumphant scream and disappeared.

ZIYI BREATHED for the first time in days. Weeks. Years. She was…

Her heart beat again.

Her stomach growled with hunger.

Her wrist hurt, where Jack was hanging on to it.

Her mouth no longer tasted like sugar and funeral flowers.

"Jack," she breathed. "I'm — me."

Jack swung around and stared at her for a moment, then

dropped her wrist like it was burning. "Ziyi. You're Ziyi again."

Ziyi swallowed. Her throat hurt a little. She could hear something like a scream in the back of her thoughts, but did not know why. "Is everyone okay?" She gasped as Jack hugged the breath out of her, all of a sudden. "Oh."

"I've been doing that a lot lately," Jack breathed into her shoulder. "Ziyi."

"I'm sorry," said Ziyi. "I didn't really think before I —"

Jack kissed her, and Ziyi completely forgot what she was going to say next.

"WHAT DID YOU DO?" Dennis demanded of Kai.

"Tell you in a minute," said his infuriating boyfriend.

Prince Zuo-lin loped towards them and swung an arm around each of their shoulders. Dennis couldn't even find it in him to be irritated. "That's new," Zuo-lin noted, nodding across the room to where his sister Ziyi (no longer a fairy) was making out fiercely with Corporal Jack.

"Not as new as you'd think," said Dennis. He blinked. "Speaking of new…"

There was a group of strangers standing at the edge of the ballroom. A small woman, with dark hair and bright eyes. An older version of her, perhaps a brother, with long hair falling in his face. A tall dark soldier behind them… no, that one wasn't a stranger. That was Saladin Teh, Sarge's old friend.

"Oh," said Dennis slowly, figuring things out.

"Yeah," said Kai. "I guess so."

"I don't get it," said Zuo-lin.

Sarge burst in through the doorway, looking wild. Back in his civilian clothes, not the Hound uniform from the other reality. "What the hell is going on around here?" he demanded, then stopped with a broken look on his face.

"My friend," said Saladin Teh, holding out his arms in greeting. "It's been a long time."

The woman threw herself at Sarge, murmuring words into his chest.

The dark-haired man hung back, looking embarrassed, but Sarge pulled him into the hug too. He looked delighted and annoyed and confused all at once.

"That one used to be Master Foxglove," Kai said in an undertone. "And the woman, that was Miss Clover. They all came back. They're human."

"So what?" said Dennis. "Are you saying that wasn't part of your grand plan?"

Kai looked bashful. "I didn't have a grand plan. I had a last minute improvisation which worked out surprisingly well."

"Speaking of which," said his twin sister, glaring. "Where is my magic? If you let that summer witch mother of yours get her hands on it…"

"I don't think she'll get near it," said Kai. "I, uh, sort of, when we were coming back. Had a thought. Redirected it somewhere safe."

"How safe?" Camilla demanded.

"A really safe place for magic that's used to being ink, in a building with lots and lots of iron, to keep the fairies away," said Kai.

Amira — had she even existed in that other reality? — stepped out of a crowd of beautifully dressed but confused castle guests, and smacked Kai around the head. "You didn't," she said.

"Ow," he said mildly. "I'm a prince now. Behave yourself."

"Kai," said Amira in dismay. "Tell me you didn't send a

furious fairy queen and *all your magic* to the local newspaper office. We'll never hear the end of it!"

ONLY THREE OF THEM WENT, in the end. Kai and Camilla, accompanied by Queen Ella. Amira refused to join them, claiming she wanted deniability when the press corps started asking difficult questions.

Chase and Cyrus stayed behind to give dutiful farewells to the upset guests of the most eventful and confusing Solstice Gala ever held in the kingdom of Charming. The Royal Hounds stayed behind also, agreeing that anything dangerous that crossed Queen Ella's path today was going to regret it with or without their assistance.

It was a nice walk down to the town. Even if L insisted on carrying her sword bared.

"She turned the fairies human," said Camilla thoughtfully. "Something must have happened, to make her do that. She wouldn't do it to be nice…"

"Nice was never Mother's strong point," Kai said quietly. He was going to have to stop calling her that. "Maybe she didn't mean to set them free."

He had half expected to find the office of the Charming Herald in flames, or overgrown with beanstalks and roses. Some sign of damage caused by the Summer Queen of the fairies, in her frustration at being thwarted.

Maybe she had got hold of the magic after all. Maybe he had made the worst mistake of his life.

"So you used to work here," said Camilla, pushing open the door to the office. "Seems small."

"You live in a castle," said Kai. "Your perspective isn't normal."

Camilla shivered as they crossed the threshold. "It's here.

Our magic. Partly, at least. I can smell it, mixed in with all the real ink. Is that… vanilla and wet feathers?"

"Are you saying that you haven't armed a dangerous, vengeful supernatural creature with an outrageous amount of magic that she's been scheming to get hold of for sixteen years?" said Queen Ella. "Good to know. Save something for *your* birthday party."

The building was deserted. No reporters making up gossip. No editors inventing irresponsible headlines. No monochromists sniffing chemicals.

Somewhere, deep in the Charming Herald building, there was a swishing sound.

"Sounds like the presses are running," said Kai. "Come on. Let me show you. This part is pretty cool."

He opened the door, and felt the magic — his magic, Camilla's magic. Warm, hungry and waiting for them to take it back.

"Yep," said Camilla with a snort. "Pretty cool. That's so normal of you, normal expert with a normal perspective on normality."

Queen Ella looked at the loops of paper, running through the iron mechanism of the printer. "Oh," she said, lost for words. "Oh, *Kai.*"

Kai stared.

"You protected the magic," Camilla breathed. "And… she tried to take it anyway."

Yes. That was a thing that had happened. And here was the evidence, in black and white.

"WHAT DO you mean she was printed?" Dennis asked, some time later.

"I mean," said Kai hollowly. "Sending her there, into all

that iron… and the magic… and the printing press. She must have been desperate enough to try to take it and… I guess we found out why fairies hate ink. It did something to her. Trapped her. Like a monochrome print on a silver plate. Or rather, like old stories of what people thought monochromes did. All that — soul stealing sort of thing."

"She's printed?" Dennis repeated.

"A stack of forty eight newspapers, each containing an image of… well. The Summer Queen of the Fairies. It's not a flattering picture, either. There's some text too, but it's mostly undecipherable."

"I'm trying to feel bad about this," Dennis said after a moment of contemplation. "I mean, she was your mother."

"Yep." Kai had mixed feelings. Very mixed feelings.

"What did you do with the newspapers?"

"Iron chest, locked with several keys, deep in the cellars of the newspaper office. Surrounded by metal and more metal."

"I guess that won't come back to bite us for at least a decade?"

"At least. Maybe our kids can handle it." Kai did not mention that Camilla had burst into horrified laughter for at least five minutes, or that Queen Ella had to be dissuaded from impaling the entire stack of newspapers with her sword.

"You have this back." Dennis ran his fingers over the black tattoo of a castle wall, on Kai's upper arm. His skin was warm to the touch, just this side of feverish. "Nice."

"I have a few," said Kai. "Including some new ones. Pretty sure our magic isn't going to stop being ink any time soon."

Dennis grinned. "I'll look for them later," he promised.

"We poured most of the magic into the walls of the tower," Kai told him. "We're working up to taking it back ourselves, a bit at a time. Camilla is using a lot of it into her current project of de-treeing our father."

"Probably for the best."

Kai leaned his head on Dennis' shoulder, enjoying the calmness of having him nearby. Of the world making sense again. "How was your day?"

"Eh, could have been worse. I think your mother only slightly hates me now."

"Score."

"I know, right? Also, Jack was so busy making out with Ziyi's face, she completely missed Sarge being offered his old job back."

"Did he take it?"

"Nope. Enjoying his bar too much. Especially now he has some extra old army mates to help out. Turns out your Master Foxglove was Clover's brother, got caught up in wishes trying to get her back… anyway. Sarge has them back now."

"Happy endings all around then," said Kai.

Dennis went tense under his touch. "A moderately content ending would do for me."

Kai kissed the side of his neck. "Really? Moderately content?"

"Slightly satisfactory."

"Mildly neutral?"

"Or, here's a novel idea. No endings at all. Let's start something, instead."

"Yeah," Kai breathed, turning to kiss his boyfriend properly. "Good plan. Let's start something."

EPILOGUE

JUST ANOTHER DAY AT CASTLE CHARMING

THREE MONTHS LATER

The day started well. Kai awoke with a corporal in his bed, warm and drowsy. He leaned up, planting a slow kiss on Dennis' bare shoulder. "Rise and shine."

"Shining is not in my job description," muttered Dennis.

Kai added a hint of teeth to his next kiss. "Are you sure…?"

They were late to breakfast.

"WALK OF SHAME," coughed Chase into his napkin, as Kai and Dennis arrived just this side of disgracefully late to the private breakfast room that the royal siblings had negotiated for themselves, during the recent reshuffling of living quarters.

The queen gave in remarkably quickly to that one, almost like she agreed that she shouldn't have to deal with her adult children until after they'd had their first coffee of the day.

Kai reached out and flicked his brother in the sunglasses as he passed him on the way to the sideboard, where the food options were laid out for them. "Walk of hangover?"

"Shhh, not so loud," groaned Chase.

Cyrus bounced up from the table, draining the last of an orange juice glass that had been specially ordered for him, four times the size of nearly any other drinking vessel in the castle, except perhaps for the Ancestral Goblets which hung in the portrait gallery and could double as rookery helms. "Gotta go," he said cheerfully, smacking Dennis on the back as he headed out. "See you later?"

"Wouldn't miss it," said Dennis, helping himself to eggs, bacon and mushrooms.

"You know you don't have to do it," Kai said in a low voice as Cyrus powered out of the breakfast room.

"Eh," said Dennis. "It's in everyone's best interest that your mother gets a chance to beat me up every few days."

Kai could feel a familiar shiver in the air as he sat down, his magic reaching out for Camilla and finding traces of her in the room. "Cami ate already?"

"She wanted me to pass on the message that kale smoothies are especially conducive to magical control," said Chase, pushing his own toast around the plate.

"I think I'd rather turn evil," said Kai.

Chase pushed his sunglasses down, and smirked at him. "This is why you're my favourite."

CAMILLA WAS in the middle of a full meditation when Kai let himself into the tower. Their shared workroom, behind the kitchen, was a work in progress. Two of the walls were still covered with the swirling tattoo designs holding their excess magic in ink. The other two were blank. Perhaps they'd paint a mural or something on there, when the walls were no longer needed.

Kai's magic reached out for that of his sister, alert to her presence.

"Today's the day," said Camilla serenely, her eyes still closed, and her legs neatly crossed. "The season begins. Ready to catch yourself a marriageable princess?"

"Are you?" Kai shot back.

They exchanged private smiles. Life became a lot simpler for them both, once Queen Ella came to terms with Kai's enduring devotion to Dennis, as well as Camilla's equally enduring disinterest in any form of romance or marriage.

Chase and Cyrus were still in the firing line. The queen had made a public declaration that she and the king would not announce which of the elder twins would inherit the kingdom, until after both of them had chosen their future spouse. Clearly, she thought this would encourage both princes to get their finger out and accept a betrothal.

It was sweet, how hard Queen Ella was trying to be a good parent, though she still didn't quite *get* her children. Chase and Cyrus were now even more determined to hold off matrimony for as long as possible. This was going to be a long and fruitless season for the hopeful candidates.

For the younger royal siblings Kai and Camilla, it had become a spectator sport.

"Enough gossip," said Camilla. "Let's get to work."

KAI WAS STILL BUZZING a few hours later when he left the tower. Over the last few months, he and his twin had worked out a series of rules to ensure that neither of them went 'the full beanstalk,' i.e. overdosing on power. One of those rules was that they never worked for more than a few hours at a time, after which they made sure to get fresh air, avoid each other's company, do non-magical things that made them happy, and eat regular meals.

Camilla struggled with all of those restrictions except #2. After so long isolating herself from her family, her natural tendency was still to shut herself up, away from everyone. She was working on it.

Kai wandered over towards the courtyard, from where he could hear yells, bangs and the clashing of swords. Speaking of family togetherness…

"Ah, Camden," said a gentle voice, interrupting his walk. "Hold this, will you?"

Kai stopped, and accepted the basket of cut roses, along with a pair of secateurs and three individual gardening gloves. "Where do you want these, Father?" he asked, in the awful voice he found himself putting on in the presence of the king these days — polite and deferential, washed of all personality, and only a tone or two above a whisper. His Majesty did not do well with loud noises.

Some might see the changes in King Iolchas as an improvement. He could no longer be found raging at or coldly ignoring members of his family. Gone was the pomposity, the vicious streak, and the melancholy.

But here was the cost: a traumatised man who took no further interest in the throne or the governance of his kingdom. His twice-transformation into a tree (once in this universe and once in a universe of suspicious and unreasonable happiness) had worked some kind of deep and lasting damage on the King of Charming.

The worst part was, thought Kai as he trailed after his father, carrying his garden tools, it was so much easier to like this version of the king.

Camilla was dealing with her feelings of guilt and culpability only marginally better than before, which was to say at least she hadn't run away to live on a cloud with imaginary flying horses this time around. She refused to see her father, or to spend any amount of time in his presence, claiming that she needed to keep her emotions calm and settled until the magic was likewise stable.

King Iolchas did not seem to mind being ignored by his daughter. He did not mind much these days, except for aphids and other garden pests, about which he could summon quite a detailed and indignant lecture.

Chase also had little to do with the king. His own resentment at the years of neglect and cruelty could not be cast aside overnight. He was polite to the king at evening meals, the only ones that the royal family mostly shared all together, but he never opened a conversation or called attention to himself in King Iolchas' presence.

In private, Chase was harsher. Once, when drunk, he admitted that he thought their father was faking it; just another kind of abandonment. He and Cyrus got into a filthy argument about it, which neither of them spoke of again after that night.

Cyrus was certainly more willing to accept this new version of the king at face value. Kai often caught glimpses of Cyrus in the gardens, carrying tools or exchanging a few words with the quiet king.

Kai understood Chase's anger as much as he understood Cyrus' need to forgive; as for himself, he had needed to process a whole lot of feelings of guilt and culpability, not least the fate of his foster mother. In the garden, pottering around with the strangely serene King of Charming, he had found the thinking time he needed, as their life settled into the new normal.

It was amazing how okay they had become, all things considered. It would get better.

Queen Ella continued to sleep in different chambers to her

husband, and had taken on the workload of the reigning monarch with a ferocious dedication. It was clear from recent public appearances that the king was content to be little more than a figure on her arm.

If she had thoughts or feelings on the matter, she had not shared them with her children.

Up ahead of Kai now, the king stopped by a particularly laden rose bush and reached out absently. Kai placed the secateurs in his father's hand and stood well back.

Snip, snip! The dead heads fell, one after another, neatly severed. The king occasionally selected a still-blooming stalk to cut properly and lay in the basket, but otherwise was fully occupied in chopping away the dead and dying flowers.

It was autumn. The rose season in Charming was long, but coming to an end.

"I have to go," Kai said after a while, disturbing the near-silence. "The carriages are coming soon."

"Ah," said his father, giving a rare smile that was not in any way related to gardening. "Duty calls. Off you go, son."

"Did you want to join us?" Kai asked, almost surprised at himself.

The king huffed gently beneath his breath, and turned back to his work. "Not my place these days," he mumbled.

KAI FOUND Dennis where he had expected to: in the court-yard, fighting with the queen. When Zed headed home to Xix, Queen Ella had missed her sparring partner. Old Sarge came by once a week to give her a bit of a workout, but everyone else in the castle was too deferential to be any use to her.

Then, eight weeks ago, Dennis finally lost his temper with the queen and told her off in no uncertain terms about her refusal to acknowledge his and Kai's relationship.

She listened to his fury with an odd sort of smile, while everyone around them froze in horror. She tilted her head to one side. And then she said, in a challenging tone: "What are you going to do about it?"

The first time the two of them sparred together, it was a lot closer to a duel than anyone was entirely comfortable with. Kai practically expired from holding his breath too long in anticipation of the moment when one of them took it too far.

Now, they sparred for an hour every other day. And while Queen Ella had never allowed the word 'boyfriend' to pass her lips… she now referred to Dennis in public as her son's champion.

Kai would take it.

Cyrus and Chase, dressed about as tidily for a royal reception as anyone could expect of them, lounged over the railing of the balcony that overlooked the courtyard, cheering on the pair in mid-fight. Cyrus was barracking for their mother, and Chase for Dennis, but at one point they switched teams without even blinking.

It wasn't noon yet; neither the queen nor the champion would be ready to stop. They were both creatures of routine. Kai headed up the steps to join his brothers. "Really," he said to Chase. "That's what you're wearing?"

"What?" said Chase, looking down at his bright green tunic. "It doesn't have any egg stains."

"Someone wants to look like he's not trying too hard," said Cyrus with a smirk, ruffling Chase's carefully styled hair.

"Sod off, sod off," his brother yelped, shoving him away.

After a few more rounds, Ella and Dennis stopped fighting exactly on the noon chime. Kai had instituted this rule himself, because the two of them were so stubborn they would never be the first to admit they were tired. The first week they tried to spar regularly, they kept going until supper every day. Dennis had almost collapsed from dehydration.

Kai went down to claim a sweaty kiss from his boyfriend. "Get your glad rags on," he called to his mother. "There's queening to be done."

"Oh, I think the princes can handle it," she said, putting away her collection of swords into the lock box. "I'm going to take a two-hour bubble bath."

"I think you mean, read and sign fourteen different diplomatic documents," said Amira, appearing at Cyrus' elbow as if by magic.

He sputtered, looking around. "How did you get there? Did you find another secret passage?"

"It's competence," she said sweetly. "Look it up."

The queen rolled her eyes but waved Amira down to her. "I'll sign them *in* the bubble bath."

Dennis hurried off to get changed himself. It wasn't long before their visitors were due.

Kai grinned up at Cyrus and Chase as they came down the steps, half shoving each other. "It's sweet the way you and Amira think we haven't noticed."

"Noticed what?" said Cyrus innocently.

Chase rolled his eyes. "You could invite her to breakfast sometimes, you know. Not very princely to send her off every morning without so much as a point of toast."

His brother's shoulders sagged. "She won't," he grumbled.

"Ashamed to be seen with you?"

"Something like that. She says she likes me," Cyrus added, cheering up slightly. "But she likes her job more. Also, she totally thinks no one knows, please don't tell her you've figured it out."

Kai had shared cocktails with Amira and Jack two days ago, both women discussing their love life in horrendous detail. "Yep," he said with a straight face. "We'll take it to our graves. Of course, you might have to murder Chase to make sure he keeps the secret."

"That's fair," said Chase. "Shall we head out the front?"

Cyrus snorted. "Not that he's keen or anything."

Chase tripped him up, though Kai shot out a hand to steady Cyrus before he fell flat on his face.

"This is why you're my favourite," Cyrus told him earnestly.

Now it was Chase's turn to snort.

A CROWD HAD GATHERED around the front of the castle, waiting for the coaches. Reporters hustled together at the front, elbowing and stamping to get a good spot. A few uniformed castle guards stood nearby, making a vague attempt to keep order.

Because the princes were there, the Royal Hounds were too. Sergeant Jack leaned against the castle wall, offering something like a salute as the brothers approached her.

"That's what you're wearing?" she asked Chase as he joined her at the wall.

"Don't you start," he muttered.

"I like the hair, though," she teased. "Doesn't look like you're making an effort at all."

He ducked her attempts to tidy it. "Stop, woman. You're not the Sarge of me."

"Here we go," said Cyrus, straightening his own collar. "Time to go to work, boys."

The Charming Pumpkins began their rattling progression towards the castle, drawn by horses that would clearly rather be anywhere else. Lights popped, and the air filled with the familiar scent of monochrome explosions.

Questions burst out from the reporters as the first crop of princesses emerged from the pumpkin coaches. Why were they here? Who were they wearing? Which Royal did they hope to secure in matrimony? What was that weird smell of dried root vegetable?

The Princes of Charming stepped forward to do their duty: greeting the princesses, debutantes, and chaperones and handing them off almost immediately to the household staff, so they could be escorted to their assigned quarters. It had to be done quickly, because there were more pumpkins charging towards them, ready to be unloaded.

By the time the sixth pumpkin opened to reveal its cargo, Kai had a lot more lipstick all over his cheeks than he was altogether comfortable with. He glanced back at one point and saw that Dennis, freshly showered and garbed in his Royal Hound tabard, had joined Sergeant Jack. Both of them clearly found the whole thing hilarious. So, that was less to explain later, at least.

A seventh pumpkin, slower than the rest, rolled in to stop in front of them. The monochromes flashed, even before the door opened.

Prince Zuo-lin of Xix, newly restored to the bosom of his forgiving family after proving he had not murdered his step-sister, emerged from the pumpkin coach with a wide smile and a swish of his dark ponytail. Most brother-chaperones who came along for the season wore neutral clothing unless they were specifically here to catch a mate. Zuo-lin wore a floor-length tailored coat in blinding white, covered with embroidered lilies and jasmine flowers. This was a man come courting.

Without even having to look at each other, Cyrus and Kai each pushed their brother in front of them, just enough to catch Zuo-lin's attention.

The flirtation between Zed and Chase had been a source

of great amusement to everyone, in the days that followed the Summer Queen Disaster, before the imperial siblings of Xix decided they needed to return home and sort out matters with their family. Chase had spent the last few months telling everyone that it didn't mean a thing, and he didn't care whether Zed came back to Castle Charming or not.

Now, Prince Zuo-lin bowed. Prince Chase bowed back. They stared at each other. When Zuo-lin held his hand out in greeting, Chase took it in his own.

The crowd went wild.

Kai and Cyrus were almost knocked over as the press corps followed Chase and Zuo-lin up to the castle.

"How does it feel to be the least newsworthy prince in Castle Charming?" Kai asked Cyrus, laughing.

"Works for me, little brother," Cyrus grinned back.

This pumpkin coach was not empty yet. Princesses began to clamber out of it. Xixese princesses, by the looks of it, all dressed at least as prettily as Zuo-lin. Clearly their family thought thought Castle Charming was the place to be, to secure a match.

Kai couldn't argue with that.

Finally, from behind three of her sisters or cousins, Princess Ziyi emerged. She wore a less fussy version of Zuo-lin's tailored coat, in deep blue instead of white, with no flowers. She wore soft trousers that fell around her like a skirt, an old trick that Camilla had taught her for when you want to be comfortable while still appearing to follow the social rules.

Kai greeted Ziyi with a smile, squeezing her hand. Cyrus kissed her on the cheek, which drew the attention of a few of the reporters away from the Chase and Zed Show.

"Welcome home," Kai told her. "Hope you're planning to stay longer this time."

Ziyi nodded, her eyes moving past him, through the

crowd. Up by the castle, Dennis waved and grinned, knowing that he wasn't the one she was looking for.

Sergeant Jack stepped forward, looking nervous.

Ziyi ran. She lost both shoes on the steps, and it didn't slow her down. At the top, she threw herself into Jack's arms and Jack caught her in a tight hug that turned, very quickly, into a front-page kiss.

The reporters swarmed. The monochromes popped. Chaos reigned.

Kai gave his brother a friendly smack on the back and made his way around the crowd. Dennis met him halfway. They exchanged a brief, un-scandalous kiss, and no one paid any attention to them at all.

"I guess they're bored with us," said Dennis, his big hand wrapping around Kai's. "No one even asked me about the colour of your underwear this week."

"We are exceptionally boring," Kai agreed with a smile. "Long may it last."

THE REST of the day was unremarkable, in the best possible way.

THE END

ALSO BY TANSY RAYNER ROBERTS

Power & Majesty

The Shattered City

Reign of Beasts

Cabaret of Monsters

Musketeer Space

Joyeux

Merry Happy Valkyrie

Tea & Sympathetic Magic

Unreal Alchemy

Love and Romanpunk

Please Look After This Angel & other winged stories

The Mocklore Omnibus [Splashdance Silver & Liquid Gold]

Ink Black Magic

Bounty

NON-FICTION & ESSAYS

It's Raining Musketeers

Pratchett's Women

AS EDITOR

Mother of Invention (with Rivqa Rafael)

Cranky Ladies of History (with Tehani Croft)

ABOUT THE AUTHOR

Tansy Rayner Roberts is an award-winning science fiction and fantasy author, who also writes murder mysteries as Livia Day. She lives in Tasmania with her family.

Listen to Tansy on Sheep Might Fly, a podcast where she reads aloud her stories as audio serials.

Read some of Tansy's stories before anyone else when you pledge to her Patreon.

What tea is Tansy drinking? Find out when you subscribe to her excellent newsletter.

Find TansyRR

Website: tansyrr.com/

Newsletter: tinyurl.com/tansyrr/

Patreon: www.patreon.com/tansyrr/